Praise for Cressida McLaughlin

'One of our favourite women's fiction stars'
Heat

'Hopeful and hopelessly romantic . . . A gorgeous,
sweep-you-off-your-feet slice of escapism'
Red

'A warm and wonderful read'
Woman's Own

'Cressida's characters are wonderful. A delicious summer treat!'
Sarah Morgan

'Evocative and gorgeous'
Phillipa Ashley

'Uplifting, heartwarming and brimming with romance'
Cathy Bramley

'Gorgeously romantic . . . forced me to go to bed early
so I could read it'
Sophie Cousens

'I just LOVED this story. All the characters are wonderful'
Isabelle Broom

'Real heart and soul'
Sarra Manning

'The most gorgeously romantic, utterly perfect book'
Rachael Lucas

'A triumph. Breathlessly romantic, it sparkles with wit
and genuine warmth'
Miranda Dickinson

'So many perfect romantic moments that made me melt.
Just gorgeous'
Jules Wake

'A wonderful ray of reading sunshine'
Heidi Swain

'I fell completely and utterly in love . . . it had me glued to the pages'
Holly Martin

'A total hands-down treat. A book you'll want to cancel plans and stay in with'
Pernille Hughes

'Sizzlingly romantic and utterly compelling, I couldn't put it down'
Alex Brown

'Bursting with [Cressida's] trademark warmth and wit'
Kirsty Greenwood

'Funny, sexy and sweep-you-off-your-feet-romantic'
Zara Stoneley

'Perfectly pitched between funny, sexy, tender and downright heartbreaking. I loved it'
Jane Casey

'As hot & steamy as a freshly made hot chocolate, and as sweet & comforting as the whipped cream & sprinkles that go on top'
Helen Fields

'Just brilliant. Sweet, sexy and sizzzzling. It was a pure joy to read'
Lisa Hall

'A little slice of a Cornish cream tea but without the calories'
Bella Osborne

'Perfect escapism, deliciously romantic. I was utterly transported'
Emily Kerr

'Utter perfection . . . a total gem'
Katy Colins

'Sexy, sweet, and simmering with sunshine'
Lynsey James

The Cornish Cream Tea Bookshop

Cressy grew up in South-East London surrounded by books and with a cat named after Lawrence of Arabia. She studied English at the University of East Anglia and now lives in Norwich with her husband David. *The Cornish Cream Tea Bookshop* is her thirteenth novel and her books have sold over half a million copies worldwide. When she isn't writing, Cressy spends her spare time reading, returning to London, or exploring the beautiful Norfolk coastline.

If you'd like to find out more about Cressy, visit her on her social media channels. She'd love to hear from you!

 /CressidaMcLaughlinAuthor
 @CressMcLaughlin
 @cressmclaughlin

The
Cornish
Cream Tea
Bookshop

Cressida McLaughlin

HarperCollins*Publishers*

HarperCollins*Publishers* Ltd
1 London Bridge Street,
London SE1 9GF

www.harpercollins.co.uk

HarperCollins*Publishers*
1st Floor, Watermarque Building, Ringsend Road
Dublin 4, Ireland

First published by HarperCollins*Publishers* 2022
1

A catalogue record for this book is available from the British Library

ISBN: 978-0-00-850372-7 (PB)

This novel is entirely a work of fiction.
The names, characters and incidents portrayed in it are
the work of the author's imagination. Any resemblance to
actual persons, living or dead, events or localities is
entirely coincidental.

Set in Birka 11.25/14.5pt by Palimpsest Book Production Limited, Falkirk, Stirlingshire

Printed and bound in the UK using 100% Renewable Electricity by CPI Group (UK) Ltd

MIX
Paper | Supporting
responsible forestry
FSC
www.fsc.org   FSC™ C007454

This book is produced from independently certified FSC™ paper
to ensure responsible forest management.

For more information visit: www.harpercollins.co.uk/green

To anyone who walks into a bookshop and knows,
without a doubt, that it is where they're meant to be

Chapter One

Ollie Spencer reached blindly for her mug of tea. She grabbed it and took a long swallow, barely noticing that it was still too hot to drink. Her eyes were locked on her phone, on the email that had just arrived, announcing itself with its usual, gentle ping.

From behind her, where she was sprawled on the sofa in their minuscule living room, her best friend Melissa said, 'What is it? You've gone as white as the paintwork's supposed to be.'

Ollie cleared her throat and turned. That electronic ping – such a dainty noise, one she heard tens of times a day, had a big impact this time. It was a blaring klaxon, a brass band marching past the window, playing her favourite tune. As the words began to sink in, she felt a smile take over.

'It's here.' She held out her phone, even though Melissa wouldn't be able to read it from where she was. 'They've paid out.'

1

Melissa pushed herself to sitting, her long dark hair falling over her shoulder. 'Seriously? It's actually arrived?'

Ollie sat next to her, the sofa springs protesting beneath the worn cushion. 'It's real. It's a real, genuine thing that has happened – to me.' She sounded – felt – awestruck. 'Fifteen thousand pounds.'

'Hey.' Melissa squeezed her arm. Her hand was almost unbearably hot, in the middle of August in this tiny flat that never seemed to have any air, even when they opened all the windows. 'If you're feeling guilty, then stop. You're *owed* this. You couldn't work for months, and since then . . .' She let her words trail away, because they both knew what the end of that sentence was.

'I don't feel guilty.' Ollie rubbed her shoulder, which still ached sometimes, as if the bones were grinding together. Her doctor had told her that in the autumn and winter, when it was cold and damp, was when she would feel it the most. 'I know it's right. I just—' She waggled her phone. 'It's so much money.'

'Enough to do what we talked about, and then some,' Melissa said.

Ollie rested an arm along the back of the sofa, one leg dangling over the edge, settling in for a serious discussion.

'I'm moving to Cornwall,' she said. She'd meant it to come out as a question, one dripping with cynicism and scepticism, because wasn't it the most ridiculous idea? But for the last few weeks, it was all Ollie had thought about: going to the picturesque Cornish town where Melissa's granddad lived, with its curved harbour, cobbled streets and lush green countryside, and breathtaking views over the rugged coastline. It was a world away from the city

2

streets she was used to. Right now, she couldn't imagine doing anything else with the money.

The accident had been a scene stolen straight from one of those awful, predatory injury claim adverts. She'd been hurrying along a damp pavement, takeaway coffee in hand, used to the bustle of London mornings: everyone in their own bubble, focused, laser-like, on their destinations. The office block ahead had been covered in scaffolding for weeks, adding a temporary tunnel to her journey. No big deal. She had barely registered the shout, had thought, at the second of impact, that someone had slammed into her from behind. But then she'd found herself sprawled on her back on the pavement, pain radiating out from her shoulder, its intensity quickly consuming her consciousness, while concerned faces loomed over her.

A piece of metal had fallen from one floor up, had landed on her shoulder and fractured it. She had tried her hardest not to think about what would have happened if it had hit her head. The long recovery had meant months away from her job at Grady Books, and since then, she hadn't managed to get back into her stride. Her boss, Ruth – not the most sympathetic of women to begin with – had taken her injury and subsequent absence as some sort of affront, and had handed over Ollie's responsibilities: the events she loved to organise, the social media – everything that drew books and customers closer together – to her replacement, Andie.

Ollie wasn't the type to give up easily. She had tried to charm and persuade her way back into Ruth's good books, but her boss had become increasingly impatient. Andie was the new golden girl, and while Ollie was still hanging on by her fingernails, this insurance payout would allow her to let go.

She'd had legitimate reasons for claiming it. Her sick pay at the bookshop was only statutory, and Ollie couldn't survive in London for very long on that. Also, the doctor who had overseen her recovery had told her she might always have some stiffness in her left shoulder. She hadn't been able to brush the accident under the carpet, even though she'd wanted to more times than she could count.

'You're moving to Cornwall,' Melissa repeated her words, her tone defiant. 'Every single star in the universe has aligned. You want to get out of London as much as I do, and you won't get a chance like this again. If you stay here, that money will be gone in months, on rent and coffees and nights out. Instead,' she leaned forward, pressing her point home, 'you take it, you move to Port Karadow, and you help my granddad with his book.'

'While you and Tiago build a new life in sunny Portugal?'

Melissa shrugged, not looking remotely guilty. 'I love him. This is *my* fresh start, and now you have one, too. You remember how gorgeous Port Karadow is. It's got that slower pace, that living-by-the-seaside vibe you can't get enough of whenever you've visited with me; you can help my granddad get his life story typed up' – she gave a tiny, affectionate eye-roll – 'and the last time I spoke to him, he told me that there's a new bookshop opening up in the Old Post House in town. An independent bookshop, Ollie. Looking for staff! For someone to run events, be the link between the shop and the community.'

Ollie's pulse picked up. It had sounded idyllic before, but with a new bookshop she could apply to work in too? Were the stars *really* aligning? Giving her a chance to press the reset button?

She could move out of London, move away from the tiny flat that she shared with Melissa, but which was soon going to be entirely hers, including the full monthly rent payment. Move away from the job she used to thrive in but had come to hate since all the creative aspects had been given to someone else, leaving her with orders and accounts, back office functions she couldn't get inspired about. And move far away from the man she had loved but who, she had discovered in recent months, wasn't the kind-hearted boyfriend she had believed him to be, resulting in a messy, painful break-up only a few weeks ago.

'I know that look,' Melissa said. 'Don't think about Guy. It wasn't you, Ols.'

She shrugged, wanting to gloss over it. 'I was a pain in the bum while I was recovering.'

'You were bored, in agony a lot of the time, unable to work. He should have looked after you, been compassionate, not got uptight and short-tempered. I'm glad he did, though, otherwise you wouldn't have seen that side of him until it was too late. Until you were tied together.' She waggled her ring finger. 'This accident, as horrible as it was, is opening doors for you: letting fresh air blast through and clearing out the cobwebs. Make the bloody most of it, I say.'

Ollie nodded. 'You're right. Guy should have been better about it. He should have been a better person, full stop. It's good that I found out. Great, really, that things have worked out the way they have.' She straightened her spine, tucked a strand of long, cherry-red hair behind her ear. 'It's time to move on,' she added, the slow smile curving her lips like a satisfied cat.

This was an opportunity to have all the things that – cooped up in the flat during the long convalescence, her shoulder at first a fiery, all-consuming pain, then a dull, agonising ache – she had decided she wanted. The work–life balance; the green space and seaside; the calm.

'You could take Henry Tilney,' Melissa said, and Ollie looked up, surprised. The chocolate Labrador puppy, named after Ollie's favourite Jane Austen hero, was six months old now. Their flat was, arguably, too small for such a boisterous dog, but Melissa had worked from home – as a self-employed life coach – and had been able to give him all the attention he needed and take him for walks, building up the distance and his stamina as he grew.

'You don't want him with you in Portugal?' He was lying on the rug by their feet, and Ollie reached her toe out to stroke his silky fur.

'It's complicated, taking a dog out there,' Melissa said with a sigh. 'And hot, as well. I think he'll be happier in Cornwall, with you.'

Ollie rubbed her neck. 'I'll be out all day, if the bookshop job works out – wherever I end up working.'

'Granddad will look after him during the day.'

'He's eighty,' Ollie pointed out.

'Eighty-one, actually. But he's still sprightly, and if you're agreeing to type up his memoir, then he can't really complain.' Melissa grinned. 'I'll talk to him.'

'Does he even like dogs?'

'Oh yeah, loves them. He'll be made up – about all of it.'

Ollie felt a rush of something – triumph, elation, relief? She could start again at a new job in a brand-new bookshop, help Melissa's granddad, Liam, turn his handwritten history into a typed document, take Henry for long walks to the beach, getting fresh air and exercise. She could have a more peaceful, fulfilling life.

The only thing missing would be Melissa, who was following her heart and the sun to Portugal.

Ollie grasped her friend's hand. Her phone sat between them on the sofa cushion, the email with its life-changing news still open, like a talisman.

'I'm going to miss you like fucking crazy,' Ollie said.

Melissa laughed. 'You will. But you'll be living your perfect Cornish life, and you'll soon forget about me.'

'Not a chance,' Ollie said, laughing along with her. 'But it is going to be perfect, isn't it? God.' She tipped her head back, letting out a groan. 'I cannot *wait*.'

'A perfect, wholesome, Instagram-worthy life,' Melissa announced.

They swapped smiles, Ollie unsure why her friend's assessment of the move she was about to make didn't sit right with her. She pushed the discomfort aside and thought, again, how that one shocking, painful incident had given her an opportunity that she never imagined she'd get. What she couldn't do, she realised, as her mind started buzzing with plans and to-do lists, was waste it.

Chapter Two

Two months later . . .

Ollie had woken up to the soft smudge of an autumn mist feathering the view that, even though it had been hers for the last two weeks, she still hadn't got used to. There was the gentle green of the lawn outside her converted barn, then the rolling hills beyond, parting perfectly in the middle like a child's painting to reveal the grey-blue slice of sea in the near distance. The sun had risen slowly – it was noticeably taking its time the closer the year crept to Christmas – and once it was up, it hadn't been strong enough to blast away the soft grey cloak that, if anything, made the landscape even prettier.

But now the inside of her converted barn mirrored the outside, because Ollie hadn't yet fixed on the optimum number of incense sticks she needed to get the smell without smoking herself out of her own home. She swore, wafted, then gave up and pushed open the French doors, letting in a blast of October cool.

Henry lifted his nose off his paws, sniffed the air, and bounced up on his strong legs.

'No Henry!' Ollie shouted, but her dog had already rushed through the open door. 'Fuck!' At least he wasn't bold enough to stray much beyond the potted bay trees on the patio, despite the temptation of the lush, well-mown grass.

Ollie followed her dog outside and stood barefoot, hands on hips, on the cold paving slabs, while Henry bounded and yapped, running up to her and away, as if he couldn't believe his good fortune at being allowed out, into the day, so soon after waking up.

Ollie tried to look cross, but she couldn't keep the smile from her face.

She had been nervous about assuming full responsibility for Henry, but Melissa had taken him to training classes when he was a puppy, so his moments of being a terror were few and far between. And, now he was eight months old, he was settling into himself. Still boisterous and full on, but slightly less of a whirling dervish. He was a source of happiness and amusement, and while she was still trying to find her feet in her new surroundings, he was a constant. Of course, that would all change tomorrow. She had the rest of the day to get in the headspace for her new job.

Being mindful was a new approach for Ollie, and she wasn't used to it yet. In London, she had rolled from one thing to the next: a busy day at work, a book event or drinks with friends, going to a play or picnic with Melissa, dinner with Guy. She had rarely stopped to think about how she really felt, assess her stress levels, wonder whether she was doing herself – or others – any good.

Now she was determined to look after herself more – her mental health, as well as her physical. But every time she committed to half an hour of incense and meditation, of deep breathing or yoga, something went wrong. Whether it was a smoke-out, Henry deciding he needed a wee or her phone blaring because she'd forgotten to put it on silent, Ollie's attempts at living in the moment were always foiled. She hated when people let her down, but what was really unforgivable was when she did it to herself.

She scooped her hair up – long, thick and wavy, her natural reddish-brown dyed a bright, cherry red with blonde highlights – into a ponytail, and stretched her arms skywards, breathing through the ache in her shoulder.

'Hello day!' She inhaled, bringing air slowly into her belly then her lungs, the way her mindfulness app had taught her. The strong scent of patchouli wafted out of the doors and mingled with Cornwall's sea-salt air. She settled into a rhythm, closed her eyes and attempted to tune out Henry's bouncing circles and high-pitched barks, but then another voice disturbed the quiet.

'Is everything OK here? Your oven on fire, Ollie lass?' It was deep and rumbling, a strong Cornish accent mixed with a hint of the Irish heritage in Melissa's family, and Ollie already knew it well.

She opened her eyes and smiled. 'I'm good, thanks, Liam. I just lit too many incense sticks.'

'Ah. Right.' He nodded sagely.

Melissa's granddad, Liam Byrne, was the owner of Foxglove Farm – and Foxglove Barn, which she was renting from him. He was eighty-one years old but looked ten years younger, with a tall, rangy frame, mid-brown hair only just beginning to grey at the temples, and a narrow face. His dark eyes were kind, accompanying an easy manner that made him instantly approachable. Melissa had explained that he had fixated on the need to write his personal history because he was worried that his time was short, but other than a slight limp, he seemed fit and healthy.

Foxglove Farm and its accompanying barn gave off the same vibe as their owner: no longer a spring chicken, but dependable and welcoming; trustworthy. The buildings were redbrick, with mature rose bushes outside, their winter leaves glossy and thriving. It was the type of farmhouse that would appear in a lavish historical adaptation on Netflix, and it was perfectly positioned, nestled in a snug valley and surrounded by hills, but with a view of the ocean. Ollie couldn't have imagined a better place for her new start: she realised how lucky she was to be here.

'I'm still getting the hang of it,' she added, pulling the sleeves of her thin jumper over her palms. 'The right number of sticks. One day soon, though, I'll do it perfectly!'

'Never understood all that myself.' Liam slid his hands into the pockets of his sage green padded jacket. He was wearing it with a flat cap and grey trousers, and Ollie was struck by how he always blended in with the surroundings: countryside tones, a natural palette. She looked down at her neon lilac leggings. Countryside blending wasn't something that came naturally to her. 'Does it work, then?' he asked.

'The incense?'

He nodded.

'Apparently. Loads of people say it has calming, healing properties, especially if you light it when you're meditating.'

'Hard to meditate with this pup around, I bet.' Liam crouched when Henry, having exhausted his interest in the ancient yew tree at the edge of the lawn, came bounding up to him. 'Hello, Henry Tilney.' The chocolate Lab responded enthusiastically, jumping as if he was on a spring. 'Never heard of a dog with his own surname. *Northanger Abbey*'s your favourite Austen, then?'

'It's completely underrated,' Ollie said. 'It's funny *and* creepy, satirical, but still has a beautiful, genuine love story. Henry is such a laid-back hero, and sees past Catherine's eccentricities to her good heart. He's hardly ever angry with her, despite how wrong she gets things.'

'You prefer that to Fitzwilliam Darcy's hard edges?'

Ollie crossed her arms. 'I don't know why everyone loves him so much. He's so uptight. If I was an insecure woman—' she stopped herself, laughed. 'All women have insecurities, and I don't think, in real life, Darcy would be that appealing. All that stoic silence – I'd get so mad at him when he didn't just *talk* to me! Who wouldn't go for twinkly eyes and a warm smile instead? A bit of patience and kindness? That's so much hotter.' She pictured a face: green eyes below thick, expressive brows, his dark hair a tumble of curls, a soft amusement in his expression that seemed etched in, so she couldn't imagine him without it. He had one dimple, she'd noticed the last time, in his left cheek—

'You could be on to something there.' Liam's mouth quirked up. He was rubbing Henry's ears, the dog squirming as if he couldn't cope with such extreme pleasure. 'Though is Mr Knightley a good blend of the two?'

'Maybe,' Ollie said, but she had never loved George Knightley. Perhaps it was because she knew that she could be as interfering as Emma and, rather than face it, she gave all her affection to the escapism of naive Catherine Morland and her spooky houses. Besides, Catherine Morland loved books, and *that* made her Ollie's ideal Austen heroine. 'But Henry Tilney's the one for me,' she added.

'Pooch or man?' Liam pushed himself slowly up to standing. 'My joints get stiffer with each new autumn,' he said, more to himself than her.

'Pooch,' Ollie clarified, because she had traded in men for her beautiful dog, just as she'd traded in the hectic but suddenly hollow whirlwind of London for undulating hills and a barn conversion; her unsympathetic boss for a new job in an independent bookshop that actively wanted an injection of Ollie Spencer enthusiasm. She waited for the twist in her stomach, that strange mix of discomfort and attraction whenever her thoughts led her to her ex, Guy. Then, having let it intrude for a couple of seconds, she forced it away again. 'Dogs are a lot simpler.'

'That they are. You off into town today?'

'Tomorrow,' Ollie said. 'It's my first day at A New Chapter. The manager, Thea, called me on Friday to confirm. I could have started a week ago, I'm that ready to get stuck in.'

'Thea's a sweet, gentle girl,' Liam said. The look he gave Ollie was warm, but with a hint of something – warning? She hadn't started typing up his memoir, yet: he'd wanted to give her a couple of weeks to get settled first. But they'd had coffee; they bumped into each other most days, and although she'd only met him on a couple of visits with

Melissa before she'd moved down here, it seemed he'd already started to form an opinion of her.

'She seemed so nice at the interview,' Ollie said. 'She obviously loves her bookshop.'

'It's her passion; something she worked towards for years before setting up here, in Port Karadow.'

Ollie pushed her heels into the damp grass to stretch out her calves. 'And once she's got regular events happening, she'll be even busier, even more successful. I've got experience running launches and campaigns.' Perhaps not *quite* as much as she'd told Thea and Becky, her colleague, at the interview. There were only so many events one bookshop could hold, and her enthusiasm had, ever so slightly, got away from her: she'd tweaked and embellished her experience, had possibly made it sound like she ran book-related events for a large portion of London. She knew, however, that she could live up to her own hype.

'I understand that,' Liam said. 'Just . . .' He glanced away from her, in the direction of the sea, then turned back. 'Tread gently, Ollie.'

'Of course I will!' She gestured behind her, as if the gentle wafts of incense exiting the barn could back her up. She knew that she was a whirlwind of ideas and energy, and that sometimes, for some people, it was too much. But she also had a lot of good qualities, and she hoped Thea and Becky would see that. Anyway, part of her reason for being in Cornwall was to reset. She had her long walks in the countryside, and the meditation, and the whole *living in the moment* thing. 'I'm not going to waste this opportunity,' she told him.

'I know you're not one for doing things half-heartedly.' Liam put his hand on her arm. 'Come to the house for a glass of wine afterwards, if you like?'

'And you're *sure* you don't mind looking after Henry? I'm hoping to persuade Thea to have him as a bookshop dog after a while.'

Liam looked down at Henry, who was gently chewing his shoelaces. 'It'll be a treat. Honestly.'

'Thanks, Liam.'

'And maybe go easy on the incense, next time?' He winked at her, extracted Henry's teeth from his shoelace, and strolled towards the farmhouse.

Ollie sank into a perfect, cross-legged pose on the grass, and Henry put his nose in her lap.

'Is thirty-five too young for a mid-life crisis?' she asked him. His eyes were dark pools, full of emotion. '*I* don't think that's what this is,' she added, running her hands along his soft, fuzzy coat. 'Forget I said anything.'

She had turned over a new leaf: a whole tree's worth of them. She'd been given the chance to move to Cornwall, to live differently, to start again in a new bookshop and help her best friend's granddad with something that was important to him. She appreciated Liam's concern, his suggestion of caution, but she was good at what she did.

She lay back on the grass, the washed-out blue of the sky above her dotted with cotton-wool clouds.

She had embraced change, and now all she needed to do was settle into it – at A New Chapter, and in Port Karadow. She had left everything she knew behind: her best friend was in Portugal with her toy boy, her other

15

friends were carrying on with their London lives, though they had promised to call regularly, to even visit someday in the future, and her parents were happily retired in Yorkshire, no doubt planning their next cruise. Ollie had gifted herself an enviable life in Cornwall, in a beautifully converted barn with a hint of sea view, and she was determined to make the most of it.

Henry nudged his nose under her chin, and she wrapped her arms around him and closed her eyes, absorbing the sensations of this one, specific moment. Ollie Spencer was a new woman and, if she was honest, she was looking forward to getting to know herself again, too.

Chapter Three

It felt strange walking into town without Henry bounding along at her side, but Ollie couldn't take him with her today. For her first day at A New Chapter, she had put on a long, wine-red skirt below a black silk blouse, and finished it off with her caramel coat and her leather boots. Her hair was loose around her shoulders, only the front strands pulled back from her face and secured with a butterfly clip.

It had been misty again when she stepped outside, the air damp enough for her to feel it against her skin. It was invigorating, and exactly what she needed to help her focus on her first day. Ollie wanted Thea and Becky to like her: she wanted to be seen as part of the team.

She walked along the country road, the tall, thick hedges on either side starting to turn from green to red and russet, the birdsong lifting her spirits. She knew this route now, knew where there were dips in the road, which side to walk on so she could easily step onto a verge if a car came past.

Over the last couple of weeks she had got into a routine: getting up, putting on Henry's harness, walking along the narrow lanes, sometimes down to the beach, then into town. She picked up a coffee and, occasionally, a pastry from the independent café, Sea Brew, then went to soak up the sights and sounds of the harbour. Now, the greens and ambers of the countryside slowly gave way to the odd farm building, then neat rows of houses, then the whole town, spread out before her like a chocolate box full of enticing flavours, the harbour and sea sparkling beyond it.

Usually she would walk up the hill, out of the valley Liam's farmhouse was nestled in, then back down into town, but today she would only be going up. A New Chapter, Thea Rushwood's independent bookshop, was at the very top of the hill, in a historic building called the Old Post House that had been renovated over the summer.

By the time she turned onto the lane that led to the Old Post House, the sun had burned away most of the mist, and Ollie could feel sweat slick on her lower back. The walk had filled her with energy, and she was buzzing. She turned a corner and stopped, marvelling again at how beautiful the bookshop was.

A New Chapter stood on its own, a solid chunk of a building built in honey-coloured stone, with a gravel space in front of it big enough for several cars. The windowsills shone brightly, and the sign above the wide doorway had red, swirling font on a glossy white background. It read: *A New Chapter: Port Karadow's independent bookshop*. There were colourful displays in the windows, one an amalgamation of blues and greens and, when Ollie stepped closer, she could see they were all Cornish titles: fiction and

18

non-fiction, hardback and paperback. The other window was a rainbow assault, a display of children's books surrounded by enticing-looking toys and games. The front door was postbox red, matching the sign, and a placard outside read: *Coffee Served Here*.

Ollie took a deep breath and pushed open the door, feeling the satisfying weight of it, hearing the loud, resonant ping of a bell announcing her arrival.

When she came for her interview, she had fallen in love with the interior. A staircase ran up the middle of the large space, its wooden banister polished to a high shine. There was a wide counter to the left of it, with displays of book-marks, local postcards and leaflets alongside the till, and a neat tower of pocket-sized Port Karadow guides. The shelves were well spaced and organised. Ollie couldn't help but drink it in again now that she was a part of it; now that she belonged. It was comforting and exciting all at once; still quiet at nine o'clock, but that was to be expected – especially as the shop had only been open for two weeks.

Becky, Thea's colleague, stood behind the counter. Her long, dark blonde hair was very straight, and she had deli-cate features and pretty, large brown eyes. She gave Ollie a smile that didn't quite reach them.

'Welcome back,' she said, her low voice melodious, and unmistakably Cornish. 'I'll go and get Thea.'

'Hi Becky,' Ollie said. 'I'm so glad to be here!'

Becky nodded but didn't say anything else, and when she disappeared, Ollie turned in a slow circle, scanning the bookshop, the titles on the shelves. Outside it had promised coffee, but she couldn't see a machine or a café area, couldn't smell its rich, morning-heady scent.

'Hi Ollie!' She turned to find Thea with Becky. The bookshop owner was slim, with dark hair pulled back from her face and a warm, genuine smile. She held out her hand. 'It's so good to see you again. Have you settled in OK?'

'Like a dream,' Ollie said. 'A good one, of course – not a nightmare. Port Karadow is lovely, and so different from London.'

'I can imagine. We're very happy you're here, aren't we?' Thea glanced at Becky, and after a second, the other woman nodded. 'Let me show you the back room. You can store your bag and hang up your coat, then we'll get a coffee and have a chat.'

'I'm really keen to get started,' Ollie said. 'To pitch in wherever I'm needed, and focus on organising events. I want to help you build on the success of your launch.' She had been packing up her life in London when the bookshop had opened, but Thea had told her their plans for launch day at the interview.

'It was better than I could have hoped for,' Thea said. 'It was so busy, which I know isn't quite reflected now.' She gestured around the beautiful space, currently devoid of customers. 'It's going to take time to get known, for people to see us as their bookshop of choice, but I'm confident we can do that.'

Ollie widened her smile. 'I've been thinking about this, and a full programme of events in the run-up to Christmas, to help promote the bookshop and tie in with what Port Karadow already has planned, would give us the best possible start.'

'It's already the middle of October,' Becky pointed out.

'I know,' Ollie laughed. 'But nobody needs to know how short our lead time has been. If the events run smoothly, it'll seem like they've been planned for months.' She was used to staying on her toes, and if she was in charge this time, there would be no limits to what she could achieve.

'And you have firm ideas about the type of events you think we should be putting on?' Thea's expression was hopeful, and Ollie felt a spike of adrenaline. She could bring real value to this place.

'I have *tons* of ideas,' she said. 'I know we talked about it at the interview, but since then I've been looking into the town, the community, and I read the recent interview with you in the local paper. Port Karadow already has a great reputation at Christmas, with the returning lights pageant, and we need to make sure A New Chapter is right at the heart of that activity.'

'It's good that you're ready to get stuck in,' Thea said, smiling. 'Though I still need to show you how everything works.' She gestured for Ollie to follow her further into the bookshop.

'A New Chapter isn't the same as a fancy London bookshop,' Becky said, before they could move. 'We don't have the same goals, the same customer base, or the same budget. It doesn't follow that what worked for you there would work here.'

'I appreciate that,' Ollie said. 'But I've got a lot of experience promoting books and understanding readers, and I also have a lot of contacts—'

'Here we go.' It was muttered, but loud enough for Thea and Ollie to hear.

Thea shot Becky a look that was concerned rather than angry, then turned to Ollie with a smile. 'Contacts?'

'Publishers and publicists,' Ollie explained. 'If we wanted to get a particular author here, for example.

21

Some of the writers who set their books in Cornwall would be ideal.'

'Let's talk about it in a moment,' Thea said. 'I want to give you the grand tour, and show you the events space.'

Thea led her to the storeroom at the back of the shop, where Ollie left her coat and bag, and then took her on a tour of the building. Once they'd been through the expansive downstairs, with the fiction and children's sections, they climbed the grand staircase in the centre of the space.

'I noticed that you have a sign outside that says coffee's served here,' Ollie said.

'We do serve coffee,' Thea replied, 'Though it's not as we'd like it to be quite yet. I want a self-service coffee machine up here, for when we hold events, and for people who want to come and read before they decide on their purchases. It's on my to-do list, and in the meantime we're making coffees in the kitchen.' She gestured as the upper floor came into view. 'What do you think?'

Ollie let out a long breath. The space was so different to the near building site it had been when Thea had shown her around at the interview.

The room itself was beautiful, with large windows letting in the soft autumn sunshine, and showing off Port Karadow, a tumble of rooftops down to the glistening harbour, in all its pretty, seaside glory. On the left-hand side of the staircase was more shelving: the non-fiction section, Ollie could see at a glance. The space to the right was more open, with the shelving only along the wall, and displaying a selection of books with the covers facing outwards. At the back there was a raised platform, like a low stage, and at the other end of the room, under the window, there was a sofa in a bold, fuchsia fabric. There were also a couple of beanbags, but other than that, it was empty: a carpeted area brimming with possibility.

'Wow,' Ollie said. 'This is starting to take shape.'

'It's a long way from finished,' Thea explained, 'but I want to keep it flexible, so we can change the layout depending on the event, accommodate any style we want. We've got the stage, and I'll get some foldout chairs which we can store out the back.'

'It looks great already,' Ollie said, and she meant it. 'It's beautiful, and it has so much character. We should use it straight away – trial an event here.'

Thea smiled. 'Let me make you a coffee, then I can show you – hang on, what?'

Ollie turned in a slow circle. 'We should test the space out as soon as we can. It's Tuesday now: how about on Friday evening?'

Thea blinked. 'How could we possibly do that?'

'A book club,' Ollie said, thinking on her feet. 'We could just ask a few people to come, to each bring one of their favourite books to discuss. It would be really informal – the beanbags, the sofa, a couple of bottles of wine. That way we can see what they think about the shop and this space: a book club and focus group rolled into one. It doesn't need much planning.'

'You're serious.' Thea laughed. 'Who do you have in mind?'

'I can ask in town today: I only know a couple of people, but I can see if they're free. And you must have friends you can drag along.'

'I can . . . I could, I suppose. You want to do it so soon?'

'No time like the present,' Ollie said. 'A book club would

23

show that we're an event-minded bookshop, and it will take the pressure off slightly while we organise other things.'

'OK.' Thea's smile was unguarded. 'Let's do it! Let's get a coffee and tell Becky our plan.'

'Perfect.' Ollie followed Thea back downstairs, her head already racing with possibilities. Seeing the events space had unleashed her imagination, set off sparks that she hadn't felt ignite for a long time. For the first time since her accident, Ollie felt like she was in control of her destiny, that she could really make a difference. And there was something about it being in Port Karadow, rather than London, that made it feel extra special.

Chapter Four

Ollie walked from the statuesque splendour of the Old Post House, down the hill into Port Karadow's cluttered, colourful streets.

It wasn't a particularly polished town, which made Ollie love it even more. The buildings didn't match in colour or style, the shops were mostly independent with a few familiar chains, and while a lot of them had made the effort to be attractive, none looked overly upmarket. She couldn't imagine that, when it was time for the Christmas lights to go up – and that wouldn't be long now, with it being less than two weeks from November – they would all match: she was expecting a rainbow kaleidoscope, rather than a drift of white twinkles. Port Karadow embraced every style and palette, and felt welcoming because of it.

As she reached Main Street, a skittish marmalade cat approached her and she bent down, hand outstretched, but it must have smelt Henry on her boots because it changed direction, bounding onto a wall and disappearing. Once it had gone, she walked to the ironmongers. It was one of her favourite places already, with its shelves bursting with treasure, inviting her to get lost inside for hours. The owner, Maisie, was probably a couple of years younger than Ollie, and had recently given up her schoolteacher job to help her father run the shop. He was getting on and – Maisie had told her – needed to retire, even though he didn't want to.

Ollie knew all this because she'd bought picture hooks, earthenware pots and outdoor lighting from the shop when she'd first arrived. Now, Maisie was cleaning the glass of the front door, spraying and polishing, standing on tiptoes to reach the top corners.

'Maisie! How are you?' Ollie asked.

'I'm good.' Maisie paused to smile at her. 'How are you getting on at Foxglove Barn?'

'It's really looking like home, now. I've put up some photos, and got a haul of books from the charity shop to fill my bookcase. I've just about prevented my dog from chewing everything to pieces so far, too.'

'That sounds like an accomplishment in itself! If you need anything else, just pop in.'

'I will, thank you. Oh, and Maisie?'

'Yes?'

'What are you doing on Friday evening, at half-past six?'

Maisie sucked in her cheeks. 'Uhm, nothing. Sadly.' She laughed.

'Come to A New Chapter, then. We're having our inaugural book club meeting, deciding which titles to read over the next few months. Bring a book you'd love to talk about, and we'll do the rest.'

'Oh, that sounds . . . are you sure? That would be lovely.'

26

'Entirely sure. See you then!' Ollie waved and walked on, enjoying the afternoon sun painting the cobbles gold, and gently warming her cheeks. After a few more steps, she'd reached Sea Brew. Her heart rate picked up, which was ridiculous, because it was just a coffee shop. They made a wonderful chai latte and crispy, delicious sausage rolls, but neither of those things, as good as they were, made her pulse race.

She risked a glance through the window, and saw a familiar tangle of dark curls, heard a low laugh that vibrated right through her. She spent a moment indulging, as if inhaling the sweet, rich scent of a chocolate she wasn't going to allow herself to eat, then moved past the open door and into Cornish Keepsakes.

The gift shop smelled heavenly, and the sight of all the chunky wicker hampers, lined with colourful tissue paper and filled with goodies, wasn't any less enticing. There were gingham-topped pots of jam, coaster sets, bags of fudge and jars of old-fashioned, brightly coloured sweets. The smell came from an array of locally produced candles, the floral and musky perfumes mingling into a single, heady aroma.

The shelves around the edges of the shop were filled with stone and glassware ornaments made by local artists, sea-glass jewellery that winked at her. Ollie wanted to absorb every sparkle and glossy surface, to inhale the smells until her head was full of them, instead of thoughts of the man next door.

In one corner, surrounded by the soft glow of golden fairy lights, was a Christmas display. Ollie's breath caught at the beauty of it. The hamper centrepiece was packed to the brim, with a jar of brandy butter, a Christmas pudding wrapped in red foil, a box of luxury mince pies and several silvery crackers, their zig-zag ends so distinctively festive. Shredded red tissue paper spilled out of it, and nestled in between each item were sprigs of holly with plump red berries, and bundles of cinnamon sticks tied with golden twine. Ollie pressed a hand to her breastbone. She *loved* Christmas, and this display was the perfect blend of elegant and over the top, just as the festive season should be. But it was more than that. It was . . .

'What do you think? Do *you* think this is too early?'

Ollie spun round. 'Meredith! How are you?'

Meredith was a few years younger than her – in her late twenties, probably. Her soft brown hair fell in waves around her shoulders, and her warm eyes and the sprinkle of freckles across her cheeks gave her an open, friendly appearance. When Ollie had come into Cornish Keepsakes two days after moving in, to buy candles and decorative trinkets to make the barn more homely, they'd started chatting. Since then, Ollie had made the gift shop a part of her daily routine – it was next to Sea Brew, after all – and she and Meredith had struck up the beginnings of a friendship.

'I'm great! What about you?'

Ollie nodded. 'I'm really well, thanks. Just admiring your festive display.'

Meredith crinkled her nose. 'I never thought I'd be accused of getting into the Christmas spirit too early.'

'Don't tell me you're not a fan.' Ollie was incredulous. 'You work in the gift business!' Personally, she never passed up an opportunity to add more decoration, more twinkle, more *fun* to life.

'I used not to be,' Meredith admitted, folding her arms. 'I had a really tough Christmas – a long time ago, now – and I ended up dreading it. But since last year, things have changed. A whole lot, actually.' Her expression brightened.

'You and Finn?' Ollie knew that Meredith's boyfriend, Finn, was a painter.

'Me and Finn,' Meredith confirmed. 'And some other things, too. I'm ready to embrace the festive season as early, and as wholeheartedly, as I possibly can. And Adrian, would you believe, thinks I've taken it too far!' She laughed.

'I don't think that,' Adrian called from the office behind the shop. 'We just don't want to ride roughshod all over autumn. We need to make the most of every season, and you've put Christmas up before Halloween.'

Meredith rolled her eyes. 'I told you: this is one *tiny* corner to plant the idea in people's heads. My Halloween stock is arriving tomorrow, at which point I will happily fill the rest of the shop with cobwebs and dangling spiders.'

Adrian, the owner of Cornish Keepsakes, appeared in the doorway. He always looked dapper, wearing a suit and one of his endless supply of quirky ties. Today, it was green avocados on a pink background. 'Hello, London Ollie,' he said.

Ollie laughed. 'Is that a moniker so you remember who I am?'

'It was, but I don't think I need it anymore. Would you be disappointed if I dropped the London part?'

'Not at all. I don't want people thinking I'm one of those terrible interlopers. What are they called – grockles?'

'That's more for tourists, I think,' Adrian said. 'We'll just call you Ollie from now on.'

'Very decent of you.'

'How did your first day go?' Meredith asked. 'Everything good with Thea?'

'It was a great first day,' Ollie said, aware that Meredith and Thea were close. 'I'm brimming with ideas already.'

'I'm so glad!' Meredith smiled. 'Thea's so proud of the bookshop, and she's really receptive to new ideas, especially from people with different backgrounds to her. She came from the library, but you've been a bookseller.'

'I hope I can live up to her expectations,' Ollie said. 'And with that in mind, I've got the first meeting of our book club on Friday. Do either of you fancy it?'

'Friday as in three days away?' Adrian asked.

'That's right. Six thirty at the bookshop. Bring a book you'd love to talk about, drink some wine, have a chat. It's going to be super informal.'

'I'll have to check with Tillie. We might have a do to go to.'

'I think Finn and I are free,' Meredith said. 'Can I get back to you?'

'Of course. I'd love you to be there, to be a title trailblazer, but if not you can come to the next one.'

Meredith laughed. 'A title trailblazer, I love that.' She turned to the nearest shelf, rotating candles so that their names were facing outwards, as Adrian went back to his office. 'How did you get on with Becky?'

Ollie shrugged. 'She seems more reserved than Thea, but I've got time to win her over, if that's what I need to do.'

'I don't know her very well,' Meredith admitted, 'but it sounds like she's had a tough time recently. She split up with her husband not that long ago, and she's got three young children.'

'God. That sounds really hard. Maybe author events and Christmas pageants aren't her focus at the moment.'

Meredith shook her head. 'She does work at A New Chapter, though. She can't be cynical about everything Christmassy or, if she is, she's going to have to hide it well.'

'Speaking from experience?' Ollie grinned when Meredith gave her a sheepish nod. 'I know some people who have made it their life goal to be cynical about absolutely everything.'

'Things must have been very different in London,' Meredith said. 'I imagine this all feels a bit alien to you.'

'Green space and endless skies, the gentle hum of the waves, peace and quiet?' Ollie raised her eyebrows.

Meredith smiled. 'I'm not saying you were trapped in London, just that moving here must have been a big decision.'

'It's a complete lifestyle change,' Ollie admitted. 'But a great one, so far. It's as if I've suddenly got space to breathe and think, to plan things properly instead of spending my life working or commuting, or out at events. My senses aren't on constant overload, and I guess you don't notice it when you're immersed in it, but now, being away from London, the difference is startling.'

'Finn has said much the same.'

'So you've heard it before, the hackneyed scenario, all this "move to the countryside, change your life," stuff, but I suppose it's become a cliché because so many people have done it, and it works.' She chewed her lip, felt the stickiness of the red lip gloss she had put on that morning. 'I don't mind being a sheep, as long as people don't think I've come here believing I'm superior because I'm from London.' She thought of Becky's earlier accusation. 'I don't want to be a dickish sheep.'

Meredith laughed, her eyes kindling with warmth. 'Nobody thinks you're a dickish sheep.'

'Debatable,' Ollie said with a grin.

'And surely,' Meredith went on, 'when it comes to running successful book events, you *do* know best. That's the whole point.'

'I want to be part of the team.' Ollie picked up a holly sprig and rubbed her thumb against a waxy leaf. 'I'm even more excited than I thought I would be.'

'That's a good sign,' Meredith said. 'Are you going to be in Cornwall for Christmas?'

Ollie nodded, then gave Meredith an apologetic look and put the holly back in the hamper. 'The barn will look gorgeous decked out with baubles and lights. I feel giddy about having so much space to fill – I'll have to get a huge tree.'

'Are your family coming, then? That must be lovely, having the chance to host in your new home.'

Ollie smiled, not wanting to admit that the decorations would most definitely outnumber the people. Melissa was firmly ensconced in Portugal with Tiago, her parents were planning one of their yearly cruises, and, other than Guy, there was nobody else she knew well enough that they would abandon their family plans and come all the way to Cornwall for the festive holidays.

'What are you doing now?' Meredith asked, as if she sensed her discomfort and wanted to change the subject.

'Going to . . .' she cleared her throat. 'Going to get a tea in Sea Brew.'

'Oh lovely! Say hello to Max for me.' She put her hands on her hips and turned in a slow circle. 'I'd better start thinking about what I'm going to do with all these Halloween decorations when they arrive.'

'Put them *all* in Adrian's office,' Ollie said with a grin, and Meredith laughed. 'Lovely to catch up. Hopefully see you again soon?'

'We could go and get a drink sometime, if you'd like?'

'I'd *love*,' Ollie said. 'Let's do it!' She said goodbye to Meredith, then pushed open the door and stepped onto the street. '*Say hello to Max for me*,' she whispered, repeating the other woman's words.

She shouldn't even be going inside. She should stay well away from the temptation she had already told herself she couldn't give into. She needed to give herself time to properly get over Guy: she needed to be on her own for a bit. But the reckless part of her, the part that so often overruled her more sensible side, was already in charge of her feet. The sensible side gave a tiny shrug, putting up the barest minimum of fights before giving up, and Ollie turned towards the quaint, unassuming but very popular café only a few steps away.

Chapter Five

Sea Brew was charming in every way. It didn't try to be fancy or different; it didn't serve coffee in jam jars or have exclusively vegan pastries – though it did cater to everyone, from what Ollie had seen. It was an attractive café with gingham tablecloths and prints of Cornish seascapes on the white walls, and the guarantee of a friendly welcome.

When Ollie walked in, she was hit by the rich smells of coffee and butter, the salty, warming scent of pastry. The sound of grinding coffee beans filled the air, the low thrum of a pop song on the radio a background beat. Usually, there would be a young woman or man behind the counter – Ollie had been served by three different staff members so far – but today, she could only see Max.

Max, who – Meredith had told her – owned Sea Brew, and who Ollie had noticed, immediately and intensely, the very first time she'd been here, in the same way you notice a gleaming red Ferrari in a row of hatchbacks; the way a single blooming wild rose sticks out in a dense green hedgerow.

Ollie found that she was hovering in the doorway, unable to move further in or back out. It was so unlike her: it wasn't in her nature to be shy, but perhaps the logical part of her brain, the one that remembered how badly she had misjudged Guy, was telling her to proceed with caution.

Max had his back to her because she'd taken the open door from a leaving customer, and it hadn't closed properly and been given a chance to ding when she opened it again.

His hair was a tangle of curls, so dark brown they looked almost black, and his shoulders were wide, his navy T-shirt pulled tight across them. He was at least six foot tall, she thought. She couldn't see his face but she could picture it: the thick eyebrows, unusual green eyes beneath, the strong jawline that was sometimes smooth, sometimes stubbled. The dimple that appeared in his left cheek when he smiled.

She wondered if he'd noticed her: if he'd registered that she had been here almost every morning over the last ten days – usually with Henry – and chatted with his staff, exchanging a brief hello with him while he busied himself behind the counter. She didn't think, right now, that she could say a single word. It was such an alien feeling.

She heard steps behind her and turned to see a rosy-cheeked woman, her face framed by tendrils of strawberry blonde hair, wearing a waxed jacket and wellies. Ollie stepped to the side.

'You going in or coming out?' the woman asked in a broad Cornish accent.

Ollie moved further into the café, backing up against a table. 'Go ahead.'

'All right, lass,' the woman said jovially, and walked past her. 'Max, be a love and pop a sausage roll in the oven – if you've got any left this late in the day.'

Max turned, and there it was: the face that had stayed in Ollie's mind's eye long after she'd walked out of the café on every occasion. It wasn't just that he was handsome, but that he radiated warmth. His ready smile and green, crinkle-edged eyes were like open arms, compelling her forwards. His chest was partially hidden behind a black-and-white chequered apron which emphasised his tapered torso, and the short sleeves of the navy T-shirt showed off his sculpted arms. He was solid, strong-looking, but not bulky. He was—

'No problem, Lizzy,' he said. He smiled at the woman, then his gaze flickered to Ollie and his lips flattened. She couldn't blame him: what must she look like, standing against a table, frozen and mute? 'Do you want one heated up, too?' He paused for a beat, then added, 'I thought I'd get ahead of the game. No pressure, though. You might not be after any food.'

It took Ollie a second to realise he was talking to her, not Lizzy. His deep voice was mesmerising, the edges of his words softened by the hint of a Cornish accent.

'Oh – Uh. I . . . I am . . . that is to say that I would like, uhm . . .' She watched his brows draw together, his lips twitch. *For fuck's sake.* 'I'd love a heated-up sausage roll,' she managed, almost shouting to compensate for her stumbling. 'Thank you,' she added. Internally, every one of her organs shrivelled up in embarrassment.

'Good-oh.' Max leaned into the display cabinet, his tongs outstretched. 'People say they're the best around here.'

36

'That's because Beryan makes them,' Lizzy said, turning to Ollie. 'She's who Max commissions to make his cakes and pastries. She's a baking superstar, and he somehow zeroed in on her skills before anyone else, got this exclusive arrangement.'

'You don't make them yourself?' Ollie had just assumed he did.

He looked up, his gaze finding hers. 'No, baking's not a skill of mine. The business side of things is fine, and what I like most is being here, talking to customers.'

'Spending all day shooting the shit,' Lizzy said, and Max laughed.

'There are worse ways to make a living.' He stood up straight, two of the huge sausage rolls on a cardboard tray. 'And Beryan and I have a great partnership.' His smile was gentle, far from anything approaching cocky.

'I don't even know if he pays her.' Lizzy leaned against the counter as if she was as familiar with the café as her own kitchen. 'Or if it's all just charm.'

'Come on now,' Max said, opening the door of a compact oven built into the wall, sliding the sausage rolls onto a metal tray inside. 'You know I'm above board. This whole charm thing is wearing thin.'

'Is it heck,' Lizzy replied. 'If it's not charm, then it's flat-out bewitching. You can see that about him, can't you?' She turned back to Ollie, and Ollie jolted, still unable to find her footing in Max's presence, and especially when asked such a pertinent question.

'Don't drag Ollie into this.' Max moved to the smart black coffee machine, which took up a significant space behind the counter.

Ollie blinked, replaying his words. 'You know my name.'

Lizzy chuckled. 'He makes it his business to know everyone's name. Ollie, is it?'

'That's right.'

'Meredith told me,' Max admitted. He was still facing the coffee machine, and Ollie was desperate for him to turn around, so she could see his expression. 'She mentioned that you'd moved here from London, and I—' He cleared his throat. 'I commented on your dog. The chocolate Lab.'

'He's called Henry Tilney.' She wondered if he was terrorising Liam right this moment.

'Sorry?' Max said on a laugh.

Lizzy was watching them, her arms folded.

'He's named after the hero in a Jane Austen book,' Ollie explained. '*Northanger Abbey*. I got him with my friend, and we didn't want to call him something obvious: Fido or Rex or Trigger.'

'Do people call their dogs Trigger?' Lizzy asked.

'No idea,' Ollie said. 'But when I saw him, I knew. He was Henry Tilney. Now my friend's moved to Portugal, and I've moved here, and he's all mine.'

'Henry's a great name for a Lab,' Max said. 'He's boisterous, I bet.'

'Very,' Ollie confirmed. 'I need someone to drag me out of the house and pull me through the countryside: help me get to know my surroundings better.'

'Max likes hiking in the countryside, don't you, Max?' Lizzy said.

'Sometimes,' Max replied. 'What drink did you want with your sausage roll? Chai latte, as usual?'

'You know my order as well?' Ollie laughed.

38

'I pay attention,' Max said, shrugging. 'You'd like one?'

'Love one.' Ollie finally unglued her feet and joined Lizzy at the counter.

'So you're from London,' the older woman said. 'Second home in idyllic Cornwall? Escaping the big smoke for a bit?'

She sounded friendly enough, but Ollie was immediately wary. 'First home,' she said. 'Only home. I moved here a fortnight ago, and I'm not going back to London.' She was only renting Liam's barn, so she felt as if she had an escape route, but she already loved being here, and after her first day in A New Chapter, she was excited about having a new business to make her mark on. And, only two weeks in, the frantic speed of London, the city stretching all around her, seemed so distant, as if she had only seen it in a film, and never really lived there herself.

'Cornwall can seem slow.' Lizzy's tone had softened, and Ollie realised she and Max were looking at her with concern, as if she didn't understand what she'd let herself in for.

'It's deliciously slow,' she said. 'I have no complaints so far.'

'Are you in town?' Max asked, turning to check on the pastries.

'At Foxglove Barn, so not too far.'

'Oh, Liam Byrne's outbuilding,' Lizzy said. 'Finally made it liveable, has he?'

Ollie laughed. 'It's like something out of *Country Living* magazine. It's a dream.'

Max smiled at her, and their eyes locked. His were dark green: moss rather than grass, and she thought that he could absolutely have got Beryan to make cakes for him without paying her. But he was too nice for that: too wholesome, despite the dark curls and unusual eye colour that somehow gave him an air of danger. *Dangerously hot*. She wondered if he ever asked Beryan to make cinnamon rolls.

'What is it?' she asked, because he hadn't dropped his gaze and he hadn't said anything, and having all his attention on her was making her feel like she might dissolve into a puddle at any minute.

'Nothing,' he said, and looked away. 'What do you do, for work?' He took the sausage rolls out of the oven, put them on a cooling rack.

'I'm a bookseller, and I've just got a job at A New Chapter. We're going to organise events in the run-up to Christmas, bring some razzmatazz to the town.'

Max's smile showed off his dimple. 'That sounds great. Thea mentioned that she wants my help picking a coffee machine.'

'And you're putting her off at every turn,' Lizzy said, accepting a takeaway cup from him.

Max frowned. 'Why would I do that?'

'Because it'll be competition.'

'It won't be,' he said, laughing. 'She wants a Help Yourself machine for customers who want to browse. There's room for all of us.' He held out Ollie's latte to her, and her fingers grazed his as she took the cup. She noticed how tanned and strong his forearms were. He was incredibly attractive, even more so now she knew how friendly he was, how calm and considerate: even to Lizzy, who clearly made it her mission to tease him.

Then she thought of another attractive man, with blond hair and caramel eyes, his smile a little crooked, as if it was a physical manifestation of the fact that, beneath the surface, all wasn't as it should be. But she hadn't picked up on it, she hadn't realised until she was injured and in pain, and he had no time for her. His temper had frayed, his good humour all but gone when she became hard work. Her 'can-do' attitude had gone on hiatus when she'd fractured her shoulder, and his affection had left with it, and had failed to return. *Guy.* She had misjudged him so badly. She couldn't trust herself, at the moment, when it came to men. She needed breathing space.

She took a step backwards and raised her cup. 'Thank you for this.'

'Don't go without your sausage roll.' Max put them into paper bags, and Ollie felt a traitorous thrill of nerves at the thought of their fingers brushing again.

'Course not,' she said. And then, despite her need for breathing space, she added, 'Come to our first book club meet-up on Friday night. Both of you, if you're free. No need to bring anything except yourself and a book you love that you're happy to talk about. We'll provide the refreshments.'

'I'll have to check with the teens,' Lizzy said. 'The likelihood is that I'll be ferrying one or other of them to a house party somewhere. But Max would love to, I'm sure. Getting to wang on about his favourite book, and bewitch a pretty young thing at the same time.'

Ollie laughed. 'I'm thirty-five!'

'Beryan's fifty-eight, and she isn't immune to his charms.'

'Lizzy!' Max rolled his eyes. 'Do you come in here purposely to make trouble?'

'Why would you even ask me that?' Lizzy took her

41

sausage roll, lifted her coffee cup in thanks and winked at Ollie. 'Of course I do. Best part of my day.' She blew Max a kiss, then walked out of the café.

Max slumped against the counter, raising his arm up like an exhausted triathlete at the end of a race. 'Here's your sausage roll.'

Ollie grinned. 'Get a lot of mental workouts like that, do you?'

'All part of the service,' he said, smiling at her.

There was no mistaking the change in his tone, kindness shifting towards flirtation, and Ollie thought he might have more weapons in his arsenal of attraction than she could possibly cope with.

'And I do love it,' he continued. 'Talking to people. The variety, the fun. I get all the news – get to share in people's good fortune, commiserate with them if things aren't so great. Sometimes it strays towards agony uncle, but I'd much rather that than be stuck in an office somewhere, making friends with a computer.'

'Agreed,' Ollie said.

'Yeah, you're a people person too, I can tell.'

'Not so much fun talking to inanimate objects.' She laughed. 'But maybe being in sleepy little Cornwall, I'll be too starved of company, turn tail and run.' She thought of her beautiful barn, all the space just for her and Henry. Her empty Christmas plans.

'No you won't,' Max said. 'Sure, it's different here, but just think of it as quality rather than quantity.'

'That's a good way of looking at it.' When he smiled, her lips tugged upwards too, as if she was his reflection and had no choice but to mirror what he was doing.

'Anyway, I'd better get back to Henry and my to-do list.' The smell of pastry and spiced sausage meat from her paper bag was making her stomach rumble. 'What do I owe you?' She put her cup on the counter, took out her purse and her card.

'See you tomorrow?' Max said, once she'd paid.

'Of course. Before work though, rather than after. And come on Friday night, if you're not too busy. It'll be good fun.'

'I'll think about it,' Max said. 'Thanks for the invite.'

When she turned in the doorway, unable to resist a final glance, he gave her a quick salute, his head slightly angled. It was a throwaway gesture, but it was far too hot for Ollie to handle.

She rushed out into the pale October sunshine, and almost collided with a man in a fisherman's jumper who was striding up the street.

'Fuck fuck fuckity fuck,' she said, as soon as she was out of sight of Sea Brew. She had promised herself that she would focus on her new home and her work, on getting to know who she really was, before she thought about flirting or kissing or even looking at another man.

Max, she realised, had been put in her path as a challenge. It was bad enough that he ran the best café in town, but she might also end up helping Thea sort out the bookshop's coffee machine – which would mean working with him – and if that happened she would have to bury her feelings for him deep, deep down.

It would be good for her, she decided, as she walked through the pretty town, with its glistening harbour and autumn sunshine. Ollie was here to restart her life, reach her potential, and live mindfully, and men – Max very much included – were nowhere near the top of her to-do list. She had so many other things to tick off first, before she could even consider letting her attraction to him run riot.

Chapter Six

When the doorbell rang early the next morning, Ollie was making a green smoothie using a recipe she'd found on a well-being website. She looked at the radio-active green gunk in her Nutribullet – she wasn't sure the avocado had been a good idea – and went to see who it was.

A delivery man in blue overalls was standing above a large cardboard box on the doorstep. Ollie felt a skip of excitement, because she knew what this was. She thanked him, and dragged the box inside.

She manoeuvred it into the open-plan living area, which really did look like it had come straight out of *Country Living* magazine. It was high-ceilinged, with an expansive lounge area, the kitchen along one wall, and glass doors at either end. The walls were pistachio green, the woodwork – window frames, doors and beams – was pine, there was a modern fireplace with a large mirror above it, and two giant, duck-egg blue sofas facing each other.

A bookshelf was fixed along one wall, the spines a bright pop of colour in the serene space. Alongside Ollie's favourite books from London, there was the haul she'd picked up from the charity shop in Truro. A series of mysteries with bold, Seventies covers had caught her eye, a quick glimpse had told her they were set in Cornwall, and she'd ended up buying all five. She planned to delve into them over Christmas.

Ollie was just about to open the box when she heard a 'Cooee!'

'Hi Marion,' she called. 'Come through.'

Liam's housekeeper, a short, lithe woman who had so far been quite brusque with Ollie, appeared in the doorway. She was dressed in an ankle-skimming beige skirt, plum-coloured blouse and oatmeal cardigan. Her blonde hair was cropped short, and her earrings were turquoise studs.

'I saw the delivery man pull up,' she said, 'and wondered if you needed help with anything?'

'I've made it – just about.' Ollie ran a hand over the thick cardboard.

'Something nice, then?'

'Hopefully.' She knew that answer wouldn't satisfy the other woman.

Marion Proctor – who had assured Ollie when they met that she was no good at typing, and was happy to continue cleaning, and cooking Liam's evening meals – was shameless in her nosiness. Liam had said that she was indispensable, that he didn't know what he'd do without her, but Ollie thought that was as much about her company as the tasks she completed for him.

She went to get a knife while Marion fussed over a gleeful Henry, the dog lying on his back in a state of ecstasy while she tickled his tummy.

'I ordered these from London,' Ollie said, sliding the knife along the sellotaped seal. 'Having all this space, I thought I'd treat myself.' She pulled open the flaps and peered inside, and then, with a delighted squeal, reached in for the first garland.

It was a string of fabric paper chains, the material silky, the links silver, pale green and pink. Hanging from the chain were tiny, jewelled baubles in buttercup yellow and pale blue. Ollie pulled it out slowly, as if she was a snake charmer in charge of a viper, and Marion gasped.

'Goodness! That's a bit fancy.'

'It's from a specialist Christmas shop in London. I've always loved their window displays, and this year I thought I'd get some decorations.'

'Must have cost a pretty penny,' Marion said, a scolding edge to her voice.

'Some things are worth splashing out for, and I'm not going to have Christmas with zero decorations as well as no—' she caught herself, pressed her lips together, and went back to the box. 'I bought a few. Look – this one's gold and blue, and there's another one covered in fake snow.'

Marion helped Ollie take the garlands out. She made gentle cooing noises, running her thumbs over the different textures: tinsel and frosting, the smooth glass of an iridescent bauble. Ollie sucked in a breath as she saw the final garland, the one that was sheer indulgence. It was made of thick, bushy tinsel in pearlescent white, the baubles hanging from it small and mirrored, and in every colour imaginable. She would hang this one above her headboard. She brushed it against her cheek, the soft tinsel tickling her skin.

'This the Tiffany's equivalent of Christmas tat, then?' Marion asked.

Ollie laughed. 'Something like that. They're going to make this place look gorgeous, though.' She sighed happily, then noticed that Henry was about to clamp his strong jaws around one of the garlands, and hurried over, scooping them back into the box.

'You know,' she said, as the older woman helped her tidy up. 'I bought more than enough for the barn. If you wanted one – or you thought Liam might like one to brighten up his kitchen – then just say. We could have a fun time decorating the farmhouse together, put on a Christmas playlist.'

'It's October,' Marion pointed out.

'I know, but look!' She gestured to the glass doors, where the thick frost they'd woken up to was only just being burned off by the sun. 'If we put our minds to it, we could pretend it was November – December, even.'

'I don't think so,' Marion said. 'Besides, we don't go in for fancy stuff here. There's a mature holly tree out the back that Liam will cut some branches off. There are always plenty of berries left – the birds don't get them all.'

'I bet that looks lovely,' Ollie said, sinking onto her haunches. 'Let me know if you change your mind, though.'

'I'd best be off,' Marion said. 'Thank you for showing me your . . . sparkles.' She waggled her fingers, then walked out of the room.

Ollie stared at her box of indulgent goodies, the colours and textures, the way that everything shimmered and shone in an unashamedly festive way. She realised, after she'd heard the front door slam, that she hadn't told Marion about the book club meeting on Friday night.

The air was icy against Ollie's bare cheeks, though the rest of her was wrapped up in her long coat, boots, thick scarf and berry-coloured woolly hat. Henry was overjoyed at the path they had taken, round the back of the farmhouse and deeper into the countryside. It was hilly here, the ground soft after recent rainfall, the trees in compact clusters rather than never-ending stretches of woodland, so they were sometimes beneath a canopy of oranges and reds, sometimes out in the sunshine.

The inclines stretched Ollie's calves, the descents tested her knees, and she caught glimpses of the sea in the distance, the gunmetal grey sparkling whenever the sun peeked out from behind a cloud.

Everything smelled rich and musty, thick with vegetation, and birds sang in the trees. Getting out in nature, all the articles and podcasts had told her, was one of the best things you could do for your well-being, and with Henry, Ollie had a ready-made reason to.

A walk through London streets was always interesting, full of tableaux of other people's lives, and it was rich with green spaces. But if your workdays were long, and you didn't have one of those green spaces on your doorstep – only a flat with a few houseplants – you could go far too long without hearing the trill of a blackbird. Being in Cornwall, Ollie felt like she'd been picked up and put down in a different world. But it wasn't just her surroundings that had changed.

Everything she'd given value to in London had gone. Her job, which she had blithely thought she would continue to excel at; her relationship with Guy; living with Melissa. They had all, in the end, proved to be impermanent, and without them, her life had become paper thin, meaningless. Moving here had seemed like the perfect solution to her problems, even though she was having to start from scratch. It was exciting and disconcerting all at once.

She increased her pace as a hill rose in front of them, the leaf-strewn pathway weaving between spindly trees. She hurried to the top, still several paces behind her dog, and saw the Cornish countryside stretched out before her: the soft ripple of hills meandering into the distance, pockets of autumn-burnished foliage, the blue-grey line of the sea. There was a lemon-yellow cottage to her right, nestled in a steep valley.

Ollie stood with her hands on her hips and breathed in, letting the emotions rush over her. She was just starting out, so it was bound to feel strange. And so what if she'd bought expensive decorations that only a handful of people would see? Marion's words had been playing on her mind, reminding her that, despite the twinkly garlands, her festive calendar was empty. She tried to ignore the twinge of sadness, and was about to make her way down the hill when Henry started barking. He was scrabbling in a pile of leaves, his movements more frantic than Ollie was used to.

'What have you got there?' He looked up at her, panting, as she joined him, and she directed her gaze to where he was digging. 'What's this?'

It was a large stone, more of a boulder, nestled at the bottom of the hill she had just come down. There were several smaller stones around it, and fallen leaves had gathered in the hollow of earth in front of it.

Henry had clearly found something interesting in the pile of leaves, but Ollie was distracted by the exposed, smooth side of the boulder. On it, imprinted in it, but surely impossible because it was a natural rock, not a piece of concrete, was what looked like a handprint, the fingers splayed.

Ollie crouched and put her hand out, her gloves cracking as she stretched her fingers. It fitted into the ghost handprint almost perfectly, the stone cold even through the leather. Henry stopped scrabbling, and his gaze fixed on Ollie's hand.

'It's probably a fossil,' she said. 'One that looks like a handprint. Don't you think, Henry?'

Her dog whimpered.

'What were you scrabbling at, anyway?' She tried not to be too alarmed that her dog had stopped what had, moments before, seemed like the most important dig of his life, and was now sitting calmly, watching her.

She pulled her hand back and stood up quickly, her knees protesting.

'I,' she said to him, 'have been spending too much time on New Age websites.'

Henry barked up at her, then turned away from the rock and his beloved pile of leaves, bounding on ahead as if the last few minutes hadn't happened. Ollie shook her head. The sooner she got these bookshop events going, the sooner she got to know more people in the town, the better things would be. Otherwise, regardless of how many avocado smoothies she drank – and that smoothie had been truly disgusting – she wouldn't sort her life out, but instead would send herself into isolation-based madness.

Sparing only the briefest glance at the strange stone, Ollie followed her dog, who seemed entirely carefree as he cavorted in the mud, delighting in the acres of land stretched out ahead of him, and they made their way towards the silvery shimmer of sea in the distance.

Chapter Seven

By the time she was getting her washing in from the line in the garden behind the barn, Ollie's confusion had faded. The handprint must have been a natural anomaly, and she'd imagined Henry's strange behaviour.

'Hello there,' called a familiar voice over the redbrick wall.

Ollie dropped her pyjama shorts into the basket and turned to see Liam resting his forearms on the wall. 'Hi Liam, how are you?'

'Grand, love. What about you?'

'I'm good! I had Marion's help with a delivery this morning.'

'I heard.' He gave her a wry smile. 'Marion is quite strong on tradition. You're certainly giving her some things to think about.'

'And talk about?' She grinned. 'I think having your ideas challenged is a good thing.'

'So do I, and speaking of ideas, when shall we get going on my book? I appreciate that you've just started your new job, but two weeks is surely enough time to settle in?'

Ollie pretended to be outraged. 'I would have started a week ago! I was waiting for you to come to me.' A blackbird hopped onto the wall, bounced a few steps towards them, then flew off into the mature trees, peeping loudly.

Liam chuckled. 'I know, lass. I know.' He gestured behind her. 'Henry's looking worn out.'

Ollie turned to see that her dog, who had come outside with her, was lying flat-out beneath the rotary washing line. 'We just had a good walk,' she said. 'Although . . .'

'Although what?'

'I found this stone,' she rushed. 'It must have some kind of fossil in it, because I thought, for a few minutes . . .'

'Kerensa's handprint,' Liam said. 'That's what you found, isn't it? The handprint pressed into the stone, about twenty minutes' walk from here, at the bottom of a steep slope?'

Ollie's pulse skipped. 'It's an actual *thing*, then? I thought I must be imagining it. Who's Kerensa?'

'She's the subject of a local legend,' Liam explained. 'If now's a good time, we can go to my study, I'll tell you about her, and we can get started on my manuscript. Of course, you can take away my scribbled notes, but I've been told my handwriting leaves a lot to be desired.'

'I don't mind working in your study. I'll bring my laptop.'

'Finish what you're doing and come to the back door in ten minutes. This place is rife with myths and legends, and you've just stumbled on your first one.'

'There's a whole story behind the rock?'

'There's a story behind everything in Cornwall,' Liam said. 'Bring Henry with you, and I'll see if I can rustle up some biscuits.'

'You're on.' Ollie hurried back to her basket of washing, eager to get it inside.

Not only was she intrigued by the farmhouse, and how Liam lived in that big, solid building all by himself, but she was delighted that her discovery had a story behind it, that some underused part of her mind hadn't assigned meaning to something inconsequential.

And, she thought, as she un-pegged her tea towels and stepped around her sleepy Labrador, what better way to root herself in her new home than to find out some ancient legends about it? The more she knew about Port Karadow, the more she would feel a part of it.

The inside of Foxglove Farm was as she'd imagined it. Red stone floors and dark tones throughout, though the forest green and navy walls were accented by glossy white doors, and while the windows looked old, with thin glass, they were large and let in a lot of light. The whole effect was cosy rather than sullen and unwelcoming.

Ollie followed Liam down the corridor, Henry staying close to her side, until they emerged into a room that could have played the library in an adaptation of *Beauty and the Beast.*

'Bloody hell,' she blurted.

It had a deep-red carpet covered with an intricately patterned blue-and-gold rug, and other than the door, the fireplace and the large picture window that looked out on the front lawn, the walls were lined with floor-to-ceiling bookshelves. There was a large, solid-looking desk in the middle of the room, and a leather sofa beneath the window. It was entirely different to the clean lines of her modern barn, but if Ollie had a room like this, she would never leave it.

Liam strode to a shelf and ran his finger along a row of books. The shelves reminded Ollie of her parents' house, though they seemed more organised, with the obviously older spines higher up, newer books lower down. It was a treasure trove, one she could get lost in for hours – days, probably.

'Decades worth of collecting,' Liam explained, glancing over his shoulder at her. Henry settled himself in a corner, and Ollie wondered if he'd found where the heating pipes ran beneath the floorboards. 'I'm looking for a specific book.'

'Related to Kerensa?'

'Exactly. I had it recently, I'm sure.'

While he searched, Ollie breathed in the familiar bookish smell, luxuriated in the soft carpet beneath her feet, and listened to her dog's gentle snuffles. There was a stack of notepad paper on the desk, the edges crinkled as if they'd been thumbed through often, a brass, anchor-shaped paper-weight keeping them in place.

She was about to ask him what had made him want to write a memoir, when he held out a small volume to her. 'Here we go.'

Ollie took it. It was old, the cover made out of a thick, rough-to-the-touch material somewhere between leather and cardboard. The edges were frayed, the blue-grey colour faded to silver in patches. She squinted at the gold lettering on the cover: *Myths and Legends of Port Karadow and the Surrounding Area.*

'This little area has its own book?' she asked. 'There are that many legends in this part of Cornwall?'

Liam nodded. He was watching her, a hint of amusement on his face.

'And one of those is related to the handprint I saw? I thought I was losing the plot: I mean, it could have been anything.'

'But it looked like a handprint, didn't it?'

'It really did.' She laughed. 'Who was Kerensa?'

'She was a young woman who worked in a grand stately home at the southern tip of Cornwall, close to Land's End. The house isn't there anymore, because in the years after Kerensa worked there, its position on the clifftops became precarious. The family left before it tumbled, brick by brick, into the sea, but Kerensa had fled the property long before then.'

'Why?' Ollie rested a bum-cheek on the corner of the desk.

'She'd been seduced by the master of the house, despite the other female staff warning her of his reputation. She was young and pretty, and believed the things he told her.' Liam sighed. 'They were discovered together by the master's wife, and although it wasn't a surprise to her, Kerensa was too beautiful to stay. She was thrown out, with nowhere to go and no references in her favour.'

'What did she do?'

'She journeyed up the coastline, looking for somewhere, someone, who would give her shelter, employ her in any role. She was always moved on, told to try this place or that, none of the households willing to take her in themselves. She became exhausted, cold, malnourished. She had to forage for food.'

57

'Did she die?' Ollie cleared her throat. It was just a legend, she told herself. It wasn't real.

'Hold your horses,' Liam said gently. 'When Kerensa was close to giving up, she encountered an old woman along the area's most well-used highway – a highway in those days was an earth track, of course, not a tarmac road. When Kerensa asked about jobs in the area, this woman told her about a place nearby, where she would find food and warmth, friendly faces and a job: where she could make a difference and be part of a family again. The woman sent Kerensa on her way with hope, rekindled energy, and a smile that she hadn't used for a long time. The house she was heading for wasn't too far from here, though Foxglove Farm wasn't built until a hundred years after Kerensa made her fateful journey.'

Liam paused, and Ollie realised she was holding her breath. She was desperate to find out what had happened to this young woman. Even Henry had raised his head, his chocolate eyes gazing at Liam. The deep timbre of his voice had captivated her dog, too.

'Did she make it?' Ollie's own voice was a whisper.

Liam shook his head. 'Her spark went out ten miles from the place she'd been seeking, and as she sank to the ground, she stretched her hand out, pressing her open palm against the flat rock she'd fallen beside. There was no reason to, of course: it was stone, it couldn't possibly hold her impression. But somehow, it did.

'She was found by the owners of the house the old lady had sent her to. They were out riding, and came across her lifeless body, arm still outstretched. They gave her a proper burial, even though they hadn't known her. And the lady of the house said that she had seen the girl's handprint in the stone, had laid her own hand over the indentation, and felt an overwhelming surge of hope, of happiness.

'You see,' Liam went on, shifting slightly where he stood, 'even though Kerensa never made it to her new home, the old lady she met had given her hope, and her last hours were filled with the anticipation of that welcome, a renewed sense of purpose, rather than despair and hopelessness. It was the strength of those feelings that she imprinted into the rock, and it's said that anyone who presses their hand over where hers rested will achieve something they've long dreamed of but not dared to hope for: that their luck will change.'

'But she didn't make it,' Ollie said, fighting a swell of emotion. 'She was so close, and she didn't get there.'

'No,' Liam replied, 'but sometimes the *hope* of something is as important as the thing itself. She realised she wasn't entirely alone, because there was a family who would look after her. She died with that hope inside her, and she left it in the handprint for others to find centuries later.'

Ollie stood up, pacing to the window. 'But if that's the case, if it's magical, then why is it just *there*, hidden in the woodland? Why doesn't it have a National Trust car park or an English Heritage plaque?'

'Because if everyone knew about it, then the magic would be lost,' Liam said calmly.

'Really?' She slumped onto the sofa. 'So . . . so now that *I've* put my hand against hers, I'm supposed to get what I want?'

'What is it that you want, Ollie?' There was a definite twinkle in Liam's eye, now.

She bit her lip. 'I want to belong. To build a life here, and to make a difference at the bookshop.' *To feel less alone,* she added silently.

Liam pointed at the book she was still holding. 'Time will tell if you get it. Port Karadow is full of these stories, and a lot of the legends have their origins in the land surrounding this farmhouse. You could seek out more of them on your walks with Henry.'

Ollie looked down at the small hardback. 'Thank you.'

'Now, shall I see if Marion's happy to fetch us some tea and cakes? Then I could set you off on typing up *my* history.'

Ollie nodded. 'If the way you told Kerensa's story is anything to go by, then this typing project isn't going to be a chore at all.'

'Why's that?' Liam asked.

'Because you're a wonderful storyteller. I felt every moment of Kerensa's journey, and I can't believe she didn't make it.' She swallowed the lump in her throat. Could pressing her gloved hand against a stone really have a bearing on her future?

'Let me go and see about that cake. And then, chapter one.'

'Chapter one,' she repeated with a smile.

Liam left Ollie in his study while he went to talk to Marion, and she looked down at her hand. She decided that she really must have been on too many New Age websites, because already – just being in Liam's study, being so welcomed by him – she was starting to feel a little bit more like she belonged, and was wondering if there might actually be some truth to the legend of Kerensa's handprint.

Chapter Eight

Between closing time at A New Chapter and the start of the book club on Friday, Ollie walked down to the harbour to stretch her legs, and pick up the supplies she needed from Main Street. Clouds were racing across the sky, hiding then revealing the late afternoon sun like a faulty Jack-in-the-box, and the sea went from twinkling to dull grey, then back to twinkling.

It was so beautiful. Even now, only ten days from November, she could picture this place under warmer, heavier sunshine and with an idyllic holiday atmosphere, and, as it was, it wouldn't be too long until it was fully decked out for Christmas.

Ollie walked back up the hill, her tote bag heavy on her shoulder, her insides a mess of nervous excitement. She checked her hair which, that morning, she'd pulled into an elaborate bun with plaits feeding into it, and glanced at her reflection in the window before pushing open the bookshop door.

'Do we know how many people are coming?' Thea asked. She was carrying two bottles of wine up the stairs, while Becky followed with a couple of foldable chairs.

'I'm not sure,' Ollie admitted. 'Meredith said she and Finn were coming, and I think Lizzy is – I met her in Sea Brew. Maybe Maisie, too, though she didn't confirm. Adrian and his wife, Tillie, have another event to go to.'

'OK,' Thea said. 'Ben can't make it, but I think Sylvia is coming.'

'Sylvia?' Ollie asked, following them up the stairs.

'She used to live here, before the renovation. She ran the post office with her husband, and everyone in Port Karadow knows her. Since I've taken over the building, she hasn't exactly lost interest in what happens here – she's not shy about voicing her opinions.'

Ollie thought of Marion's endless curiosity, and grinned. 'Sounds familiar. I bought scones, by the way.'

'Scones?'

'And jam and cream. I thought we could offer everyone a cream tea with their wine.'

'It's all a bit haphazard,' Becky said, unfolding the chairs then gesturing around the room.

It looked eclectic, with its mix of seating – the beanbags alongside the flimsy chairs, the sofa under the window – but Ollie didn't think that was a bad thing. 'We're just trying to get some people here to talk about the bookshop, get the reality of events and book clubs on everyone's radar.'

'Did you run a book club in your last place?' Thea asked, as she arranged glasses on the table.

'I wanted to,' Ollie admitted, 'but my boss didn't think it would work. She said there would be no consistency, that book clubs were more suited to front rooms and friendship groups than bookshops.'

'Well, if it helps,' Thea said, 'this was a bedroom until a few months ago.'

'And Port Karadow is very different to London,' Ollie added, her hands on her hips. 'The community's smaller, tighter. If we do well tonight, then we'll get the same faces coming back next time, along with a whole load of new ones.'

'Are you all right if I head off?' Becky asked. 'I need to get the kids.'

'Of course. Ollie and I can manage.'

Becky said goodnight, and Ollie went back to her tote bag, taking out a small box that she'd purchased from Maisie half an hour before. 'It's never too early for fairy lights,' she said, pulling the long, LED trail out of the box. 'And these are gold. I thought we could drape them along the bookshelves.'

'Perfect.' Thea took the other end and, together, they unwound them. 'We'll match the twinkliness of the town.' She gestured to the window, where dusk had fallen and the lights of Port Karadow stood out, like a dense blanket of stars, beyond the glass.

Lizzy was the first to arrive, followed by Meredith and her very blond, very smiley boyfriend Finn. Ollie poured them glasses of wine, and told them to help themselves to the scones and toppings.

'I've got a stew in the oven,' Lizzy said. 'If I'd known there was all this, I would have left Martin to fend for himself.'

'We were going to get fish and chips,' Meredith added. 'This is as good, if not better.' She loaded her scone with jam and cream, and went to speak to Thea who, Ollie couldn't help noticing, was looking anxious.

'Hello!' Maisie was the next to arrive. 'The lights look great.'

'They do, don't they?' They had given the upstairs space a celebratory feel that would last long after Christmas was over. 'Help yourself.' Ollie gestured to the refreshment table, and Maisie grinned and went to get a plate.

'Do you think this is it?' Thea asked, ten minutes later. 'I was sure Sylvia was coming, but maybe her daughter wasn't free to drive her over.'

'Six is a great number,' Ollie said. 'And tonight's just an introductory session. Discussing how the club will work, picking the first book. After this we can promote it properly, get more people interested. Then, next time, the chairs will have been delivered, and it will be—'

'Look who I found outside, Theophania!'

Ollie and Thea both turned, and Ollie's stomach swooped as she watched their two new guests reach the top floor, their cheeks pink from the cold.

The woman who had spoken was in her seventies, Ollie guessed, with a smart grey bob and sharp eyes. She was slender, neatly put together, and looked particularly tiny next to the man whose arm she clutched. But that was because Max was tall and wide-shouldered, and his curls gave him extra height.

'I didn't realise you were coming,' she blurted, and the woman gave her a curious look.

'You must be Ollie Spencer,' she said, letting go of Max and striding forward with her arm outstretched. 'I've been hearing all about you.'

64

'All scandalous I hope,' Ollie said with a grin, which faded quickly when the other woman raised an eyebrow. 'Are you Sylvia?'

'Of course I am. Thea told you I was coming, didn't she?'

'You're our VIP,' Ollie said. 'Come and have a seat. Would you prefer the sofa, or a chair?'

'Sofa,' Sylvia said. 'God forbid you make me sit in one of those things.' She flung a hand at a beanbag, and Finn got off the sofa, kissed Sylvia on the cheek, then moved to one of the chairs.

'Would you like a scone with cream and jam?' Ollie asked. 'A glass of wine?'

'If you're offering,' Sylvia said. 'Red wine, and don't scrimp on the cream. There's nothing worse than a scone with a paltry amount of cream.'

'And make sure the jam's on top,' Finn added.

'If she gets that wrong,' Sylvia said, 'then I don't care what Max has told me. She doesn't belong here.'

Ollie's step faltered as she walked to the table. She felt a hand gently cup her elbow.

'Don't worry,' Max whispered into her ear, sending a pleasant shiver down her spine, 'I'll make sure you get it right.'

'This is supposed to be friendly and informal,' Ollie murmured back. 'But I get a feeling my first event for A New Chapter is going to be a bit of a challenge.'

'Nothing wrong with a baptism of fire,' Max said, sounding amused. 'And if you can handle Lizzy and Sylvia in the same room for a whole evening, then you're set for anything.'

Ollie exhaled, blowing a strand of hair off her face. 'I'd better get this scone perfect, then: start off on the right foot. Finn said I should put the jam on the top?'

65

'Which is one of the reasons you should take anything Finn Becker says with a pinch of salt.'

'He's messing with me?' Ollie tried to keep the outrage out of her voice.

'He's a joker,' Max said. 'Stick with me, and you'll be fine.'

'I might hold you to that. So jam first, cream on top?'

'And be extra generous with the cream, remember. You do that, and I'll pour the wine.'

By the time they were all settled, Ollie and Max – as the last two to sit down – on the beanbags, she was feeling ever so slightly frazzled. But, she reasoned, this was her first event here, it had been mostly spontaneous, and if there weren't any challenges then it wasn't the right job for her. Her last one, at Grady Books, had plummeted from the dizzy heights of a dream role into days of abject misery, and she wasn't going to let that happen here. That meant she had to be positive, and stay in control. Alongside understanding what Thea wanted, if she also got to know the locals – especially the prominent ones who had a voice in the town – she could find out what would work for them, too.

'Good evening, everyone,' she said. 'I'm Ollie Spencer, and welcome to the introductory session of A New Chapter's book club. This is our first, informal event, and I hope that, together, we'll be able to come up with a book list we can use for future sessions. In my experience, nothing works better than getting a mixture of people together, finding out their favourite books, and going from there. If our initial selection isn't varied enough, we can adapt it as we go.'

'Book clubs can get rowdy with too many people,' Lizzy pointed out.

'That's true,' Ollie said. 'But not everyone will be able to make it here for the monthly sessions. My plan is to promote our book club to the whole town, then have the discussion online as well as in person, so whoever wants to join in is able to.'

'That does sound grand.' Lizzy treated Ollie to a warm smile.

'What are the rules?' Finn asked. He was holding *Rivers of London*, the first book in the Ben Aaronovitch series. It was a good choice: popular and imaginative.

'They'll be guidelines more than rules, I hope. This is supposed to be fun, after all. And of course, whatever the book list is, we'll make sure we have enough copies here so that anyone who wants can buy one. I was thinking, Thea,' she continued, 'that we could get stickers. They could say something like: *A New Chapter Book Club Pick*. We can pop them on the copies, so that anyone who buys one has that sense of belonging. They're not too expensive if you order in bulk.'

'That's a brilliant idea.' Thea scribbled in her notebook.

'Max says you're from London,' Sylvia said, then took a dainty bite of her scone.

'That's right. I've worked in bookshops for a long time, and I'm delighted to be here, working in Thea's.'

'You like reading, then?' Sylvia asked. 'You're not just one of those fancy consultants?'

'Not at all. I love books, and reading, and I want other people to have the opportunity to love books, too – whatever kind they want. Nobody should be put off by literary snobbery: all that matters is that they choose the books that interest them. That's why I want us to come up with a diverse reading list for our club: it's why I invited you all here.'

'Why us, though?' Finn asked.

Ollie shrugged. 'Because I didn't want to waste time, so I went with the people I knew, and I asked Thea to do the same. After the first few sessions, we can ask other people to choose the books. I just needed a few trailblazers to get us off the ground.'

'Well, I'm honoured,' Lizzy said, folding her arms.

Ollie gave her a grateful smile. 'So, what I thought we could do, is take it in turns to say why we've picked our book, why we think it would appeal to our Port Karadow friends.' She knew Thea had a copy of *The Picture of Dorian Gray* by Oscar Wilde, and could see that Lizzy was clutching *The Vanishing Half* by Brit Bennett. 'Meredith, I can't see what you've brought. Why don't you—?'

'What other events are you going to put on here?' Sylvia asked.

'All sorts,' Ollie said. 'Readathons, book-swapping events. It shouldn't just be me, Thea and Becky shouting about the books we sell, or authors giving talks – though those are great. We should be giving customers a platform, too.' It was a horrible phrase: *a platform,* and she wrinkled her nose in distaste, but she didn't know how else to say it.

'At her interview, Ollie suggested a Book Wars tournament,' Thea said, grinning. 'That's something we're definitely going to do.'

Ollie laughed. 'That's one of my more off-the-wall suggestions, but it could be brilliant.'

'What's Book Wars?' Max asked. His beanbag was next

to hers, and with their legs outstretched, her knee kept brushing against his.

'It's where two people each have a set amount of time to argue the case for their chosen book. There should be a theme every time, some kind of similarity, so Stephen King versus Dean Koontz, or a classic versus a modern retelling, like *Pride and Prejudice* and *Eligible*, or two books with the same title that are completely different. The audience gets to decide who has made the better argument. It's fun, and a good way to sell books.'

Thea leaned forward. 'Once we've got this part of the shop finished, and I've got a mic and speakers installed, I'm doing it. We could have it as a monthly, or even weekly, thing. Whoever wins each round comes back, until we've whittled it down to a grand final.'

'A Book Wars league,' Ollie said, excitement bubbling through her at the thought. 'We can talk more about it in a bit. Meredith, do you want to—'

'What are you doing for the Christmas pageant?' Sylvia asked. 'I assume you'll be having something spectacular. It's on the twenty-third of December.'

Ollie exchanged a glance with Thea. 'I was thinking of an author reading and signing,' she said. 'Someone who writes books set in Cornwall. Mysteries or thrillers, potentially – something that fits with the time of year. But tonight, we're just picking titles for the book club.'

'Who would you choose, if you could have absolutely anyone here?' Maisie asked.

'Oh God.' Ollie rubbed her forehead. 'There are so many great authors who write Cornish stories. Of course, it will depend on who's available. I haven't talked to Thea or Becky about that yet. It's exciting, though!'

'If you can get anyone to come, of course.' Lizzy frowned. 'Just before Christmas, all the way down here. It's a big ask.'

'A *huge* ask,' Sylvia added, tutting.

'I'm sure Ollie can do it,' Max said. 'Ollie, I forgot to bring my book with me, but I was going to pick *In Cold Blood* by Truman Capote.'

'That's an excellent choice,' Ollie said, 'a controversial classic that everyone will have an opinion about. Right.' She wrote it down in her notebook, and let her knee nudge Max's in a silent thank you. 'Meredith, what's your choice?'

Meredith reached into her handbag and, after a long, loaded pause, pulled out a brightly coloured hardback. '*Something Wilder* by Christina Lauren! Ollie, this book is so brilliant.'

'I recommended it to her,' Thea said, grinning. 'It's like *Romancing the Stone* and *Indiana Jones*, and it has the most incredible love story.'

'Oh God, that one,' Finn said, tipping his head back, eyes on the ceiling. 'She's already read half of it out to me.'

'Not *half*,' Meredith protested. 'Just some of the good bits.'

'Don't you think it's a bit far-fetched?'

'Not at all. It's exciting and dramatic and hugely romantic.' They stared at each other, the air between them fizzing with tension.

'This,' Ollie said, after she'd taken a moment to soak up the atmosphere, 'is what we want. Books people will be passionate about, one way or the other. We want disagreement, challenges, love and hate. *Something Wilder* will be perfect.' She wrote it down. 'Lizzy, tell us about your choice.'

With the evening finally on track, Ollie was able to steer any wayward discussions back to book choices, and they went round the circle, everyone talking about what they'd picked and why. There were questions asked – a lot from Finn – wine drunk, and scones eaten.

Night fell, the lights inside the bookshop burned more brightly, and Ollie let the twin joys of contentment and anticipation wash over her. This, she thought, was going to work. She wondered if Max was thinking the same, because he gently kicked the sole of her boot with his navy Converse. She *loved* Converse shoes. It wasn't fair that he was wearing them. He had to have *some* flaws – didn't he?

As the night wore on, and they fell into a heated debate about *The Thursday Murder Club* by Richard Osman – 'Why would you ever want your crime to be cosy?' Sylvia asked – and Thea topped up everyone's glasses, Ollie wondered if she was charmed. Had finding Kerensa's handprint, as ludicrous as it sounded, given her what she wanted? Had she been gifted her desires by a woman who had died tragically, hundreds of years ago?

She still had to win over Becky, who she was sure didn't agree with her approach, perhaps mistrusted her solely because she had come from London, and she knew it would be hard to resist Max, with his beautiful eyes and his kindness. They could, she realised, be characters in an epic fantasy series that she had to overcome before she could get to the treasure: The Defier and The Temptation.

She had enjoyed her first delve into Liam's life history, his scrawled notes as compelling as his story about the poor woman who had lost her life all those years ago. She felt comfortable with him, and now – her two fantasy characters aside – this job looked like it would be as fulfilling as she'd hoped, with problems to navigate and events to orchestrate, and everything, for the next couple of months, with a twinkly, festive vibe.

She caught Max's eye and he smiled at her, his green irises almost luminous beneath the glowing fairy lights. She felt a flutter low down in her stomach as she returned it. This, she decided, was going to be a bigger test than she'd first anticipated, but alongside the trepidation, there was hope. Liam, Marion, Thea and Max, Meredith and Finn. Maybe Maisie, Lizzy and Sylvia – and possibly Becky one day, too. She was building connections, forging friendships.

It felt like a new start.

Chapter Nine

O llie spent her Sunday firming up how the book club would work. She had everyone's title choices, and a plan to promote them online as well as at the bookshop. Thea had agreed that they would get generous stock in of each book, and design stickers for the covers. They had gone with Maisie's choice, an anthology of ghost stories called *The Haunting Season*, for November, as it fitted with the time of year, and would appeal to a wide audience. Who didn't love a ghost story in winter?

She had her laptop open, and was sitting on the thick carpet in the barn, eating a bacon sandwich while Henry chewed on Boris, his seemingly indestructible warthog chew toy. A Constantly Christmas radio station was playing through her computer, and her festive garlands shimmered in the sunlight streaming in through the glass doors. It was calm, quiet, and exactly what Ollie had been hoping for when she moved here.

Her gaze drifted over the titles on the bookshelf, and she wondered which book she would have chosen. There had been enough options on Friday, and she hadn't wanted to impose her own suggestions. Now, however, she realised they were missing a book set in Cornwall.

She scooted over to the small selection she'd bought in the charity shop. She'd been drawn to them because of their bright, Seventies covers, and when she'd picked one up she'd seen the words: 'A Cornish Mystery' emblazoned on the back. Now, she trailed her finger along the spines, and her brain stuttered as she read the full title of one of the books: *The Legend of Kerensa's Handprint: a Roskilly and Faith mystery* by Bryan Mailer.

'What the hell?' she whispered to Henry, pulling the book out. The cover showed a stylised illustration of woods, hills and the sea, a stone with a handprint etched into it in the foreground. It was a bright design, mostly blues, greens and yellows, which gave it a cheerful, unassuming look. Right now, however, Ollie was feeling pretty bloody spooked. The name Kerensa hadn't rung a bell when Liam had mentioned it the other day, but then she'd bought this set of second-hand books without paying much attention to the titles – beyond noticing that they were set in Cornwall.

She scrambled to her feet and hurried to the kitchen, where her handbag and its contents were spilled over the central island. She found the book of legends Liam had given her and took it back to her spot on the carpet.

She examined both books, frustrated when she couldn't find an author's name on the small volume of legends, almost as if it was an encyclopaedia, but they'd kept the compiler anonymous. Her charity shop find was undoubtedly fiction:

a mystery story, starring a young policewoman called Megan Roskilly, and an older, jaded historian called Faith. It was part of a series, and this one was clearly centred around the legend Liam had told her, the handprint she'd stumbled across. Had Bryan Mailer written his series around famous local legends? Did they sell them in A New Chapter? She would have to ask Thea. For now, she needed to find out if—

Her phone beeped and she grabbed it, expecting a photo of Melissa with Tiago in sun-drenched Portugal.

Instead, there was another name on the screen.

Max.

They had exchanged numbers on Friday night, when Thea had said it would be a good idea if they worked together to source the coffee machine for the events space. Her stomach flipping, she read his message:

Hey Ollie, it's Max. How about Tuesday morning? We could meet at the café and I could give you a rundown of the options. ☕

She replied immediately:

Tuesday morning is great. Looking forward to it! Ollie. xo

Smiling, she returned to the compilation of legends and the mysteries she'd bought, picking up the first Roskilly and Faith novel. Soon, as was so often the case when she started a new book, she was lost inside the story, and didn't come back out again for hours.

* * *

'Fucking fuck!' The words exploded into the still morning air and frightened a pigeon from a nearby tree. Henry barked at its departing form, and Ollie had the urge to shout an apology after it. 'What am I even doing?' She looked at her dog, who, even when he was excited, had those sorrowful dark eyes that made her either worry for his state of mind, or feel pitied by him.

She gripped the little grey book, juggling it between her hands while keeping a tight hold on her phone, the maps app open on the screen. She was meeting Max in less than an hour, but right now she was on the outskirts of Port Karadow, in a patch of land behind the northernmost houses, clambering over rocks to get to the ruins of a church that, she had to admit, looked like something out of a horror film.

She had discovered that, of the five mysteries she'd bought in the charity shop, four of them had corresponding legends in Liam's book. She hadn't had a chance to ask him about them yet, whether he knew of the series, and right now she was intent on getting to the bottom of the facts – or the real-life locations of the legends, at least.

She had spoken to her parents on Sunday night, found out that they had booked to go on a Scandinavian cruise over Christmas. They had asked her to accompany them, as they often did, and she had turned them down as always – though this time, with a new job that would only get busier in the run-up to Christmas, she had a more legitimate excuse than usual.

Now she knew for certain that her parents were going to be absent over Christmas, she had begun to settle to the idea that, in all probability, she would be spending it alone. Despite the connections she was making here, it was likely that everyone would already have plans, and that she wouldn't be an ideal fit for any of them. But it was fine. It was only one day, only one year. Nothing at all, in the grand scheme of things.

What she *was* struggling to settle with, however, was her attraction to Max. Ever since his innocuous message on Sunday, she had been on a countdown to the meeting this morning. She fancied him, undeniably and overwhelmingly, and she had resolved to stay relationship free, at least for the time being. Those two things were warring inside her, like pumice stones grating against each other. She knew nothing about him or his relationship status. He might be married to a gorgeous woman, or to a man. He might be committed to being single, and it was entirely possible that, even if none of these things were true, he wasn't attracted to her. They had only met properly twice. He had been friendly, but then so had she. No big deal.

All these rationalisations should have comforted her, but she still felt unsettled, and she had woken up at five o'clock that morning, when the world was dark and wintry, and hadn't been able to go back to sleep. So she had decided to follow one of the legends in the book, to distract herself with something intriguing. The one she'd picked, because it was close to town, was a ghost story.

St Ethel's church. The ruins she was skirting round had, supposedly, one winter's night over a hundred and fifty years ago, been the site of a horrific battle: screams and shouts were heard, the rhythmic sound of horses' hooves, the crackle of flames. It sounded horrendous, but it also hadn't been real.

Giving up on her juggling endeavours, Ollie gazed at the sea for a moment, spread about below her and closer than it was from her barn, the way it shimmied and shivered in the weak morning light. Then she found a piece of the churchyard wall that was still intact, and perched on it while Henry skirted the uneven ground, nose down, tail up. She opened the book, her eyes scanning the tiny print.

'Listen to this,' she called to her dog. '*When the alarmed villagers rushed out on that dark night in 1872, some of them hefting weapons, others with buckets of water to quench the flames, they found St Ethel's church poised and silent, the horrific sounds fading as if swallowed by the sea.*' She shook her head. '*Except for one unusual thing. There was a light glowing from within, bright enough to make the stained-glass window beneath the bell tower shine.*' She looked up. There was nothing left of the stained glass now.

'*The rector had been one of the first to hear the commotion, and he unlocked the door but found only darkness. The light was gone, and nothing of the phantom battle remained. This author has done extensive research into the area, and can find no battle to speak of, none that could have played out here, its haunting echo carrying through the years. But, if you go walking in Port Karadow late on the first of December, and stray too far from the welcome glow of the Christmas lights, be sure to avoid St Ethel's church. Even in its ruined state, those lost soldiers might still be searching for shelter.*'

Ollie swallowed, a chill running down her spine. She would have appreciated a hug with her dog, but he was sniffing the church wall, no doubt searching for something a lot more solid than ghosts.

'*This author,*' Ollie repeated, checking the front of the book and the title page, even though she had already examined it thoroughly. 'It doesn't say who the author is, though.

How can a book not have an author?' She was flicking through the pages, trying to find clues, when her phone buzzed on her knee. 'Shit!' She grabbed it before it fell onto the rocky ground. 'Hello?'

'Ollie? Hey. It's Max.' Even his voice set off tingles inside her.

'Oh! Hi. Am I late? Sorry, I—'

'No, I'm early. Are you on your way to the café?'

'I'm five minutes away, near St Ethel's church.'

'The ruins? What are you doing there?'

Ollie glanced at the book. 'Come and meet me, and I'll tell you.'

'OK.' He sounded intrigued and amused, and Ollie grinned at the phone. 'Give me ten.'

'See you soon.' She hung up.

She was coming round the side of the ruins, having done a circuit and found only signs that someone very real had been using the site as a party venue, when she saw him. Short navy jacket, dark jeans, a blue and white-striped scarf wrapped around his neck. He was holding two takeaway cups, which perked her up as much as the sight of him. There wasn't much in the way of wind, but there was a bitter chill in the air.

Henry spotted him too, and raced forward, barking.

'Henry, no!' She had a vision of him jumping up and Max being covered in scalding coffee, but her dog, while clearly excited, didn't raise his paws, and simply danced around the café owner with unbridled joy.

'Hello.' Max put the cups on the wall and crouched, ruffling Henry's fur. He looked up when Ollie approached. 'He's very well behaved. Have you been training him?'

79

Ollie felt a flush of pleasure at the compliment, even though it wasn't hers to accept. 'My friend, Melissa, took him to classes when he was a puppy. Since then, I've read a few books, tried to keep him on track that way.'

'Why am I not surprised that you put your faith in a book?'

Ollie laughed. 'I do have a bit of a thing for them.' She almost added that she'd been reading books on how to retrain herself, too.

Max stood and handed her a cup. 'So what are you doing out here?' He gestured at the discarded beer cans. 'There are a lot of beautiful walks around Port Karadow, but this place is less salubrious. The council try and keep it clean, but they can't always stay on top of it.'

'What do you know about it?' Ollie lifted the lid off her cup and blew on the hot liquid, inhaling the rich, milky steam. 'Thank you so much for this.'

'What do I know about the church?' Max shrugged. 'Not a whole lot. It's ancient, obviously, and falling down. Some people think it should be cordoned off; that it's not safe.'

'You don't know anything about the phantom battle?'

Max laughed. 'What? No, I've never heard of a phantom battle. Have you been going too hard at the incense?'

Ollie failed to hide her surprise. 'Who told you I'm an incense fiend?'

He ran a hand through his curls, but didn't look away. 'I'm sorry. It was Lizzy. She heard from Marion, that—'

'Of course.' Ollie waited for the stab of embarrassment, but the only thing she felt was amusement. 'Did she also tell you about my overpriced Christmas decorations?'

Max smiled, his discomfort dissipating when he realised she wasn't offended. 'They sound great. If you can't be over the top at Christmas, when can you be?'

'Cheers to that.' Ollie tapped her cup against his. 'You'll have to come and see them.'

'I would love to, but right now I need to know about this ghost battle. I've lived in the area my whole life, I go walking round here, but it's news to me.'

'You obviously haven't seen the book.' She waved it in the air. 'An oracle on all the mythical corners of Port Karadow.'

'Is that so?' Max raised an eyebrow. 'Come on then, tell me.'

'We need to get Thea a coffee machine.'

'We can do that afterwards. You can't dangle something like this in front of me and then change the subject.'

'OK then,' Ollie said, unable to draw it out any longer because she was, in fact, desperate to tell him. 'Here it is.'

She put her cup down and turned to the right page: 'The St Ethel's Church Haunting'. She sat on the wall again, cleared her throat, and started reading out loud. After a moment, Max perched on the wall alongside her, his gaze fixed on her while she read. She was glad it was a cold morning, because his attention was like a heater, fanning warmth in her direction.

When she got to the end, he was shaking his head, an awed expression on his face.

'So? What do you think?' she asked.

'I think it sounds completely terrifying, and we should come back on the first of December to hear the phantom hooves for ourselves.'

Ollie laughed. 'You're serious?'

Max paused, considering. 'Partly. I mean, why wouldn't we, when it's hardly an effort to get here, and we could end up hearing something extraordinary? How have I never heard this before? Where did you get this book?'

'Liam gave it to me.' She held it out for him to take. 'He had it in his study.'

Max inspected it, his long fingers turning the pages, his movements reverential in the face of the book's age. 'I've heard that his study's incredible. You must be like a kid in a sweet shop.'

'I am a bit,' Ollie admitted. 'He's been so kind to me. And, hey, I found a series of Cornish-set mysteries in a charity shop just after I moved here, and the characters go around investigating crimes connected to local legends like this one. They're by an author called Bryan Mailer. Have you heard of him?'

Max shook his head. 'Should I have?'

'I don't know. The stories in these mystery novels, and these legends, correspond. The author must know the area well.'

'Or he had a copy of this book. Are they recent?'

'They were published in the Seventies. I looked him up online, and the series is all he wrote. It looks like he was popular at the time, so I wondered if you'd heard of him. I love that he took his inspiration from the landscape round here.'

Max looked up from the book. 'Like you were saying on Friday, loads of writers set their stories in Cornwall.'

'It's a rich source of inspiration, that's for sure. I've been thinking about the events at the bookshop.'

'High on your success of the other evening?'

She grinned. 'Thank you for helping me keep that on track; I was worried Sylvia was going to interrogate me all night. Next, I want to do a ghost walk: a tour of Port Karadow, dictated by the legends in here.' She tapped the cover. 'Bring everyone back to A New Chapter at the end, and they'll load up their tote bags with mysteries and ghost stories. I'm going to see if I can get some of Bryan Mailer's books in, too.'

'You're not resting on your laurels, are you? Is your mind always this busy?'

'I want to make A New Chapter the most successful bookshop in Cornwall,' she admitted. 'No time to rest on anything – not laurels, and definitely not my bum.'

Max laughed. 'Fair enough. I suppose part of that success includes getting a coffee machine installed?'

'Exactly.'

He stood up and gave the book back to her. 'We should probably get going, then. I thought we could look online, I can show you what I think would work, and then, if you take those ideas to Thea, we can go to the wholesalers later in the week so you can see them in all their chrome and plastic glory.'

'Sounds ideal. Thank you.'

'Happy to help.' He blew on his fingers. He didn't have gloves on, and Ollie had to resist the urge to take hold of his hands, to warm them between her palms. Instead, she clipped Henry's lead onto his harness, and they left the ruins of St Ethel's church behind and walked into town. The colours were subdued beneath a grey sky, but Port Karadow was no less charming.

'How long have you been running Sea Brew?' Ollie asked.

'Close to four years,' Max said. 'It was a bit of a gamble to begin with. There was an old guy, Serge, running the café, but he was retiring and wanted someone to buy it. I'd just . . . I'd given up my other business and was looking for something new. The people part played to my strengths, and I thought the rest I could learn, or employ experts to do, like Beryan with the cakes.'

'It's a great café,' Ollie said, 'and it's obviously successful. I'd say the gamble paid off.'

'Yup.' Max laughed. 'I got lucky.'

'It sounds like you worked hard for it. What was the business you gave up?'

'I used to be a personal trainer.'

Ollie glanced at him. They were at the bottom of Main Street, only a couple of minutes from Sea Brew, and she was wondering just how many challenges the universe was going to throw at her. Because not only had she failed to find any flaws in Max's personality, now she was faced with images of him in gym gear, his muscles glistening with sweat, his voice commanding in a way she hadn't heard it so far.

'Bit of a change,' she said, trying to keep her voice light.

'Yeah, I basically did a three-sixty. From helping people get in the best shape of their lives, to tempting them with buttery, sugary cakes.' He laughed. 'Sometimes, though, life throws you a curveball, and you just have to catch it as best you can.'

Ollie was about to ask what his curveball was – her shoulder choosing that moment to ache, as if on cue – when they reached Sea Brew. The door was closed against the cold, one of the servers Ollie recognised standing behind the counter.

'OK?' Max gestured at her shoulder. She hadn't realised she was rubbing it. It had become an automatic response, like a tic she couldn't control.

'I'm fine,' she said, dropping her hand. 'Are *you* OK?'

She hadn't meant to ask it, but there was something in his expression she'd never seen before, as if only 80 per cent of him was with her, the other twenty a long way away. So far, whenever she'd been with him, he'd been wholly present: warm and attentive, the sun around which everyone else orbited. It was disconcerting seeing him on edge, even if it was mostly intuition that told Ollie he was uncomfortable.

'I'm good,' he said. 'Just thinking about the past. It's hard not to, sometimes.'

'Do you want to talk about it?' As she said the words, a voice inside her head said, *Nope. Danger.*

Max paused on a breath, as if he'd been about to reply but then changed his mind. 'Let's get the coffee machine sorted first,' he said. 'But I wouldn't be wholly against it, as long as it's an even exchange.'

'What do you mean?'

Max reached out and took her right arm, the undamaged one, and pulled her forwards. A voice behind called, 'Thank you!' and only then did Ollie realise she'd been blocking the café door.

'If I tell you why I went from PT to café owner,' Max said, 'you have to tell me what's up with your shoulder. And also why you swapped London for Cornwall. That's a drastic move in anyone's book.'

'From coffee machines to deepest secrets,' Ollie said with a laugh. '*That's* a drastic move.'

Max grinned at her. 'We started the day talking about haunted churches. I think our relationship has already broken the confines of its original boundaries.'

'Maybe it has,' Ollie said, and she really, *honestly*, hadn't meant to sound so flirtatious, but Max's green eyes shone, making up for the lack of sunshine, and now she was so close to him, he smelled incredible: like a herb garden and coffee shop rolled into one. She couldn't decide which of her senses was getting the better deal.

'So,' Max said, blinking quickly and dropping his hand, as if her flirting had made him wary. 'Coffee machine.'

'Coffee machine,' Ollie repeated, inwardly cursing herself. 'Do you think we could find one that makes these chai tea lattes?'

Max laughed and pushed open the door, gesturing for her to go ahead of him. 'You don't ask for much, do you?'

'Why not reach for the stars?' she said. 'You might fall short, but there's always a chance that you'll make it first time.'

Max paused in the doorway, his gaze sharp on hers. They stayed that way, something shimmering in the space between them, until a customer came up behind Max and said, 'Excuse me,' and he was forced to move out of the way.

Ollie walked into the coffee shop, her heart beating a hectic rhythm in her chest, her dog quietly content at her side, oblivious to the tension surrounding them like falling snow.

Chapter Ten

It had felt good walking into A New Chapter after her meeting with Max, with a solid selection of self-service coffee machines to show Thea. She felt as if she'd survived, somehow. She hadn't jumped on him, she had remained professional, and they'd had fun, even looking through a fairly dry catalogue. But she'd also done what she needed to, and it showed Thea that she could be dependable, that her skills weren't just about conjuring up event ideas.

The next morning, with Thea in the office and Becky dealing with new stock, Ollie spent time serving customers. She smiled at two women who came in with damp hair, which made her think of Meredith, and her love of sea swimming. She shivered just as one of them came up to the counter.

'Excuse me, do you have the latest Ruth Ware book in stock?'

'Do you mean *The It Girl*?' Ollie asked. 'It's so brilliant.'

'That's the one. My partner's a big fan, but he hasn't read that one yet.'

'Let me see if we have it. If not, we can order it in and it should arrive in the next couple of days.' Ollie clicked through the system on the computer, checking their stock levels.

'Thank you,' the woman said, then added, 'You're new here.'

'That's right. This is my second week.'

'Not Cornish, though.'

Ollie looked up. 'Yorkshire born and bred, but I lived in London for over a decade. Now I'm trying out Cornwall.'

The woman nodded. 'There's often resistance to incomers turning the place upside down, but new blood isn't always a bad thing. We wouldn't have this place if it weren't for Thea.'

'I hope I can make a difference too.'

'In what way?' The woman raised an eyebrow. 'What do you bring to the table?'

'Years of experience, endless enthusiasm and some great publishing contacts.'

The customer smiled. 'I like a woman who knows what she's worth and isn't ashamed to announce it.'

Ollie laughed. 'What's the point of keeping it hidden? There are too many demands on everyone's time for us to figure each other out without help.'

'Stand out from the crowd.' The woman nodded. 'Who gets to the end of their life and says, "I wish I'd made less of an impact?"'

Ollie grinned. 'Too true. Oh, here we are. We can have it in for you by Friday, if that's any good?'

'Ideal. Thank you.'

'No problem.' Ollie took the woman's details, and ordered the book in. At least, she thought, as the customer went to join her friend, not everyone was against her being here.

In fact, it was only Becky's disapproval she'd come up against, and that had faded since the first day.

She wanted her presence to be a blessing rather than a curse. What she didn't want was to end up as one of the legends in Liam's compact tome: the woman hounded out of Port Karadow for imposing her city views, left to die an undignified death in the icy harbour, her ghost rising every night as darkness fell, terrifying people out getting fish and chips as she gave them book recommendations from beyond the grave.

The thought reminded her that she needed to talk to Thea about her ghost walk idea. There wasn't any time to lose: Halloween was five days away.

'We can absolutely get a well-known author here for the Christmas event,' Ollie said, several hours later. 'Anyone would be lucky to have an invite from us.'

Thea sat forward. 'I appreciate your confidence, but it's a long way to come from London, for just a few hours. What would we be offering *them*?'

They were upstairs, in the not-quite-finished events space, rain beating against the large windows. The spotlights in the ceiling and the fairy lights Ollie had bought made it seem bright and cosy, so that she could almost pretend there was no rainstorm, that she wasn't going to get drenched on her walk home.

'We'd be offering them a beautiful Cornwall location and a twinkly, atmospheric event, full of book lovers dying to lap up their latest novel. I know you think it's a big ask, but if we pick an author who sets their books here, then of course they'll be keen!'

'We could pick someone who already lives nearby. Fern Britton, Liz Fenwick or Veronica Henry. One of them would be amazing!' Thea's eyes lit up.

'They would be great, of course: the audience is ready made. But what if we were even more daring? What if we went with someone who doesn't live nearby; who doesn't come here very often. Someone unexpected!'

Thea's expression didn't match the excitement Ollie was hoping to inspire. 'I'm not sure.'

'Let me have a think, give a few people a call and see what's possible.' Ollie's list of publicity contacts wasn't massive, and it was likely to be out of date now. But Thea didn't need to know that, and there were a couple of people she thought she could rely on. They just needed to fix on the perfect author: someone who was a big draw but was also approachable, and who would be happy to travel to Port Karadow close to Christmas Day.

'Thanks, Ollie,' Thea said, smiling. 'How has today been? Becky said you were getting the hang of the till.'

'It's all straightforward, so no worries there. And I had another idea – a Halloween ghost walk. I know it's only a few days away, but I'm sure we could drum up enough interest.'

Thea frowned. 'How would that work?'

'I would lead our group of intrepid customers round a few spooky places in town – I've got a book of local legends that Liam gave me – then bring them back here, where they will inevitably purchase horror stories and books on local hauntings.'

'Wouldn't you need to learn all the ghost stories before-hand?' Thea asked. 'That's not easy.'

'It'll be fine. I've got the legends, and mostly I can just wing it.'

Thea sighed. 'Ollie—'

'I know it's another quick event,' she cut in, 'and that there isn't much time to prepare, but we need to make the most of all the opportunities the calendar offers.'

'You really think you can run an *entire* ghost walk, all by yourself?'

'I would *love* to run an entire ghost walk,' Ollie assured her. 'We've got the Halloween theme in the children's section, but why don't we have a table in Fiction, too? I've already written a list of books we can order in. Just say the word, and I'll do it.'

Thea gave a tiny nod. 'OK then, but I don't want you stretching yourself too far. We need more space to plan things.'

'And after this event, we'll have it. But with this and the book club, there's no cost except our time, and they could generate some good sales, and show people that A New Chapter offers a diverse range of events. In future, I'll be more on top of things, but just because Halloween and Christmas are rushing towards us, it doesn't mean we should ignore them. I was thinking ten pounds a ticket for the ghost walk, fully refundable if we don't get enough interest, and it'll include a drink when they get back here afterwards.'

Thea laughed. 'You've already planned it all out!'

Ollie grinned. 'I wouldn't be very good at my job if I didn't come prepared.'

'So when you come in tomorrow, you'll have a list of authors and their publicists' contacts for the Christmas meet and greet, and you'll have sold ten tickets for our ghost walk?'

Ollie opened her mouth, her thoughts stumbling, and then noticed the gleam in Thea's eye. 'You had me for a minute. Give me until Friday, at least!'

'That's only two days,' Thea pointed out.

'It's Halloween on Monday, so we haven't really got a moment to lose.'

'No.' Thea peered through the banisters as heavy footfalls sounded on the stairs. 'You're right.' Then her face split into a grin, and Ollie twisted on her beanbag, making sure she didn't fall out of the dent she had created for herself. She understood why Thea was smiling.

The man who stepped onto the upper floor had short, chestnut hair, and his dust-covered T-shirt – where was his coat on this cold, wet day? – showed off a strong, lean torso. He looked serious until he saw Thea, then he smiled, and it was as if he was two different people: the Brooding Thinker and the Handsome Charmer.

'Hey,' he said, as Thea got out of her beanbag and went to greet him.

'Hi.' That single, tiny word conveyed a level of familiarity it didn't take a rocket scientist to interpret. The man bent and gave Thea a quick kiss, then she turned and pulled him across the room. 'Ollie, this is Ben, my boyfriend. Ben, meet Ollie, our firecracker from London.'

'Firecracker?' Ollie laughed as she pushed herself out of the beanbag and shook his hand.

'Oh God! Sorry!' Thea covered her eyes. 'It's your red hair, and the fact that you think anything is possible. I didn't mean to insult you.'

Ben gave Thea a fond look.

'Firecracker is a massive compliment,' Ollie said, winding

a strand of hair around her finger. 'When I went to the hairdresser, desperate to cover up my mousy brown, I asked for a combination of copper and fire engine. They did a really good job, so I've stuck with it ever since. I'm hoping I can find a hairdresser in Cornwall who can keep it going.'

'It's beautiful,' Thea said.

'And I'm not remotely offended. I'm going to have to work extra hard to live up to the name now, though.'

'I was going to ask if you're settling in OK, but it seems like you are,' Ben said.

'Of course! How could anyone fail to feel at home in Port Karadow?'

'So true,' Thea said.

Ollie noticed that they were holding hands, Ben rubbing his thumb over the base of Thea's palm. The gesture was so intimate that Ollie felt a stab somewhere close to her heart. Things had never been like that with Guy. Or maybe they had, at the beginning, but she had erased all the good memories because of what had come after.

'I'll leave you to canoodle,' Ollie said, and headed for the stairs.

'Oh no, we weren't—' she protested, but Ollie waved her away.

'Say no more! I want to find the best place for my ghostly table, anyway.'

She hurried down the stairs and to the back of the shop, where the brightly coloured children's section had its own, smaller beanbags, a vibrant red carpet that contrasted with the rest of the shop's dark blue, and book-related cuddly toys peeping out between the books on the shelves.

A young girl and boy were kneeling at the tot-sized table, drawing on paper with wax crayons, and an older boy – still only around eleven years old, Ollie thought – was sitting on the carpet, reading a book and holding a giant cuddly spider that, despite the smile on its face, gave Ollie the creeps.

'You all doing OK in here?' she asked.

The older boy glared at her for a second, then went back to his book. The girl at the table turned her wide-eyed face to her and said, 'Yes thank you, miss.'

Ollie smiled. 'Let me know if you need anything. Are your mum or dad in another part of the shop?'

'*I'm* looking after them,' said the older boy.

'Of course, but you're still quite young. Is someone picking you up? Has one of you got a phone, so I could give them a quick call?'

'Mummy says it's OK,' the little girl whispered. Her pale brown hair was still blonde at the tips, and she looked so young, her eyes creasing with sadness. Ollie thought she might be about to cry, and had an urge to back up, hands out, and extract herself from the situation. But these were young children: they couldn't be here alone.

'And where is mummy?' she asked. 'Maybe we should get her, just to be on the safe side.'

'Mummy *is* here,' said a voice from behind Ollie, and she turned to find herself face to face with Becky. 'They're fine here until closing. I'm keeping a close eye on them.' She grabbed Ollie's arm and pulled her out of the children's section. Ollie's shoulder throbbed, but she didn't say anything. 'And,' Becky continued in a hissed whisper, 'my job would be a lot easier if you were behind the till, where you were supposed to be.'

'I'm sorry,' Ollie said. 'I was upstairs, talking to Thea.'

'Yeah, about your glitzy events, I know. The thing is, though, that there are a lot of mundane tasks that have to happen too. It's not all about booking celebrity authors and draping the shop in frilly decorations.'

'I know that,' Ollie said, keeping her voice calm. 'And I *am* sorry. I didn't realise they were your children. They're gorgeous.'

Becky stared at her, but then something inside her loosened. 'Yeah, well. The after-school club isn't running for the next couple of days because they're short-staffed. This is the only place for them to go.'

'It's a good place,' Ollie said. 'It must seem like paradise to them.'

'Meg and Billy are OK, but Dylan wants to be out playing with his friends, or at home on the Xbox.'

Ollie nodded. 'It must be tough.' She had no idea, really, but she could see Becky wasn't pleased with the situation.

'Yeah,' Becky said, the single word dripping in sarcasm, as if she knew exactly how clueless Ollie was. 'You going back to the till? There's some postal orders need sorting.'

'Of course. And listen, Becky—' But the other woman had walked away, crouching down next to her two youngest children, her demeanour instantly softer.

Ollie watched her for a moment, sighed, and went to make a start on the postal orders.

Chapter Eleven

Try one hour without your phone. Leave it on the other side of the room and don't be tempted to touch it.

It was one of the suggestions in the mindfulness book Ollie had bought after her accident, when she couldn't work and everything she tried to do at home – read, binge Netflix series – had been overwhelmed by the searing ache in her shoulder that painkillers barely touched. At the time, she had been seeking out distractions rather than trying to abandon them, but she'd thought mindfulness and meditation would help her focus on something other than the pain.

Now she was trying to bring calm back into her life. The only problem was, she had distilled her favourite tips from the book into the notes app on her phone, which was rather unhelpful when she was trying not to use it. What also wasn't helping was her chat with Melissa. She didn't want to leave her friend's message unanswered while she was right there, on the other end of her device, albeit hundreds of miles away.

Melissa had responded to her tale of wandering round a haunted church with a 😱, even though she had downplayed the meeting with Max. Melissa knew all about Guy, and about how Ollie had resolved to stay single. Even from Portugal, her friend would hold her to her word.

Ollie returned to the pile of paper she was cutting into strips. Her expensive garlands shimmered in the soft evening light, her living space homelier with them in it, but she couldn't help thinking about what Becky had said, the derision in her voice when she'd mentioned glitzy events and frilly decorations.

Ollie loved glitzy, and she wasn't opposed to frilly, but that didn't mean she couldn't be versatile.

She took a strip of paper, curled it round and stapled it, creating her first link. She was about to pick up a second when her phone chimed. She expected to see another message from Melissa, but there was a different name on the screen: Max.

She grabbed the phone.

When was this battle supposed to be? Looking into the church. Mx

Ollie grinned and typed a reply.

There never was any battle. The author researched it and came up empty. Are you a detective now? 🕵️ xo

The 'xo' was her automatic sign-off, but the moment she'd pressed 'send' she questioned it, as she was doing with everything that related to Max. It was an unsettling feeling, second-guessing herself. She saw he was typing, and her paper chains were temporarily forgotten. Henry was laid out on the carpet, sleeping the sleep of the happily exhausted, and Ollie could hear the high, tuneful song of a bird somewhere outside.

Max's next message appeared:

You have to admit it's intriguing. I feel bad that there's a big chunk of history I don't know.

Come with me next time I explore one of the legends – or on my ghost walk, on Monday night? xo

Maybe I'll do both. Let me know when and where on Monday.

Ollie blew her sleepy dog a kiss, and replied:

6pm Monday, leaving from A New Chapter. Thea loved the coffee machines btw. We're good to go with next steps. xo

Ah yes! That's what I really meant to msg you about. ☺ Great news. Mx

Ollie tried not to read too much into the inference that he was keen to spend time with her – he just wanted to learn more about Port Karadow's history – and went back to her paper chains.

Half an hour later a rap on the door was followed by bustling footsteps, and Marion appeared in the doorway, a cardboard box in her arms. She assessed Ollie, lying splayed out on the carpet, her snake of book-print paper chains coiling around her.

'Bit different to your fancy swags.' Marion gestured to the blue-and-silver garland hanging along the mirror above the fireplace.

'I wanted to try something else,' Ollie admitted. 'For the bookshop.'

'Is that what this is for, too?' She waggled the box. 'It was delivered to the main house. Liam was about to open it when I noticed the name on the address label.'

'I did put Foxglove *Barn* on there, didn't I?' Ollie scrambled to standing, just as her festive playlist went from Michael Bublé to Eartha Kitt. 'Santa Baby' was, without a doubt, Ollie's favourite Christmas song.

'Delivery drivers get confused, and some are just plain lazy.' Marion put the box on the kitchen island, and stood, waiting.

Ollie realised that she was expecting to take news of what was inside the box back to Liam. Or perhaps she had a Port Karadow WhatsApp group that fed gossip to the entire town, stories running back and forth like electric currents.

'What if this is a delivery from Victoria's Secret?' Ollie asked, switching the kettle on.

'What's Victoria's Secret? Some other fancy-pants decorations boutique?'

'Not quite.' Ollie put two Yorkshire Tea teabags in mugs. 'Although, in a way, I suppose it is.'

'What do you mean?'

'It's an upmarket lingerie shop. Lots of lace and silk and sultry colours.'

Marion shook her head. 'Women decorating themselves for men, then.'

'I would argue that it's often women decorating themselves for themselves,' Ollie countered. 'There's nothing wrong with wanting to look nice for yourself; to prance around your bedroom feeling good.'

Marion raised an eyebrow. 'I'm not one for prancing. My husband, Adam, probably wouldn't notice if I spent a small fortune on a pair of knickers.'

'Don't get them for him, then. Get them for you.'

'When did we go from boxes turning up at Liam's to fancy underwear?'

Ollie poured boiling water into the mugs. 'You should look them up online. But I promise you, this box *isn't* full of lacy bras and thongs.'

'What *is* inside, then?'

Ollie decided that if she wanted to order anything remotely personal in future, she would have to get it delivered elsewhere. 'Let's have a look,' she said.

It felt a bit like Groundhog Day, getting a knife to slice open a box while Marion watched on. She undid it, put a hand in and rifled around inside. She pulled out the first item and handed it to Marion.

'A little plastic tube. What does it do?'

'This.' Ollie took it from her and cracked it in half, and the mute plastic suddenly glowed red, casting an eerie light on the older woman's face.

'What's it for?'

'A ghost walk I'm leading through the town on Monday night. It's a Halloween event, for A New Chapter. Everyone who comes will get one of these.'

'Why?'

'Because they're fun, and because it's going to be dark, and it's a good way of keeping control of my ghost hunters. You should come!'

'I don't think so.' Marion sipped her tea. 'Ghosts and hauntings and whatnot aren't my thing.'

'Ooh, that reminds me.' Ollie took *The Legend of Kerensa's Handprint* off the bookshelf, and brought it back to the kitchen. 'Have you heard of this author?'

Marion squinted as she read the title, then turned the book over and read the back. While she did, Ollie took a photo of the glow sticks and sent a message to Max with the caption: Look what just arrived! xo

'Can't say I've heard of this Bryan Mailer person,' Marion said. 'This looks like a provincial little novel.'

Ollie felt a stab of disappointment. 'According to the internet, he was really popular in the Seventies and Eighties. But neither you or Max have heard of him, even though his books are set in this part of Cornwall.'

'I prefer a saga, myself.' Marion put the book down, disinterested.

'I found Kerensa's handprint when I was out walking,' Ollie went on. 'And this is an entire novel based on that exact legend. It's twenty minutes' walk from here!'

Marion shook her head. 'As I said, I don't go in for ghosts and hauntings. What I *am* interested in, after you mentioned it, is this Victoria's Promises site, or whatever it is. I haven't treated myself for a long time, and I'm curious about it.'

'You're serious?' Ollie laughed, and went to get her laptop. Showing her landlord's housekeeper around the Victoria's Secret website was not something she'd had on her bingo card when she'd been planning her move to Cornwall.

By the time Marion had left Ollie to it, her pockets lighter but with a gleam of satisfaction in her eye at treating herself – *not* Adam – to some luxurious new underwear, Ollie had almost forgotten the other woman's dismissal of the Cornish mystery. But the novel was still sitting there, on the island, and as she went to put it back with its friends on the bookshelf, she wondered how anyone local could fail to be interested in it.

Bryan Mailer had got his inspiration from Port Karadow and the surrounding area. There was a whole novel based around a rock formation twenty minutes from the farm. It was exciting, surely, even if you weren't an avid reader. What she hadn't been able to discover from her internet search was where Bryan Mailer was now. He'd written the books a while ago, but that didn't mean there wasn't a trail of breadcrumbs Ollie could follow.

As she returned to her paper chains, she thought that Liam, at the very least, would know about him. He had the little book of legends, after all. As she settled herself back on the carpet, Henry lifted his head and gave her a sleepy, curious look.

'You missed an interesting online shopping session,' Ollie told him. Henry rested his nose on his paws, nonplussed.

An hour or two later, after the sky had darkened and Ollie was making herself beans on toast, her phone pinged.

You got glow sticks?! Are we going to a Nineties rave? 😎😆

Laughing, she typed a reply:

They're for the ghost walk. You're still coming, right? xo

Wouldn't miss it!💀 You're spending your evening working, then? What a surprise. 😳

Ollie looked at her paper chains. She was working, sort of, but Max didn't need to know that. She had picked the locations she would take her wannabe ghost hunters to on Monday night, and wasn't remotely worried about being a temporary tour guide – especially knowing Max would be there, too. In fact, she felt giddy at the thought of spending another evening in his company, and it was this giddiness that – much later, after she'd calmed down considerably – she would blame for what she ended up typing next.

The glow sticks arrived, that's all – it doesn't mean I'm working. I've been on the Victoria's Secret website, which is very much *not* work! xo

As soon as she'd sent it, she closed her eyes in despair. She went to hit 'delete for everyone' but the ticks had already gone blue. 'Fuckity fuck biscuits,' she said to her dog. Henry stared balefully at her, as if he knew just how much of an idiot she'd been. Perhaps Max didn't know what Victoria's

Secret was? Was that remotely plausible? She thought probably not, and anyway, he'd been looking up the ghostly battle earlier. If he was curious, he'd research it.

She couldn't leave it like it was: her fingers flew across the screen.

Please ignore that last message! xo

What message? 😉 There are a hundred different things I could have replied to this, but I'll quietly forget about it instead. Speak soon. Mx

Ollie sagged, relieved, against the sofa, even though the traitorous part of her brain couldn't help wondering what some of his replies might have been.

Chapter Twelve

Halloween dawned full of soft, autumn sunshine. It was the nicest day they'd had for a while, the sea shimmering a rich, sapphire blue as Ollie walked into town, carrying her box of glow sticks. It wasn't giving off the spooky vibes she needed for her event later, but at this time of year, any sunshine was welcome.

Inside A New Chapter, her Halloween table was piled beautifully with Laura Purcell and Michelle Paver novels, some real-life ghost stories and books of local hauntings. The sign above it read *Haunting Reads* and she'd draped it with fake cobwebs.

'Hi Becky,' she said, putting her box down. 'Is there an update on the numbers signed up for tonight?'

Becky clicked through screens on the computer. 'There are fifteen, now. Three up from yesterday.'

'Amazing! Are you coming?'

'No, I haven't got a babysitter, so I'm doing trick-or-treating instead.'

Ollie sighed. 'I used to love trick-or-treating when I was little, and back then I just had a plastic bowl and was only allowed to visit the three neighbours my parents had checked with in advance. It's got so much bigger.'

'It's all Americanised,' Becky said. 'Not sure it's that great, actually, promoting ghouls and villains to our kids.'

'I suppose if they stick to children's characters – the Worst Witch and Harry Potter – then it's OK. It can get out of hand easily, though. My walk tonight will focus on Cornish history – local hauntings – and books.'

'And glow sticks,' Thea added, taking one out of the box. 'I used to love these.'

'I've got way too many for tonight, so you can fill your boots.'

Becky and Thea both snapped a stick, the crackle and burst of colour as they ignited incredibly satisfying.

'Ollie,' Thea said, waving her luminous green stick at her. 'I know you're getting ready for tonight, but have you had any more thoughts about our big Christmas event?'

Ollie pressed her lips together, trying to suppress a grin. 'What about . . . Sophia Forsythe-Hartley?'

'Seriously?' Thea looked alarmed rather than delighted. 'Mega famous thriller author with a hugely popular Cornwall-set series? She wouldn't blink at a bookshop like ours, let alone come for an event here.'

'That's not true,' Ollie protested.

Thea shook her head. 'Her book tours include America, Scandinavia, Australia. In London she does Waterstones Piccadilly and Daunt Books, and occasionally she has events at places like the Festival Hall. She wouldn't come here.'

'We won't know that until we ask her.'

'We can make a pretty informed guess,' Becky muttered.

'Are you really confident we could get someone like that here?' For the first time, Thea sounded concerned, as if she'd reached the limits of her belief in Ollie's can-do attitude. It was understandable, because it was a world away from ghost walks and book clubs, but that didn't mean they couldn't try.

'I know someone who knows her editor,' Ollie said, tilting her chin up. 'What harm can a phone call do?'

'No harm,' Thea said. 'But don't mention this to anyone else, please. Nobody beyond our inner circle, OK? Not until it's more than a pie in the sky idea. I don't want to get anyone's hopes up, or have anyone laugh at us.'

'Nobody will laugh at us,' Ollie replied. 'But I won't say a word, not to another soul. I know you say it's pie in the sky, but we *want* to aim for the stars, don't we?'

Thea leaned on the countertop. 'Did you know that I've wanted to run a bookshop since I was ten?'

Ollie took a glow stick out of the box, cracked it, and was satisfied when it shone a bright, almost eye-aching blue. 'I knew it was a dream of yours, but I didn't realise you'd had it that long. You must be so proud of what you've achieved.'

'I am,' Thea said. 'Really. I love this place already, and I'm so happy to have you, and Becky, here. But my ambition stopped at running a successful, loved bookshop by the sea, with customers who trusted my stock and my recommendations, and kept coming back. It's a busy job, there's so much to do behind the scenes as well as day to day, which is why I wanted *you*, someone with different experience, who could help us reach readers and the community in different ways.'

'That's what I'm doing,' Ollie said.

Thea smiled. 'You are. Already, you're doing so much. I love your ideas, and I love your energy, but I'm not aiming for the stars. I'm aiming for Port Karadow, Cornwall, with some online customers further afield. I want us to hold popular events, and I want us to be ambitious, but I am not after stretching ourselves – me or you or Becky – too far or too hard. I don't want to promise anything I can't deliver. Do you get it?'

'Of course I do,' Ollie said. She got it, but that didn't mean she agreed with it. Why not aim further than you thought possible, just to see where you landed? But Thea was her boss, someone who had turned her passion into a reality. She had fulfilled an incredible dream, so it made sense for Ollie to listen to her, learn from her. She could not fuck this up.

'Come to me with any ideas,' Thea said, 'but please always speak to me before you act on them. This town is way too good at spreading rumours.'

Ollie smiled. 'I'd noticed.'

'I don't want anyone to think we're too big for our boots. We need to grow into them first.'

'I guess I'm not known for my caution,' Ollie said.

'And I'm not known for my risk-taking – launching this place aside, but that was still mostly calculated. Let's meet somewhere in the middle.'

'Middle sounds good. For now, anyway.' She grinned, Thea laughed and Becky – though Ollie only just caught it – rolled her eyes. She would have to convince both of them that she wasn't being too ambitious, that she was only doing what Thea had asked her to do. Sophia Forsythe-Hartley was not too big for this bookshop. 'Does anyone want a cake from Sea Brew?' she asked. 'I'm thinking of doing a run.'

'Dylan told me that Max is coming on the ghost walk,' Becky said.

'That's right,' Ollie replied.

'He wanted to go, but I can't bring Billy and Meg along: it's too late for them, which is why I'm trying to tempt them with trick-or-treating instead.'

'Does Dylan know Max well?'

Becky shrugged. 'Max helps out with the school football team when he can. Dylan worships him.'

Something twisted in Ollie's gut. Of course Max helped out with the football team at the local school: he was genuine and kind, and he used to be a personal trainer. Did that mean his kindness towards her was just that? He'd tried to be friendly to a newcomer, and she'd taken it too far? She thought of their recent message exchange, and squeezed her eyes closed.

'Is he coming as a customer, or a helper?' Thea asked.

'He's bought a ticket,' Ollie said. 'Why?'

Thea shrugged. 'His main goal in life seems to be helping people out, so it wouldn't surprise me if he wanted to help you, too.'

'He seems really lovely,' Ollie said, unable to resist the opportunity to talk about him.

'He's so charming,' Thea added, shaking her head. 'Like Becky says, he helps out with the football team, he organised this barbecue cook-off in the summer with Marcus Belrose, the chef who runs the Happy Shack. He's fully invested in the town, and so sweet with it. I find it entirely unfathomable that he's single.'

Ollie rearranged the pile of bookmarks on the counter. 'Maybe he had a bad break-up? Or – what if he's like a small-town celebrity? He's *so* charming and hot, he runs a popular business in the heart of Port Karadow, he has women constantly throwing themselves at him and he's just exhausted by the whole thing.'

Nobody spoke for a moment, and Ollie looked up.

'Beats me.' Becky shrugged. 'I chat to him, sure, but mostly about how Dylan's getting on. We've not really gone there with each other's hopes and dreams.'

Ollie was surprised how relieved she felt at Becky's ambivalence. Then she realised Thea was giving her a curious look. 'What?'

'*So* charming and hot?' Thea repeated.

Ollie rolled her eyes. 'Nothing I said is untrue. There's no point in me trying to backtrack.'

'Fair enough.' Thea bit her lip. 'So you're off to Sea Brew, are you?'

'If that's OK,' Ollie said. 'I don't *have* to go, though.'

'No, I'd love something.' Thea's smile was uncharacteristically mischievous. 'I got up late and didn't have time for breakfast this morning.'

'Yes, boss,' Ollie said, grabbing a tote bag from behind the counter. She could definitely do with some fresh air right now. She tried to ignore the fact that her pulse was already starting to thrum at the thought of seeing Max.

* * *

The window of Sea Brew was a mass of cotton-wool webs, oversized plastic spiders, and skeletons, with a few cute-looking ghosts thrown in to soften the horrifying effect. Ollie stepped inside and Max, who'd had his back to her, turned around.

She gasped, and he grinned.

'What do you think?' he asked.

'Terrifying,' she said, although that wasn't the first word that came to mind.

His skeleton outfit was made up of a tight-fitting onesie that showed off all his muscles, despite the black-and-white design. He'd painted his face white with deep, dark eye-sockets, and he hadn't bothered to restrict his curls. Even as a Halloween character, he was disarmingly sexy, and the chequerboard apron remained firmly in place. He was a House of Horrors monochrome delight.

'I hope you're wearing that tonight,' she said.

He laughed and shook his head. 'No way. It's surprisingly thin, and I don't want to take attention away from the tour guide.' He gestured to her. 'This is just for today.'

'Because you wanted a day of not being harassed by small children?'

His eyes flashed. 'I'm only borderline scary.'

'If you say so.'

'I can't afford to put off my younger customers, because I've got a whole load of homemade sweets to give away. Anyway, all the kids I've seen so far have been a hundred times more terrifying than I am.' He reached under the counter and held out a large tin full of beautifully crafted pumpkins, skulls and ghosts, all made out of marzipan.

'Did Beryan make these?' she asked, taking a ghost.

'Of course. How's the ghost-walk prep?'

'So far we've all cracked a glow stick, but there's nothing left to do, really. My walk is sorted, and I've got a table of haunting reads to lure customers in afterwards. If anyone tries to walk out without buying something, I'll threaten to lock them inside A New Chapter with the ghost.'

Max shook his head. 'You're shameless, you know that?'

'I'm a bookseller. My job is to sell books.'

'Also, I didn't know the Old Post House had a ghost.'

'Your supernatural knowledge of your home town is severely lacking, Max.'

'That's why I'm coming tonight. You'll tell me all about it?'

'Of course. Right now, though, I need to buy pastries.'

Max gestured to the croissants, pains au chocolate and Danishes laid out in the glass case. 'Pick your poison.'

'I hope that's not a special ingredient in recognition of what day it is.' She leaned over, taking her time choosing. 'I need to get this right. The way to a woman's heart is through her stomach.'

'Whose heart do you need to reach?'

She sighed. 'I'm trying to convince Thea and Becky that we can be as ambitious as we want with the bookshop. They're fine with the book club and ghost walk, but anything more . . . elaborate, and they don't seem keen.'

'That's surprising,' Max said. 'I thought Thea was pretty open-minded.'

'It's understandable that she's being cautious, I suppose. Her shop's still new, and she cares about it. She just . . . she wants me to rein in my ideas. Paper chains instead of fancy garlands.' That was the best metaphor she could come up with, because she had promised Thea she wouldn't tell anyone about her suggestion of getting Sophia Forsythe-Hartley to come to the shop. 'But I could aim for satin paper chains, I suppose. Everyone loves a bit of satin, don't they? Can I have a custard cream Danish, an almond croissant and a pain au raisin, please?'

She looked up when he didn't reply.

'Yeah, of course.' He lifted a hand, as if he was going to rub his face, then must have remembered the face paint and ran his fingers through his hair instead. 'Warmed up?'

'Please.'

He turned away from her to put the pastries in the oven. 'I'm guessing there was nobody to rein you in with the Victoria's Secret purchases, though.'

Ollie went entirely still, a warmth pooling inside her that clashed with the warning signs flashing in her head. She hadn't expected him to bring it up: she'd been embarrassed about the message ever since she'd sent it to him. She opened her mouth, about to tell him that it was Marion who had bought things from Victoria's Secret, but realised she didn't want to bring anyone else into the conversation.

'No,' she said softly. 'Nobody else had any say in those.'

'Right.' Max's voice was like gravel, and he cleared his throat before turning round. The white face paint was thick, so she couldn't tell if he was blushing, but the way he looked at her – it made her breath stall somewhere between her lungs and her mouth.

'Not sure what Thea would say if I took those purchases into A New Chapter and showed them off.' Her laugh sounded strange. 'Glow sticks are much safer.' She smiled, but he didn't return it. Instead, he took a step closer to the counter, closing the space even though there was still a barrier between them.

'Ollie, I'm so sorry. I shouldn't have—' He was cut off by the bell dinging and a small fleet of squealing children running through the door, accompanied by two frazzled-looking mums.

'Trick or treat!' the children shouted in an unruly cacophony, and after that Max was too busy with customers to finish his sentence, handing over Ollie's pastries with what could have been an apologetic look – though it was hard to tell through his skeleton veneer – and a quick hand squeeze.

Ollie stepped out into the cool October air, and started the climb back to A New Chapter, wondering how she was supposed to focus on anything after that encounter. She thought that Victoria's Secret and sexy skeletons would always, from this day on, make her think of Halloween.

Chapter Thirteen

As Ollie waited in the bookshop for her intrepid ghost-seekers to assemble, the ones who'd already arrived cracking their glow sticks and looking at the books, she realised how perfect Halloween was as a lead-in to Christmas. There were celebrations, parties, the outlandish decorations and dressing up. It was all so Americanised now, as Becky had said, but it still felt like a dress rehearsal or, at the very least, a warning: *a more extreme version of this is coming, so you'd better be ready.* There were a few days to prepare for fireworks night, and then it was all uphill – or downhill, depending on your point of view – until Christmas.

Her ghost-walk attendees ranged from young to old, eager-looking to trepidatious. Some were here to be entertained, some to be scared, and it was Ollie's job to achieve both. The bookshop, with its lights turned low to enhance the spooky atmosphere, filled up, until all the ticket holders apart from Max had arrived.

'Good to go?' Thea asked, handing Ollie her coat. 'I'll be here when you get back, ready to help you sell hundreds of terrifying books.' She widened her eyes, and Ollie laughed.

'We're going to be rushed off our feet. I—'

The bell dinged and Ollie turned just in time to see Max hold the door open for Dylan, then come in after him. She smiled at him and he smiled back, but there was wariness there, too. She hadn't forgotten their earlier conversation – how could she? It hung between them, like a Halloween mist.

'Good evening, everyone,' she said, clapping her hands. 'Happy Halloween! Welcome to the first Port Karadow ghost walk. Tonight isn't only special because of the date, but because we are in one of the country's – if not the world's – most haunted places. Cornwall has so much history, so many mysteries nestled along its coastline, and deep in its forests, its buildings and ruins. Have you ever,' she went on, dropping her voice, 'felt a chill on the back of your neck when there was no wind? Sensed eyes burning into you when you were convinced nobody was there?' She took a step towards her group. 'Heard footsteps or whispers when you knew you were alone?' She paused, waiting for the nervous titters to die down. 'You'll need to be on high alert for all those things tonight, because I am about to take you to some of Port Karadow's spookiest places. I can see some of you are prepared.' She gestured to a young family, the parents smiling behind two children dressed as ghost-busters, their jumpsuits with the famous symbol sewn onto the breast pockets. 'The rest of you? You'll just have to take your chances.'

Ollie pulled her coat tighter around her, clutched the book of legends to her chest, and swept through the small crowd to the front door. She thought she heard a familiar voice whisper 'Terrifying,' as she passed, and made a mental note to tease Max afterwards. The fact that he'd brought Dylan with him, when Becky said she couldn't get a babysitter, proved that they did have a bond, and that Becky trusted him implicitly.

Outside, darkness was beginning to fall, and as she led her group to St Ethel's church – close by, and with a dramatic story that Ollie knew well by now – they passed pumpkin lanterns on stoops, the flickering tea lights visible through eye sockets; orange and black bunting; a string of ghost-shaped lights in a window.

The air had that tantalising, smoky tang that was so reminiscent of autumn: of piles of leaves and conkers, card-board cups full of milky hot chocolate, the sizzle of roasting hazelnuts, the sticky sweetness of toffee apples. The sun was a pale streak along the surface of the sea, crowded by the gathering clouds, its light eerily orange, as if it wanted to match the day's decorations. It was, Ollie decided, one of the most stunning things she had ever seen.

Her group were enthralled by the ghostly battle at St Ethel's church, the young ghostbusters running round the walls, fake Proton Pistols held high, and Ollie went over the top with her dramatic pauses, delighted when the eyes of her guests widened with fear and anticipation. It was fun, telling spooky tales, and she understood why Liam had been so keen to tell her about Kerensa's handprint, rather than let her read it from the book.

'Onwards,' she said, after she'd told the group everything she knew about the phantom battle, with some embellished details of her own. 'If you're keen, you can come back here on the night of December the first, and experience the ghosts for yourselves.'

'Not a bloody chance,' said a short, robust man who Ollie had mentally assigned as the bouncer of a local night-club. Perhaps she had misjudged him.

As she slipped through the crowd to reach the front, their next destination the town's picturesque harbour, she passed Max and Dylan.

'Having fun yet?' she asked in a low voice.

'S'all right,' Dylan said, shrugging.

She caught Max's eye and they exchanged a grin. It seemed she would have to work harder.

She had been worried that the harbour would be busy with people eating fish and chips, enjoying the light display created by the bobbing fishing boats, their cabins softly aglow, but as she walked onto the pathway in front of the water, she could see they were the only ones there. Perfect.

The water was an inky, murky blue, and the cloud cover had blocked out the richness of the night sky, obliterating any chance of moonlight or stars. As she waited for her group to assemble around her, tendrils of mist slunk across the sea towards them. Was this Kerensa's doing? That particular legend was too far out of town for Ollie to include tonight, but ever since she'd heard the story, her thoughts had tripped back to the young woman whenever she had a stroke of good fortune.

She turned, so she had her back to the railings, her small group facing her with eager expressions. 'Port Karadow harbour,' she said. 'There's no better place to eat chips or candyfloss, that box of doughnuts from Sea Brew, or slurp down your hot chocolate. You get the fresh air, seaside soundtrack, an unbeatable view. On a sunny day, it's busy with tourists and locals. But,' she went on, softening her voice, 'how many of you come here after dark? I don't mean on pageant day, or to watch the New Year's firework display. I'm talking about on a night like this.'

There was silence from her audience, and then a teenage girl who had come with her boyfriend, said, 'Why wouldn't we come here at night?'

'Because you don't want to catch sight of the Lost Fisherman,' Ollie said gravely. 'Seeing him is a sign of bad luck: one you won't be able to shake off for a whole year.'

'What does he look like?' This was the smaller of the two ghostbusters, standing at the very front and looking up at her, blinking his surprise.

'He appears as a light, drifting across the still waters of the harbour,' Ollie said. 'When you look more closely, you'll see that there's no boat attached, that the ship's lantern is almost all that remains of him. He died, you see. Took his boat out when a terrible storm was forecast, confident that he knew the sea better than anyone, could navigate all her moods and tantrums, knew how to survive her at her worst. He realised, as his boat sank below the waves, that he was mortal, just like everyone else.'

'What do you mean, the lantern is *almost* all that's left of him?' This had come from Max. His dark curls fell over his forehead, and his hand was on Dylan's shoulder, the boy standing in front of him.

'As well as the light,' she said, holding his gaze, 'you can hear his halyard, clanging as if the storm was still raging.'

She was overjoyed when she saw Max's Adam's apple bob: she was getting to him. 'It's a frantic, upsetting sound,' she continued, 'one that foreshadows his fate. If you hear it, or see the light, then bad luck is inevitable. The year ahead will be full of trouble, of sadness. Best, one would say, to avoid this place after da—'

'Oh my *God!* The light – there! Look!'

The single, screeching voice was soon joined by other exclamations, and Ollie spun to face the water, her eyes searching . . . searching . . . There. *Shit.* A lump solidified in her throat as she watched the soft glow hovering above the water, moving from north to south, weaving between the stationary boats that were clearly visible.

'We have to go!' another voice joined in.

'The Lost Fisherman!'

'Holy fuck!'

Ollie squinted, frantic. It couldn't be real. She couldn't have conjured up a bloody ghost just by talking about it. Her group were restless behind her, some on the verge of abandoning the walk altogether.

'It's not—' She couldn't say it wasn't true: she didn't want to break the spell. But if everyone ran, if they didn't come back to A New Chapter, she would be accused of terrifying their customers and sending people *away* from the bookshop. She focused on the light, peering closely, because it couldn't be real, could it?

A hand landed on her good shoulder, squeezing gently, and she knew, without looking, that it was Max. She kept scanning the harbour, her breath lodged in her throat, and then – there.

'It's not the Lost Fisherman!' she shouted, spinning round, trying to break through the commotion. 'It's a rowing boat, a late-night fisherman who is very much alive. See? Come and look – come on.' She beckoned them all forward, called to the young couple who had run as far as the nearest bench. She coaxed them back, as if they were skittish kittens.

Everyone stepped up to the railings, peering through the night, and at that moment the tiny rowing boat – so small and dark that it was almost invisible – reached a bigger fishing boat. The glowing lamp spotlighted the smaller craft and the grizzled fisherman sitting in it. There were sighs and murmurs of relief, the bouncer whispered, 'Fucking hell,' and a couple of people laughed nervously, their voices frayed with fear.

'It seems, ladies and gentlemen, boys and girls,' Ollie said, surprised she could hear herself speak over the pounding of her heart, 'that we have been spared the sighting of the Lost Fisherman, and have instead had an encounter with the *brave* fisherman. Who wants to row out to sea in such a small boat, in the darkness? Not me, that's for sure.' She exhaled, her breath puffing out a cloud into the night air. 'Everyone suitably terrified?'

There were a few 'yup's, some mutters of assent, and Ollie rolled her shoulders, kneading the left one when it protested.

'Excellent. I promise that our next spot is a little less traumatic. Ghostly, but much more benevolent. Who's heard of Clotted Cream Cottage, at the edge of town?' A few hands were raised, and all eyes were back on her. Thank God for that. Never mind the story of the Lost Fisherman, she had been close to inventing her own Port Karadow legend: The Lost Bookshop Customers. That, she was sure, was the most frightening of them all.

When they made it back to A New Chapter, some of her guests picking up their pace as if it was a refuge they'd been searching for for days, Ollie held the door open and let everyone go ahead of her. Thea was there to greet them, offering elderflower cordial or glasses of wine, and Ollie watched, gratified, as most of them swarmed to her carefully curated Halloween table.

Dylan and Max were the last to enter, and Ollie waved them through the open doorway with a flourish.

'That was awesome,' Dylan said. 'Max was really scared!'

He frowned. 'Not true. You were the one who jumped when that rowing boat appeared.'

Dylan laughed, turning to look up at him. 'It was *you*!'

Max sighed. 'Maybe it was me. Let's not tell anyone else though, hey? Got a book in mind you want to get?'

Dylan grinned. 'Mum says I can choose one.'

'Off you go, then. I'll take you home in five minutes.'

They watched as Dylan rushed to the Halloween table, rather than heading for the children's section.

'He seems like a great kid,' Ollie said, following Max further into the shop.

'He is. He's had a tough time of it since Becky split up with his dad, and he's a lot older than his brother and sister, which makes things harder. Becky thought it would be good for him to come tonight, and I was here anyway, so . . .' He shrugged, his gaze leaving hers as he glanced around the shop. Then he turned back to her. 'Ollie—'

'You don't have to say anything,' she rushed.

'I stepped over a line.' He moved closer to her and dropped his voice. She knew he was trying to apologise, but seriously? The low tone, the sudden lack of space between them? It wasn't getting any *less* seductive.

'I brought it up in the first place, and I shouldn't have.' She glanced behind her to check that nobody could overhear them. Thea was busy at the till, and she knew she needed to join her.

'I just . . .' he started, and Ollie had a moment of blind panic. If he told her he was attracted to her, if he admitted he'd been thinking about her in lacy underwear, she would be entirely lost – like that bloody fisherman. She would be lost to the charms of a decent man, rather than a storm, but it would still swallow her whole.

She blinked the thought away and said, 'Are we still on for Thursday?'

Max paused, then nodded. 'Of course.'

'Good! Only, I need to help Thea, otherwise she'll drown in a sea of customers.'

His shoulders dropped, and she wondered whether he felt relieved or defeated. 'Sure. I need to see where Dylan's got to.'

Ollie's hand moved of its own accord, squeezing his upper arm. She could feel how firm his bicep was, even beneath his coat. 'Please don't worry, Max. I honestly didn't mind you saying that. I mean, I – it doesn't matter. It was . . . it was nice.' She winced. *Fuck*. That's not what she'd meant to say at all.

She gave him a quick smile and left him there, hurrying over to the counter to help Thea. But she had seen the look on his face just before she'd abandoned him, the way his lips had parted ever so slightly, his eyes darkening. He hadn't looked confused or alarmed, and the only way she could describe it – the only way she could think to – was that, after she'd admitted to him that she had *liked* him referring to their underwear conversation, that she had thought it was *nice,* was that he'd looked at her hungrily. Perhaps kind, charming, *so sweet with it* Max was a little bit dangerous, after all.

Chapter Fourteen

The next morning, the rain was coming down in sheets. 'Hello, November,' Ollie said, as she pulled back the curtains over her French doors. 'Thanks for this.'

Henry looked up at her and whimpered, and Ollie, knowing she would have to change again once she'd been outside, put her wellies and a waterproof jacket on over her pyjamas and took him for a short walk before breakfast. The cloud cover kept the cold at bay, and even though she wasn't exactly toasty, she got back feeling exhilarated rather than chilled to the bone.

By the time she'd had a hot shower, then milky coffee and toast with peanut butter on, the rain had abated slightly, and she thought she might make it to work without becoming a drowned rat.

There was still a heavy drizzle, and Ollie got into town in half her usual time. She had an umbrella and kept her head down, but she could feel the rain soaking her trousers from the knee down, and watched droplets land on the sleeves of her coat like a thousand tiny jewels.

Today, more than ever, she needed a proper drink from Sea Brew, rather than the instant coffee she'd get at A New Chapter. She hadn't been able to sleep when she'd eventually got home after the ghost walk. Max's expression just before she'd left him played as the lead track in her thoughts, along with her triumph that the walk had dipped towards disaster, but she'd been able to rescue it.

Those victories were the best kind. If you could claw your way back from near-failure to resounding success, then you were achieving; you were learning. It had given Ollie the confidence to go online, find out the name of Sophia Forsythe-Hartley's editor, dig deeper for the format of the publisher's email addresses, and write her an enthusiastic email about A New Chapter, and about how much they would love Sophia to launch her new book there in December.

She didn't think she was defying Thea, exactly: she was simply making enquiries. Her spontaneous events were bringing sales and recognition to the bookshop, and an author launch had the potential to be huge. But it couldn't be done at the last minute: she had to give it the time, effort and energy it deserved.

She reached Main Street and slowed her pace, the cobbles ahead slick and precarious, even against her low-heeled boots. She walked carefully, every step placed with precision, her eyes on her feet, so when someone crashed into her she jolted backwards and squealed in surprise.

'Jesus Christ!' The voice was loud and male, and as she raised her umbrella she saw a dark figure reel away from her, clutching his face.

'Oh my God! Are you OK?'

The man bent over, rubbing his eyes. He was dressed all in black, his chosen protection against the weather a rather ineffectual leather jacket, and his dark hair was dripping.

'Are you all right?' she repeated, when he didn't respond. 'You should have been looking where you were going!'

Ollie felt a spike of anger. 'I should be saying that to you. I *was* looking where I was going: I didn't want to slip on the cobbles. Where were *you* looking that you managed to crash, with full force, into my umbrella?'

'I was in a hurry,' the man shot back, his face still obscured by his hand.

'Oh. *Well* then. It's clearly all my fault.'

'Jesus, this hurts,' he groaned.

Ollie sighed and, spotting the overhang of a shop doorway, dragged the man over to it.

'Do you still have both your eyes?' she asked, because he was making a lot of fuss.

'I don't know!'

'Let me have a look, then, if you're incapable of knowing whether one's been gouged out by how it feels.'

'There's no need to be sarcastic.' This was more of a grumble, and the man slowly lowered his hands, revealing his face. It was one Ollie recognised. Marcus Belrose, the famous chef who'd opened his Happy Shack in Port Karadow earlier that year. He had a reputation for being arrogant and a hard task-master, and so far Ollie had seen nothing to dissuade her of those rumours. He had a neat goatee around his pursed lips, and his eyes were dark and, unsurprisingly, still in place.

'Your left eye looks a little red,' she said, 'but you're not even bleeding.'

127

'What do you mean *even?*' His gaze was direct, and not entirely pleasant.

'You're being rather over dramatic.'

'It was incredibly painful and a genuine shock! Who are you, anyway?'

Ollie laughed. 'What's that supposed to mean? *Who am I to be walking these hallowed streets? Who would dare to bump into you, Marcus Belrose?*'

He stared at her. His eye was quite red, she conceded, but there was no need for him to be an asshole. 'I'm sorry,' he said shortly. 'What's your name?'

'Ollie.' She held out her hand. 'Ollie Spencer. I moved here a few weeks ago. I'm working at A New Chapter.'

He nodded and grasped her hand. 'Gorgeous little shop.'

'With big ambitions,' she said, still rankled by his attitude.

'Oh yes?' He raised a supercilious eyebrow.

'Of course. You came to Port Karadow with big plans, there's no reason we shouldn't have them, too. In fact, I'm running a programme of events, and I know you haven't released a cookbook since you moved here, but what do you think about joining forces? We could hold a cooking class in the Happy Shack, get the attendees to make one of your recipes – led by your charming self, of course – and A New Chapter could sell copies of your books.'

Marcus folded his arms, the leather of his jacket squeaking. 'This is your pitching technique? Jab me in the eye, tell me I'm being a baby then coerce me into running an event so you can sell books?'

'Your language is inflammatory,' Ollie said. 'But yes, basically. Except, if we're splitting hairs, *you* assaulted *my* brolly.'

Marcus's eyes gleamed, and Ollie got the sense he was trying not to smile. 'Let me think about it. We'd need a meeting to sort out logistics. The Shack's not set up for cooking classes.'

'I bet if you shifted a few things around it could be. Don't you have an open hatch so everyone can see your chefs at work?'

He narrowed his eyes. 'You haven't eaten there yet?'

'I've only been here a few weeks,' she said again. 'Give me a chance.'

Marcus nodded, and she could see he was considering it. 'Let me talk to the team, and I'll get back to you in a couple of days. Number?'

Ollie resisted rolling her eyes. 'Come up to the bookshop: that's where Thea and I will be. I need to go or I'll be late for work. Put some ice on that eye if it still feels like it's about to fall out – you must have some at your restaurant.' She patted him on the arm, then, before he had a chance to reply, she stepped out from under the awning and walked up to Sea Brew, leaving him gawping after her.

'I don't know if it's a good idea.' Thea's large, worried eyes looked at Ollie over the rim of her coffee cup.

Ollie shrugged. 'I know Marcus can be a bit of an asshole, but he's close to being a genuine celebrity in Port Karadow. He's got the confidence to run an event, and he'll have customers eating out of the palm of his hand if he bothers to turn on the charm.'

'I know he'll be good at it,' Thea said. 'Ben worked with him over the summer, on his beach barbecue truck. He said that when Marcus tones down the peacocking, he's actually OK.'

'What are you worried about, then?' Ollie had been pleased with her quick thinking, literally bumping into the town's celebrity chef and using it to her advantage. But even this idea, it seemed, wasn't the right one.

'How are we supposed to promote A New Chapter, if the event you're suggesting isn't *at* A New Chapter?'

Ollie's gaze flicked to Becky. She'd said it calmly enough, but there was something about her posture, the way she was holding her coffee cup – the coffee that Ollie had bought her – so precisely.

'We'd be there, though,' she replied. 'We could get a pull-up banner for events we host elsewhere. Or maybe we *could* do it here? It will depend on the recipe, but it doesn't need to involve ovens or fancy hobs. You can get so many plug-in options these days. Why don't we do that, instead?'

Thea rubbed her cheek. 'It could be messy, and over-complicated.'

'I bet Marcus wouldn't let us sell any cookbooks that weren't his,' Becky chipped in. 'Which limits us a lot.'

Ollie swallowed down her frustration. 'He wouldn't be able to stop us selling anything. The point of every event is that, alongside whatever books we're actually promoting, customers always end up buying a book they saw reviewed online, or one their friend told them about. Marcus couldn't prevent that happening.'

'He might try,' Becky said.

'How are the Book Wars plans coming along? And the book club?' Thea asked brightly.

'I've promoted the November choice for the book club on our Facebook page, and I've put up a post about Book Wars, to find some willing competitors. I've ordered the

130

chairs for upstairs, and I'm going to the wholesalers with Max later this week to buy the coffee machine.'

'That all sounds great, Ollie.'

'I'm also going to have the details of the first quiz locked down by the end of the week. I'll start easy; general knowledge with some book questions thrown in.'

'Sounds perfect,' Thea said. 'And don't discount the Marcus Belrose idea. If he can come up with something easy that we could cook here, we'll go ahead. Let's have a look at those banners you mentioned, too. Ten minutes after work – the three of us?' Thea turned to Becky. 'Is the after-school club back on this week?'

'Yeah,' Becky said. 'I can spare ten minutes, but no more than that.'

'Wonderful. Right, let's get back to it. It's publication day for a big chunk of pre-Christmas titles this Thursday, so let's think about rejigging the window display. We could start to bring in some Christmassy bits, too. Ollie, are you happy to look into that?'

'Of course.' She thought of her growing pile of book-themed paper chains at home. She would need to bring them in on a day when it wasn't raining, or her hours of slicing and stapling would be for nothing.

'Not from Selfridges though, OK?' Becky grinned at her and Ollie smiled back. She didn't know if it was a good-natured joke, or a barb meant to sting her. Whatever it was, she realised she still had a long way to go before she and her colleague could be considered amicable, let alone on genuinely friendly terms.

Chapter Fifteen

'Is that Yule log bunting?' Ollie asked, even though Max was busy behind the counter and had his back to her.

They hadn't seen each other since their *moment* at the bookshop after the ghost walk. She'd been hoping to see him in Sea Brew after bumping into Marcus Belrose, had planned how to defuse the tension between them, but he hadn't been there. For a ridiculous moment Ollie had thought that he'd decided she was too difficult to deal with, and had left the café in the capable hands of his staff so he didn't have to see her.

But it was Wednesday morning and here he was, in all his curly-haired, broad-shouldered glory. She had breathed a sigh of relief as she'd stepped through the door, then grinned at the sparkly, festive bunting: Christmas puddings alternating with robin-topped Yule logs and mince pies, all with a healthy dose of glitter. The problem with Yule logs, however, was that they were an indistinct shape.

Max turned, his smile widening when he saw her. 'Are you questioning my decoration choices?'

'It's just that they could be *actual* logs, especially with the robin on top.'

'I'll pass that onto Jasmine, the young girl who made them. I'm sure she'll be delighted.' He raised an eyebrow, and Ollie laughed.

'I'm not trying to be cruel. Forget I said anything.'

'Something else we both need to forget?' His voice had dropped, and he looked faintly embarrassed. 'Look, Ollie, what I said the other day—'

'Please, Max. It's done. You've already apologised, and you really didn't need to in the first place. Marcus Belrose has more reasons to say sorry to me, and I was only in his company for ten minutes.'

'Marcus Belrose? What did he do to you?'

'Not a whole lot. He's a pompous dickhead, though, isn't he?'

Max pressed his lips into a thin line, a look of displeasure on his face that Ollie had never seen before. It was like the lamp you always keep on at home, even when it's bedtime or you're going out, being unexpectedly switched off.

'Unless he's your best friend?' she hedged.

'Not at all,' Max said immediately. 'We've crossed paths a few times. We were judges for a barbecue competition in the summer, but we're certainly not bosom buddies. Are you sure he didn't do anything to upset you?'

'It was fine.' Ollie waved his concern away. 'He walked into my umbrella and had the temerity to blame me. I came to soothe my rattled nerves with a latte, but you weren't here.'

'You still got the latte, though?' Max bent over, re-arranging the sausage rolls to close a gap.

'Of course, but it wasn't the whole experience: something was missing.' She hadn't meant to sound so sincere.

He looked up at her, a smile slipping back onto his face. 'Good to know I'm getting *something* right.'

'Of course you are. And I wanted to check we were still on for the trip after work tomorrow?'

'Sure. I'm knocking off early, though the place we're going to is open until eight. And there's a Christmas market in a village on the way back, if you fancy it? We can only have so much fun looking at coffee machines.'

Ollie's heart skipped. 'Sounds great. Shall I bring my car in?'

Max shook his head. 'My house is a five-minute walk. We can go in mine.'

'Thanks. I'll meet you here, then?'

'Yeah. Ollie . . .'

'Max?' She waited for him to continue, then felt her phone buzz in her handbag. She didn't recognise the number on the screen, so she answered it before it cut out. 'Hello?'

'Is that Ollie Spencer?'

'Speaking.' She mouthed an apology to Max, then walked to the window.

'Excellent. This is Arabella March, Sophia Forsythe-Hartley's editor. I received your email.'

'Oh? Oh! That's . . . I'm glad it got to you without a hitch, and thank you for taking the time to phone me back.'

'It's not a problem. I've discussed your proposition with Sophia, and she's very interested in the possibility of an event at A New Chapter. Her schedule is packed, as you

134

can imagine, but we were hoping you and Thea Rushwood would have an online meeting with us, sometime over the next few weeks?'

'Of course! That would be wonderful.'

'Excellent,' Arabella said again. 'If I send over some dates when Sophia's free, then perhaps you could get back to me in the next couple of days?'

'I will absolutely do that.'

'Grand. Good to talk to you, Ollie.'

'You too, Arabella. Thank you for your call.'

When they'd said goodbye, Ollie almost bounced back to the counter.

Max was looking at her expectantly. 'Good news?'

'Potentially. An author I'm desperate to have at A New Chapter wants an online meeting with us, to discuss holding an event.'

'That's great, isn't it? You look part elated, part terrified.'

Ollie tugged her ponytail, the adrenaline rush of Arabella's call fading as she realised what this meant. 'When I spoke to Thea about it, she wasn't too keen. She said we shouldn't be aiming for such big-name authors, in case we got every-one's hopes up and then it fell through.'

'But you went ahead anyway?' Max looked amused rather than concerned.

'I thought if I could confirm the event and go to Thea when it was a done deal, she'd see that we *can* be ambitious. We can get whoever we want, because we're a stunning independent bookshop in a popular, idyllic town and we shouldn't put any restrictions on ourselves.'

'And now you've done that,' Max said. 'You've proved it to her.'

Ollie laughed. 'I really haven't. There are so many places where this could fail, between now and Sophia Forsythe-Hartley stepping through the bookshop doors. And she wants to meet with me *and* Thea via Zoom, so I can't present it as a done deal – unless I go ahead without Thea, and I don't think that's wise.'

Max grinned. 'Surely a half-done deal is better than no deal? You've got nothing to lose from an online meeting, and a Christmas event with a bestselling author to gain. Thea will see that.'

Ollie pressed a hand to her forehead. 'Thea's going to be mad that I went ahead behind her back, but she'll be extraordinarily happy with me once she's calmed down, won't she?' She dropped her hand. 'Right. It's all going brilliantly. No need to worry! Now, what were you saying to me before Arabella's phone call interrupted us?'

Max was smiling at her, his expression slightly dazed. 'Sorry?'

'You were saying something before my phone rang. You went all serious, said "*Ollie*" in that deep voice that means you're about to be profound.'

He shook his head, and she could see he was struggling to hold in his laughter. 'I *was* about to say something important.'

'Go on then. What was it?' She beamed at him, feeling the charge between them, a shimmer like a phantom set of Christmas tree lights, sparkling and infinitely desirable.

'I've decided something,' he said. 'There's a caveat to me helping you and A New Chapter out.'

Ollie folded her arms on top of the glass display case, and rested her chin on them. 'I knew this was too good to be true. Come on then, Max. What condition are you placing on your help?'

He leaned against the coffee machine, his hands on his hips. 'Once you've got good coffee up at the bookshop, you won't need to come here anymore, will you?'

Ollie frowned. 'You told Lizzy that you weren't worried about us being competition.'

'It's not the competition I'm worried about,' he said. 'We offer a lot more here, refreshment wise, than you ever will at A New Chapter. And I don't sell books, so competition isn't a concern. What I'm actually, genuinely worried about is not seeing you anymore. Or, not as frequently, at least.'

Ollie's heart thudded, her mouth drying out in a second. 'I'm never going to stop coming into Sea Brew, Max,' she said. 'And I'm sure Thea and Becky won't, either. As you say, we're never going to replicate what you have here: I don't think any of us are considering baking sausage rolls or Danishes, not even on special occasions.'

He stepped forward. 'So I'm guaranteed to have your custom? Your company, still?'

'You are,' she said, her voice scratchy. 'And I presume that sometimes – and not just tomorrow afternoon – you have a life outside of Sea Brew?'

'I do,' he replied. 'Your point is . . . ?'

'My point is that my company and my custom don't have to go hand in hand. We could see how tomorrow goes, and then, maybe, we could plan to see each other again, without the interests of A New Chapter being part of the equation.' *No no no,* the cautious side of her brain screamed. *What are you doing?*

'Are you saying, Ollie Spencer,' he murmured, closing the gap further so that they were both leaning on the glass, only the display case separating them, his face so close that she could see the different shades of green in his irises, smell that heady, herby scent, feel the gentle puff of his breath on her hand, 'that you'd consider spending time with me as a friend? Away from the café?'

Ollie swallowed. If she stood up straight, he would be within kissing distance. She imagined that even kissing him on the cheek would be a transcendent experience. He was by far the most attractive man she'd ever come into contact with.

'I am,' she said. 'I would. Consider it, I mean. I may have been considering it for quite a long time prior to this conversation.'

She saw him swallow, then his lips lifted into a gentle smile. 'Good to know. Very good to know. Chai latte?'

'Please.'

She watched him go through the routine he must have performed tens of thousands of times, his movements deceptively smooth, while she knew both of them were trying to return to a state of normality: to café owner and customer. But things had changed between them. A whole evening in Max's presence, beneath the fake-snow-covered awnings and twinkly lights of a Christmas market, stretched ahead of her like a delicious promise.

The voice of reason was still shouting at her, trying to warn her, but right now Ollie couldn't bring herself to pay attention to it, not even for a second.

'I just need to introduce Thea to it casually,' she said later that evening. She was in Liam's study, the fire crackling gently, a berry-red Anglepoise desk lamp spotlighting the stack of written notes while she typed the words onto her laptop.

Liam was on the sofa, a glass of red wine glowing in the light from the flames, and Henry was stretched out on the rug. A few well-placed decorations in here, Ollie thought, and it would be a Christmas grotto of magical proportions.

'Introduce Thea to what?' Liam asked. 'And can you really read my notes, type them up, and talk at the same time?'

'Sort of. I only need half my attention for the copy-typing. I'll check everything for errors afterwards.'

'Whatever works best for you, lass. So, introduce Thea to *what*? Unless you were thinking out loud?'

She grinned at him. 'Introduce Thea to the very real possibility of holding an event with Sophia Forsythe-Hartley. She's dubious about having such a big author in A New Chapter. She and Becky are both new to bookshop events.'

'Thea worked in a busy library for years: I don't think she's clueless.'

'That's not what I mean. I just need to help them see . . . what's *this* word? Oh, hang on. Parsimonious? Parmesan? Parliamentarian?'

'Let me see.'

'Oh no, I've got it! *Partridge*. That makes much more sense, considering you're talking about growing up on the farm, hiking in the countryside as a boy.'

'It would be somewhat off the wall if parmesan had suddenly come into it,' Liam said drily.

'You could have been having big, Italian-style farmhouse dinners. Gnocchi and spaghetti, pesto and bolognese, all topped with flurries of parmesan.'

'In rural Cornwall in the Fifties?'

'Fair enough. OK, so. Getting back to it.' She kept typing, one half of her focus on the notes, the other half on what she was saying. 'Of course I don't think Thea's clueless – *or* Becky. They know what they're doing, but they have set ideas about what's achievable. I just need to show them what's possible, then they'll see I'm not talking out of my backside.'

'And Sophia Forsythe-Hartley's the woman you're going to use to do it?'

'Exactly. There's no reason why A New Chapter shouldn't have a slice of the big pie. Why should it get stuck with the dry little canapés? Oh – speaking of authors with Cornish books, have you heard of Bryan Mailer?'

There was a moment's silence, then Liam said, 'Who?'

'He wrote a series of Cornish mysteries in the Seventies. I found some in a charity shop, and you will *never* guess what one of his books is based around?'

'If I'll never guess, you'd better tell me.'

Ollie looked up from her laptop. 'Kerensa's handprint! Can you believe it? This Bryan Mailer has written a series of fictional mysteries, with two characters called Roskilly and Faith, and they're all based around genuine local legends. He hasn't written anything for years, but he was popular when the books came out.'

Liam shifted slightly on the sofa. 'What does this mean for your programme of events?'

Ollie shrugged. 'Nothing, really. It's just interesting, don't you think?'

'It's certainly that. Cornwall is full of places with hidden meaning, so it's not a huge surprise that an author –

especially several decades ago, before every other writer used our fair county as inspiration – took their beginnings from what was already here: Kerensa, the Lost Fisherman, all those stories.'

'Oh my God,' Ollie said, laughter bubbling out of her. 'Speaking of the Lost Fisherman, I have to tell you what happened on Monday night!'

'I'm all ears,' Liam replied, taking a sip of wine. 'But before you do – about Thea.'

'What about her?'

'Perhaps her caution about the events is twofold. She might be protecting you, as much as her and her bookshop.'

'What do you mean?'

The quiet before he replied was punctuated by the sizzle of logs collapsing into embers as the flames licked at them, and the tap-tap-tap of Ollie's fingers on the keyboard. The window was covered with heavy, emerald-green curtains, keeping out the night, and it felt like the safest, cosiest cocoon.

'Thea is a kind-hearted soul,' Liam said eventually. 'She moved here from Bristol, started a business, and to begin with not everybody was enthusiastic. Some folk are fully on board with the regeneration of Port Karadow, but I'd wager that most would prefer it to come from locals. Thea and the council worked together on the Old Post House, which was in her favour, but she still got some nasty comments directed at her, and some said behind her back. Her fella, Ben, is also a relative newcomer to the area. She knows what it feels like to be welcomed with less than open arms.'

Ollie rubbed her cheek. 'So if I go in all guns blazing with promises of Sophia Forsythe-Hartley, people will think

I'm trying to shake things up: that I don't think Port Karadow, or A New Chapter, are good enough as they are?'

'I'm playing devil's advocate, but some locals might see it that way.'

'I get that,' Ollie said. 'But I've read more than one article where Sophia's been seen as a hero of sorts, in the way she portrays the county; how accurate her history is. Cornish people *love* her.'

'Aye, that they do. So, on the other side of the argument, if you promise to bring her here, then it all goes wrong, you'll have a bit more than egg on your face.'

'A whole omelette?' Ollie laughed.

'With mushrooms and cheese, and chips to accompany it.'

Ollie pointed a finger at him, her shoulder giving a brief twinge and then settling, perhaps calmed by the warmth in the room. 'Got it. I will tread exceptionally carefully, and if Thea says it's a no-go, then I'll stop.'

Liam was quiet for a moment, then he said, 'Life is full of the unexpected, of things going right just when you think they're going to collapse in a heap, and vice versa – everything is smelling of roses and then . . . well, it fades to nothing.' He was staring at the fire, as if he could divine meaning from the particular dance the flames were performing.

'You sound like you're speaking from experience,' Ollie said softly.

He chuckled. 'Of course I am. I'm eighty-one. My other grandchild, Colm – Melissa's brother – has lived in Australia for a decade, and I've not spoken to him for nearly as long. We used to get on, and I regret what happened between us. There have been some other disappointments, too, of course.'

'Want to talk about them?'

He frowned, shook his head. 'It's long in the past, lass. Dreams come and then they go. You have to buck yourself up, get back on the horse. What I suppose I'm saying, is that resilience is one of the most important skills you can have – in any job: in life. Hardly anything works out the way you imagine it will, and you need to be able to adapt. That's it, really.'

'Bouncebackability,' Ollie said.

Liam laughed. 'A word I haven't heard, but a good one.'

'I'll get a little badge.'

'You'll do OK, Ollie,' he said. 'I know you will.'

She nodded. 'Thank you.' Already, she had come to value Liam's opinion, to see him as a surrogate father – or grandfather. It mattered, that he believed in her. She returned to the stack of paper, glancing at the next couple of sheets. 'Right, you,' she said. 'Silence, please. These next few pages are dense with detail, and I don't want another parmesan incident.'

'Terribly sorry to have distracted you so,' Liam said deferentially.

'Apology accepted. Just don't do it again.'

Liam raised his glass, Ollie did the same, and they smiled at each other from opposite sides of the room. With a growing sense of contentment, Ollie returned to her typing.

Chapter Sixteen

When Ollie met Max after work the following day, he greeted her with a cheerful smile. There was no lingering look, no attempt at another apology, and her overriding emotion was relief. She needed to keep a clear head, and that was becoming increasingly difficult around him.

'Ready to choose a Nespresso machine?' he asked, pulling on his coat.

'A *Nespresso* machine?' she stuttered. 'Do they really—? I thought they were for domestic kitchens.'

'I'm joking,' he said. 'Come on.'

They walked through the streets of Port Karadow, and it was already evident that Halloween was behind them and Christmas was in front. Twinkling lights had been strung up inside some of the houses, creating a cheering golden glow that not even the most staunch of Christmas deniers could complain about.

'You live near the café?' Ollie asked, her hands deep in her pockets.

'Only five minutes away. It's handy when I press the snooze button too many times.'

'I can't see you as an over-snoozer.'

'Why not?'

'Because you're so . . . sparkly. So full of energy.'

Max laughed. 'Sparkly isn't a compliment I've had before, but I'll take it.'

'Better than charmer?' She was thinking of Lizzy's comments that morning in Sea Brew.

'It seems kinder. Charmer has an air of . . . I don't know. It's slightly seedy, somehow. I hope I don't ever come across as seedy.'

'You really don't,' Ollie said. A light drizzle filled the air, not enough for an umbrella today, but she could see tiny droplets landing in Max's curls, could feel it wisping against her skin. 'I have never thought that, not even for a second.'

'That's a relief. Here I am.' He gestured to a solid-looking terrace, the bricks in a golden hue that seemed so typically Cornish. The tiny front garden had been paved over, and there were a few pots with unrecognisable plants in, their winter foliage subdued. The front door was a smart grey with a square of stained glass, the blues and purples vivid in the afternoon light. An Audi was parked outside, its gleaming black paintwork suggesting it was well cared for.

'This is you?' Ollie tried to see in his front window, but all she got was a reflection of the street, the room behind it too dark to make out.

'I'd offer you a drink before we go, but if we want to fit in the wholesalers and the Christmas market we should step on it.' He unlocked the Audi and held the passenger door open, and Ollie climbed into the pine-scented interior.

An hour and a half later, Ollie had, with Max's invaluable help, chosen the perfect self-serve coffee machine for A New Chapter. She'd spoken to Thea, who had given her permission to make the order, and then Max had driven them away from the industrial park, back towards the coast, and suddenly they were at the top of tall cliffs, a village nestled below them, a patchwork of rooftops and a curved, sandy bay. It was beautifully quaint, a typical Cornish seaside community, and even though it was evening, the beach was busy – not just with people, but with vehicles and stands: a Christmas market.

The light was fading, turning the sky a deep, inky blue, and Ollie could feel the anticipation of the unusual setting, all its festive promise, like a slowly expanding balloon in her chest.

'This is Porthgolow,' Max said, as he drove slowly down the steep hill into the village. 'It's smaller than Port Karadow, but it has the Cornish Cream Tea Bus.' He gestured at a glossy red, vintage double-decker that had pride of place. 'The owner runs food fairs and festivals, and this year she's expanding, having the Christmas market on weekdays, as well as at weekends.'

'It's beautiful,' Ollie said, craning her neck to look at the stalls, already busy with customers. Christmas music competed with the steady thrum of the waves, the low hum of talking and laughter.

Max parked in the car park next to the beach, then turned to her as he shut the engine off. 'Ready?' She didn't think she was imagining the trepidation in his voice. Was he thinking that this felt like a date, just as she was?

'Absolutely,' she said, because she wasn't tentative or trepidatious. She was Ollie Spencer, and she could handle an evening with a hot guy at a Cornish Christmas market without totally losing her head. Or, she thought, her heart.

They stepped over the low metal barrier onto the beach. The sand felt firm, with only a slight give, beneath her boots. The air was biting, with the added sharpness of being close to the sea, and above them, on the north side of the cove, a glass building gleamed with golden light, like a star on top of a Christmas tree.

'This is amazing,' Ollie said, as they let the market swallow them, a thick blanket of festive sights, smells and sounds. Between the food trucks selling burritos and beers, cocktails and crepes, there were little wooden huts reminiscent of traditional German markets. The log designs were rustic, and the strings of fairy lights and fake snow, with the grey-blue sea in the background, made it seem magical.

People strolled between stalls holding cups of hot chocolate or mulled wine, and children in brightly coloured hats and scarves wove between adults, giddy with the knowledge that Christmas, with its presents and chocolate and end-of-term excitements, wasn't far away.

'I know it's only the third of November,' Max said, 'but it doesn't feel like it in here. It's a proper Christmas wonderland.'

'What are you hoping to get?' Ollie asked, quick-stepping to keep up as he strode towards the nearest stall. It was full of wooden carvings: aeroplanes and donkeys, bowls and spoons, boxes with intricate patterns on the lids. Wooden hearts, stars and doves hung from the ceiling, some with details picked out in metallic paint, others plain, letting the grain show through. Their silky, colourful ribbons announced them as tree decorations, and Ollie was tempted to buy one of each design.

'Nothing in particular,' Max said. 'I just thought we could soak up the atmosphere.'

'You're a fan of Christmas, then?'

He smiled. 'I'm not obsessed with it, but I love how celebratory it is, how over the top it can be. I love things like this.' He gestured to the bustle and glow surrounding them. Ollie looked down, and was surprised to find sand on the ground, rather than snow.

'I do too,' she said. 'I love that it's the perfect excuse to be as silly as you want. And I'm sure I can find inspiration for the bookshop here. What about Sea Brew? I'm guessing you won't stop at Yule log bunting?'

'Of course not. I'm going to ease into it, though. I don't want the café looking like an exploded cracker factory at the beginning of November. Have you heard any more from that author's editor?'

'Nope. I'm sure she'll send over dates soon enough. Do you want a mulled wine?'

'Depends how strong it is. I'm driving us home.'

'Let's see what festive drinks are on offer.'

They found the bar truck, and Ollie bought Max a Black Forest gateau hot chocolate, and herself a mulled wine. With darkness descending and the drizzle soft but persistent, it felt perfect, somehow: as if snow would have been a cliché, but the rain was just enough.

'How are you liking Liam's barn?' Max asked, when he'd bought them cinnamon sugar pretzels to go with their drinks.

'I love it. It's calm, and quiet, and I've got so much space! Sometimes I get the urge to lie on the carpet and starfish.'

Max grinned. 'Why don't you?'

'I'd get trampled by a dog, who just keeps getting bigger. Anyway, I have zero complaints. It's so different to my poky London flat – I mean, obviously.' She rolled her eyes. 'Do you live on your own?' It was the first time she'd asked, even in a roundabout way, about his relationship status. Of course, he could live with his parents, but somehow she didn't think that would be the case.

'Yeah,' he said. 'I like having my own space, and I'm too old for all that house-share rubbish: someone else's plates filling the sink; passive-aggressive arguments about toilet paper.' He shuddered. 'It's just me and Oxo.'

'And Oxo is your child? I must say, that's an unusual name. Boy or girl?' She glanced at him, and he laughed and elbowed her gently in the ribs.

'Oxo is my cat.'

'Why?' She was laughing now, too.

'Because I like cats.'

'No, I mean why *Oxo*? How did you end up naming your pet after *stock cubes*?'

'It's short, it trips off the tongue. It's a step up from calling him Cat.'

'I bet he's thrilled.'

'Honestly? I don't think he's that bothered.'

'Well *I* think—'

'My lovelies! Care to step into our festive photo booth?'

They turned, distracted by the woman who had called out to them. She was standing inside her wooden stall wearing an elaborate elf hat. Her dangly star earrings brushed her shoulders.

'No thanks!' Ollie called.

'Just five pounds for an instant print-out and digital copy of your Polaroid strip. You'll have magical memories you can keep forever, and they're perfect for those personalised Christmas cards.'

'Oh, we're not—' she started.

'That would be great,' Max said, at the same time.

Ollie looked at him.

'It'll be fun,' he said. 'Come on.'

'Max, no!' She laughed.

'Ollie, yes.' He held out his hand. 'What about Christmas giving you an excuse to be as silly as you want?'

'I can't believe you're using that against me.'

'Not *against* you. *With* you.'

She stared at him, at his green eyes dancing with amusement and hope, his ungloved hand reaching out to her. Ollie took a breath. It felt like a leap; a decision that was about so much more than a strip of photographs. She took his hand.

'Great,' he said quietly.

'Wonderful! Come in, my loves.' The woman beckoned them inside, where most of the space was taken up by the type of photo booth common to post offices and railway stations. A red curtain with a stocking motif covered the entrance.

'This is a single person booth,' Ollie pointed out.

'You can cosy up. Now, adorned or unadorned?' The woman held up reindeer antlers and a Santa hat.

'Your call,' Max said.

Ollie swallowed. 'Unadorned.' When her eyes caught his, she wondered if she'd made the wrong decision: taking out the idiocy, distilling it down to something more serious.

'You go in first,' the woman said to Max, 'and your gorgeous girl can follow.'

'Right.' Max cleared his throat and pulled back the curtain. He stared at the low stool, suddenly looking like a man on his way to the gallows.

'Feeling particularly silly?' Ollie asked him.

She watched his shoulders rise and fall in a breath, then he stepped inside the booth and sat down. He held his arms out to her, though she noticed that he couldn't quite meet her gaze. She didn't blame him.

She stepped forward, and had nowhere to go except down, onto his jean-clad thighs, her legs between his open ones. She sat slowly, wincing, and Max brought his arms around her waist. On his lap, she was slightly higher than him, and he spoke into her ear, his breath tickling her neck.

'This was a really stupid idea, wasn't it?'

She smiled down at him. 'Have you *ever* seen a two-person photo booth?'

'I just thought—'

'First photo coming in three, two, one!'

The flash came while they were looking at each other. Ollie had time to shift her position, turning towards the camera in time for the second flash. The third one, she felt Max put his head on her shoulder, thought he was probably making a face at the camera, so she turned, intending to say something, but he must have been about to speak to her too, and she found her lips millimetres from his.

'Oh.' She exhaled, drowning in his green gaze as the flash came for the final time.

'All done, lovelies!' The woman sounded very far away.

Max turned his head, and though Ollie didn't think their lips were touching, it had, somehow, become very hard to tell. If she leaned forward, even a centimetre, they would be kissing, and then—

'We should go,' he whispered, while at the same time tightening his arms around her waist.

'OK,' she murmured.

He shifted position, and before he let her go, Ollie was sure – almost 100 per cent – that he'd let his lips graze along her jaw. But had he really done it, or had she imagined it? When he dropped his arms she stood abruptly and pushed through the curtain. She smiled at the woman, while every nerve ending in her body was tingling, jumping, alive with what Max had just done. He *had* done it, hadn't he?

She watched him take his wallet out, slide out his card, ready to pay, give the woman his email address so she could send him the photos. Ollie touched her jaw, but already the moment had become a mirage. Had it really happened, or had she imagined it because she had wanted it to?

The woman handed Max their photo strip and, before showing her their pictures, he took her hand again and dragged her out of the stall.

'Come on,' he said. 'Let's go and get a drink.'

'I thought you couldn't because you were driving?' But she let herself be pulled along by him.

'I'll get fizzy water with ice and a slice. At least that way, I can pretend it's gin.'

'OK then,' Ollie said, laughing as they wove their way through the drizzle-soaked Christmas market, thinking that the evening couldn't possibly take any more unexpected turns.

Chapter Seventeen

There was a pub called the Seven Stars across the road from the beach, and Max led her into its warm, bustling interior, to a corner booth that seemed to be waiting for them. The window was fogged up, the view of the market and the sea beyond distorted. Max had his sparkly water with ice and a slice, and Ollie had a large glass of white wine.

'What made you come to Cornwall?' he asked, almost as soon as they sat down. It was as if he was studiously ignoring what had just happened. Were they going to keep having these moments of closeness, followed by a sort of silent denial?

'I had a cosy encounter with a man in a photo booth, and couldn't face him afterwards,' Ollie said, scrutinising him as she sipped her wine.

Max chuckled, his gaze firmly on the scarred wooden table. 'Yeah. That was . . . not my brightest spark of spontaneity.'

'You didn't enjoy it?' Ollie pressed.

He looked up, and she saw his cheeks were flushed. 'I did, but I feel like I forced you in there; forced you to sit on my lap.'

Ollie shrugged. 'I could have refused to come in with you. I said no at the beginning because I thought you wouldn't want to do it. When you held out your hand . . .'

'What?' he asked quietly.

'I didn't want to say no after that. Not at any point.' She wanted to ask him if he'd kissed her jaw, or if it had been the phantom of her longing, but she would sound like a needy sixteen-year-old. So she decided he *had* done it, then consigned it to history. 'And I came to Cornwall because my friend Melissa, who's Liam's granddaughter, told me he needed someone to type up his life story for him.'

Max raised his eyebrows. 'You left London, moved all the way to Cornwall, to type up the memoir of your friend's granddad?'

'OK, it's a little bit more complicated than that.' She paused as a group of men bustled into the pub, almost tripping over each other in their haste to get to the bar. They were wearing long red and white scarves, like a lacklustre *Where's Wally* stag-do. She turned her attention back to Max. 'I fell out of love with my job in a London bookshop, mostly because my boss lost faith in me. I split up with my boyfriend, who . . .' She cast around for the right way to put it, 'he wasn't there for me, when I needed him the most. He showed his true colours, and they weren't the glorious rainbow I thought they'd be. Then I got a windfall, and it gave me a rare opportunity to change things up: that cushion that gives you time to find a new place, put down a deposit, all the moving costs. It all came together, and Port Karadow – with Liam and his memoir, the job advert for A New Chapter – seemed to be the answer to my problems.'

'Seemed to be?'

'Oh, it is! So far, anyway.'

'I'm sorry about your boyfriend,' Max said, 'and about your boss losing faith in you. Those things must have been hard.'

She nodded. 'They were a bit of a pickaxe to my confidence – but not for long. I was off work for a while, and when I came back . . . somehow everything had moved on, and I couldn't, for whatever reason, keep up. You know when something's tainted, and you feel as if, even if you *could* claw your way back to where you had been, it's gone beyond the point of no return?'

'Yeah, I understand that,' he said quietly. 'Why were you off work?'

'Some scaffolding fell on me,' she said, and watched Max's eyes widen in alarm. 'I'm OK, obviously. Completely fine. Mostly, anyway.'

'Your shoulder?' Max asked, his brows drawing together.

'I – oh.' She was rubbing it again. 'Yes. I fractured my shoulder, hence being off work, hence ending up with a windfall that let me move here.'

'Does it still affect you badly?'

'It gets stiff and sore when it's damp. And cold. Maybe I should relocate to the Bahamas.' She laughed, but he was frowning. 'It's OK, honestly.'

He shook his head, as if clearing his mind of unwelcome thoughts. 'You know, spending time with you, you'd never guess you'd had such a hard time of it.'

156

'Who wants to be a victim? I'd much rather get on with things, focus on the positives. There's no lasting damage apart from a few aches and pains. It could have been so much worse.'

He nodded, his gaze intensifying. 'You don't mind living on your own in that barn?'

She took a gulp of wine before replying. 'What do you mean?'

'You're sociable. Fun. I expect *you* wouldn't mind a house-share.'

'Are you kidding? I'm not sharing my toilet paper with anyone. Besides, you're sociable too. You're fine with just you and Oxo, and I've got Henry, *and* Liam next door, and don't forget Marion, who is intent on helping me open every package that lands on my doorstep.'

The colour rose in Max's cheeks, and she knew he was thinking about Victoria's Secret purchases.

'Why did you stop being a personal trainer?' she asked, letting him off the hook. 'Did you get an injury, too?'

'Sort of.' Max picked up a beer mat and started shredding it.

'What does "sort of" mean?'

'I got something called myocarditis,' he said. 'It's inflammation of the heart.'

'What?' Her reply was croaky, his words, spoken so matter-of-factly, shocking her.

'It can happen to anyone,' he went on. 'But younger people, especially if they're particularly healthy, can get it. That's what happened to me. And I recovered – I'm fine now. But my specialist suggested that, while I *can* exercise, being a personal trainer, being involved in such intense activity, so frequently, was a risk. I decided I didn't want to risk it.' He shrugged, but Ollie could see his pulse beating in his neck: it looked like it was racing.

'I'm so sorry,' she said. 'Can I – do you mind if I ask about it?'

'Not at all. I'm not trying to hide anything.'

She sat back in her chair, then worried that Max would think she was distancing herself from him, so she sat forward again. Beneath the table, she stretched out her legs and, when she found his, unashamedly tangled them together. She saw the surprise on his face, but then it settled into something softer, as if he understood what she was doing.

'How old were you?' she asked.

'Thirty-two. It was four years ago.'

'And if you were a PT . . . I've always thought that was more about shouting at people, getting them to do the exercise, than doing it yourself.'

He nodded. 'That's a large part of it, but you have to be able to teach all the latest routines and workouts, know the science behind it, keep up with your clients. And I was fitness obsessed, to be honest. I wasn't a *do as I say, not as I do* trainer. It was easier for me to walk away.'

'And open up a café? From getting people fit, to getting them fat.'

He laughed, and Ollie was pleased. It was clearly a difficult topic, and she didn't want to bring his mood down.

'Everything in balance,' he said. 'That's my motto. And it fulfilled the thing I loved most about being a trainer, which is talking to people, being sociable. In a lot of ways, it's even better, because I meet a lot more people, I get to serve customers all day. Some I see several times a week, others I only meet once. But I make them happy: less hungry; more fulfilled. When I was a trainer, my clients were mostly happy in the long term, but when they came to see me? Not so much.'

'Was it a lot of tough love?' she asked.

'Oh yeah. I wasn't there to go easy on people. I worked them hard.'

His words sank into her like syrup. She didn't want her mind to follow the path it was heading down, so she took another large gulp of wine and said, 'If you don't mind me saying, you still look pretty . . . healthy.'

He nodded. 'Apart from not killing myself in the gym, I'm leading a completely normal life. There's a chance of it coming back, but it's slim.'

'What happened when . . . when you got it? Do you mind me asking?'

He shook his head. 'I'd been feeling ill for a few days: bad nausea, and like I couldn't take a proper breath. It was January, so I thought it was flu, but then, one day – I'd just got home from the gym – I felt off. Strange in a way I can't really describe. Then I started seeing flashes of light, had darkness at the edge of my vision. Then I woke up in hospital.'

'Shit. That sounds so scary. Were you living alone then, too?'

'No, I was living with my girlfriend. I was lucky she was there, even if we didn't last much longer after that. My recovery was slow, and I guess – well, it was a lot for her to take on board.'

'You too, though!' Ollie couldn't help saying. 'You *more* than her.'

He shrugged, smiled at her, and she knew he didn't want to go down that road.

'Anyway,' she went on, 'when I said you looked healthy, I didn't just mean that you don't look like an ill person. You still look . . .' She bit her lip, then leaned over and squeezed his bicep. They'd taken their coats off in the pub, and he was wearing a speckled blue long-sleeved T-shirt that hugged his torso.

He raised an eyebrow, amused. 'I look . . . ?'

She rolled her eyes, but she was glad he was making her say it: bringing lightness and flirtation back to the table. 'You look like you still take care of yourself. Like you could be Mr May in the Port Karadow Hot Business Owners calendar.'

'Is that something you're bringing in next year?'

Ollie pursed her lips. 'Definitely considering it, now that I've invented it.'

'Keep me in mind.'

'You're at the top of the list. If I can't find anyone else, you'll have to dress up in different outfits for every month. And when I say *outfits*, I mean togas, swimming shorts, maybe just a big bunch of sunflowers covering the pertinent bits for August.'

'I can almost see your cogs turning.'

'This actually might have to happen, now. But what I'm saying is, you look incredibly fit.'

He grinned, then rubbed his knuckles against his shirt. 'I try my best,' he said, but then his smile slipped. 'I walk a lot, and I do yoga every week, at a class here in Porthgolow, in fact. At Crystal Waters, the hotel on top of the cliff. I try and stay healthy without pushing myself.'

'Sounds good,' Ollie murmured. Her thoughts were racing – not with made-up calendar poses – but with all the things she wanted to say to him. She would never have guessed he'd been through something so traumatic. *Inflammation of the heart.* He hadn't said as much, but the fact that he'd had to change his career, his whole outlook, made her pretty certain that it was a serious, possibly life-threatening, condition. And there she'd been, griping about her aching shoulder. 'But you're always so sunny!' That was her next thought. Sadly, it had also burst out of her mouth.

Max's gaze was serious. 'I have a lot to be thankful for. The fact that I've recovered, that I've found something else I love doing. That I live where I do. That people ask for my advice about coffee machines, and I end up here, having early Christmas drinks with fiery booksellers.'

'I'm very thankful for that, too,' Ollie said, emotion unexpectedly clogging her throat. She had given up trying to find Max's flaws. Every new revelation made him go up in her estimation.

'Come to yoga with me one weekend, if you like?'

Ollie didn't have to think about it. 'I'd love to. And next time I hunt down one of those legends, you have to come with me and Henry to find it.'

'Absolutely,' he said. 'I'm glad we've got a plan.'

'Why?' Ollie asked, as they clinked glasses, sealing the deal.

'Because I was starting to panic, scrambling for an excuse to see you again, outside of chai tea latte time.'

Ollie's laugh revealed her delighted surprise. 'Well, now we've got two whole reasons, both of which could be recurring.'

161

'It's a relief,' he said. 'I feel like the pressure's off.'

'It is.' Inside, she was dancing. Her cautious voice had backed off, as if it knew a lost cause when it saw one. She couldn't sit still. 'My round. Want another pretend gin and tonic?'

'I'll risk a coffee this time.'

'Brave man.' She stood up, intent on making her way through the festive throng to the bar.

'Oh, and Ollie?' She felt Max's hand gently wrap around her wrist, and turned to look at him. 'Back there, in the photo booth?'

'Yes?' She held her breath.

'I wanted to kiss you, properly. But like everything else about that particular episode, it went disastrously wrong. I'm not giving up, but give me time to regroup?' He looked so contrite, so hopeful, so *handsome*.

'OK,' she said, struggling to keep her voice even. 'I'll give you a second chance.'

'Great. Thank you for being so considerate.'

With another nod and smile, Ollie turned away from him and, feeling as if she had almost superhuman energy, wove her way through the crowd to go and get their drinks.

Chapter Eighteen

'The first thing we need to do is take stock of what we've got on the trestle tables in front of us. And don't forget, there are many variations of the fajita recipe. All veg, meat and fish are welcome: it's the sauce that makes this my own, personal, very special creation.'

'Righto!' Lizzy waggled her fingers over the selection of peppers, onions and mushrooms on her table. Laid out next to them was a raw chicken breast, several purple tortillas, and a selection of herbs and spices.

Ollie, standing at the side of the room, couldn't help glancing around Thea's beautiful events space, with its sofa pushed into the corner, the bookshelves with Marcus Belrose's cookbooks facing outwards, the tables with their little portable hobs on. Portable hobs, in a bookshop. There was one sink upstairs, in the storeroom behind the stage. The deep blue carpet was new and plush and pristine. Had this been a good idea? Now it was happening, she wasn't sure.

The confident chef was standing in front of eight eager participants, and Ollie couldn't fault the way he had kitted out the session. He had provided plentiful, good-quality ingredients – not to mention bringing the cooking apparatus – as part of the event fee. It was just so . . . so crammed in. She could hear the usual bookshop sounds downstairs: the bell pinging, customers asking Becky questions, the crackle of paper bags as purchases were made. Having Marcus here, with an array of food, the smells of a kitchen, felt wrong. But it was happening now, so she just had to get to the end without any disasters.

'We want all the vegetables cut into strips,' Marcus said. 'Thin strips that retain a bit of crunch and can be properly coated in the sauce.'

'Thin strips,' Meredith murmured. Her head was bent, her grip strong on the knife's handle.

Finn, at the table next to his girlfriend, seemed less dedicated. He was looking around, seeing what everyone else was doing, and hadn't touched his own ingredients.

'The excellent thing about this recipe,' Marcus went on, pacing backwards and forwards on the low stage – he had chopped his vegetables in record time, which Ollie thought was a bit show-off – 'is how versatile it is. How *quick*. You have your family over just before Christmas, you want something easy, but still tasty, to satisfy them. With this, you can prepare and cook the veg, the proteins, then lay them out for your guests to help themselves, assemble their own fajitas.'

Ollie sighed. It wasn't exactly rocket science. Why had she propositioned Marcus? She wanted to get back to the book club, to Book Wars. To happy, wholesome, book-focused events. Marcus went through the steps of creating the sauce, and she zoned out, gazing out at Port Karadow, at the rooftops dusted with sunlight. She'd opened the window before the event had started, and a fresh breeze slipped in, diluting the culinary smells.

'Oh my God,' Meredith said, breaking through her thoughts.

'This is a bloody wonder,' Lizzy added. 'I'm going to baste my turkey in it on Christmas Day.'

'I *love* this sauce,' announced a young woman called Candy, who had chosen the trestle table at the back of the room.

Even Finn was staring at his pan with awe, a spoon in his hand. Ben, Thea's boyfriend, who had worked with Marcus and was apparently an excellent cook, was frowning at his concoction. Ollie watched him add a splash of maple syrup, then stir and taste, his face a mask of concentration.

'This sauce will take your fajitas from bog standard to brilliant,' Marcus said, stirring the contents of his own pot languidly. 'Your dinner party guests will be clamouring for more. You can adjust the quantities to enhance the sourness or sweetness, just as Ben's doing.' Ben looked up, clearly surprised that he'd been singled out. 'And the great thing is it works with chicken or beef, fish or halloumi. It's great on jackfruit, if you want a vegan option.'

'I could stand here and eat the whole pan,' Meredith told him.

Marcus's smile was snakelike. 'Coat your fillings in it, and you'll have quadruple the pleasure. Right. Now the sauce is done, we need to cook the main ingredients. This will vary depending on what you've chosen. Flash-fry the strips of steak, but give chicken and halloumi a slower, steadier cook. I'll come round and give you individual instructions, and while you're waiting, keep tasting that sauce: get it perfect for *you*. We're all chefs, now.'

'I don't think I'll ever be a chef,' Finn said. 'But I'm going to make these fajitas at home.'

'Oh Marcus,' Meredith said, 'I could kiss you! Finn's pancakes are the best, but after that he runs out of steam.'

'Pancakes and fajitas are all I need in my repertoire,' Finn replied. 'Both crowd pleasers.'

'Meredith pleasers,' she corrected. 'What should I do with my tuna, Marcus?'

'Show it the heat for just a few seconds,' Marcus said, striding over to her table.

Ollie sniffed the air, wondering if someone had let their sauce caramelise, because something really smelt as if—

'Oh my God!' Candy squealed from the back of the room. She was waving her spoon in the air, flicking drops of sauce onto the walls and carpet. 'Oh shit!'

Ollie rushed over because she did *not* want Thea's events space to be covered in sauce, however brilliant it was. The chatter died around her as everyone turned to look, and she realised that the sauce was the least of her worries. She had time to wonder how it was possible to leave a piece of kitchen towel on a portable hot plate while it was switched on, and not notice it, but then her brain and body stalled as flames shot into the air. Candy stepped back, catching her long, flowing dress on the edge of the table and dragging it with her. The cosy sofa was just behind her and—

'No!' Ollie ran forwards, arms outstretched, as Candy dropped her spoon on the floor and the table tipped. The flames licked and flickered, threatening to consume everything in their path, but then Ben was there with a pan of water, throwing it onto the hot plate, dousing the fire. Ollie sighed, her mouth open to thank him when Candy's pan of sauce teetered, wobbled, and then slipped off the table, turning in mid-air and landing, with a loud, wet thunk, on the beautiful fuchsia sofa.

'Oh my God!' Candy slapped her palms against her cheeks. 'I am so, *so* sorry!'

'It's OK,' Ollie murmured, even though, at that moment, it didn't feel like it was. 'Thank you, Ben.' She gave him a grateful smile, because even though this was a disaster, at least the bookshop wasn't on fire.

'No worries.' Ben looked down at the stricken sofa and ran a hand through his hair. 'Bloody hell, though.'

Meredith came to stand alongside Ollie, and then Finn appeared, clutching a roll of kitchen towel and the hand soap from the upstairs sink.

'We'll get it out,' he said brightly. 'Don't worry.'

Ollie bit her lip. The pretty events space looked like a herd of reindeer had trampled through it: the abandoned tables, sauce splattered on every surface, the charred kitchen roll and ruined hotplate still smouldering. The air smelled of burn, and not the nice, autumn crackle or the open fire smokiness, but the you-shouldn't-even-try-and-cook-toast, what-are-you-doing-in-the-kitchen? charring. Ollie glanced over her shoulder. Marcus looked furious. Well, she thought, sod him. He and his ego would have to get over it.

'It's OK,' she said again to Candy. 'Really. These things happen.' And this one had happened because she'd been stupid; spontaneous; over-enthusiastic.

She heard footsteps on the stairs, and turned just as Thea bounded onto the top floor. 'The coffee machine's here!' she announced. 'Do you think there's enough room for . . .' Her words fell away at the same time as her smile, her eyes widening as she took in the scene in front of her.

'All right pet,' Lizzy said brightly. 'Come to see the carnage?'

Behind Ollie, Candy started to sob.

Two hours later, the events space was almost back to normal, though the smell of burnt paper still hung in the air – despite the icy wind they'd let in by opening all the windows – and the sofa had a stain on it that looked decidedly distasteful. Ollie thought that if the coffee machine hadn't turned up, and was currently being installed by two very cheerful technicians who had been happy to wait while they cleared up, then she might, actually, be out of a job. She would, she thought, look for beautiful throws online, and find one to cover the sofa.

'We sold three cookbooks,' she said to Thea, trying to muster up a smile.

Thea sighed. 'These things happen, I guess.'

Ollie closed her eyes. She had never heard her boss sound so cold, or so defeated. 'I am so, so sorry,' she said. 'It didn't work: you were right about that. It was an honest-to-God disaster, but I promise you I've learned my lesson.'

Thea nodded, her lips pressed together.

'I'll make it up to you,' Ollie continued. 'Should I just—'
She gestured to the sofa. Perhaps if she went over the stain again, or got some industrial strength fabric cleaner—

'Could you see what's happening in the children's section?' Thea cut in.

'No problem!' Ollie hurried down the stairs, her heart beating double-time. She *would* make it up to her boss. Perhaps if she told her that Sophia Forsythe-Hartley wanted to hold her launch here, Thea would forgive her for the morning of chaos and destruction. Though best to give her a little bit of time to recover, before she dropped that particular bombshell.

When she reached the children's area, she saw that Becky's children were here again. Dylan was sitting in a corner, reading a book and casting weary looks at his younger siblings, who were arguing over a colouring book. The pot of felt tips had already been a casualty, and the pens were littering the carpet. One, with its lid off, was tantalisingly close to being ground in and leaving a bold, purple stain. Ollie decided that she had had enough of unwelcome stains.

'Anything I can help with?' she asked, raising her voice. 'Hey, Dylan.'

'Hey.' He glanced up at her for a nanosecond.

Alongside Becky's children, there were two young girls with blonde hair and matching coats, crouched on the floor with a book between them. A woman, the girls' mother, Ollie presumed, was browsing the romance section nearby, her gaze continually flitting over to them.

'I want to colour the duck,' Billy said.

'The castle!' Meg protested. 'I do the castle!'

'We could get you each a book?' Ollie suggested. 'That way, you can have your own pictures to colour, then at the end you can show each other what you've done. How about that?'

'That won't work.' Dylan's tone was dismissive.

Ollie looked at him. 'Why not?'

'Because they always want what the other one has.'

She thought for a moment. 'So we get two copies of the same book.'

Dylan gave her an appraising look and a tiny shrug, then went back to his YA novel.

Ollie crouched and browsed the shelves, looking for a colouring book they had two copies of. If she fixed this, would it help to make up for what she'd done? Would Becky mind her buying books for her children?

She felt a tug on her ponytail and looked round. One of the blonde girls was smiling up at her. 'Hello,' she said.

'Christmas!' the girl shouted.

'It will soon be Christmas,' Ollie said, nodding.

'No! Christmas!' She pointed at Ollie and bounced up and down on her knees.

Ollie frowned and looked at the shelf. None of the colouring books had a Christmassy theme.

'She's pointing at your tinsel,' Dylan said.

'Oh!' After everything that had happened, Ollie had totally forgotten. She'd found a stray bit of blue tinsel at home that morning and, in anticipation of the cooking class, had woven it around her ponytail. She pulled it out and handed it to the girl.

'I *love* Christmas,' Billy said, walking on his knees to join them. 'When I'm older, I'm going to cover my *whole house* in tinsel!'

'Twinkle lights.' Meg opened and closed her fists to make five-fingered stars.

Ollie watched as the blonde girl draped the tinsel over her sister – her twin, surely – as if it was a wig.

'I'm not going to have tinsel,' Dylan said, putting his book down and scooting closer.

'What are you going to have?' Ollie asked. 'What would your ideal Christmas decorations be?'

'Paper chains, I guess. You can have them printed with anything. I'd have football crests on mine.'

'Good call,' Ollie said. 'What about books?'

'What *about* books?' Dylan sounded so exasperated, it took all of Ollie's self-restraint not to laugh.

'What about if your paper chains were printed like the pages of a book?'

Dylan shrugged. 'All right, I guess. Not as good as football, though.'

'Glitter!' one of the blonde girls said.

'Glitter is very important, especially at Christmastime.' Ollie nodded sagely.

'And hot chocolate!' Meg shouted, pointing over her shoulder.

'For decorations?' She smiled and turned around to see what Meg was pointing at. All the breath left her body, replaced by several thousand excited butterflies and a strong urge to ask for a hug.

'Hello,' Max said.

It had been just over a week since their trip to the Christmas market, and although she'd seen him in Sea Brew every morning, and they'd arranged to do yoga together this weekend, Ollie's body had not stopped responding to the sight of him. If anything, her reaction was getting more extreme.

'Did you order a hot chocolate, Meg?' Ollie asked. 'Excellent choice. I didn't realise Sea Brew did personal deliveries.'

Max laughed, gesturing to the takeaway cup he was holding. 'This is coffee.'

'Well,' Ollie said. 'Our new coffee machine has just been installed, and is being set up as we speak. By tomorrow, we should have our own selection of highly desirable drinks.'

'Which means you don't have that choice right now. I thought I'd pop in, see how your event went. Hey, Dylan,' he added.

'Hi Max!' Dylan scrambled up, and Max ruffled his hair. 'Doing OK, buddy?'

He nodded. 'Better than Ollie.'

'Why's that?' Max asked, shooting her a confused glance.

'Mum says she totally ruined the event with that chef guy. Set stuff on fire and all sorts. Mum said it was a bloody disaster!'

Ollie clamped her mouth shut to stop it falling open.

Max's frown deepened, though she thought his clenched jaw was, perhaps, to prevent himself from laughing. 'Is that right?' he murmured.

'It wasn't my finest hour,' she said quietly, and suddenly, she felt exhausted. All the adrenaline, the energy it had taken to remain upbeat after Marcus had stormed out, taking his cooking equipment with him, and Candy had been ushered out of the bookshop in tears, Meredith's arm around her shoulders, left her. Her shoulders sagged, the left one twinging mercilessly.

172

'Want to take a breather?' Max asked in a low voice.

'I don't know if I can.' Ollie gestured behind her.

'Hot chocolate!' Meg said again, and this time she was joined in her chorus by the other children.

Max gave a dramatic sigh. 'Hot chocolates, eh?'

'Yes!' shouted five voices, even Dylan sounding excited now that Max was here.

'Right. Let me check with Becky, and – are you these girls' mum?' he asked the woman hovering beside the romance books.

'I am. If they're being badly behaved—'

'Not at all.' Max held up a placatory hand. 'If I come back with hot chocolate from the café down the hill, would you be happy for them to have one? If they're lactose in-tolerant, or . . .'

'No, that would be lovely,' the woman said, looking surprised. 'Thank you.'

Thea appeared behind Max, her expression softer than the last time Ollie had seen her. 'You going to get coffees?' she asked. 'The men upstairs say we'll be fully functional in half an hour, but I don't know if I can wait that long.'

'You don't mind?' Ollie asked.

Thea's smile was hesitant. 'Of course not. I should think you could do with the fresh air.'

Ollie felt a swell of gratitude, and for the second time in five minutes, she had the strong urge to hug someone. 'Thanks, Thea.'

'We'll catch up later this afternoon, OK?'

'Of course. What would you like from the café?'

'Do you do tequila?' she asked Max, grinning at him. 'A hot chocolate would be great for me, too. Thanks.'

'What would you like?' Ollie asked the blonde girls' mum, checking that she had her purse in her pocket.

'Oh!' The woman pressed a hand to her chest. She was very pretty, but the dark circles under her eyes were pronounced, and Ollie got the impression she'd brought her children to the bookshop to give herself a few moments of calm. 'I couldn't possibly—'

'We're turning this into a bit of a tea party,' Ollie said. 'The last round of drinks from Sea Brew before our own coffee machine makes the café, and this guy,' she pointed at Max, 'completely redundant.'

He laughed. 'Thanks for that.'

Ollie couldn't resist. Her relief at Thea's olive branch, and Max's reassuring presence, were making her giddy. She put her arm around his shoulders and squeezed. 'He knows he's safe, or he'd be showing more obvious signs of worry. What would you like? I'm getting a round in. *I'm* buying,' she added, when she saw Max was about to protest.

Once she'd collected orders from everyone in the shop who looked like they weren't rushing away, she stepped outside, holding the door open for Max.

'So Dylan wasn't exaggerating, then?' he asked. 'About the Marcus Belrose event?'

'Not even a little bit,' Ollie said with a sigh, recklessly slipping her arm through his. 'I thought my job was on the line for a while, there. If I'd set fire to the bookshop, it would have been game over.'

'If you'd set fire to the bookshop,' Max said, 'all that would have mattered would have been getting you and everyone else out safely.'

'Good thing it didn't happen, then. For so many reasons.' She smiled up at him, and he glanced down at her. He stopped walking, bringing them to a halt on the steepest part of the hill.

'You know you're allowed to make mistakes, right?'

'Not ones involving hotplates and fajita sauce in cosy bookshop nooks.'

'Even those ones,' Max protested. 'Cut yourself some slack, Ollie.'

'I need to do so much better next time: show Thea that she can trust me 100 per cent.'

Max sighed, then leaned over and planted a swift, gentle kiss on her forehead. 'I'd better make this the best round of hot chocolates I've ever produced, then.'

'You don't need to fight my battles,' Ollie said as they started walking, as she slipped her arm through his again. Her forehead was tingling where his lips had been.

'I'm not. I'm just here to help. Hot chocolate is my territory, so let me do this, OK? At the next event, you'll come out guns blazing and everything will go brilliantly, but right now . . .' Max squeezed her closer. 'You can lean on me. Just for the next half an hour or so.'

Ollie didn't know what to say. She was trying to be so positive, defiant in the face of adversity, but Max could see how much the morning's catastrophe had dented her spirit. She didn't know how to convey her gratitude, so she just held his arm more tightly, whispered 'thank you' to him. They walked down the hill together, Port Karadow harbour appearing in front of them in all its chilly, steel-blue glory.

Chapter Nineteen

The Crystal Waters spa hotel was Ollie's kind of place. It sat on top of the cliffs in Porthgolow, where they'd been only ten days before for the Christmas market, and was as luxurious up close as it had been when she had stood, looking up at it, from the beach.

The building was a combination of warm, honey-coloured stone and glass, and before they'd even stepped through the automatic doors she felt her pulse settle. Because, it turned out, even when the bookshop you worked in was in a quaint seaside town, and especially if you had pissed off your boss and an influential celebrity chef by ruining their event and setting fire to things, it could feel quite stressful.

'Max Holden,' Max said to the young woman at reception. 'I'm here for the ten o'clock yoga class. I phoned a couple of days ago to say I was bringing a guest.'

'Wonderful,' the woman said, typing quickly. 'And you know where to go?'

'I do. Thank you.'

'Have a good session.'

'Thanks,' Ollie added as they passed.

They walked across the elegant, understated foyer, and her gaze was drawn to the sea, visible through the glass wall at the back of the room, beyond sloping gardens that, even in November, had plants that provided architectural interest. 'This place is stunning,' she said.

Max held open a door that led to a stairwell. 'It's not bad, is it? It has one of the highest-rated spas in this part of Cornwall, and they run excellent classes, too. Janine, the tutor for this session, is great.'

'She's happy for all abilities to take part?'

'Absolutely. You won't feel out of place, I promise.' The smile he gave her was warm and encouraging, and she felt it spread through her, welcome when she only had a thin hoodie over her yoga gear.

They emerged into a studio a level below reception, that looked out on the gardens Ollie had been admiring. There were yoga mats laid out, and golden spotlights in the ceiling cast a gentle glow over the space. Several other people were getting settled, placing water bottles next to their mats, and a tall, lithe woman with curly hair was holding her phone close to a sound system. There was a bright, electronic ping as it connected wirelessly.

'OK?' Max asked. 'Where do you want to be? Front, middle or back?'

'Back,' she said immediately. 'It's where I'm most comfortable.'

'You were a back of the bus girl at school?' He put his rucksack down and took off his trainers. 'I can see that about you.'

Ollie laughed. 'Busted. Though it was a little country bus, going from rural Yorkshire into Scarborough, and there wasn't a whole lot of rebellion.'

'I thought I detected a hint of Yorkshire in your accent. You can sit down, stretch out.' He gestured to the mat next to his.

'Oh! Yes.' She pulled off her hoodie and shoes, and sat on her mat. Her matching yoga top and leggings, bought just before she'd moved to Cornwall, were black with large, shimmery gold stars all over them. They had promised her *ultimate comfort and precision* while performing the most demanding yoga poses. Sadly, she hadn't got much further than mountain pose and downward dog, and now, looking around, seeing Max in his navy joggers and loose grey T-shirt, the other attendees in their distinctly un-flashy outfits, she felt like a total plum. Still, if there was one thing she prided herself on, it was her ability to style it out.

'You look great,' Max said, his hand resting on hers so briefly, she thought she must have imagined it. She realised he hadn't said it to be flirtatious, but because, somehow, he could see her hesitancy, the realisation that her outfit suggested a level of competency she couldn't live up to, and had wanted to reassure her. *One flaw,* she said to herself. *Let this man have one flaw, or it's going to be very hard for me not to follow him around like a smitten puppy.*

'Right then,' said the curly-haired woman, who she presumed was Janine, from the front of the room. 'Ready to get flexible and find some inner peace?'

'Yes,' Ollie said, her voice rising above the others. Inner peace was something she could sorely do with right now.

'From here, we're going to transition into crow pose. That's right, you know what to do. Strengthen your elbows, press your knees either side of them, and then . . . lift your feet off the ground. One by one if you need to.'

Ollie was crouching, bent forward, but now she was supposed to lift her legs off the floor, with only her straightened arms supporting her? She hopped a couple of times, her nose angling towards her mat, but it seemed like something her body was fundamentally opposed to doing.

She looked at Max, and saw that he was doing it. His arms were lean but strong, the rest of his body positioned as if he was about to dive-bomb into a pool, but raised from the ground. Only his hands were on the mat, but there was no sign of strain in his face; he looked genuinely serene.

Ollie couldn't help thinking about what he'd told her in the pub: what he'd had to give up, because his heart had become inflamed. It was a silly way to think about it, she knew, but if there was anyone whose heart seemed fully functional – stronger and healthier than other people's, even – then it was Max.

'I don't think you should do this one,' he said. There was a faint tremble in his voice, the only sign that he was exerting himself.

'I don't think I *can* do this one.' Ollie bounced her feet up once, twice. It seemed impossible.

'No, I mean because of your shoulder. It's not strong enough. Don't hurt yourself, Ollie.'

'OK,' she murmured. She knew he was right, even though she had wanted to keep up with the class. Her shoulder had started to ache the moment she'd lifted a foot off the floor. She sat on her mat and took a deep breath instead, pushing away her frustration. She had loved that aspect of the class; using the full capacity of her lungs, which she was sure she never did day to day. 'How are you still doing that?' she asked Max.

'I've been coming to this class for over a year.'

'And this time you get to look after me, too.'

Max put his feet on the mat. 'You should never push through an injury, however much you think you're capable.'

She nodded. 'Thank you. I feel like I've had an extra tutor helping me. I got Janine *and* Max.' She smiled, but even though he returned it she saw a flash of something else cross his face: was it sadness? Regret? Shit. He couldn't train people anymore, and he had clearly loved it.

'Max, I'm sorry,' she whispered, as Janine instructed them to lie on their backs for the last part of the class.

'What for?'

'For saying that. It must be hard—'

'Nothing to apologise for,' he whispered back, and reached over the space between their mats to squeeze her arm. His palm was hot, and even though Ollie was sweating, she welcomed his touch. As they finished with a period of calm breathing, lying on their backs on their mats – which seemed like an endeavour in not falling asleep – she wondered if there was anything Max could do that she wouldn't welcome. That, in itself, was not an entirely welcome thought.

* * *

180

'Let me buy you a coffee before we go back.' They had returned to the hotel's reception, where a small queue at the desk suggested some people had been wise enough to escape for a calming break before their festive to-do lists kicked in. With these surroundings, the beach and the sea, the hot-tub perched on the cliff outside, who could blame them?

'Sounds good.' Max gestured to an opening off the foyer, where Ollie could see metal chairs and tables, a cosy-looking bench in front of the huge, sea-facing window.

'This is gorgeous,' she said as they stepped inside. The room was opulently furnished, with brightly coloured cushions on the chairs, a gleaming bar along the far wall, and gold and ruby garlands hanging from the ceiling. There was a tree in the corner adorned with matching baubles, and the room seemed to shimmer with warmth and possibility.

'Where do you want to sit?' Max asked.

'The window seat, obviously.' A waiter was with them in moments, and they ordered cappuccinos and a plate of festive Florentines. 'Big question,' she said. 'Does the coffee here live up to Sea Brew's standards?'

Max smiled. His dark curls had tightened along his hairline, and his face had a healthy, post-exercise glow. Ollie tried not to think of his heart, beating away inside his chest, and whether it was behaving itself. He'd told her he was fine, now. She had to let it go.

'What do you think?' he asked.

'I think that of *course* it's not as good, but that you'll be incredibly polite about it, anyway.'

Max laughed. 'It's almost as good. I am begrudgingly impressed with the coffee here – but then I am with everything in this hotel. What did you think of the yoga?'

Ollie sighed. 'I think it's a stealth exercise. It presents itself as this calming, easy discipline, where you can gain flexibility, strength and mindfulness without almost dying, then it sneaks in things like the crow.'

'You can't take that as a failure,' Max said. 'I know you'll frame it that way, that you're critical of yourself, always trying to do better, but you broke your shoulder, Ollie.'

'How do you know I'm thinking of it like that?'

'Because I know you,' he said simply.

Ollie tried not to read too much into it. 'OK. I won't see it as a failure.'

'See it as an adjustment, instead. You've had to adapt your plans due to the circumstances. So often things are out of our control. Think of your Marcus Belrose event.'

She put her head in her hands and groaned. 'I *was* in control of that, though. And I almost set Thea's bookshop on fire.'

There was a polite cough, and she sat up to let the waiter put their coffees and biscuits on the table. They reached out to take a Florentine at the same time, their fingers brushing. The chocolate and nut discs glistened under the soft lights, their tops adorned with syrup and cranberries.

'One burned paper towel isn't a building fire,' Max said. 'It didn't go well, but Thea's sensible: she's not going to hold one misstep against you. The book club and the ghost walk were successful. Those were spontaneous; you adapted to the circumstances and made the most of them.'

'I suppose so. But I need to be doing *more*.'

'And I bet you've already thought of a hundred new ideas.' He gave her a gentle smile. 'Though I hope one of them's not to buy all the customers hot chocolate on a regular basis, like you did the other day, because you'll bankrupt yourself before the end of the year.' He bit into a Florentine.

'That is *not* my plan,' Ollie said. 'Besides, we have our own drinks machine now. It has a hot chocolate setting, and we've put the powder in. Customers can press one button – two, if they want fancy syrup – and make their own hot chocolates.'

Max shook his head sadly, and she laughed.

'You were the one who helped me get the best machine! Anyway,' she went on, 'I want to get everyone involved, and Christmas is the ideal time to do it. A bookshop doesn't only have to focus on books, does it? As long as we're holding events – and as long as it's not bloody *cooking* – people are bound to buy something.'

'So what's next? Other than me asking Beryan to add Florentines to her list of treats for Sea Brew. These are delicious.'

Ollie nodded while she nibbled on one. They were amazing. 'Paper chains,' she said. 'Paper chains and Sophia Forsythe-Hartley.'

'You're going for opposite ends of the spectrum?'

'And everything in between. I have to make A New Chapter the most talked-about place in Port Karadow – for all the right reasons. To do that, I need to cater for everyone.'

Chapter Twenty

The following Tuesday, Ollie found herself knocking on Max's front door at seven o'clock in the morning, trying not to think about what he looked like in pyjamas, or whether, in fact, he wore any.

When he answered, however, he was fully dressed, already doing up his coat and wrapping his stripy scarf around his neck. 'Morning,' he said, and Ollie's reply got stuck in her throat. He was too gorgeous for words.

'Hey,' she said eventually.

'Hi. Hi.' He directed this second greeting to Henry, who was almost vibrating with excitement, his tail wagging madly. Max crouched and gave him a vigorous stroke, and Henry buried his nose in Max's neck, licking him with abandon. 'OK,' Max laughed. 'I get the picture. I'm looking forward to this, too.'

'It's suitably frettish today,' Ollie said, holding up the little grey book of legends. They'd made the plan to explore one of the legends as they were munching Florentines in

184

Crystal Waters' opulent snug, and the weather forecast had turned out to be right, for once.

'That's important, is it?' Max asked as she led them down his road and then right, away from the centre of town and towards the coast.

'Yup. The sea fret is a crucial part of today's local legend.' She'd seen the thick mist coming in off the sea a few times since she'd been in Cornwall, but was still surprised by how suddenly it could roll in, how it could make the landscape, even her dog, sometimes, disappear.

'I haven't been this intrigued since a red-haired woman and a chocolate Lab walked into Sea Brew a little over a month ago.'

Ollie laughed, hoping it would cover the sound of her clattering heart. He'd been intrigued by her the first time he saw her? 'Firstly,' she said, 'that sounds like the start of a joke: *A redhead and a chocolate Lab walk into a café . . .* And secondly, why was I so intriguing?'

'I'm intrigued by all my new customers,' Max said, but he stuttered slightly at the beginning of the sentence, and Ollie wondered if he was covering for himself. They walked in silence for a while, the space between them charged.

'We're just down here: the beach marked by a standing stone.' Ollie gestured to the stone, which was about shoulder high and in the shape of a roughly carved obelisk. It marked the point where scrubby heathland turned to sand.

'You've been here before?' Max asked, pulling his scarf tighter.

The sea fret was blocking out the first rays of the sun, and the air was icy. It was the type of day where, in Ollie's old life, she'd have pulled the duvet up and stayed in bed

185

until the very last minute. But here she had Cornwall, in all its varied, beautiful forms, and Max, who was willing to accompany her on her legend quests.

'I had to come and find it beforehand,' Ollie explained, 'or we would have ended up wandering aimlessly until we had to go to work, and we would have failed our mission.'

'Mission?'

'Mission,' she confirmed. 'Come on. This way.' She led him towards the water, the ground going from spongy to soft beneath their boots, the visibility narrowing even further as they got closer to the sea.

'This is a ghost story all by itself,' Max said, shuddering. 'I can hear the waves, but I can't see them.'

'Imagine if we were peering through the mist, and a figure walked out of it towards us: a dark shape with glowing, empty eyes.'

'Jesus. Is that the legend we're tracking down today? I wouldn't have come with you if I'd known that.' He turned around and made to walk away.

Ollie laughed and pulled him back. 'No, I just invented that. It would be creepy though, right?'

'Too creepy,' Max murmured. 'So, come on then, what are we doing here?'

'Right, well this is Stone Cove. I expect it's named, imaginatively, after this strange stone. And legend has it that one of the most devastating shipwrecks off this stretch of coast happened close to here. In the eighteenth century, a trade ship called *The Scarlet* crashed into rocks during a storm and sank, losing hundreds of lives, and produce that was being relied upon.'

'Grim,' Max said. Their pace had slowed, and Ollie wondered if he was as nervous as she was about walking deeper into the impenetrable fog.

'Very grim,' she replied. 'But the story in this book says that on foggy or misty days – days where there's a heavy sea fret – some of the lost souls come onto the beach, and leave behind unusual auger shells.'

'Auger shells? The cone-shaped ones? I thought they were common along here.'

'Not the ones left by the shipwreck victims. Apparently they're larger than most, and a different colour: white, with a blueish, pearlescent hue. Supposedly that's the tears of those who were lost, and their family members helpless on land, knowing there was nothing they could do to save them.'

'God.' Max shivered. 'This is all very miserable for this early on a Tuesday morning.'

Ollie faced him. 'You know those books I told you about? The mysteries by Bryan Mailer? One of them is based around this legend. Roskilly and Faith find a dead body on this beach and have to investigate, and it gets tied up with the auger shells legend.'

'Have you read them all, now?' Max asked.

'Nope. I'm up to number four, and I only have five. There are four more, but I need to get them on AbeBooks because they're out of print.'

'Has anyone else heard of this mystery author?'

Ollie walked further onto the beach, Max keeping up with her, which was a good thing because she didn't want to lose him in the fret. 'Lizzy has – she's read them *all*, said she devoured them years ago. I need to speak to Thea, see if we can get them stocked in A New Chapter. It's strange that Liam and Marion, who I would have picked as the first people to know about him, both drew a blank when I brought him up.'

'Liam hasn't heard of him?'

Ollie shook her head. 'Not a whisper.'

'Are they particularly grisly?' Max picked up a stick and threw it for Henry. The dog ran after it, barking into the fog.

'They're dark, but they're funny, too. The characters are memorable – they're always arguing, which lightens things up, because the subjects *are* on the sombre side. I mean, I've never come across a myth or legend that hasn't got some sort of tragedy woven into it.'

'There must be *some* with happy endings,' Max said. 'Surely.'

He walked towards her, and Ollie felt a growing pressure in her chest that she thought must be anticipation. They'd seen each other several times since he'd admitted he wanted to kiss her, but since then he'd backed off, as if he regretted the confession. Now, though, she didn't know if it was the eerie light cast by the sea fret, the sense of danger – however imagined – or her own excitement at being on this strange hunt with him, but she thought she could see something new in his expression: a hunger that hadn't been there on Sunday, when they'd done yoga together; the hunger she'd seen at the end of the ghost walk.

'You,' she said, her words slightly breathless, 'are a hopeless romantic. That makes *so* much sense.'

'Why would that make sense?'

Ollie walked backwards, more to encourage him to keep moving than to distance herself from him. 'Because you're always so kind, so generous. You've got so much . . .' she was about to say *heart,* but didn't know if that would be OK '. . . warmth in you. It stands to reason that you'd believe in happy endings: in love.'

'Don't you?' he asked.

'Not recently,' she said, and then, because she didn't want to taint their morning with thoughts of Guy, she added, 'and I think that, even if a legend does have a happy ending, there has to be tragedy somewhere along the way. It has to have emotional weight, otherwise how have these things lingered for so long? Kerensa's handprint, the phantom battle at the church, the Lost Fisherman. They exist because of the emotion those people felt. It was too much for mere mortals to handle, so some of it got left behind.'

'That makes sense,' Max said, taking another step towards her. 'But why does the emotion have to be negative? Aren't there any legends in your book that talk about over-whelming, all-consuming love: a love that wasn't lost or ripped away?'

'I don't know,' Ollie admitted. 'I haven't read them all yet. But if there *is*, then the lovers will have been through trials to get there. You can't have an epic love story without challenges. Two people like each other, they fall in love, the end. There's nothing epic about that.'

Max shook his head, and this time he stayed where he was. When he spoke, his voice was quieter. 'I think that's the most epic thing of all. When there are over six billion people on this rock, the fact that, over and over again, two people can find each other and experience a love so deep, so profound, that they're desperate to spend the rest of their life — their one life on this earth — with that person. No other drama is needed.'

Ollie swallowed. His eyes seemed so bright in the gloom, as if they were a beacon she could always turn to, could find in the fog, to keep her safe. 'I hadn't thought about it like that,' she whispered. 'I had never—'

She stepped backwards, and her foot rolled over something, unbalancing her.

Max was there in a flash, gripping her arm, steadying her. Pain stabbed through her shoulder, and her wince was automatic. Max let go. 'Sorry,' he said. 'I'm sorry, I had no—'

'It's OK,' she rushed, not wanting him to think that she didn't like him touching her. 'Just my stupid shoulder. What did I roll on, though?' She bent down, the whistling wind and the crash of waves filling her ears, and then she saw it: a white and blue shell, its curves perfectly proportioned, its pearlescent surface gleaming, even though the sun was hidden. How could nature create something so beautiful? 'Oh my God!'

Max stood in front of her. 'You planted this.'

'I did not! I would *never* do that. Do you really think I'd be able to navigate my way to this exact spot, to place it and then come back to it, with this sea fret going on?'

'You admitted you'd been here earlier, to check you'd got the location right.'

'Max,' she said, laughing. 'This is not a stitch-up. I swear on Henry's life.' Her dog, who had returned to them with his stick in his mouth, dropped it on the sand so he could bark at her, then rushed towards Max. 'No, Henry—' she started, but an icy wave hit her so suddenly that the words were shocked out of her.

Max swore, pulling her forwards, but it was too late.

Under the cover of the sea fret, they'd got too close to the shallows, and a wave had snuck up and broken over her knees. She looked down to see water dripping off the hem of her coat in steady rivulets. She was already beginning to shiver.

'We need to go now,' Max said. 'You need to get dry, get warmed up.'

'I'm about thirty minutes from here,' she replied, her teeth chattering.

'We'll quickstep it.' He put his arm around her shoulders, pulling her into his side as they started walking. 'Make it in twenty-five.'

'I didn't plant that shell, Max. I wouldn't know where to get one from.'

'I know that really. But it's just . . . it's crazy, isn't it?'

Ollie shrugged. 'Or whoever wrote the book of legends found these beautiful, unusual shells on this beach,' she held up their found treasure, 'and created a story to fit the discovery.'

Max glanced down at her. 'Don't ruin it,' he murmured, and planted a kiss on her forehead. 'Come on, let's step it up a gear. I don't want to think about how cold your feet are right now.'

'They're a bit chilly,' Ollie admitted. What she didn't add was that, after his kiss, as brief and platonic as it had been, she was already beginning to feel warmer.

*   *   *

It felt a little bit strange and a whole lot intimate having Max in her home.

She tried seeing it from his perspective: the cool colours and clean lines, mostly tidy, but with a little bit of her personality thrust into each space; her latest read, *Ten Years* by Pernille Hughes, on the table next to the sofa; a *Food for the Soul* cookbook open at the 'Bountiful Brunch' recipe on her book stand in the kitchen; the weighty Christmas garlands draped over everything.

'Make yourself a coffee, if you want.'

'Don't worry about me,' he said. 'Just go and get in a hot shower.'

'OK.' Of course she didn't need his permission, but she liked his concern, the care he was showing her. And right now, despite her well-crafted leather boots, her feet were soggy blocks of ice. She hurried up the stairs, intensely aware that her bedroom was on a mezzanine, visible from downstairs in a style typical of barn conversions. She grabbed fresh trousers and underwear and hurried into the bathroom, letting the shower fill with steam before she stepped into it.

She stayed in there until the warmth returned to her skin and she could feel her toes again. She took her time dressing and looked at herself in the mirror, condensation fogging the edges. She thought that, if this had been London, the period of her life before she'd met Guy, she would have turned on the charm, encouraged Max into her bedroom, even though they were both due at work.

She didn't know if it was Max who was different from the other men she'd been attracted to, or if *she* was different – after Guy, and after moving to Cornwall – but the last thing she wanted was to make a move that might scare him off, that might turn something with potential to last – whether as a friendship or more – into something fleeting and, ultimately, disastrous.

With Max, she realised, she didn't want instant gratification, she wanted long-term satisfaction. She drew a heart in the corner of the mirror, wondering if it would leave an imprint after the steam had faded, and went to join him.

The smell of coffee filled the barn, and Henry was gnawing on a bone she'd bought him the day before. Max was leaning against the kitchen counter, sipping his drink. He stood up straight when she appeared.

'How are you feeling?'

'Much warmer,' she said, as he handed her a mug of steaming coffee. 'Thanks for coming back with me. You didn't have to, and now you're going to be late to Sea Brew.'

'Molly's opening up. One of the perks of owning the business is that I get to be flexible. You, on the other hand . . .'

Ollie glanced at the wall clock. 'Shit. I'd better let Thea know I'm running late.'

'If you tell her you were attacked by the sea and had to come home to change, I'm sure she'd understand.'

'I hope so.' She picked up her mobile, about to call A New Chapter, when it rang in her hand. She answered automatically. 'Hello?'

'Is that Ollie Spencer?'

'Speaking. How can I help?'

'This is Arabella, Sophia Forsythe-Hartley's editor. We spoke before?'

'Yes! It's lovely to hear from you. How are you?'

'All good at this end, and phoning with excellent news. Sophia is very keen to discuss your proposed launch event at A New Chapter, and would love to Zoom with you and Thea Rushwood at three on Friday. I'll send you a link.'

'That's . . . amazing!' Ollie grinned at Max, and then Arabella's words thudded into her consciousness. 'You mean *this* Friday?'

'I do indeed. We're so looking forward to hearing your ideas for her event. It would be such a boon to hold it in Cornwall.'

'Yes, of course,' Ollie said faintly. 'That's . . . wonderful. I'll – I'll tell Thea this morning. And see you online in, uhm, three days' time!'

'Marvellous.'

Arabella rang off and Ollie was left with the phone still gripped to her ear.

'Good news?' Max asked. 'Or . . . ?'

'Very much *good*, and very much *or*.'

'OK.' He laughed. 'Do you – are you all right?' His face creased in concern. 'Maybe you should call Thea, let her know you need a day in bed—'

'Sophia Forsythe-Hartley and her editor are Zooming with me and Thea this Friday,' she rushed, partly because she couldn't quite believe it, and also because she wanted to cut off Max's suggestion about staying in bed, which was not remotely helpful right now.

He smiled. 'That *is* good, isn't it? But then . . . Does Thea know? That you've been in touch with her, even?'

Ollie reached for her coffee and took a big gulp. 'She's certainly about to find out!'

Max put his mug down and stepped forwards, and before Ollie realised what he was doing, he wrapped his arms around her. 'She'll be over the moon,' he said into her shoulder. 'Once she's got over the shock.'

'I hope you're right,' Ollie murmured. 'It's only a few days after the Disaster with Marcus Belrose.'

He laughed gently. 'Is that the official title?'

'It is. And we don't need a sequel anytime soon: Disaster with Sophia Forsythe-Hartley, swiftly followed by the third in the trilogy: Ollie Spencer Looks for a New Job.' She slid her arms around his waist, relishing the feel of his solid torso, his strong arms wrapped around her, the soft fabric of his jumper. She inhaled his herby, smoky scent, and rested her cheek against his collarbone.

'It won't come to that,' Max whispered into her ear.

Looking over his shoulder, Ollie could see that he'd placed their mythical shell carefully on the mantelpiece, next to where she'd slid the strip of Polaroids from the Christmas market into the mirror's frame, anchoring the photos there so she could see them every day. It was that gesture, even more than his hug and his words of reassurance, that made her realise how much trouble she was in: she'd accidentally found a man who, despite all her plans to focus on herself and her job, was far too good to ignore.

Chapter Twenty-One

The quiz was on Friday night, the same day as Thea and Ollie's Zoom call with Sophia Forsythe-Hartley and her editor. Ollie had turned up at work early, with a soft, mint-green throw that she knew would look beautiful draped over the sofa, and high hopes. This, she decided, was going to be a good day. The cooking class was a blip, and she was ready to get back on track.

'So,' Thea said, greeting her with a smile. 'A bit of a Friday, huh?'

'A huge Friday,' Ollie replied, closing the door of the bookshop to block out a strong wind that had made the leaves dance on her walk in, and was, right this moment, whipping the water in the harbour into impatient white horses. 'This is for you. Us.' She held out her tote bag.

Thea took it and looked inside, her neat brows furrowing. 'This is a bit different to Sea Brew sausage rolls.' She took the throw out and unfurled it, her eyes brightening. 'It's so beautiful.'

'It's to make amends, to you *and* the sofa.'

Thea folded the throw on the counter, then put it back into the bag. 'You didn't need to do that. Last Friday was a tough day, but if everything went absolutely perfectly all the time, I'd start to get suspicious that we were living in some kind of Matrix.'

Ollie laughed. 'True. But it happened because I wasn't properly prepared. I'm discovering that impetuousness and event planning don't always go together.'

Thea pursed her lips. 'Maybe not, but there's a fine line between impetuousness and enthusiasm, and I definitely don't want to lose your enthusiasm. Shall we go and see what this looks like?'

'Sounds great.' Ollie followed her up the stairs, glad that she'd started the day off well. She decided that things could only get better from here on in.

Max had been right: Thea had been over the moon about the very real possibility of Sophia Forsythe-Hartley holding her launch event at A New Chapter, as soon as she'd got over the shock. Ollie had been relieved, along with having a lingering, unfamiliar sensation of being able to be vulnerable in front of someone: she was surprised it had happened with Max so quickly.

Usually, she aimed for positive and bubbly, and kept her work-related insecurities on the inside: a problem was simply a challenge to be faced, nothing to dwell on or worry about. But the event with Marcus Belrose had shaken her, had made her realise how much she cared about succeeding here, in this town and with these people. Having Max there to reassure her, about that and about her communication with Sophia's editor – to tell her Thea would be pleased

– had meant more to her than, initially, she was prepared to admit even to herself.

'Let's have the table here, the chairs behind it,' Thea said that afternoon, when they were getting ready for their Zoom meeting. 'It would be good to show off the view, but if we do that we'll be silhouettes. If they want a virtual tour, we can just pick the laptop up.'

'We should include a tour, I think.' Ollie made Thea and herself coffees using their new, slinky machine, then brought them over to the table.

'This is a big thing, isn't it?' Thea said, as she added another hardback to the pile beneath the laptop. 'It could make a real difference.'

'Yes! But don't forget that it's a big, *positive* thing. I messed up with the Marcus Belrose event, but this one . . . this one will be stellar.'

'Stellar,' Thea repeated, seeming to like the word, and when Arabella and Sophia appeared on the screen, sitting in a bright space with white bookshelves behind them, Ollie heard her whisper it under her breath.

Arabella was whip-thin, with a dark, glossy bob and wearing a smart purple shirt. Sophia was curvier, with dyed blonde hair and slightly too much blusher, but she had warm blue eyes and a friendly smile. A pair of glasses dangled on a chain around her neck, over a cream blouse.

Ollie made the introductions, then they got down to business.

Sophia had a jolly tone and laughed frequently, and her enthusiasm was clear. She was like an elegant Mrs Christmas, Ollie thought, feeling a thrum of excitement as she pictured her gracing A New Chapter during the festivities. Arabella was kind but cautious, which was to be expected, and they spent a while talking about Sophia's upcoming book, *The Forgotten Shore*, and the inspiration behind it. When the author brought up how mystical their part of Cornwall was, Ollie couldn't help jumping on it.

'There's so much folklore around here.'

'Yes, of course,' Sophia said. 'The place is chock-full of ancient stories. You can get lost, fall down endless rabbit holes. I don't mean literally, of course – though that is very possible, too.' She chuckled, and Thea and Ollie joined in.

Ollie leaned closer to the screen. 'Have you heard of an auth—'

'How would you go about promoting the event?' Arabella asked, and Ollie sat back.

'Let's start with social media,' she said smoothly, hiding her disappointment at being cut off. 'And our newsletter. Then I can tell you about the Port Karadow Christmas pageant, and how we're going to tie Sophia's appearance in with that. There's almost too much to go through,' she added, laughing.

Sophia beamed, and looked at her editor. 'Marvellous,' she said.

Ollie tried not to be too smug.

By the time people started filing in for the quiz, the bookshop was buzzing, Ollie and Thea high on their success. Even Becky had seemed pleased that they'd secured such a high-profile author, though her enthusiasm was tempered, as it always was, with caution and practicalities.

'We need to start selling tickets soon,' she said. 'There's not much more than a month to go.'

'I've already got the newsletter written,' Ollie replied, 'and the social media posts. Once we've pinned down the details – the exact timings, and how much we want to charge – it'll take the press of a few buttons to get it out into the world.'

Becky folded her arms. 'You were confident they'd say yes, then?'

Ollie grinned. 'If they said no, it was half an hour of my time wasted. If they said yes, then we'd be ahead of the game. It made sense.'

'It's *all* positive,' Thea said, putting an arm around each of them. 'All of it. Now let's take that energy into tonight, make our first quiz as much of a success as the Christmas event is going to be.'

'Do we mention it?' Becky asked.

'Until we've firmed everything up, which should be on Monday, we stay quiet.' Thea mimed zipping her lips. 'It's our secret, OK?'

'OK,' Ollie and Becky said in unison, and when Ollie caught the other woman's eye, she was delighted to get a brief smile in return.

Nothing, Ollie reasoned, an hour later, could go wrong at a quiz. There were no hotplates or naked flames, no pitchers of tomato-heavy, oil-based sauce to be flung about, no possibility of mistaken ghost sightings that would have everyone screaming and running away in terror.

The events space was full, six teams of up to six people crowded round tables, all with determined expressions and poised pens because, Ollie knew, if you went to a quiz, regardless of the topics or the quality of the prizes, it was almost impossible not to be competitive.

Finn, Meredith and Ben were on a team with Adrian and his wife Tillie, Lizzy had brought someone who Ollie guessed was her husband Martin, and two lanky teenagers who had the same rosy cheeks and tawny hair as her. There were quite a lot of people she didn't recognise, which could only be a good thing, and then there was the team made up of Liam, Marion and Max.

She didn't know why they'd decided to join forces, except that she'd been eager for them all to come, and it was quite likely they already knew each other, considering how close-knit Port Karadow was. Regardless of what had brought them together, it was lovely to see Liam at a community event, and it was lovely to see Max full stop.

She had to stop her gaze drifting to him every five minutes, because she was supposed to be running the show. She would give almost anything to know what the three of them were talking about in between rounds. But their presence didn't stop her from asking the one question she'd included with a slightly ulterior motive. She watched everyone's faces as she read it out, her stool on the low stage at the front of the room giving her an elevated position.

'Which author wrote the Roskilly and Faith series of Cornish-based mysteries in the nineteen seventies, which used local legends as the inspiration for the plots?'

She held her breath, hoping she wouldn't be met with a sea of blank faces, or the quizzers looking at her with the disappointment of hearing something that was beyond their knowledge base. She felt a spark of excitement when heads bent over tables, and she heard the whisperings of conferred ideas. When she caught Max's eye, he frowned at her, but she saw amusement there, too. Obviously she had gifted their table a point, but she wanted to see how many other people in the town had heard of Bryan Mailer.

The outcome, when they went through the answers at the end, was a lot better than she'd hoped. Most of the teams recognised the name, and in some cases it was more than that.

'Oh I loved those mysteries.'

'Knew the answer right away: easy-peasy.'

'I think we've got a couple of his books on the shelves in the back bedroom.'

'Someone told me he was a recluse who lived near here; tied up in legends and not much else.'

Ollie listened to their comments, storing them away for later. And afterwards, when the prizes had been awarded – to a team made up of people Ollie didn't yet know, who called themselves The Port Karadow Crusaders – and everyone was milling around the bookshop picking up Christmas presents, Ollie's prepared table of Bumper Quiz Books getting a lot of attention, Thea brought it up.

'Customers sometimes ask me for those Roskilly and Faith mysteries, but they're out of print.'

'Really? Maybe we should get some second-hand copies in, then. They're great stories.'

'You've read them?' Thea asked, as she slid a stack of paperbacks into a customer's *Fall Into A Good Book* tote bag.

'Four so far. They're so engaging, and they're super local. I think we should look on AbeBooks. I know we don't have a second-hand area right now, but I don't think that matters.'

'They'd be great for the Cornish section,' Thea said. 'I'll look into it.' She handed the customer her receipt, and wished her a good night. There were only a couple of people left in the shop, the clock ticking round to ten o'clock.

'We could do it together, if you like?'

Thea paused, then smiled. 'Sounds good. And Ollie . . . ?'

'Yup?'

'Tonight was brilliant. Really fun, and busy, and profit-able.'

Ollie's grin was unabashed. 'I know! I'm so bloody happy.'

'And there's so much to look forward to,' Thea continued. 'On a night like this, not too far from now, when the view is even twinklier, we'll have Sophia Forsythe-Hartley in this building, reading to a packed-out audience from her new book.'

Ollie nodded, and they both stared out of the window at night-time Port Karadow shimmering with life, the soft, firefly glows of the boats in the harbour contrasting with the brighter street lamps and lit windows. Ollie offered up a silent thanks that things were on track again, that she was being productive for Thea and the bookshop: that she was back.

Chapter Twenty-Two

'Do you want to come over tomorrow?' That was what Ollie had blurted to Max as he was walking out of the door after the quiz, after she'd told him he wasn't allowed to stay and help clear up, because he was a paying customer.

His eyes had widened, perhaps because it wasn't something they'd planned. Not a yoga session or a legend hunt to hide behind, just her asking, straight out, for his company. But then he'd nodded, smiled gently, and asked her what time to come.

Now she was waiting for him, Henry lying on her feet and a cup of calming camomile tea clasped in her hands. She had done some breathing exercises, cherry-picked the most relaxing yoga poses from their class on Sunday – which did *not* include the crow – and now she was sitting here, hoping he'd turn up soon, because nerves were bubbling inside her gut like porridge in a saucepan.

When the knock on the door finally came, it startled her so much she almost spilled her tea.

She opened it and found Max on the other side, his smile wide, his curls windblown.

'Did you walk here?' she asked.

'It seemed a shame not to.' He stepped inside when she moved back to let him in. 'There are some really interesting walks round here; lots of trails to follow.'

'I feel like I've only found about two per cent of them,' Ollie admitted. 'What do you want to drink? Tea, coffee, beer? Or I could open some wine?'

'A beer would be great, thanks.'

'Come in, take off your coat, make yourself at home.'

He followed her into the living space, and Henry came bounding up to meet him, ready for another round of Max's affection. Ollie got beers out of the fridge and popped the tops.

'Liam's done an amazing job converting this place – I meant to say the other day.'

'Did you see it before it was renovated?'

'Once, but a long time ago. He used to have the odd garden party in the grounds, the kitchen garden out the back. He kept this place as storage, from what I can remember. Old lawn mowers, tents, that sort of thing.'

'Then "amazing" doesn't begin to cover it,' Ollie said, laughing.

She put the beers on the coffee table, then returned to the kitchen and shook some sweet chilli crisps into a bowl. She settled on the sofa next to Max, turning towards him. She was wearing jogging bottoms and a hoodie. It was her weekend uniform and she'd put it on automatically, even though she'd invited him here.

'Cheers.' She held out her bottle.

'Cheers.' Max clinked his against it. 'Does Liam look after Henry while you're at work? He seems docile now, but I expect he can be a handful.'

'Liam and Marion tag team,' Ollie said. 'He told me that Marion's been taking Henry on walks to tire him out. Sometimes I wonder why she's here: it doesn't seem like Liam needs all that much help, and if she can fit in long walks with my dog, then she's clearly not rushed off her feet.'

'Her husband, Adam, commutes into London during the week,' Max said. 'So I think it's probably about company, for both of them. Liam must be lonely, rubbing along in that big old house by himself. It was good to see him at the quiz last night – I wasn't sure he'd come, but I think they did it for you. They're both glad you're here.'

Ollie's throat thickened at the suggestion that Liam and Marion had come to the quiz for her. They both knew about the disaster with Marcus Belrose, and she was touched by their show of support. Instead of saying as much, she deflected. 'For typing purposes and deliveries to interfere with. Perhaps they're having a clandestine affair?' She waggled her eyebrows and sipped her beer. 'No, forget I said that. Just because they spend time together, it doesn't mean it isn't platonic.'

'I expect you're not the first person to speculate about it, though.'

'*You* don't think they're having an affair, do you?'

Max held his hands up. 'I have no opinions on the matter. Except that Marion talked about Adam a lot last night: she seems devoted to him. And Liam's quite a bit older than her.'

Ollie nodded. 'Well, then. It just proves that men and women can be friends. There doesn't have to be anything romantic, or physical, involved.'

'There doesn't *have* to be,' Max repeated, and the atmosphere in the room shifted. No matter that it was an airy, high-ceilinged space with French doors at both ends; it suddenly felt tiny. Ollie's attention fell to Max's lips. They were slightly parted, a faint shadow of stubble along his jawline.

'So, Sophia Forsythe-Hartley is launching her new book at our big Christmas event,' she said brightly, trying to break the tension.

'I knew she would be.' Max nodded.

'No you didn't.' Ollie whacked him gently on the arm. 'You're only saying that after the fact.'

'Not true. I knew your enthusiasm would win her over.'

'Flatterer.'

'I'm being honest,' Max said, laughing. 'But I'm really pleased for you. You must be thrilled that she's agreed to it; you all must be.'

'Thea is.' Ollie picked up a handful of crisps and munched through them steadily, her thoughts returning to the bookshop. 'Becky . . . well, the jury's still out. Or, to be more precise, she's still not convinced by *me*.'

Max frowned and put his bottle on the table. Ollie noticed that the hem of his jeans was ripped, and that he was wearing white and red-striped socks. 'Why not?' he asked.

Ollie rolled her eyes, trying to make light of it. 'She sees me as the classic London interloper, with fancy ideas and no clue about the issues facing the locals. She thinks I

207

should be doing more for them, not burning down the bookshop with fancy celebrity chefs.'

Max shook his head. 'But you're doing so much. Your Book Wars idea, the book club, the quiz. And everyone wants a bit of glamour in their lives sometimes, whether that's going to a posh dance in Truro, doing yoga at a spa instead of in your living room, or an event with a famous author at a bookshop.'

'I know,' Ollie said, 'but my events so far . . . they're bringing in the same crowds. To start with – with the book club, especially – I went to people I knew, and now I need to widen the reach of A New Chapter. It needs to be better known, a bigger part of the community.'

'So, what are you thinking?'

Ollie felt nervous, suddenly. She was starting to realise how much Max's opinion, his response, mattered to her. 'Well,' she said, 'remember what I said to you when were at Crystal Waters?' She got up and hurried up the stairs to the mezzanine. She found the long – far too long – snake of book-print paper chains she'd tidied away up there and, when she realised they were a monumental trip hazard, wound them around herself. She walked down the staircase, slowly and deliberately, making sure she didn't tread on any of the links.

Max kept his eyes on her as she descended. 'A paper chain dress?'

She grinned. 'I might have got a bit carried away. Making paper chains is really soothing, so in the evenings, while I've been watching TV or listening to music, I've just been adding to it. And it made me think – we could run some Christmas decoration workshops for children. We get so many in the shop, but a lot of them, the younger ones especially, don't always want to read. They want to draw or colour, be active.'

Max lifted one of the links. 'Wait, are these *books*? Isn't this the equivalent of treason in your world?'

'I printed the pages from the internet,' Ollie said. 'I didn't rip them out of real books: I'm not a monster. But that's the beauty of them. You can have any design you want: no limits.'

Max tugged gently, the chains making a pleasing, shivering noise as she moved, and then she was back on the sofa, next to him. She realised that some of the links were beneath her, undoubtedly squashed, but she didn't care.

'So you're going to get the kids who come into the bookshop to add to your record-breaking paper chain trail?' he asked.

'Paper chains are just one idea. And one event isn't going to make a difference: I can hear Becky telling me that right away.'

Max shook his head. 'Don't let Becky dictate your entire events programme.'

'It's not just about Becky, though. I want the bookshop to work for the whole town. I'm going to get this right, Max.'

'You're already working so hard.'

'That doesn't mean I can start coasting now. Besides, it's coming up to Christmas, and I *cannot* get the Christmas events wrong. Running workshops for children would bring in their parents and carers, and it would give them somewhere different to go – something they could get excited about that would give the adults a break *and* make them more aware of the shop. We could do readings, colouring in, other crafts.'

'I can't see Becky being against that.'

'I hope not,' Ollie said. 'We always had traditional events at the last bookshop I worked in: author readings and signings, the occasional charity quiz. Port Karadow is so . . .'

'Different?'

'Friendly,' Ollie said. 'It's a proper community, and the bookshop – especially because it's in the Old Post House – feels as if it's right in the centre.'

Max smiled at her. 'Do you turn every problem into an opportunity to make things better?'

'Isn't that what all the best people do?' She thought of Max's own challenge: being forced to give up his entire career, the way he'd used it as an opportunity to start Sea Brew, becoming successful and loved in the town after dealing with such a serious health issue.

He picked up the trail of paper chains, wound the loose end around Ollie's back, and tugged again, more firmly this time. Ollie had stapled them together, so they held fast, and she took his hint, leaning towards him. She put her hand on the sofa cushion next to his knee.

'Would you call this a problem, or an opportunity?' he murmured.

Ollie swallowed. 'What? Being tied up in paper, next to you on the sofa?'

He nodded. His gaze held hers, and she could see the gentle rise and fall of his chest.

She licked her lips. 'I suppose some people might say it was a problem – the whole being tied up bit. But having you here, next to me . . . of course that's a good thing. But an opportunity? I suppose—'

Max dropped his head, exhaling a laugh.

Ollie blinked, the spell broken. 'What is it?'

He looked up at her. 'My flirting needs a whole lot of work.'

Her insides flipped. 'I disagree.'

'You actually thought that was seductive, what I just did?' He waggled the paper chain, and Henry lifted his head. Ollie wondered if it sounded similar to her rattling his treat jar.

'I was enjoying it,' she said. 'I wasn't thinking *what an idiot,* or anything.'

Max grinned. 'Good to know.'

'I guess sometimes,' she went on, her heart pounding, 'flirting is overrated. Sometimes it's less hassle to bypass it completely.'

'What do you mean?'

'I mean . . . this.' She closed the gap between them, reached a hand up to cup Max's jaw, and pressed her lips against his. His hesitation lasted for a second, and then he was responding, moving his lips against hers, sliding his fingers into her hair and tugging at the hairband to release her ponytail.

Kissing Max, Ollie had enough brain power to realise, was like a white-water rapids ride, and floating in an infinity pool all at once; fireworks and a cosy fire; simultaneously calming and earth-shattering. He was strong and steady, his intent – after that first breath of hesitation – was undeniable, and it gave her the confidence to kiss him back with all she had.

Max pulled back slightly, so he could whisper against her lips. 'This is better than flirting.'

'I think so. I certainly hoped it would be. Actually, I was fairly confident.'

'Were you?' He kissed her again.

'I was,' she murmured. 'Glad I was proved right.'

'Me too, Ollie,' Max said, pulling her closer, changing the angle of his head to get better access to her lips. 'Me too.'

Chapter Twenty-Three

On Monday, Ollie stood looking up at A New Chapter, at its honeyed stone and the colourful, elegant window displays. It was a clash of old and new that was somehow harmonious. Could children's workshops really work here?

Ollie knew that more complicated events like this required a lot of thought. There were safeguarding concerns, extra rules and guidelines to follow, but she had spent most of Sunday researching similar events: the groups they held at the library in Truro, other bookshops that ran successful children's sessions.

Her nerves followed her all morning, and while she had planned to sit Thea and Becky down properly and talk it through with them, they all ended up at the shop counter at the same time, and Ollie's mouth decided there was no time like the present.

'I was thinking we could have craft sessions for children upstairs.'

Thea's expression was curious. Becky narrowed her eyes.

'Making Christmas decorations to start with,' she went on. 'Paper chains are fun and easy, the materials are cheap, and they'd all have something festive to take home at the end. If it works, we could move onto bauble painting – I've found kits you can buy online. If they're popular, we could do them on a regular basis.'

Thea was nodding, like a solar-powered toy in soft evening light.

'When were you thinking?' Becky asked.

'I was hoping you'd help with that,' Ollie admitted. 'I don't know what time of day would work best. Right after school, early evening, or should we limit these things to the week-ends? It has to work for the parents and carers, too.'

'After school is great, as long as they can get from school to here.'

'Something as simple as story time would be popular, too,' Thea added. 'Especially with the pre-school kids. And parents love it, because it gives them a bit of a breather. A coffee and a browse round the bookshop while we're in charge of their toddlers.'

Ollie felt the first flutterings of possibility. 'I don't want to turn this place into something it's not, but we have the resources – refreshments, a customer toilet – to run more regular events for the community. We're a bookshop first, of course, but . . . anyway. It's just an idea.' She sipped her latte – coffee rather than chai tea – and decided it was good, but not as good as the drinks at Sea Brew. Though those couldn't be beaten, because they came with added Max.

Her insides warmed at the memory of their make-out session, how hot it had been, but also how natural, considering they hadn't known each other that long. It could have easily led to more, but she was determined to do things the right way. She hadn't managed to stay away from him – she'd already let herself off for that: staying away from Max was a lost cause – but she could take things slowly, get to know him better before hopping into bed with him.

She thought Max must feel the same, because after they'd finally come up for air, they'd talked more about Ollie's ideas, planned their next legend hunt, and then he'd left, saying he didn't want to abandon Oxo completely.

She'd floated her way through her typing session with Liam, though her ability to multitask meant that he hadn't realised she wasn't entirely present, and since then she'd been counting down the hours until she could see Max again.

'I think it's a wonderful idea,' Thea said now. 'We don't want to overstretch ourselves – we've got a lot of preparation to do for our star author launch – but two children's sessions would be doable. Becky, are you happy to help Ollie with those?'

Ollie realised she was chewing her lip. This was the most nervous she'd been since the day of her interview, when her whole future hung in the balance.

'I guess I could,' Becky said. 'There's a lot to consider.'

'I was hoping you could help me with the details,' Ollie replied. 'I don't want to get things wrong right at the start – it's hard to claw your way back when you do that, and I care about this place, about its reputation.' Her words were as subtle as a sledgehammer, but she hoped Becky would see that she was committed to being better, less narrow-minded.

'Sounds good,' Becky said. She had her arms folded tightly, and wouldn't hold Ollie's gaze for long, but Ollie still took it as a win. She wanted to be friends with these people; to feel like this new life was really hers, rather than the experiment it sometimes felt like. She wanted to belong in Port Karadow, and it seemed as if, finally, she might be heading along the right path.

Later, in Liam's sumptuous study, with the fire crackling and a glass of port on the desk beside her, Ollie turned to the next chapter of his life history.

As she typed up stories about his youth, about him growing up on the farm, the opportunities and the loneliness he'd experienced, her thoughts returned to A New Chapter. What other crafts could they do in the upstairs space? It wasn't huge, after all, and wouldn't take a whole classroom's worth of children.

'You're like one of those newfangled robots they were talking about on the news,' Liam said. He was on the sofa, idly turning the pages of a book. Ollie had got used to this: sometimes they talked about the stories in Liam's manuscript, or Ollie's job, or the legends she was discovering, and sometimes there was an easy silence, broken only by the sounds of typing and the dancing flames.

Ollie looked up from the screen. 'What do you mean?'

'Your typing seems automatic, your eyes are moving back and forth as if you're computing a hundred things a minute, and your shoulders are up around your ears. Are you OK, love?'

'Of course.'

'Not too much burning the candle at both ends, going to work and coming here, walking that pooch of yours in between? Not too much legend-hunting?'

'I love those legends,' she admitted. 'And – God, that Lost Fisherman one – I told you, didn't I, that we almost saw him on my ghost walk? I planned it a bit too well and nearly lost all my customers before they had a chance to stock up on Stephen King novels.'

Liam rubbed the back of his neck. 'Perhaps you did see him.'

Ollie frowned. 'What do you mean?'

'What are ghosts, if not things that seem out of place, that make no sense within the context? If you hadn't waited until that fisherman's rowing boat had been spotlighted, then you could have said that you'd seen him. Who's to say that the legend didn't originate from people in exactly the position you were in?'

Ollie sat back in the leather chair. 'Huh.'

'We all assign meaning to things that have none: that's human nature. And that's partly, surely, what legends are.'

'You're wise beyond your years.'

Liam laughed. 'Wiser than I should be at eighty-one?'

Ollie kneaded her shoulder, trying to massage away the ache. 'I was frantic when I saw it. Not because I was scared, necessarily, but because of how my guests were reacting, and—'

'And if you hadn't had the patience to debunk it, they would have held on to their terror and run away from your walk, which would have been seen as a disaster because it didn't generate any book sales, and instead generated unkind gossip about your so called "friendly ghost walks". *Then* you would have been able to say: "I encountered the Lost Fisherman, and look how my luck changed for the worse, right afterwards." Meaning, see? It's everywhere.'

'And what does *this* mean,' she said, indicating the cosy study, their friendship.

'It means you have generosity, and energy, in abundance. Even as things get busy at the bookshop, you're still happy to spend time with me, to do my typing.'

'Of course I am,' Ollie said. 'And it's not just out of obligation, either. I love spending time with you, and I'm intrigued by your memoir. I would never think to do anything like this. Are you hoping to get it published when it's finished?'

Liam chuckled, swirling his port around in his glass. 'Good God, no. Nobody would be interested in the tales of an old codger like me.' Then he added, so quietly that she almost missed it, 'Not any more, anyway.' He looked up, smiled at her. 'No, lass. It's just for posterity, and ink fades after time. At least if it's on a computer, it isn't likely to disappear.'

'Well, I think tons of people would want to read it: you're more interesting than you give yourself credit for.' She returned his smile, then glanced at the shelves, the paperbacks and hardbacks all organised neatly, reaching right up to the ceiling. It certainly felt as if she and Liam had been meant to end up together, rubbing along on the Foxglove Farm estate, surrounded by books. Everything in her life felt weighted with meaning, but perhaps that was because, in some respects, it was all still so new. She was less than two months into her Cornwall life, and a whole lot had happened already. So much for the slow, easier pace she had been craving. Ollie smiled to herself, and kept on typing.

Chapter Twenty-Four

When Max knocked on the door the following evening, Ollie was in the common but undesirable state of having filled the whole barn with incense smoke.

She'd lit some sticks when she'd got home after a frantic day at the bookshop, people starting their Christmas shopping in earnest, and a delivery van getting blocked in in the parking area, resulting in a grumpy driver and fractious customers. Thea had handled the situation calmly, but it had left a pall of irritability over the shop, rather than the joyful atmosphere Ollie had come to expect. She had tried to change the mood, had considered leading everyone inside the shop in a five-minute meditation, but had decided to help Thea sort out the storeroom instead.

Now, as she hurried to the front door, she tried to waft the rose-scented smoke away. It hung in thick, stubborn clumps in the air.

'Hello! come in,' she said. Was it obvious how pleased she was to see him?

'Hey.' Max handed her a bottle of wine, stepped into the hall and bent to take off his shoes. He looked up at her as he undid his laces, and his smile made her breath catch. She didn't know if she would ever get used to it. Raindrops sparkled on his coat and in his curls, and she wanted to wrap him up in her arms.

'Sorry about all this.' She waved her arms as she led the way into the living space. 'Shall I open the wine now? I'm making tacos, if you'd like some? Spicy chicken, peppers and onions. Sour cream and cheese.'

'You didn't have to cook, but they do sound delicious.'

'Just be glad that this smoke is from my incense and not the oven.'

'I'm glad to be here, with you.'

Ollie, her back to him as she got out glasses, smiled into the kitchen cupboards. 'How was the café today?' she asked as she poured the ruby-red wine.

'Busy,' Max admitted, sitting on the sofa. 'It feels like everyone's upped their game, as if they've suddenly realised Christmas is coming and someone's pressed a panic button.'

'That's what the bookshop was like.' Ollie came to join him, resting her shoulder against the back of the sofa, her whole body turned to face him. 'Customers are getting impatient, unhappy if they have to wait a couple of days for a book to come in. I love how busy it's getting, I just wish everyone would be a bit more considerate of their fellow shoppers.'

'You didn't have a bookshop brawl, did you?' Max widened his eyes comically.

Ollie laughed and shook her head. 'A driver got blocked in, the owners of the cars doing the blocking said they should wait for ten minutes – that sort of thing. Have you ever had a café fight? Gingham tablecloths whipped off, cream buns used as ammunition?'

'In Sea Brew? Never. Our customers are unwaveringly happy.'

'Loving your self-confidence,' Ollie said. 'But then, I'm always happy when I'm in Sea Brew, so it's probably justified.'

'You might be slightly biased, though.'

'Because I'm in a . . . kissing relationship with the owner?'

Max grinned. 'Kissing relationship? I've not heard that one before.'

Ollie shrugged. 'I'm not sure what else to call it.'

'Does it have to have a name?' Max asked, his smile softening. 'Whatever it is, I'm really enjoying it. Being here, spending time with you.'

'Me too. And I just . . . are you OK if we take it slowly? I don't want to rush into anything.'

'Rushing never did anyone any good. Just look at the hare and the tortoise.'

'So you want to be tortoises together?'

'I'd love to be tortoises together.' He leaned forward and kissed her, briefly, on the corner of her mouth. Ollie felt a delicious shiver go through her, followed by a sense of contentment that, she realised, she hadn't experienced in a long time.

'So, tacos.' She got up quickly, unsure what to do with the feelings, knowing that if she stayed on the sofa, gazing at Max for too much longer, she'd blurt something out, some overshare that would knock their newly determined tortoise relationship off course. 'How spicy do you like them?'

'I'm OK with spice,' Max said. 'What can I do to help?' He followed her into the kitchen, and they prepared the food together, behaving, Ollie thought, as she switched on the oven, got out salad and sauces and spices, as if they'd known each other for years.

'Are you going to be here for Christmas?' Max asked, once they were sitting at the kitchen island, their tacos fully loaded on their plates. He picked one up and bit into it.

Ollie nodded, taking time to eat her mouthful, wondering how she could be honest without alerting Max to her worries about spending it alone. 'It seems a shame not to be, now that I've got this place so beautifully decorated.' She gestured at her shimmering, opulent garlands.

'Do you have family coming down, then? And when I say down, I don't know where they are, but I guess you can't get too much further south than here.'

'My parents still live in Yorkshire, but they're going on a Scandinavian cruise over Christmas.'

'Oh. Wow.'

'I know. They invited me to go with them, but I can't because of the bookshop. Besides, going on a cruise with your parents in your mid-thirties . . . seems a little bit like a sign that you've given up.'

'Not necessarily.'

'Have you ever been on a cruise with your parents?'

'My parents don't go on cruises. They tend to go to Spain or Greece if they go abroad, but they're near some great beaches: they live just outside St Ives.'

'Are they retired?' Ollie asked, putting a slice of escaped pepper back in her taco.

'My mum's an illustrator,' Max explained. 'She exhibits some of her drawings in galleries in town, and gets commissions for children's books and greetings cards, that sort of thing. Dad used to be a landscape gardener, but he gave up a couple of years ago. He still does triathlons, even though he's sixty-eight.'

'Is that hard for you? Did you compete alongside him?'

'I used to,' Max said. 'It was something we enjoyed doing together, but we've swapped that for barbecues and beers when I go and see them.' There was a pause, which Ollie wasn't sure how to fill, and was relieved when Max did it for her. 'I missed it, like I missed all the things I had to give up after my illness. But, in some ways, slowing down has been the best thing for me, even if the reason I had to do it wasn't exactly welcome.' He put his elbows on the counter and leaned towards Ollie, his expression turning serious. 'I know we haven't known each other very long, but I've noticed that, even when you're trying to relax – the incense, walks in the countryside – you're always working hard at it, as if it's another thing you need to tick off a list.'

Ollie picked up a taco, put it back on her plate. 'I'm the kind of person who will always be busy, unless I remind myself that I need some breathing space. I *have* put some of those things on a list – it helps me remember to do them.'

'But even on your walks, you're intent on following these local legends—'

'You're interested in those too,' Ollie pointed out.

Max nodded. 'I am. It's fun, and that shell is a great find.' He pointed to where it still had pride of place on the mantelpiece. 'But what would you be doing this evening if I wasn't here? Research for more events at the bookshop?'

Ollie sighed. 'Part of the reason I've been doing that is because I'm still finding my feet here. I spend time with Thea and Becky at work, I know Meredith a little bit better now, and there's Liam and Marion – and you, of course. You're here now, you were here on Saturday, but if I just . . . If I always call on you, then . . .'

'Then what?'

They gazed at each other over the island.

'That whole thing about moving too fast?' she said.

He nodded.

'The more you come over, the less I want you to leave. But tonight's a work night, so . . .' The implication of her words hung between them, and she saw Max swallow.

'It's different on a work night?' he asked gently.

She nodded. 'I've said it, now: that I want us to take things slowly. And having you to stay when I've got work the next morning isn't a good idea. I need my beauty sleep, and if you were here . . .'

Max cleared his throat. 'Right.' The silence fizzed between them as they focused on their food. Ollie wondered if she'd pushed things too far, bringing sex into the conversation.

'Have you heard about Christmas Yule logs?' Max asked, when he'd finished eating.

'You mean chocolate-covered cakes in the shape of tree stumps: the things you have pennants of strung up above your café counter?'

'Sort of,' he said, 'but I don't mean the chocolate ones. I mean the real ones: their origins.'

Ollie shook her head.

'They were originally a Germanic pagan tradition,' he explained. 'People would go out into the forest on Christmas Eve, find a large log and drag it back to their house, adorn it with ribbons and paper decorations and then light it, in the hopes that it would burn throughout the twelve days of Christmas.'

'Huge fire risk,' Ollie pointed out.

Max rolled his eyes. 'Back in the *olden days*, when fires were the only way of heating houses, and the fireplaces were huge and made of stone and surrounded by less flammable material than we have now, fires often stayed alight for days.'

'Aren't you the history scholar with all your *olden days* knowledge?'

'Do you want to hear this, or not?'

'Of course I do. Sorry. Please, go on.'

'Right. Well, over the years, as with all these things, variations of the tradition have emerged, but the one that stuck in my head is that, while the Yule log burned, the household respected the fact that it was a holiday, and didn't do any work.'

Ollie narrowed her eyes. 'I see what you're getting at, but I'm dismissing it instantly.'

Max laughed. 'Which bit?'

'The bit where families stopped working while the log was alight. There is *so* much to do at Christmas: buying and wrapping presents; days of food preparation; carol singing and cleaning the house in anticipation of visitors.' She tried not to fixate on the fact that the only people she'd be cleaning her barn for were her and Henry. Still, they deserved to have the best on Christmas Day, even if it was just the two of them.

'But if the log's lit on Christmas Eve,' Max said, 'then your presents should already be bought and wrapped, you can have all the food prepped so it's straightforward the following day, and I'm pretty sure carol singing doesn't count as work. We could get Meredith to do the singing anyway, and bring all her choir friends.'

'It sounds like you're turning this from a hypothetical into an actual,' Ollie said.

Max looked alarmed. 'Oh no, I didn't mean—'

'It's OK, I was joking. I'm sure you have plans for Christmas. But,' she leaned forward, 'you *have* given me an idea. We could introduce some kind of Yule log related offer at A New Chapter. I could find an appropriate-sized log, put it next to the coffee machine – not light it or anything, because we've already established that fires in a bookshop are a *recipe for disaster* – do you think Marcus would like that pun?' She shook her head. 'Anyway, I could make a sign telling people to take the Yule log challenge: half an hour away from their busy, pre-Christmas schedules to read a book. We could put some of our most tempting titles upstairs, near the sofa, and lure people into having a rest. If they started reading a book they loved, they'd probably buy it. What do you think?'

Max didn't reply. Instead, she watched, confused, as he wiped his hands on the kitchen towel she'd put out, then stood up and walked around the island, until he was standing in front of her stool. Ollie swivelled to face him. He tapped her knee, and she widened her legs so he could step in between them. He was centimetres away, staring down at her, trying – and failing – to look solemn.

'Ollie Spencer,' he said, putting his hands on her shoulders. 'Do you know why I told you that story?'

Ollie stared at him. 'Uhm . . . because you're concerned that I'm working too hard, making everything an item on my to-do list, and not chilling out enough?'

'Correct,' he said, smiling. 'And what was the first thing you did when I told you about it?'

'I questioned your credentials as a history professor?'

'Aside from that.'

'I . . . uh. Oh!' She laughed. 'I came up with a way to use it at A New Chapter.'

'You did,' he said. 'You took my suggestion that this might be a good way for you to slow down, and instead, you used it as a way to add something else to your never-ending list of things you need to get done.'

'I did, didn't I?' She bit her lip, the action unapologetically flirtatious, and watched his eyes darken.

'You're going to be trouble,' he murmured. 'I can tell already.'

Then he lifted her off her stool and carried her to the sofa, his strong arms making her feel almost weightless. By the time he'd thrown her on the cushions and bent his head to kiss her, tickling her sides at the same time, she was laughing uncontrollably, Henry barking from his spot on the rug.

It wasn't, she thought, as she gave into his kiss, quite cold enough for her to light her own fire yet, but she loved the idea of striding into the forest, harvesting a Yule log,

227

setting it aflame in the fireplace. She would watch the ribbons smoulder and disappear while she committed to a few hours of relaxation. And when she imagined it, of course Max was by her side, always close enough to touch.

Chapter Twenty-Five

The first of December seemed like an auspicious day to be holding the first Christmas decorations workshop. They'd got through a successful, boisterous and well-attended book club meeting the previous Friday, and the discussion about *The Haunting Season* was continuing online, most people loving the different ghostly stories. Ollie, however, had swiftly turned her attention to the next event, and when the children started arriving at just after three on Thursday afternoon, her nerves threatened to take over.

'We're just upstairs,' she said to the bearded man wearing a scarf covered in penguins, who was holding the hands of three young children. 'Becky will get you set up.'

After promoting the event on A New Chapter's Facebook page, and to anyone who brought children into the shop, the spaces had filled up quickly. Now the tables in the events space were laid out with magazines, a selection of Christmas wrapping paper, and child-friendly glue and scissors. Ollie and Becky had spent the previous afternoon, in moments when the shop was quiet, hanging up Ollie's book-themed paper chains so their young customers could be inspired.

'Oh wow!' she heard a girl shout, and her jingling nerves tipped towards anticipation. If they could make this work, alongside the flashier events that she firmly believed should be a part of the bookshop's future, then perhaps she really could please everyone.

'OK, Christmas elves,' she said, ten minutes later, once she'd explained how to make the decorations, 'I want to see the most creative chains you can come up with. Nothing is off limits, apart from your clothes – and your parents' clothes.' There were giggles, a couple of groans from the older children, then the space became a hive of activity. The adults supervised the use of scissors, and the sound of slicing – and ripping – paper filled the air.

'I want mine to be pink,' a sandy-haired boy said to his mum.

'OK, then. What about this paper?' She held up a roll of wrapping paper covered in flamingos.

'Yes!' the little boy shouted, and then, when his mum explained what birds they were, spent a long time trying to say the word *flamingos* before he gave up and began cutting strips.

'I thought you said more parents were coming,' Becky said, walking over to stand next to Ollie. 'This isn't a great ratio of children to helpers.'

Ollie frowned. 'I think a couple of parents have been drop-offs, when they originally said they'd stay.' She watched a young girl pick up a pair of scissors, her small hands struggling to cope with the finger holes, before a mum swooped in and helped her slide them on. 'It's looking OK to me,' she added. None of the children had to work alone for long, which was surely the main thing.

'To *you*,' Becky said sharply. 'Everything looks OK to you, though. That's the problem!' She sighed, muttered, 'For fuck's sake,' and strode to the other side of the room. Ollie went to help two brothers with their black and silver paper chains, an unsettled feeling taking up residence in her gut.

For the rest of the session she flitted between tables, praising and helping, finding the right colour or image in the old magazines she'd collected. Everyone seemed to be enjoying themselves, chains of links covering the tables and spilling onto the floor. Ollie was struggling to see the problem.

'Is it Christmas now?' a little girl called Amy asked Becky.

'Nearly,' she said. 'Have you been thinking about what you'd like from Santa?'

Amy held up her paper chain, which had six links. 'Some of these!'

Becky smiled. 'You know what? You can take those home with you. You made them, and you can hang them up wherever you'd like to.'

Amy's look of wonder seemed to light up the whole room, and Ollie had to give Becky credit: she didn't think anyone else would notice that, under the surface, she was furious.

She stayed busy, helping the children cut paper and glue their strips together. Whenever she felt a prickling sensation on her neck, she thought it was probably Becky watching her. She was hurrying between tables, carrying a roll of blue, mermaid-design wrapping paper, when Thea put a hand on her arm.

'This was such a good idea,' she said. 'Paper chains are the most fun decorations: I think all the adults are having a huge nostalgia hit.'

'Becky says there aren't enough of them. Adults,' she clarified, when Thea looked confused.

'She was happy when we went through the list earlier.'

'A couple of parents haven't stayed, just dropped their children off. The ratio's wrong, apparently.'

Thea squeezed her arm. 'Let's talk about it afterwards, OK?'

'OK.' Ollie nodded. She felt slightly sick. The situation reminded her of when she'd returned to Grady Books after her accident, and Ruth had started to question her decisions. It was the eroding of people's trust in her – although with Becky, she'd never had it in the first place. But events, groups of people having fun and being inspired, were supposed to be her forte. 'I just want to help make the bookshop successful,' she said to Thea. 'I'm honestly trying my best.'

'I know that,' Thea replied. 'You're enthusiastic and full of energy, and everything will be trial and error to begin with. We'll talk to Becky: we'll sort this out. Are you settling in OK, in the wider town? Port Karadow is a wonderful place to live.'

'It's so different to how I imagined it would be,' Ollie admitted, 'and I did a lot of daydreaming once I'd made the decision to move here. It's different in a good way, though!' She thought about Max kissing her on the sofa, the fire that burned between them – like their own, personal Yule log – and how, with every new encounter, it was getting harder for her to keep her hands off him. She could tell that Max felt the same, but was respecting her request to take things slowly.

'I'm so glad,' Thea said. 'This is going to be my first Christmas here, and I can't wait.'

'Are you and Ben doing a lot of partying?'

Thea grinned. 'I wouldn't say partying, exactly, but we're going to make the most of everything that's happening in town. I'm going out for drinks and pub grub with Ben, Meredith and Finn tomorrow night, actually. Do you want to come?'

'Oh,' Ollie said. 'I don't know . . .'

'You could bring Max too? I know you and he have become quite friendly.'

Ollie thanked her lucky stars that when her cheeks heated, her skin colour didn't change much, otherwise she would be a Belisha beacon right now, and someone might position her on the harbour wall to stop boats from crashing into it.

'I'll ask him,' she said, aiming for casual. 'I don't know if he'll be free, but I'd love to join you.'

'Fab! I'll let the others know. We're going to the Sea Shanty, one of the pubs in town. It's impossible to get a table at the Happy Shack in December.'

'Not sure I'd be up for bumping into Marcus Belrose on a night out anyway,' Ollie said, her smile slipping. She didn't need any more reminders of her recent failures. 'Pub grub and a few drinks sounds perfect.'

'Excellent. We'd better get back to the gluing, do you think?'

They returned to the throng, helping small hands make Christmas paper chains, while Port Karadow twinkled in all its December glory outside the windows.

*   *   *

An hour later, the children who had been so frantically productive, little fingers covered in glue and paper links rustling, were silent. They were sitting on the floor, facing Thea, who was on the sofa – the elegant mint-green throw covering it – her back to the window. It was close to five o'clock and almost dark, only a faint line of amber above the horizon in the distance, the lights of the town a scatter-gun of gold against the shadowy buildings.

The children had mugs of warm hot chocolate sprinkled with marshmallows, the accompanying adults had cups of tea or coffee, and all was quiet while Thea read them *The Polar Express*, her steady voice ringing out, perfectly creating the soothing, train-like rhythm of the story. It was clear to Ollie that she'd done this before – even *she* was captivated, and her thoughts had, until that moment, been in a tailspin: would Max want to join her and the others at the pub? Would Becky *ever* be happy with what she did?

As the story came to an end, she and Becky got out the paper bags decorated with stars, snowmen and Christmas trees that she'd ordered online, and together they helped the children carefully pack their decorations, coiling their chains of shimmery links into the bags.

'You can't just let helpers not turn up,' Becky whispered, her smile fixed in place. 'Not when it's a kids' event.'

'They left without telling me,' Ollie said. 'When they booked their tickets, I logged the parents who said they would stay and help out, and we had enough people. I have their emails.'

'Emails don't mean anything. Why didn't you check everyone against the list when they arrived with their children? Something could have gone seriously wrong.'

234

'It didn't, though—'

'That's not the point!' Becky spun to face her. Her smile had gone, and her eyes were glittering with anger. 'You can't just do whatever you feel like and expect everything to work out. That's not how the real world works!'

Ollie floundered, searching for a reply. 'I'm sorry,' she said eventually. 'I'll be more careful in future.'

'Next time, we'll sign people in together, OK? Make sure we're not putting our customers, or the bookshop, at risk. There are rules about this sort of thing, you know. God,' she added, 'even I didn't think you'd be this stupid.'

'Right,' Ollie murmured, because what, really, could she say to that?

They went back to lowering paper chains into bags, Ollie's heart pounding erratically. It was as if she could feel her confidence, usually so robust, shrivelling to nothing. She wondered if anyone could see beyond her painted-on smile to the shame that was slowly filling her up, drip-drip-drip, like water from a broken tap.

Chapter Twenty-Six

The Sea Shanty was full of character, with hardwood floors, a warped but varnished bar, the chairs round the dark wood tables a mismatch of styles and ages, but all softened with plush cushions. There were framed photographs covering the walls, a mixture of colour, black-and-white and sepia, showing Port Karadow through the ages: a row of fishermen, arms crossed, in front of their boats at the harbour; Main Street looking similar to today, but with people in Victorian dress strolling along the cobbles; the Old Post House when it was the town's post office rather than A New Chapter, a young couple standing outside.

The pub-friendly smells of beer and chips lingered in the air, a jukebox played sporadically in the background, and there was a rowdy, pre-Christmas atmosphere that made their table of six – nine, if Ollie included Henry Tilney, Meredith's beagle Crumble and Ben's dog Scooter, lying beneath it – have to raise their voices.

'How do you like Port Karadow?' Finn asked, once they had greeted each other and clinked their glasses together. Ollie felt like she knew Finn and Ben a little now, since they'd been at some of her events. Events that, for tonight, she was trying very hard to put out of her mind.

'I love it a whole lot,' she admitted. 'It's busier than I imagined it would be at this time of year. I had the impression that a lot of seaside towns shut down over winter, but if anything, Port Karadow has more life now than when I arrived in October.'

'Christmas is a big thing here,' Meredith said, and Finn kissed the top of her head, his grin unabashed.

'What was that smile for?' Ollie asked.

'Meredith used not to be a fan of the festivities,' Ben told her, and Ollie remembered Meredith admitting as much, when they'd been talking in Cornish Keepsakes one day. 'Finn brought her round last year, with some kind of wacky Christmas challenge.'

Meredith sat up straighter. 'I brought myself round, thank you very much. Finn might have been . . . instrumental in showing me the positive side of mince pies and bells on woolly hats, but if I hadn't wanted to change, I wouldn't have.'

'It was like Christmas rehab,' Finn said, which earned him a glare from his girlfriend.

'Shouldn't that be *anti*-Christmas rehab?' Thea pointed out. 'Otherwise you would have been weaning Meredith *off* Christmas.'

'Semantics.' Finn waved a dismissive hand.

'Not really,' Thea said, frowning. 'You're saying the opposite of what you mean.'

'Thea is a word pedant,' Finn explained to Ollie.

'I care about language, as I'm sure Ollie does, also being a book lover.'

'I do,' Ollie said, 'and it *should* be anti-Christmas rehab. That's not being pedantic at all. Scrooge rehab, maybe.'

Finn sat back in his chair. 'Fine. But whatever the right term is, Meredith is fully in the swing of things this year, and I think the pageant's going to be even bigger.'

'It was fairly impressive last year,' Max said, wrapping his hands around his pint glass. Ollie got stuck gazing at his long fingers, and when she looked up, she saw that Thea was watching her closely, an amused expression on her face. 'Meredith worked with the council to organise it,' Max told her. 'Her friend Anisha is on the planning team, and together they put on this incredible event. There were stalls, a parade, a carol concert. I told you that Meredith sings in a choir, didn't I?'

'You sang in front of the entire town?' Ollie asked, turning to her. Meredith nodded, and she and Finn exchanged a look that she couldn't interpret. 'I read about the pageant on the website. It sounded amazing.'

'And A New Chapter's going to be part of it this year,' Thea said. 'With Sophia Forsythe-Hartley.'

'Oh yes,' Ben said. 'A month ago, I had never heard of this person. Now I'm reading one of her books.'

'You are?' Meredith asked, laughing.

'Thea suggested I get myself clued up before the event. This is clearly a big deal.'

'Are you enjoying it?' Finn asked.

Ben nodded, his expression thoughtful. 'It's not my usual genre, but it's already got me gripped, and the sense of atmosphere – the descriptions of Cornwall – are spot on.'

'Interesting,' Finn said. 'Maybe I need to get in on the act.'

'You should start with the first book in the series,' Ollie said, 'because it makes much more sense if you read them in order. We've got good stock in the shop at the moment.'

This event *had* to go well. She had clearly messed up with the decorations workshop, even though Thea hadn't seemed as concerned as Becky about her mistake, and she was only just back in her boss's good books after the cooking disaster. She shouldn't be assigning so much meaning to it – she thought of what Liam had said about finding meaning everywhere – but she was already seeing Sophia Forsythe-Hartley as her Christmas saviour.

'This launch is going to be the talk of the town,' Ben said. 'I was doing a job at Cecily Talbot's house the other day, and—'

'Cecily Talbot the Instagram influencer?' Ollie asked, surprised.

'Yup. She lives a couple of miles out of Port Karadow. Anyway,' he went on, 'we were chatting, I mentioned Thea and the bookshop, and she said she'd already bought her ticket for the Sophia event. It looks like it's going to be at least as big as the Christmas pageant.'

Ollie sat back. 'Cecily Talbot lives *here*, and she knows about our event?'

'And, obviously, the bookshop,' Thea said. 'I meant to tell you, but it's been so busy the last few days, I forgot.'

'Wow, though.' Ollie took a large sip of wine, and felt Max's hand on her waist.

'OK?' he whispered in her ear. His breath tickled her skin in a way that made her feel warm all over, but couldn't quite dispel the sudden flare of anxiety. She'd come to rely on Max over the last few weeks, but she'd been too ashamed to tell him about the dressing down Becky had given her. She had made an obvious, careless mistake, and she couldn't bear him thinking badly of her.

'Course.' She turned to give him a reassuring smile. He was so close, and he looked so concerned and so handsome, his dark brows lowered, his lips slightly pursed. Her brain was a few seconds behind her body, and before even she'd realised what she was doing, she'd leaned in and kissed him. As soon as they touched, she was reluctant to move away, and what started out as a peck became purposeful and lingering. When she pulled back, Max was looking at her with surprise and – she hoped she wasn't misinter-preting – happiness, and her heart was pounding.

She turned back to the rest of the table, and saw that they were all grinning. Thea caught her eye and winked. The day before, her boss had described Ollie and Max as 'quite friendly', but it seemed she had already suspected it was more than that.

So much for taking it slowly, she thought, as Max went to get another round, and the conversation turned to festive plans and menus, and the horrifying idea of a Christmas Day swim in the sea. Still, it wasn't her fault, was it? She wasn't sure anyone would be able to resist the charm, the looks, the downright goodness of Max Holden. She was just lucky that he seemed to like her, too. In the same way Meredith had needed Scrooge rehab, perhaps Ollie needed a sanctuary away from Max, before her feelings for him burrowed right through her and settled in for the long haul.

The problem was, she had absolutely no inclination or desire to stay away from him. It was already far too late for that.

'Are you sure you want to walk me home?' Ollie asked, when they'd split into pairs and said their goodnights outside the pub. The cold December air was hazy with mist, a quiet settling over the town the further from the centre they got.

'I'm not letting you walk home alone,' Max said. 'I'm fully aware that you're an independent woman who can take care of herself, but the walk to Foxglove Barn is creepy enough in the dark, and with the added fog, it's terrifying.'

'So what you're saying,' Ollie replied, nudging him then slipping her arm through his, 'is that you're walking me home because, if you were in my position you'd be frightened, so you assume I am, too.'

'Exactly,' Max said, laughing. 'Also, I wouldn't be able to look at myself in the mirror if I left you here and let you walk alone.'

'I realised late last night that we missed the ghost battle at St Ethel's church.'

'That was last night?'

'Yup.' But she hadn't been in the mood after the decorations workshop, anyway.

'Shit,' Max said. 'I guess there's always next year.'

'And plenty more legends,' Ollie pointed out. They were quiet for a few moments, then she said, 'What about when we get to mine? You're going to leave me and do the walk – that you've already admitted you're scared of – back to yours, all alone. What about *me* looking at *myself* in the mirror?'

'I'll be fine,' Max said. 'You're my priority.'

Unable to come up with a pithy response, Ollie let her arm drop and laced her fingers between his instead. Max's skin was warm – gloveless, as usual – and she squeezed his hand, feeling the thrill of their touch go through her. She could think of one way that neither of them would have to do any solo walking, but she didn't want to overstep.

'It was a good night, wasn't it?' she said instead.

'It was great,' Max agreed. 'I knew them all a little before tonight, Meredith the best because her gift shop is so close to Sea Brew, but they're all good company.'

'You didn't know Finn and Ben that well? You seemed so comfortable with them.'

'They're both quite new to the area. Finn's been coming to Port Karadow for years, but only moved here properly last Christmas, and Ben bought his cottage in February, I think. It's probably my fault that it's taken this long for us to get together, but sometimes running a café, all the stuff behind the scenes, the days end up being longer than you expect. I have you to thank for tonight.'

'You don't really,' she said, as they reached the end of a residential street, the road ahead a fathomless, countryside dark. Ollie was suddenly extra glad of Max's presence, of his chivalry. 'Thea invited me tonight, and suggested I invited you, too. She had the impression we were good friends.'

'I wonder what that impression is now?'

Ollie grinned. 'Maybe they think we're just *really* good friends, or that kissing on the lips is something us la-di-da London bookish-folk do.'

Max laughed. 'I'd prefer it if they thought we were together.'

Ollie sucked in a breath. When she'd released it, she said, 'You do?'

'Don't you?'

They were in almost total darkness now, the road they were walking down only turning from pitch black to shades of grey as Ollie's eyes adjusted to the gloom. The temperature was dropping, and her breath was coming out in clouds, mingling with the swirling mist. She thought of the abandoned church, the ghostly figures that had, perhaps, materialised last night to fight a long-forgotten battle. She pivoted on her heel to face Max, and he stopped abruptly.

'I do,' she said, pressing herself into him, speaking the words against his lips. 'I want everyone to know we're together.'

'Good.' Max angled his head down and feathered his lips against hers. As he deepened the kiss, he wrapped his strong arms around her, sheltering her from the night.

Ollie couldn't remember the last time she'd felt so safe, or so desired. She couldn't remember the last time a man had made her feel so untethered, so desperate for his touch. Being in his arms, letting herself be kissed and kissing Max back, with the feel of his lips and his taste, his delicious scent, consuming her, she wasn't afraid of the dark anymore.

Chapter Twenty-Seven

By the time they made it back to Foxglove Barn, Ollie was tingling with anticipation. Even before their kiss on the roadside, she had decided that she didn't want Max to walk all the way home after dropping her off. Even if she hadn't been fully committed to their relationship – and it was a bit alarming how much she already was – it wouldn't have been a kind thing to do. The sofas in the barn were huge and comfortable, and she had spare blankets and pillows, so there were options if he wasn't feeling the same way she was.

The glow of the barn's outside lights, the old, proud farmhouse gleaming through the mist, and the sense of comfort she got from seeing them, made her realise how much she already thought of this place as home. Henry hurried ahead, tugging on his lead, and Ollie let herself be pulled, pulling Max in turn.

'What's the rush?' he asked, hurrying to keep up with her.

'I don't know, better ask my dog. Oh, hang on . . .' When they got close to the doorstep, Ollie realised there was something on it. A delivery that had arrived while she'd been out? But evening deliveries were unusual, and she couldn't think of anything she was waiting for. 'What's this?'

Henry was sniffing it, his tail wagging.

'It's a . . . Oh my God!' She laughed as she bent over, examining the large, solid log resting on her doorstep, a red ribbon tied around one end, a green ribbon around the other. She felt the bark, rough and cool beneath her palm. It smelled of the forest, of rich soil and damp. There was a tag hanging off the green ribbon, and Ollie crouched so she could read it.

Life is too short to spend every moment working or worrying. Mxx

She looked up at him. He was wearing a distinctly sheepish expression.

'I dropped it off here before I met you at the pub. I hadn't . . .' He rubbed the back of his neck. 'I didn't think ahead: the fact that you'd be walking back here on your own, so I'd end up coming with you. I wanted you to find it and light it tomorrow, spend your Saturday doing things for you, instead of researching book events or whatever it is I'm sure you've got planned.'

Ollie stood up and slid her fingers inside the pockets of his jacket, so she could drag him closer. 'Are you saying that you got home from work, then drove here – after you knew

I would have left to get to the pub – put this log on my doorstep, drove back home, then walked to the Sea Shanty?'

Max nodded.

'And before that, did you chop down the tree yourself? In the forest, with an axe? Then take it home and tie fancy ribbons around it? Because, if so, that's the most conflicting mix of Alpha male and softly sentimental that I've ever come across, and honestly, it's making my heart flutter.'

Max laughed, the sound low and gravelly, which made the fluttering – that she hadn't been lying about – intensify. 'I went into the woods and found the Yule log,' he admitted. 'I didn't want to cut down a tree if I didn't have to, and this one was waiting for me, as if it was fate.'

Ollie nodded. 'But would you have cut down a tree for me, if you hadn't found one?'

He bent his head towards hers. 'I would.'

'Right.' She sounded breathless, as if *she* had chopped down a tree. 'And this whole relaxing thing: the thing I'm supposed to do while the log's burning?'

'Yes?' Their sentences were only 50 per cent words now, the rest coming out as sharp exhalations. Henry was pawing at the door, and Ollie stepped back to unlock it, to release her dog from his harness and let him inside.

She turned back to Max. 'What constitutes relaxing, exactly? I mean, if I were to kiss you while the log was burning . . . Then, if I wanted to take that kiss further, maybe take off your coat, or even more layers?'

'Mmm hmm?'

'If I were to give in, and touch you in all the ways I've been imagining over the last few weeks, would that be against the rules of the Yule log?'

246

Max stared down at her. She thought that his green eyes were a shade darker than usual. 'You know,' he said, 'I don't think any of those things would be.'

'No?'

He shook his head. 'Sex is a release, isn't it? Considered a good way of de-stressing.'

It was taking all her willpower to keep their conversation going. 'Is that what we'd be doing, then? De-stressing?'

'Among other things,' Max whispered. 'Except that, all the times I've thought about kissing you, touching you, it hasn't been because I wanted to relieve stress. I have yoga for that.'

'What has it been about, then?' Ollie pulled him forwards, so they were standing in her doorway, the backs of her ankles pressed up against the Yule log.

'It's been about giving in to my feelings for you,' Max said. 'Seeing if being with you physically is as good as I've been imagining; if it brings me as much pleasure as I get spending time with you. And, mostly, it's about seeing if I can make you feel good: as good as you make me feel.'

'Those are all excellent reasons,' she said, her lips close to his. 'They chime with my own, in fact.'

'That's . . . I'm glad. So do you want to take the log inside and light it?'

'Yes.' She nodded. 'Yes please.'

'OK.' When Max's next kiss came, it was so full of purpose, so all-consuming, that Ollie was surprised they were able to pause long enough to make it inside, that she had the forethought to settle Henry in his bed with a dog treat and a fresh bowl of water.

Max put the log in her fireplace, pulled the ribbons off, surrounded it with crumpled newspaper and lit it. They stood, watching as the paper caught fire, and the flames, after a few moments, licked across to the thick trunk of wood, the scent of forest filling the air.

Then Ollie turned to Max, stretching up as he bent his head, their lips meeting, his fingers tracing the bare skin of her back, underneath her top. She felt herself burning, melting at his touch, as if the fire in the grate had reached out and sparked her too. As they gave in to their feelings, as they lost their clothes and inhibitions, Ollie discovered that Max, just as she'd imagined, just as he'd hoped, could make her feel *so* good: better than she could remember feeling for a long, long time.

When Monday morning arrived, Ollie was still in a blissful stupor that she had thought nothing could break through. Max had stayed with her all weekend, only returning home briefly on Saturday afternoon to make sure his cat was fed and watered. He told her that, most of the time, Oxo did his own thing anyway, and he knew of at least two neighbours whose houses he visited, so he was never starved of food or affection.

While he was gone, Ollie had spent an hour at the farmhouse, typing up Liam's manuscript while he sorted through one of his bookshelves, scowling and grumping as he flung books into a box.

Ollie had allowed his behaviour to penetrate her fug of happiness.

'What are those?' she'd asked.

'Books.' It was uncharacteristic of Liam to be so short with her.

'I can see that,' she'd said softly. 'What are you doing with them?'

'These ones serve no purpose. They're going to the Oxfam in Truro.'

'What are they?'

'Just silly stories. They're decades old, out of print and irrelevant. Don't concern yourself with them. Tell me what you and Max have been up to.'

Ollie had smiled stupidly. 'There's not much I can say without going into details I'm not inclined to share, and I'm certain you don't want to hear.'

'That good, eh? He's a decent young man, that Max. Not had an easy trot of it, but that makes you appreciate the good parts even more, doesn't it?'

'It does,' Ollie had agreed. She had thought back to the night before, when they'd stripped each other's clothes off and made it to her bedroom, and she'd hesitated, her hand against Max's chest.

'What is it?' he'd asked. 'If you want to stop, if you've changed your mind, then we can—'

'It's not that at all,' she'd rushed. 'Just . . . is this OK? Can you, after your illness—'

He'd placed one hand over hers where it rested on his hot skin, over his heart, and tipped her chin up, making sure she was meeting his gaze. 'I'm fine,' he said. 'I promise. I will let you know if I need to stop, or go slow, but I can't see that happening unless it's to make this better between us. You don't need to worry, OK?' He'd pressed a kiss to her forehead, and Ollie had felt her admiration for him, her attraction to him, swell inside her, as if her own heart was expanding now that she'd let him into it.

Max, she'd realised, as she typed up a particularly emotional part of Liam's memoir, about his grandfather dying and the grief that had snuck up on him unexpectedly, lived life to the full. He was always positive, as if each day he got to welcome in and see out was a bonus. She could learn so much from him, and thought that everyone should behave that way: celebrating every joyful thing, however tiny, because nobody knew what was around the corner.

When Max had got back from town, Liam had invited him in, and the three of them had sat around his farmhouse table, eating chunks of cheese on crusty bread and drinking a red wine that he'd produced from his wine cellar, and which he told them was a rare vintage.

On Sunday, Ollie and Max had lived in a cocoon. The Yule log was still burning in the fireplace, so, he had informed her, they weren't allowed to do anything but spend time together. So that's what they had done, eventually taking Henry for a walk in the fields surrounding the farm, even the cold, persistent drizzle unable to burst their contented bubble.

So when Monday came around, the realisation that they had to get up, leave the barn and go into work, was a shock.

'Are you coming back here tonight?' Ollie asked, kissing Max's shoulder.

'If you want me to.' He rolled over so he was facing her, and rubbed his eyes.

'I very much do.'

'I'd better check on Oxo, but I'll do that this morning when I go home to change.'

'Perfecto. And then we can—'

She was interrupted by her phone blaring noisily from the bedside table. She turned, fumbling to pick it up. The alarm clock told her that it was just after seven.

'Hello?' she said, feeling a spike of fear that something had happened to one of her parents, or Melissa in Portugal.

'Ollie? It's Arabella March, Sophia Forsythe-Hartley's editor. I wondered if you had time to go through a couple of details about the event with me?'

Ollie gave Max an exasperated look. He parried it with a grin, then began tracing lazy circles on her hip with his finger.

'O-of course,' she said. She glared at Max, but he just made his touch more ticklish. 'What is it you'd like to check?'

'There are a few risk assessment concerns that Sophia and I have, but it shouldn't be a problem to clear those up *at all*. Just best to nip them in the bud now, before the event.'

'Risk assessments?' This time she and Max swapped perplexed frowns. 'Of course. I'm at home right now, so if you could email me a list, I can look into it as soon as I'm with Thea at the bookshop. I can get back to you before lunch, as long as I don't need to chase down any more details to answer your questions.'

'Fabulous! I'll get those through to you right now.'

'Great! Thanks. Good to speak to you, Arabella.'

'You too, darling. Bye for now.'

After she'd hung up, Ollie stared at her phone.

'Everything OK?' Max asked. 'Who wanted to know about risk assessments?'

'Arabella, Sophia's editor. I'm sure it's fine – they just want to check everything's in place before the event later this month.'

'Whatever questions they throw at you, you're more than up to the task.' He leaned over and kissed the spot he'd been drawing on, and Ollie happily surrendered to his touch. After a whole weekend together, she didn't think she'd ever tire of being this close to him. Everything, she decided, was wonderful. Arabella's call wasn't anything to worry about, and if she worked hard enough, she could get herself in Becky's good books. After all, she'd never shied away from a challenge, and she wanted life in the bookshop to be as harmonious as her home life was starting to become. Being here in Port Karadow, she decided, as Max trailed his lips lower down her body, was nothing short of blissful.

Chapter Twenty-Eight

Thirteen days of Max, Ollie thought, as people filed into A New Chapter, the smell of cinnamon lingering in the air from the mini wreaths that dotted the space, joining the excited chatter of people who were anticipating a fun evening, but weren't quite sure what they were getting. Thirteen days since she'd given into her feelings for him, and he'd shown her that he was as committed, as besotted, as she was. And, she realised, it was only nine days until the Christmas pageant, and their big event with Sophia Forsythe-Hartley.

'Are you trying to pull apart the decorations?' Becky had an amused look on her face, but her tone had an edge which, by now, Ollie was very familiar with.

'Oh!' She let go of the mini wreath that, during her absent-minded musings, she had started to dismantle. 'Shitballs.'

Becky smiled. 'Just don't start pulling pages out of the books, and we should be fine.'

Ollie returned her smile, but couldn't help the slight sinking feeling in her stomach.

The wreath-making had been their second, more ambitious crafting event, and it had attracted a lot of attention after word of the paper chain workshop got out. They'd put a booking form on the website, and had filled the spaces in a day. Ollie had checked and double-checked that the parents who said they were staying really meant it – had probably made a few of them worry that she was losing her marbles – and had ticked everyone off on her list as they arrived.

Since then, Becky had been noticeably warmer with her, and she didn't want to do anything to upset that, because the better they worked together, the more the bookshop would benefit. Unfortunately, some of it might be out of her hands.

Arabella had been in touch several more times since she'd asked about the bookshop risk assessments. Ollie had sent her the information without telling Thea, mostly because she didn't want to worry her boss that, after their successful Zoom meeting, Sophia's editor was suddenly beginning to question things. And she'd been right to not tell her, she decided, because the challenges were *still* coming. Only that morning she'd had a phone call from Arabella, asking about the proposed rail enhancements on the west coast line in the week before Christmas.

'It says there's a possibility of thirty-minute delays on all journeys to Cornwall,' Arabella had said. Ollie had hurried into the stockroom, glad that Thea and Becky were busy with customers.

'I'll look, hang on.' She had searched for the information while the little green lozenge at the top of her screen told her the phone call was still active. 'It says it's only until the twentieth,' she'd said. 'Our event is on the twenty-third.'

'You know how these things can drag on,' Arabella had replied.

'Isn't Sophia due to arrive at lunchtime? I expect you've got her a flexible ticket, and if she gets an earlier train, that should give her some extra leeway in case there's a hold-up.'

There had been an uncomfortable pause, then Arabella had said, 'I'll see what we can do. She's leaving London frighteningly early as it is.'

'Let me know if I can help from this end,' Ollie had said brightly, though she didn't think asking Great Western Railway to change their entire schedule of track repairs was within her control.

Now, as customers arrived for the first Book Wars clash, she couldn't help the nagging feeling that Arabella was trying to find fault with their event; reasons that it wasn't the perfect launch venue for her author after all. If that happened, Ollie honestly didn't know what she'd do.

'Mum, Mum!' An eager voice broke through her reverie, and Ollie looked up to see Dylan, and then someone who made her forget all her author-related worries in an instant. Max returned her smile, his green eyes keeping her captive.

'What is it, sweetheart?' Becky asked.

'Max said he'd let me work in the café with him after Christmas.'

Max held his hands up. 'That's not *quite* what I said. I'm not advocating child labour.'

'He said I could come and see how it all works, that he'd show me how to make a cappuccino and how he does orders and stuff.'

'If he's interested,' Max said to Becky. 'He can hang out with me for an hour or two. Though he said he wants to open a restaurant, so I wonder if Marcus would be a better fit.'

Becky stroked her son's hair. 'You're very young for work experience, but if it's just a couple of hours, I can't see the harm.'

'Max is the coolest,' Dylan said, then glanced at him, his cheeks reddening. 'I'd rather find out from him than that Marcus guy.'

'Only if it's OK with you,' Max said to Becky. 'And I thought it would be better in January, after the Christmas rush is over.'

'Thank you,' Becky said. 'That's very kind of you. Come on, Dylan, let's get you a drink.' She led her son towards the stairs.

Max put his hands on Ollie's waist and kissed her. 'Hey.'

'Hello. That was very nice of you.'

'I'm always happy to help out, and Dylan's a good kid. I'm surprised he's here, though.'

'Becky said he could come as long as he's on his best behaviour. We should be wrapped up by eight, and I've told Finn and Maisie that they're not allowed to swear while they're pitching their books.'

'Which ones are they doing, do you know?'

Ollie grinned. 'Because it's nearly Christmas, they're both doing books called *The Snowman*. Maisie is advocating for the book by Joe Nesbo, and Finn's trying to sell us on Raymond Briggs.'

Max blinked a couple of times, and she watched, gleeful, as her words sunk in. 'Fuck off,' he said, quietly. 'A twisted crime thriller against a much-loved children's book?'

'I said *no* swearing, Max,' she chided. 'Isn't it great, though? I can't wait! Do you want wine? We've got tiny little glasses of wine.'

'I would love a tiny little glass of wine. This is really what you expected for Book Wars?'

'It's better than I'd hoped,' Ollie said, taking his hand and pulling him through the crowd, smiling and saying hello to people as they passed. The bookshop was getting fuller, customers browsing the shelves, slow to make their way upstairs. Exactly as it should be, she thought, as she heard the beep of someone tapping their credit card against the reader to make a purchase. She took two glasses of wine from Andrea, and handed one to Max.

'The point of Book Wars is that anything goes,' she explained. 'It makes sense to have a link between the titles, but that link can be anything – film adaptations with the same actor, same publication day, whatever – and if the books themselves are completely different, then even better. The challenger has to say why their book is best, why it deserves to win the face-off, and having a murder book against a children's book is perfect.'

'Finn's doing the Raymond Briggs?' Max raised his eyebrows. Ollie nodded.

'Then it's going to be hilarious.' He sipped his wine, and looked at her over the rim of the glass.

'What?' Ollie asked, laughing. Whenever she was around Max, she felt as if her cells were shifting. It was as if, being in his presence, every part of her was happy, but also reaching: she wanted to be better when she was with him; she wanted to be the best person she could be, for him. She wanted to keep him forever.

'Did I ever tell you that you're a genius?' he said.

'Um, definitely not. And I would have called you out on it, too, because it's *so* far from the truth.'

He sighed. 'Do you really want me to go through all the reasons I think the label of genius applies to you?'

Ollie leaned closer. 'Are some of them things you shouldn't be mentioning in a packed bookshop?' They had stayed with each other every night since that first Friday, and Ollie was already dangerously close to never wanting to wake up alone again.

'Possibly,' he murmured. 'Maybe we should talk about it later.'

'As long as I'm not tiring you out too much.' She fluttered her eyelashes at him.

'Never,' he said adamantly.

She'd meant it as a joke, but she realised he did look tired. His skin, which she automatically thought of as quite tanned even though it was winter, seemed paler, and he had dark smudges under his eyes. But the café was busy: it was a frantic time of year for everyone. Perhaps she should get another Yule log, and that weekend they should do nothing but loaf and watch Christmas films.

'Look at this,' Max said, gesturing around him. 'Look how packed A New Chapter is at six o'clock on a cold Wednesday in December. It's like a party.'

Ollie accepted his change of subject, deciding that she would ask him later how he was really feeling. 'Book events should always be a party. Books should be celebrated every chance we get.'

'I hope Thea realises how lucky she is to have you,' Max said quietly. 'I do.'

'I was just thinking the same about you,' Ollie whispered, her heart squeezing. But she couldn't help worrying that Thea might not think she was particularly lucky if her new employee couldn't follow through with the grand launch event she had promised to arrange.

Twenty minutes later, the events space was full. The spotlights were turned down low, only the ones above the stage at full power. The room was adorned with mini wreaths and paper chains, and Becky had put sprigs of holly on the shelves, nestled between the display books. Tonight, those display books were copies of *The Snowman*, both the heart-warming, emotional children's tale and the terrifying thriller. Ollie hoped they would shift a lot of both.

The space smelled of coffee, as it always did up here now, and beyond the tall windows, Port Karadow glittered in the darkness. Ollie took a moment to absorb it: this event, that she'd been imagining even before she'd moved to Cornwall, finally happening here, in A New Chapter. A small part of her wondered what would go wrong this time, but she realised that if she started to think like that, then she was lost. She had to hold on to her confidence: she couldn't let this job go the way of her last one.

Finn and Maisie stood on the modest stage, facing the crowd. Finn was wearing a Santa hat with a bell on the end, and a Christmas jumper depicting a snowy scene with skiing penguins, and Maisie was wearing a long, flowing dress with a peony pattern.

Ollie jumped onto the stage between them, and the murmuring dissolved into silence.

'Good evening,' she said, 'and welcome – or welcome *back* – to A New Chapter. Thank you for joining us on this crisp, pre-Christmas evening for the first round . . .' she paused, drawing out the moment, '. . . of Book Wars! On my left we have Maisie, who will be extolling the virtues of *The Snowman* by Jo Nesbo, a crime thriller about missing women and girls, and on my right we have Finn.' Finn gave a little bow, and a few people chuckled. '*He* will be trying to get you on side with his choice of *The Snowman* by Raymond Briggs, which features, you'll be unsurprised to hear, absolutely *no* missing women and girls, but actually, when you think about it, a missing boy.' This time, the laughter was louder and more widespread.

'Two more different books you couldn't hope to find, and I am honestly *buzzing* for this competition! How can you compare the two? How will you, our audience, decide between them? Because we're putting ourselves in your hands tonight: you will be the ones to cast your vote, and choose who makes it through to the next round. Earlier, we got Finn and Maisie to do a Rock, Paper, Scissors best of three, because we are the epitome of sophistication here at A New Chapter, and Finn is going first. Finn?' She gestured to him. 'Tell us why we need to vote for your chosen book.'

With that, Ollie hopped off the platform, allowing Finn to take centre stage, and went to stand at the side of the room.

Finn rubbed his hands together and offered his audience a wide smile, his blond curls glinting beneath the spotlights.

'Good evening, Port Karadowans,' he said. 'I'm going to start by setting the scene for you. Imagine, if you will, finally making it home after this event, hurrying up the stairs to your sleepy children, who you left with the incredibly reliable babysitter, hoping it's not too late to read them a bedtime story. Their eyelids are flickering, you turn to the picture book on the nightstand, finding the place where you left off last time. You flick through the pages to the part where the boy looks out of the window at the snowman he created, full of wonder that it's still standing in the dark, wintry night, and then his eyes fall on . . . a set of bloody footprints.'

A couple of people gasped, and Ollie could see that everyone was hanging on his words. His voice was loud and clear, showing no sign of nerves. She had guessed, the moment he said he wanted to take part in her Book Wars competition, that he'd be brilliant.

'Your precious time with your child,' Finn went on, sadness edging into his tone, 'gone. Because someone took something as innocent, as wholesome, as a winter snowman, and turned it into a story about death. Is that really what you want?'

Ollie could see Meredith staring at her boyfriend open-mouthed, and Dylan, looking positively gleeful at being there, turned to grin up at his mum. Becky smiled at him and put her hand on his shoulder. Maisie was watching Finn closely, her steely gaze suggesting that, while Finn had started well, shocking the crowd and making them laugh, she had something good to follow with. Ollie couldn't wait to find out what it was.

Thea was standing against the back wall, her arms folded. She looked relaxed, as if she was enjoying Finn's pitch, but Ollie knew she would be watching carefully, assessing, deciding whether this event was right for her bookshop. Next to Thea was Ben, and next to Ben was Max. When

Ollie's eyes drifted to him, as they so often did, she saw he was already looking at her.

He mouthed something that it took her a moment to process, her whole body tingling with pleasure when she did: *You're brilliant.*

It was almost as good as if he'd mouthed those three little words, the ones that, despite the newness of their relationship, she was finding it hard not to say when they were alone together. She settled for mouthing back, *You are, too,* then returned her focus to the stage, where Finn was transforming a beloved children's book into a bloodthirsty nightmare to prove that crime and misery weren't what you needed at Christmas. Ollie's heart was so full of hope and happiness that, even though she loved a gory thriller, right now she had to agree with Meredith's boyfriend.

Afterwards, when the events space was beginning to empty, customers clutching copies of their preferred *Snowman* book – and in some cases, both – Ollie decided that this event, at least, could not have gone any better. No young children with scissors and not enough parental help, no little fires anywhere – let alone everywhere – no real-life ghosts threatening to send their customers away. It had been funny and engaging, and people were buying so many books. So, so many books.

'This was a great idea,' Becky said, as they both watched a young woman walk past holding a copy of Jo Nesbo's *The Snowman,* plus the new Imran Mahmood thriller and the Lindsey Kelk hardback that had arrived just in time for Christmas, and which Ollie planned to read over the holidays.

'It's gone well, hasn't it?' she said. 'I'm so relieved.' She hadn't meant to sound so emotional, but she hadn't realised quite how much she'd been hoping for Becky's approval after all that had gone before. 'And Finn was a gracious loser, too.'

'Maisie was definitely better,' Becky said, holding her hands up to Dylan, indicating that he had ten minutes to browse, 'and you never know, maybe your Sophia Forsythe-Hartley event will go well, too.'

Ollie's heart pounded. 'That's the plan!'

Becky shrugged. 'I read the first book in her Cornish series. It's really good.'

Ollie cupped her hand behind her ear. 'Say it a little louder for the people at the back.'

Becky laughed and rolled her eyes. 'It was good, OK? And for the record, I don't have anything against author events, I just don't think they're the be-all and end-all.'

'I agree,' Ollie said. 'The last bookshop I worked in was focused on the big names, and I suppose that's where I saw the success – the packed shop and café. But this – Book Wars, the crafting events, are almost more satisfying, and they're still selling a lot of books.'

Becky nodded. She opened her mouth, then paused.

Ollie raised her eyebrows. 'Go on.'

'I was thinking,' Becky said, 'we could plan some more crafting events in the new year. If you wanted to?'

It took all Ollie's self-restraint not to jump up and down. Instead, she nodded sagely, and said, 'I was thinking jewellery making, actually. There must be somewhere that will let us hire some cute little flame throwers. That kind of thing always goes well here, don't you think?'

Becky folded her arms and let out an exasperated sigh. Ollie grinned, and the other woman struggled to stop a smile slipping onto her face.

As Ollie went to help Thea and Andrea behind the till, she wondered if, finally, she was starting to get things right.

Chapter Twenty-Nine

Classical Christmas music was playing in the background while Ollie typed up Liam's manuscript on Friday evening. Liam was in his usual place on the sofa, and Henry had been upgraded to lap dog – allowed to lie along the cushions, his head on Liam's knee. Marion was dusting the shelves because, she'd said, she'd come in earlier, knocked a book off with her elbow and almost choked to death on the resulting cloud of dust.

The fire was an orange glow in the grate, and the decorations that Liam had finally put up – green and silver foil garlands, the type that unfolded like a slinky – twisted slowly in the heat. Ollie had a cup of hot chocolate next to her laptop, its last marshmallows dissolving into sugary blobs. It felt companionable, as if they were an odd family, and didn't need to fill the silence. But Marion, Ollie knew, didn't hold silences for long.

'Is your Max coming round again tonight?' she asked.

'Oh. Yes, I hope so. He's meeting Beryan, planning the schedule of café treats for the next two weeks, then he'll come here.'

'He's getting to be a permanent fixture,' Marion observed.

'I hope so,' Ollie said again. 'The barn, the bookshop – all my walks searching for legends – everything's better now he's in my life. Permanent fixture sounds good to me.'

'Is it all a bit fast, though?' Marion reached up to dust a higher shelf, sending a sprinkling of fluff – snow, Ollie thought, trying to turn it festive – raining down.

'Not to me.'

'Leave her be,' Liam said gently, his nose still in his book. The cover was dark red, an old-fashioned hardback, and Ollie couldn't read the white lettering down the spine. 'Max is one of the most genial people in Port Karadow: I can't think of a better pairing.'

'Thank you,' Ollie said. 'That means a lot.'

Liam waved a dismissive hand. 'You don't need my approval: it's entirely up to you what you do with your life, though I'm very glad to have you next door, and doing my typing. Not to mention that I get to see this rascal.' He rubbed Henry between his silky ears. The dog stirred, but didn't wake from his nap.

'I'm not saying I dislike Max,' Marion went on, 'far from it! It's good to be cautious, that's all.'

'About what?' Ollie asked. 'Relationships? Life? *Underwear*?'

The older woman turned to her with wide eyes. 'I don't . . . I just—'

'Sorry, Marion.' Ollie sighed. 'I shouldn't have said that. But the man I was with before Max, when I was living in

266

London, was completely different – and not in a good way. By the time we broke up, I didn't understand why I'd ever thought I loved him. He wasn't that great to me.'

Marion got off the stepped stool she'd been dusting from, and Liam put his book down. Even Henry woke up, looking at Ollie as if, even though he couldn't understand her words, he could sense the feelings associated with them.

'I don't want any sympathy,' she said, swallowing. 'I'm just trying to explain why me and Max – why, even though it might seem fast to some people – feels right. Why wait, when we've been honest with each other? I just want to embrace it.'

Marion squeezed her shoulder. 'In that case, I'm glad. And perhaps it's time for *you* to treat yourself to some new underwear: it can work wonders for your self-confidence, you know.' She waggled her eyebrows and Ollie laughed.

'Wasn't it me who told *you* that? Right now, I'm not sure there's room for improvement.'

Marion chuckled. 'Aren't you the lucky one.'

'We're both lucky, Marion,' Ollie said seriously. 'Me *and* Max.'

'Would someone like to explain what's going on?' Liam's brows were lowered in confusion.

'Absolutely not,' Marion chided. 'When Ollie mentioned underwear, you should have realised it wasn't a discussion that included you.'

Liam flung his arms in the air. 'You're being incredibly cryptic, and I'm bamboozled. Not to mention that we're in *my* study.'

'We're both working for you, in one form or another,' Marion pointed out. 'Allow us our feminine asides.'

Ollie sighed. 'Basically, Liam, my relationship with Max is flourishing, and good quality underwear is excellent for your self-worth.'

'I'm not sure I need new boxers,' Liam muttered.

'I'd better check on those cookies in the oven,' Marion said, throwing him a horrified look. 'Hot chocolate is elevated by a delicious cookie.'

'Hear hear!' Ollie raised her mug as the other woman bustled out of the room, then returned to her typing. She wondered if she'd ever get to the end of the manuscript. But the thought of finishing, of having no reason to spend evenings with Liam in this glorious room, gave her a pang of sadness. She would have to think of other reasons to pop by.

'What are you doing tomorrow night?' he asked, as if reading her mind.

'Oh.' Ollie looked up. 'I think Max and I are staying in, apart from a walk we were thinking of going on at dusk, to hunt down another of the legends in that book.'

'Which one?' Liam asked, his eyes bright with interest.

'The one about the couple on the hill. Do you know it?' She laughed. 'Silly question: you know them all. It's such a tragic love story, and the fact that they've been seen, so clearly, even though it was a dark night . . .' She shook her head. 'It's only a short walk from here. Have you ever . . .?'

'Have I ever seen them?'

Ollie nodded.

'Once, a long time ago. At least I think I did, but it was the middle of the night, misty, all the usual caveats. I know the legend says they appear as clear as day, but I'm sure it overdramatises.'

'Why do you say that?'

268

'Because if it was true, people would have gone along with cameras and their modern phones and captured the ghosts.'

'Perhaps they can't be captured, though.' Ollie leaned forward, the keyboard protesting when she hit a random combination of keys with the heels of her hands. 'Perhaps they can only be seen with the naked eye: as fleeting as their love was.'

'It's a sad story, isn't it?' Liam said. 'Very *Romeo and Juliet*. Two families, one Cornish, one from London, at loggerheads over the farmland the incomers were taking over, their dominance over the cattle sales in the area.'

'And nobody knows if the young man really killed himself?' Ollie kept her voice low. It seemed wrong to gossip about it. So many legends had their origins in truth, even if the drama, the emotion, had been twisted out of proportion.

'They don't.' Liam sighed. 'They found him early one morning, lying in the dewy grass, a mile from his house, but the cause of death was never established. Of course, in those days, medical understanding was nowhere near as good as it is today. There could have been any number of natural causes that ended his life far too early.'

Ollie shuddered. 'Maybe we'll stay in and watch a romcom instead.'

Liam slid his bookmark between the pages of his book and closed it. 'I've got an even better idea.' His voice was louder than before, as if he wanted to expel the sadness from the room, and Henry startled awake. 'Why don't you and Max come for dinner? No obligation to do any typing at all: just good food, wine and company. We got on well at the quiz, and when he came here the other day. Now he's become so important to you, I'd like to get to know him better.'

Ollie smiled, a flush of pride warming her insides. She wanted to show Max off to everyone, shout from the roof-tops that they were together, and she couldn't think of anything better than spending Saturday evening in this hug of a house, talking and laughing with the two men who had come into her life since she'd moved to Cornwall, the Christmas decorations shimmering.

She was determined to help Max relax this weekend. She could see that the pre-Christmas rush at the café was taking its toll, and she wanted to look after him.

'I'd love to,' she said, 'and I'm sure Max would, too. Thank you, Liam, that's so kind of you.'

'It would be my pleasure. You're inspiring me to extend my social contacts, to get out and about in town more than I have been recently, especially now it's furnished with such a good bookshop. This is a good next step.'

'You're coming to the Sophia Forsythe-Hartley event too: no excuses allowed.'

Liam saluted. 'Yes, boss.'

'Let me know what I can bring tomorrow,' she said, and Liam was shaking his head when Marion returned, bringing a tantalising aroma with her.

'Orange cookies with cappuccino icing.' She put the plate of cookies on Liam's desk. They were piled high, their light brown icing glossy. 'A unique flavour combination, I'll grant you, but it works.'

Ollie didn't hesitate, and when she bit into the biscuit, a riot of flavours exploded on her tongue. 'Ohmygosh,' she mumbled. 'Marion, these are incredible.'

'Good.' She looked at the floor. 'Got to try and keep up with Beryan, even though she's getting paid for her bakes.'

'You know I think yours are superior,' Liam said, taking a cookie from the top of the pile.

'Max doesn't,' Marion murmured, and Ollie and Liam exchanged a glance. Was Marion annoyed that he had picked Beryan as his baker, and not her?

'Come for dinner tomorrow night,' Liam said. 'I've invited Ollie and Max, and you should be there too – Adam as well, if he's free. But not a crumb of cooking.'

'What will you do then, order in?' Marion sounded horrified.

'I make a mean shepherd's pie when I set my mind to it, which isn't very often at all. But I'm going to make the effort.'

'Honestly, Liam, we could bring nibbles—'

'No.' Liam cut Ollie off. 'I'm going to do this properly. I'll quite enjoy it, I think.' He smiled to himself, and now it was Ollie and Marion who exchanged a glance.

'Adam's at the rugby club tomorrow night, so he won't be able to accompany me,' Marion said. 'I'll come, but I'm going to make more biscuits – especially if Max is going to be here.'

'It sounds like you want to impress him,' Liam said.

'What if I do? Max is a lovely young man, as you said, and I don't think it would do to get on his wrong side. Not because of how he'd react, you understand,' she added quickly, 'but there are those people who draw you to them, aren't there? People you want to know, because they radiate warmth, somehow. Max is one of those.'

Ollie grinned. 'I know exactly what you mean. Perhaps we should agree to dial our adoration down a notch tomorrow night, though, or we might make him uncomfortable.'

'Good idea,' Marion said, taking a cookie. 'But I'm still going to bake biscuits. Let him see just how good I am.' She nodded decisively, then strode out of the room.

Ollie bit into her second cookie, and returned to her typing. It was comforting, she thought, to know that she wasn't the only one who had fallen for Max's charms so completely. She remembered that day in Sea Brew, all those weeks ago, when Lizzy had accused him of bewitching everyone. Was he the type of person to end up as the subject of a legend, breaking hearts across the land, being remembered as an ethereal, almost magical human being, perfect but ultimately unreachable? But, Ollie told herself, as she moved another page of Liam's manuscript to the 'done' pile, *she* had reached him: she had grabbed hold of him, and she didn't want him in a legend – not when they all had tragedy, loss or hopelessness at their core.

No, she decided. Max Holden was real, not mythical, and she wanted him by her side for as long as possible.

Chapter Thirty

'Tell me what Christmas treats you and Beryan have cooked up.' Ollie's voice was still sluggish with sleep as she lay in Max's arms in bed the following morning.

'She's making cranberry scones,' Max said, 'and cinnamon and brandy butter doughnuts. Turkey and stuffing rolls, to go alongside the usual sausage and cheese, and miniature chocolate Yule logs encased in salted pastry.'

'Uhhh. It's the last one that's blowing my mind. Rich, chocolatey Yule log inside crisp, salty pastry. When can I try them?'

'Monday, but you can't buy them all up, because I want my other customers to enjoy them, too.'

'One of each won't be too many, though?'

'Of course not. I'll get Beryan to do a special batch, just for you.'

'Charmer.' She kissed his arm, and he laughed gently.

This was something she could get used to. Already, having Max in the barn felt completely comfortable. The kitsch garland with its rainbow baubles shimmered along the headboard, the living space now boasted a huge real Christmas tree that she and Max had bought and then decorated together, and the radio in the kitchen, that she'd put on when she went to make coffee, seemed to be playing Michael Bublé's Christmas album in its entirety.

Ollie wasn't sure if it was words or emotions clogging her throat. She knew how she felt about him, she wanted to tell him how much she had come to care for him, but she didn't want to put him under any pressure. He was already having to face Liam and Marion for dinner later, and even though they weren't Ollie's parents, they were a sort of surrogate pairing, and she knew that Marion, especially, wouldn't hold back with questions now that she and Max were together. Ollie wanted to be honest, but she didn't want to scare him off by being too full on. Besides, he was working so hard, and even though he'd been as fun, as attentive, as always, she could tell he was tired.

'I think we should do as little as possible today,' she said.

'Sounds good to me.' Max turned onto his side, so he was facing her. 'What *little as possible* did you have in mind?'

'*The Muppet Christmas Carol* and *Con Air*, then take Henry for a walk in the afternoon before we go to Liam's.'

'*Con Air*?' Max's brows drew together. 'I'm trying to remember something Christmassy about it, but I'm coming up empty.'

'It's just a great film. Ridiculous, but great.'

'Can I pick a film too?'

'Of course. As long as it's not miserable: I don't have time for miserable.'

Max smiled. 'In films, or life in general?'

'I try for both,' she said, wrapping her arm around his waist. 'It's not always possible, of course, but at the moment it's working out OK.'

'OK, huh?' Max pulled her closer. 'Good to know.'

She rested her head against his chest, and felt his heart beating against her ear. It was fast, a hurried rhythm, as if he could feel the emotion that hung between them, too. 'Definitely not feeling miserable right now.' She kissed his warm skin.

'Ollie, I . . .' He pulled back, so he could look at her. His brow was furrowed, a mess of dark curls falling over his forehead. Her breath caught, and she wasn't sure if it was because he was so gorgeous, or because of the hesitation in his voice.

'If you're about to end things,' she whispered, 'then don't.'

'What?' His eyes widened. 'No! I wasn't! I was . . . I don't know if I can—' Henry's loud bark drowned out Max's words, and the next minute the dog's front paws were on the bed covers.

'You're not allowed up here!' Ollie sat up and pulled the sheet against her chest.

'It's possibly not his fault if you left the stair gate open when you went to make coffee,' Max said, folding his arms behind his head.

'I'll get up in a minute,' Ollie told her dog sternly, then turned to Max. 'What were you going to say?'

'It can wait until later.' When she pouted, he laughed, leaned up to kiss her, then swung his legs over the side of the bed. 'If we're going to fit all these films in before dinner, we'd better make a start.'

'I seem to remember you having a go at *me* for being too organised about relaxing,' Ollie said, following him to the bathroom.

'The woods out back will be decimated by all the Yule logs the two of us are going to need.' Max pulled her into the shower with him and turned it on, the ice-cold water making her squeal. He wrapped his arms around her until it warmed, the gentle steam circling them until Ollie was cocooned by it, and by the man who, she had already come to realise, she was hopelessly in love with.

The four of them sat around Liam's sturdy dining table, Henry lay in front of the fireplace, and their talking and laughter drowned out the classical Christmas music in the background. Liam had decorated the table with sprigs of holly from the tall tree behind the farmhouse, and candles flickered gently down the centre, their berry-scent thickening the air.

Ollie cradled a glass of mulled wine, the heat warming her palms, while Liam dished out huge helpings of shepherd's pie from an orange terrine that was still sizzling from the Aga.

'It's not very festive, but it's the one thing I know how to do well,' he said, as he handed Max a full plate, and Marion added a spoonful of broccoli and green beans.

'It smells delicious,' Max said. 'Thanks for inviting me.'

'It's good to see you again, son.' Liam served himself last and sat down, pulling his chair close to the table. 'Especially as Ollie's been going on about you so much. You've been a ghostly presence here anyway: much better to have you in the flesh.'

276

Ollie dipped her head, hiding her smile. She couldn't even be annoyed at Liam's teasing, because it was all true.

'Is that so?' Max held his arm out, across the table, and Ollie took his hand. 'I expect everyone in Sea Brew feels the same, except that Ollie turns up at least once a day, so they get to see the object of my affections.'

'You're the talk of the town,' Marion said, spearing a broccoli floret with her fork. 'The word *besotted* has been used on more than one occasion.'

Ollie didn't want Max to feel awkward, so she changed the subject. 'Liam, I spoke to Melissa earlier, and she told me she was going to be in Portugal for Christmas. Will you see her mum?'

'Briony's in Edinburgh with her husband,' Liam said. 'I had been hoping to see Colm, Melissa's brother, but he's delayed his flight again.'

'Is he still in Australia?' Ollie had met Melissa's younger brother a few times, years ago, when she and Melissa had been getting to know each other in London, but then he'd moved to Sydney. He'd been there for close to a decade.

'At the moment,' Liam said. 'He's moving back to the UK, but I don't know if he'll come back to Cornwall, or if he's planning on living somewhere else. Briony says he's told her very little, and I think I mentioned before, I haven't spoken to Colm myself for several years.'

'That's so sad.' Ollie remembered Liam saying he regretted what had happened between them, and wondered how serious it was. 'Maybe you'll get to see him in the new year?'

'Possibly,' Liam said, but from the sad droop of his mouth, Ollie got the impression he didn't think it was very likely.

'I need help,' Max announced, breaking through the pall that had fallen over the table. 'From all of you.'

'With what, my love?' Marion asked.

'Next week at Sea Brew,' he said. 'I need to decide whether to be Santa, or a snowman. I've got both outfits, I just need to choose one. If I'm Santa, will that confuse the children who come in? The snowman onesie's quite warm, but the temperature's expected to drop tomorrow, and stay properly cold until after Christmas.'

'Snowman *onesie*?' Marion said sharply.

'Snowman onesie,' Ollie repeated, unable to hold back her laughter. 'Oh God, Max, it has to be that one! Aside from making your young customers question why Santa Claus is working in a café when he should be preparing for his annual around the world trip, everyone needs the joy of you in a snowman onesie.'

'You think?' he asked, his eyes twinkling.

'Absolutely. *I* need that, anyway. And I would put money on me not being the only one.'

Marion sipped her wine and said, 'And what, may I ask, does one wear beneath a snowman onesie?'

Max opened his mouth to reply.

'I'm rather concerned, Marion,' Liam cut in, 'about your sudden obsession with underwear. Let us refrain from telling each other about our choice of delicates.' He shook his head, as if clearing some unwanted image, then looked between Ollie and Max. 'I want to hear which legends you've been researching.'

'Oh yes,' Marion said, folding her arms. 'Because ghosts and misery are a much better topic of conversation.' She rolled her eyes, and Ollie had to look away from Max,

278

worried that she'd explode into a fit of giggles. She could see that he was struggling not to laugh too, and felt his foot gently nudge hers under the table.

'This is such a great room,' Max said, as he, Ollie and Liam settled in the study after dinner. Marion had left them to it, saying she needed to get home to Adam.

'It needs a good clear-out.' Liam poured them glasses of brandy from the decanter, the newly lit fire beginning to take hold. 'The curtains are being eaten by moths, and some of the older books could go the same way.'

'Some of these must be decades old,' Max said, craning his neck to look at the higher shelves.

'Centuries, even,' Liam replied, but when Max turned to him in surprise, he grinned.

'I've been desperate to investigate all the books,' Ollie said, 'but Liam won't let me.'

'That's not entirely true now, is it? I said when the manuscript was typed up, I'd let you loose in here. If I give you access now, you'll get sidetracked and won't ever go back to my stories.'

'That's actually a fair point,' Ollie said. 'Max, what are you doing?' She laughed as he moved the stepped stool, which Marion had been using to dust the evening before, and climbed up it. It had three steps, with a wider platform on top – far from being a proper library ladder.

'I'm just having a look.' He pressed his fingertips into the shelves as he scanned the rows of books.

'Be careful,' Liam said. 'There may be some old tomes up there, but I'd warrant there are a fair few spiders too, despite Marion's dusting.'

'I can't see any spiders, but there are . . . wait a minute. What are these?' He pointed to a row of books on the highest shelf. They were bare hardbacks, Ollie could see, in complementary shades – pale green, blue, mauve – and had gold lettering and a matching publisher's stamp on the spine. They looked like part of a set, though from where she was, Ollie couldn't read their titles.

Liam put his drink down. 'Now, hang on, son. Not the ones right up there.'

'Ollie,' Max said, 'you remember when we went on that walk to the beach?'

'Come on, lad.' Liam stepped forwards just as Max stretched, reaching up as high as he could, to where the books were nestled on the uppermost shelf, their tops brushing the ceiling.

'Do you mean when we found the shell?' Ollie asked. 'What about it?' Why didn't Liam want him to see those books? Or was it simply that he didn't want Max reaching up precariously like that? Something about the situation suddenly felt off.

'You told me that . . . that Liam had never heard of him.' Max's voice was straining as he stretched. He sounded out of breath.

'Heard of who? Please be careful, Max.' Ollie put her drink down and went to stand behind him, reaching her arms up as if she could stop him falling, were he to tip back. But then a book fell, missing her by inches and landing on the carpet with a loud thwack. She put her arms up automatically, covering her head. Henry barked and bounded over to the steps.

'Max? What are you—' She looked up, and her words died in her throat. He was leaning against the shelves, his forehead resting on the books, his hand pressed against his chest. 'Max?'

'It's just . . .' he started. His voice was indistinct, his breaths short. 'Just a little . . . dizzy.'

Ollie swallowed a sharp slice of fear. She climbed onto the steps, so she was just below him. 'Hey, come on.' She tried to keep the panic out of her voice. She could see that he was pale, and that beads of sweat had broken out on his forehead. 'Can you come down?'

His breathing was too shallow, and Ollie gripped his arm, squeezing roughly. When he looked at her, his gaze was unfocused.

'We have to get you down,' she said, feeling the sharp prickle of impending tears.

'I'm fine,' he said. 'I'm . . .' He shut his eyes, and Ollie tightened her grip. She tugged, not knowing if it was the right thing to do, but desperate to get him off the steps. If he fell from where he was, he could hit his head on the desk – anything. She glanced behind her, but she couldn't see Liam, and she didn't have time to find him.

'Max, *now*.' She held out her other hand.

He turned and took hold of her forearms, and she stepped backwards slowly, finding the step below her by feel, terrified that she'd slip and bring them both down. Henry was whining, and she could hear him padding backwards and forwards, agitated, on the rug.

'You're OK.' She held Max's gaze. 'You're fine.' His breathing was harsh, and the colour had drained from his face. He didn't reply, and she thought he must be using up all his energy on staying upright.

Ollie stepped backwards again, bringing Max with her, the relief overwhelming when her foot met the soft rug. She coaxed him down the last step, and when they were both on solid ground, she half-walked, half-dragged him to the sofa, settling him on it as gently as she could.

'Sorry,' Max said, though it was more of a whisper, his eyes fluttering closed.

'No, Max,' she said. Somewhere between reaching the bottom of the steps and the sofa, her tears had begun to fall. 'No, no, it's OK.' She felt in her pockets for her phone, but couldn't find it. It was as if her worry had obliterated the rational part of her brain. She stroked his curls back from his damp forehead. 'I don't know what to do,' she admitted with a quiet sob. 'Please don't go to sleep.' But Max didn't reply, even when Henry put his head in his lap.

'I've called an ambulance.' Ollie jumped, then looked up to find Liam in the doorway, holding an ancient mobile phone. 'They're ten minutes away. Is it myocardia Max had?'

She could only nod, then watch as Liam spoke into the phone, his voice low and urgent.

She turned back to Max, taking in his pale face, his fluttering eyelids, the air coming out between his lips in pointless, shallow exhales. His chest was rising and falling too rapidly, and her own fear was like iced water rushing over her, freezing her insides and making her immobile. But no. *No.* She couldn't afford to panic now: not when Max needed her.

She took his hand, lying limp at his side, and threaded her fingers through his. She squeezed, trying to send warmth and love into him with her touch. 'I'm here,' she told him. 'I'm here, don't worry. I'm not going anywhere, and neither are you. It's all going to be fine.'

She wished, more than anything she'd wished for in her life up to that point, that if she said the words enough times, they would turn out to be true.

Chapter Thirty-One

The paramedics arrived in a blur of efficient questions, going straight to Max with their equipment and their steady hands, checking his vitals and asking her, and Liam, to tell them exactly what had happened, and what his history was.

Ollie told them he'd suffered with myocarditis four years before, but had been healthy since then. She felt like an imposter, because she hadn't known him long, and she didn't know if she was getting the details right. But, more than that, she felt guilty. Had *she* caused this? Had she forced him to spend too much time with her, taken up afternoons and evenings that he usually spent quietly? Was it her fault his illness had come back? She didn't know enough about it, and she didn't know what to do. He looked so pale, so unlike the smiling, funny, twinkly man she loved, and she felt as if her fear was about to burst out of her, like an alien through her chest. She wanted to claw at her skin, to get it out, to do *something* to stop this.

'I'll drive you to the hospital,' Liam said, his hand on her arm.

'What? Why? But I—' She couldn't tear her eyes from Max, who had been moved onto a stretcher, and was about to be taken out of Liam's cosy study, the fire still flickering, their untouched glasses of brandy glowing amber, to a cold, sterile ambulance.

'I'll drive you,' Liam said firmly. 'Marion's coming back: she'll look after Henry.'

'Can't I go in the ambulance?'

'I'm afraid not,' the taller of the two paramedics said. 'We're taking him to the Royal Cornwall. Go to A&E there, and ask at the desk. You'll get an update as soon as the doctors can provide one.'

Ollie nodded. She let Liam lead her out of the study behind the paramedics, let him pull her to the barn's front door, while she stared after the uniformed pair, and Max, still and silent on the stretcher. After prompting, she told Liam where her coat was, and watched in a daze as he settled Henry in his basket. Her dog was clearly distressed – he loved Max almost as much as she did – and, blinking herself out of her fug, she went and fussed over him, stroking him and whispering soothing words into his soft, floppy ears. She was surprised, somehow, when one of her tears landed on his chocolate brown fur.

She sat in the passenger seat of Liam's Range Rover, night-time Cornwall passing in a blur, the heater's harsh whirr filling the silence. She kept replaying the moment the book had fallen to the floor, her confusion when she saw Max leaning heavily on the shelves. She remembered earlier, when

285

she'd pressed her ear to his chest and felt his heart racing. She had thought it was because of the emotion between them; a pattering, Disney heartbeat that proved he was lovestruck. She was a fucking idiot.

Liam led her to a hard grey chair in the waiting room of the Accident and Emergency department, then disappeared. When he came back, he put his arm around her shoulders. 'There's no news yet,' he said gently. 'But I'm sure we'll get some soon.'

Ollie pressed her lips together to try and keep her feelings inside, but she wasn't strong enough. 'It's my fault,' she blurted.

'Of course it's not,' Liam said. 'It's usually caused by an infection: it's nothing to do with how Max has been living his life. If he's had it before, he's probably more susceptible to it returning.'

'But he should be taking care of himself. And with me, he's had all of his usual café stuff to deal with, then we've been going on these long walks and . . . and all the time in bed together, it's . . .' She couldn't even feel embarrassed. Her pain and worry, her guilt, were taking up all the space.

'It is *not* your fault,' Liam repeated. 'And Max looks after himself. He's careful, he's responsible, and—'

'And he just collapsed,' Ollie said. 'Because of me.'

'Ollie. *Ollie.* You can't think that. You have brought Max nothing but happiness, that's as clear as day. As soon as he's awake, he'll tell you the same thing. Now, do you think you can handle some pigswill coffee, or a can of Coke?'

'I'll get it,' Ollie said, standing abruptly. 'I need to do something.'

Liam looked up at her. She could tell that he was trying to remain positive for both of them, but there was a deep furrow between his brows that told her he was just as worried as she was.

She found the coffee machine and got two cups, shoved several sachets of sugar into her pockets, and then navigated the meandering corridors back to the waiting room, to Liam and any news there might be. She wondered if the doctors had Max's details and had called his parents, if they were driving through the night from St Ives, frantic with worry. She wanted to shrink inside herself, but instead, she gripped the plastic cups tighter, even though the heat of the liquid inside scalded her palms.

When she turned the corner and saw a figure standing in front of Liam, it took her a few seconds to work out who it was. She inched closer, wondering if she should find somewhere else to wait, because she wasn't sure she had the brain capacity to speak to Becky.

Before she could decide, the other woman spoke. 'Marion called me. You know how much Dylan loves Max, and I . . . I wanted to see how he was.'

'There's no news yet, pet,' Liam said. 'And I'm not sure how much we'll be told, as we're not family.'

'And what about her?'

'Sorry, I—'

'Ollie,' Becky said. 'I bet she gets to find out, to go and see him.'

Liam shook his head. 'I don't think so, Becky love. I think the doctors will call his parents, and it'll be up to them to say who can see him: and Max, of course, when he's awake.'

Ollie could tell, from her words and the way she was saying them, that Becky blamed her, too. She turned quickly and hot coffee sloshed over the rim of the cup, burning her. She gasped, and Becky spun to face her.

'Where were you when it happened?' she asked.

'In Liam's study. He was trying to get a book down, and—'

'You do realise this wouldn't have happened if it wasn't for you,' Becky said.

Ollie pressed her lips together.

'That's not true,' Liam replied for her, his tone straddling the line between gentle and forceful. 'Nobody could have foreseen this. And let's not do Max the disservice of suggesting his life is in someone else's hands.'

'But the way they've been carrying on.' Becky flung an arm in Ollie's direction, and she flinched. She put the cups on a chair, trying to arrange them on the flattest part of the plastic seat so they didn't tip over.

'Becky, come on now,' Liam said.

Becky clenched her hands at her sides. 'Dylan is devastated, did you know that? I only told him Max was unwell, and that was enough to set him off—'

'So am I!' Ollie couldn't hold it in any longer. 'Don't you think I'm devastated, too? Don't you think I already feel guilty, that I'm worried I spent too much time with him, asked him to do too much?' She tried to gather her breath, to stop the flow of tears. 'I love him, and I can't even find out what's happening.'

She rubbed her eyes and slumped into an empty chair. One of the coffee cups teetered, and then tipped. Ollie watched the hot, murky liquid spill over the seat and then, when it reached the edge, drip slowly and steadily, drop after drop, onto the cold linoleum floor.

It was much later, long after Becky had gone, and after she and Liam had watched a man and woman – the man with Max's dark curls, the slender woman with greying blonde hair knotted in a bun, their faces etched with concern – being led by a member of hospital staff into a smaller waiting room, that a nurse told them they'd be better off going home.

'He's in the best possible hands,' she said. 'As soon as there's an update, and as long as Mr Holden's parents agree, we'll call you.' Her smile was kind, but Ollie felt defeated. She nodded, took a deep breath, and dredged up a smile.

'Thank you,' she said. She pushed herself to her feet, and held out her hand for Liam.

When they reached Foxglove Farm, Liam turned the engine off, but neither of them got out of the car. The dashboard said it was almost seven o'clock in the morning, and the sky was shifting from the deep black of night to a sludgy, pre-dawn grey.

'Thank you,' she said, turning to face him. 'I don't know what I would have done without you – what Max would have done.'

Liam put a hand on her arm. 'You were there for him, Ollie. I know you think you haven't been strong, but I hope that when you look back on this, you'll realise that's just not the case.'

She shook her head, and the tears, which she thought she'd fully wrung out, threatened to fall again. 'What if he isn't OK?'

'He will be,' Liam said softly. 'Now, go and get some rest. Things will look brighter after a few hours' sleep.'

As Ollie put her key in the lock, she heard a robin singing from the stately yew tree on the lawn. She tried to take the hopeful notes of his tune into her heart, but all she could think of was how still Max had been as the paramedics carried him to the ambulance, and the fact that, if Becky blamed her too, then it must at least be partly true.

She woke on the sofa, still in the jeans and red top she'd worn for their dinner at Liam's house, her arms and legs wrapped around her dog. Henry's breathing was soft, interspersed with gentle snuffles, and she didn't think she'd ever been more grateful for him. She reached blearily for her phone, her heart sinking when the only notifications were messages of concern and support from Thea and Meredith. No news.

Realising it was early afternoon, she went to make herself a cup of tea and a slice of toast. As she was boiling the kettle, she saw Max's stripy scarf draped over a breakfast stool, and the fear rose up in her throat.

She called the hospital, tears of frustration spilling over when the woman she spoke to said she couldn't tell Ollie anything. She realised she couldn't stay here, drowning in worry. She would see if Liam wanted to walk Henry with her. She was about to clip on his harness when her phone rang. She almost dropped it in her hurry to answer.

'Is he OK?' she blurted.

There was a pause and then, 'I'm sorry, is this Ollie Spencer?'

'Yes! This is Ollie, are you from the hospital?'

'No, this is Arabella March, Sophia Forsythe-Hartley's editor.'

'Oh. *Oh.* Is . . . is everything OK?'

There was a short, uncomfortable laugh. 'I feel like I should be asking you that.'

'I . . . uhm.' She couldn't go into it with Arabella. 'It's Sunday – isn't it? Is everything all right?'

'Actually – and I am so sorry to do this, especially when it sounds like you have other things on your plate – but Sophia won't be able to make the event on the twenty-third after all. I hope you understand that we are both incredibly disappointed, and she has asked me to pass on her profuse apologies, but something unavoidable has come up, and we just can't rework things to make the trip to Cornwall fit. I wanted to let you know as soon as possible, hence disturbing you on a Sunday.'

Ollie remained mute throughout Arabella's speech, the words barely sinking in until she'd mumbled some kind of acquiescence, and then ended the call.

She watched as her toast popped up, the edges charred, the acrid smell filling the barn. The kettle was steaming, the sounds and smells so domestic and ordinary. She picked up Max's scarf and climbed onto the stool. She remembered that, in times of stress, the best thing you could do was breathe deeply, take air fully into your lungs.

She inhaled, and her mind filled with images of Max on the stretcher, of Arabella saying the words *profuse apologies* in her clipped, eloquent voice. Henry whined gently from the sofa, his dark, baleful eyes fixed on her, and Ollie couldn't bear it.

She folded her arms on the island, buried her head in them, and let the tears come again, soaking into the soft cotton of Max's scarf, while the Christmas robin trilled its hopeful, festive tune in the yew tree outside her window.

Chapter Thirty-Two

Nothing, absolutely nothing, was working.

Not summer rain-scented incense sticks or fresh air or meditation or ambient music. Ollie had walked all the way to the beach with Henry, and stood there, watching the swirling mass of waves, shades of blue and green and turquoise churning amongst the grey, the sky shifting from dark slate to soft smoke as clouds raced overhead. It was magnificent, breathtaking, but it reminded her of the day she and Max had found the seashell, and she'd ended up getting soaked and bringing him back to the barn. Then she worried she was too far from home, that there might be news from the hospital, and she wouldn't be able to get there as quickly as she wanted.

She strode through the countryside, the wind biting her cheeks, the colours of the landscape muted. Every bit of Port Karadow held some kind of reminder, refusing to let her turn her thoughts to something else: there were the legends she had been exploring with Max; the early morning walks she'd taken with Henry, when she'd been anticipating seeing him in Sea Brew, the chai tea latte and sausage roll just an excuse.

Already, Cornwall was her life, and Max was an irreplaceable part of it. She never wanted that to change, but right now she felt helpless. She wanted to *do* something: take food and good coffee to Max's parents at the hospital, or make sure Sea Brew could run smoothly until he got back. She wished that she could be productive, instead of wandering around the countryside like a directionless Eeyore.

The sight of Foxglove Barn should have been comforting, but the only things waiting for her inside were quiet and calm, her glittering Christmas decorations, and the absence of Max. And the worst thing was, she couldn't shake the feeling – reaffirmed by Becky – that she was at least partly responsible for him getting ill.

She was taking her coat off, Henry hovering around her legs, clingier than he'd been in weeks, when her phone rang. With her heart in her throat, she took it out of her pocket, expecting to see an unknown number. Instead, she saw that it was Thea. She thought of Arabella's call, and it took her a few seconds to answer.

'Hi Thea,' she said. She walked to the fridge and took out a bottle of beer.

'Ollie, I'm so sorry,' were Thea's first words. 'I wanted to call earlier, but I didn't know if you'd be at the hospital, or . . . Is there anything Ben and I can do?'

'We're here, Ollie,' Ben's deep voice said in the background.

Ollie lowered herself to the arm of the sofa. 'That's so kind of you, thank you. But I don't . . . The doctors won't let me see him, so I have no idea how he's doing. His parents are at the hospital, so that's good. He's not alone, at least.'

'Shit,' Thea whispered. 'Do you want us to come over? Take your mind off things until you hear?'

Ollie stared at the bottle resting on her knee. She felt guilty for the Sophia mess, too. She had got everything so wrong. 'I'm OK,' she said. 'Besides, it could be hours until there's any news. I just need to rest, I think. I didn't get any sleep last night.'

'Of course. But honestly, Ollie, if there's anything we can do – anything at all – please call me.'

'You're the best, thank you.'

'Take care.'

As soon as they'd hung up, Ollie wished she'd said yes to company. But what would they have done? Sat around together, being morose and worried? What would be the point of that?

She thought about phoning Melissa, or her parents, but what would she say? I've fallen for someone, I'm almost certain he's the love of my life, but he's had a relapse of a life-threatening illness that I might be responsible for; I don't know how he is, and I've totally messed up the one part of my job my boss was relying on me for?

She swigged her beer, the bubbles filling her throat, the taste bitter in her mouth. At least if she had a task – phoning Max's employees to sort out cover for the café, putting a bag together for him and taking it to the hospital – she would feel slightly better. But she didn't have the numbers of Max's staff, and she didn't have a key to his house. For both those things, she needed Max.

So instead, she sat on her sofa, Henry a heavy weight on her lap, and scrolled through her message chain with him. It was self-destructive, she knew that, and as she read every sweet message and funny joke, every hint that he cared about her, she felt worse. Was he awake? Did he have his phone beside him, ready to pick up when he came round? It had been in his jeans pocket: she remembered that from when she'd been sitting next to him on Liam's sofa, waiting for the ambulance to arrive.

With her fingers working faster than her brain, she typed out a message to him:

I miss you and I'm scared. Already, I don't think I can live without you. Please get better, Max. Ollie. xx

She sent it, then flung her phone onto the cushions, got up and walked to the French doors at the far end of the room. It was almost dark, the garden blanketed in shadows, the sky a dusky blue-grey, the wisps of clouds like streamers between the trees. She watched the view fade in increments, and realised she was rubbing her shoulder. She'd hardly been aware of it at the time, only worried about getting Max safely down from the steps, but now it was aching.

She stretched in front of the mirror, trying to ignore her pale skin, shadowed eyes and slightly shellshocked expression. As she rotated her shoulder, wincing at the pain, her gaze fell on the corner of the mirror, and the items that she'd slid in-between the glass and the frame.

The first was the strip of Polaroids she and Max had had taken at the Christmas market in Porthgolow, the photos telling a story of awkwardness to attraction in four, short frames. Looking at that last shot, their faces so close, lips almost touching, never failed to make Ollie's stomach flip. The second item was the cardboard tag that Max had tied to her Yule log. She pulled it out of its place and rubbed her thumb over his handwriting.

Life is too short to spend every moment working or worrying. Mxx

She bit the inside of her cheek. She couldn't stay here, doing nothing. And if she couldn't see Max, then she would go to the other person who, since she'd moved to Cornwall, had become a solid, steady presence in her life.

'Come on,' she said to Henry. He jumped off the sofa and was by her side in an instant.

She didn't bother to put her coat on, just picked up her phone and slid Max's tag and the strip of photos into her pocket. She pushed open the front door, stepped into the bitter night-time air, and walked to the main entrance of the farmhouse.

Liam might be asleep after their hospital vigil the night before, but if he wasn't, she would insist on typing up more of his book, or making a shepherd's pie with him to feed Max when he was better – anything that would mean she was being productive: anything that would stop the worries circling closer and closer, like hungry sharks, inside her head. They were getting so close to consuming her.

She lifted her hand to knock and jumped backwards when the door swung inward.

Liam looked perfectly put together in a mustard jumper and grey trousers, but she noticed that his chest was rising and falling, as if he was out of breath or upset or—

Fear crept down her spine. She opened her mouth to say something, but he beat her to it.

'I was just coming to find you, lass. Come in.'

'Is there news?' she asked, walking her dog over the threshold.

Liam led the way down the corridor and then paused, the dining room on their right, the study on their left. He turned to face her. 'Come and sit down,' he said. His smile was gentle, his voice soothing.

'Why?' She gripped Henry's lead tightly. 'What's happened?'

'I've just been speaking to Mrs Holden,' Liam told her. 'I've got an update for you, on Max.'

Chapter Thirty-Three

'So . . . so he's going to be OK?' Ollie was sitting on the leather sofa, Henry at her feet, Liam's Christmas decorations twirling gently in the breeze coming through the open window. It wasn't really warm enough for the window to be ajar, but perhaps he needed the cold to stay awake, or he just wanted to fill the study with fresh air after what had happened. She understood that: this place was Liam's sanctuary.

He pulled his chair out from behind the desk, then moved it so he was sitting in front of her.

'Max is stable,' he said, showing no signs of irritation at having to repeat himself. The first time, the words had washed over her. 'A relapse of myocarditis is very rare, apparently, so the doctors were understandably concerned. But according to Cath and Philip, Max's parents, his heart function is already starting to return to normal. He'll need to rest, to recuperate, and they're going to keep him in for a few days, but they're hopeful there will be no long-term effects.'

'But . . . he could get it again?'

Liam spread his hands wide. 'I suppose there's always that chance. I don't know enough about it, but when Cath called, she sounded relieved.'

'Is he awake?'

'He has woken up, but he's sleeping a lot, I think. I left my number with the nurse when we were there, and Cath very kindly called me, to give me an update.'

'Oh my God.' Ollie slumped forward, relief rushing through her like a tidal wave. 'He's going to be OK.'

'He's going to be fine,' Liam said softly. 'Especially now he's got you to take care of him.'

Ollie nodded. She couldn't think of anything she'd like to do more than nurse Max back to full health. She just wanted to be near him. 'When can we see him?'

'Cath's going to give me a call. Now—'

'Tea and mince pies.' Marion appeared in the doorway, carrying a tray. She put it on Liam's desk, then rearranged a side table so it was between the two of them. Then she moved a plate piled high with sugar-dusted mince pies, and two steaming mugs of tea, from the tray to the table.

'Come and sit down, Marion. Bring your own tea.'

She shook her head. 'I'm grand. Especially now we have positive news about Max. Goodness, his poor parents! You two get that sugar inside you, look after each other for a bit, and I'll be back in a while.'

'Thank you, Marion.' Ollie selected a mince pie and bit into it, relishing the crumble of pastry and the explosion of sweet, sticky Christmas flavours, the way her body craved it after hours of not eating, worry filling all the space inside her. She and Liam exchanged smiles as they ate, and the atmosphere in the room seemed to soften.

'Do you think we could take Max some of these?' she asked. 'Will he be allowed them?'

'We'd have to ask.' Liam looked around his study. 'I should have stopped him climbing those steps.'

Ollie shook her head. 'That didn't have anything to do with it, and you know that, because you reminded me last night. It would have happened wherever he was.' Her words allowed other possible scenarios to rush in. 'I think it was a good thing he was here. Imagine if he'd been at home on his own, and hadn't been able to get to a phone.' She swallowed thickly. 'No, don't imagine that.'

She put her mug down and sat forward. 'What I'm saying is, you have absolutely no reason to feel guilty. You spent so much time at the hospital telling me it wasn't my fault, so you can't assume any guilt, either. It was awful, and terrifying, but he's going to be OK. That's all that matters.' She exhaled a long breath and squeezed Liam's arm.

'Do you think you'll go to the bookshop tomorrow? I'm sure Thea would give you some time.'

Ollie shook her head, her horror creeping back. 'As long as she lets me see Max as soon as I'm able to, then I want to be there. It's a busy time, and there are some things I need to make up for.'

'What do you need to make up for?' Liam's forehead crinkled. 'I thought the Book Wars, the crafting sessions, were successful.'

'They were, mostly.' Ollie took another huge bite of her mince pie. She didn't want to tell anyone – not even Liam – about Sophia Forsythe-Hartley backing out of their event.

She had been so distracted when Arabella had called, she hadn't even challenged it, and she wanted to see if she could resolve whatever problem Sophia had. 'It's nothing to do with them, it's just Christmas . . .' Her gaze fell on an object lying on the floor. It was the book Max had been looking at when he'd collapsed, the one that he'd dropped. It was half under Liam's desk, its pale green cover ghostly against the dark swirls of the rug.

'What is it?' Liam turned to see where Ollie was looking.

'The book,' she murmured. She slipped off the sofa onto her knees, and crawled forward. Why had Max been so interested in it? He'd been asking her questions about the beach, and then . . . She picked it up, read the gold lettering on the front, and her breath stalled.

The Legend of Kerensa's Handprint: a Roskilly and Faith Mystery by Bryan Mailer.

'Wait a second,' Ollie said. 'You told me you'd never heard of him. *That* was what Max was saying to me.' She looked up at the shelf he had taken the book from. There were eight other books, all naked hardbacks, devoid of the bright covers and spines Ollie loved so much, but he had the whole series. Why did Liam have the entire series of Roskilly and Faith mysteries, when she distinctly remembered him giving her a blank look when she mentioned the author?

'Ollie,' Liam said. It came out as a sigh.

She shuffled round on the carpet. 'Why do you have these? They're . . . they're . . .' Her heart started to race as she flicked through the opening pages. 'They're first editions.'

Liam stared at her for several long moments, and Ollie had to move the plate of mince pies from the low side table to the desk when Henry, who she thought had been asleep, started to edge his nose towards it. Then she got to her feet, peered up at the shelves, and saw that, right in the corner, there was *another* set of the Roskilly and Faith series, this time with the covers on. She hadn't spotted it, hadn't . . . She frowned. The entire top shelf was made up of copies of the Cornish-based mysteries.

'Liam?' she prompted. 'I thought you said you'd never heard of Bryan Mailer.' She sat abruptly back down on the carpet, and picked up *The Legend of Kerensa's Handprint* again. She blinked.

Bryan Mailer.

Liam Byrne.

They were almost – not quite, but almost – anagrams of each other.

'Holy fucking shit,' she murmured. 'This is . . . this is you! *You're* Bryan Mailer. You *wrote* all these!'

He rubbed his forehead. 'It was a long time ago. Decades.'

'But . . . but!' She shook her head. 'I asked you! I was so excited and I told you all about them, and I . . . You don't say anything about it in your memoir!'

'You've only reached my twenties,' he pointed out. 'I didn't write these until I was in my thirties, and that still makes them nearly fifty years old. It was a small press, and they were popular at the time, but their appeal didn't last. I haven't written anything for years. There isn't a huge market for Cornish legends.'

Ollie spluttered. 'Are you kidding me? There's a massive market for these types of books, especially now, when Cornwall's so popular! Did you see how many people had heard of Bryan Mailer at the quiz? I can't *believe* you kept this from me.'

'It's so far in my past.'

'Liam! People *love* these books! *I* love these books. I know your publisher shut down, but that means you have the rights back. We could find someone else to reissue them.'

'Ollie,' he laughed.

'I'm serious.' How had he kept this from her? From everyone, surely. Max hadn't known – he'd been surprised by the discovery, too. Did Marion know, even?

Ollie loved these books. He was *such* a good writer – but then she knew that because she'd been typing up his memoir for weeks. Somehow, it hadn't twigged that they weren't just the stilted tales of an old man who wanted to preserve his life history, but the well-woven stories of someone who knew exactly what they were doing. How could she have been so stupid?

Ollie walked towards him on her knees. 'I can't believe this! You're a genuine, published author who's written *nine* excellent novels. You didn't tell me, and I didn't figure it out. I know what happened yesterday was awful, but look what Max has uncovered!' She held the book out to Liam on open palms, as if offering him a sacred treasure. 'You dark, dark horse, Liam Byrne.' She shook her head and returned to the sofa, holding his novel protectively on her lap.

Liam was staring into his cup of tea, his brows lowered.

'What's wrong?' she asked. 'If you think I'm going to involve you in my events at A New Chapter, then you're absolutely right.'

'It was all such a long time ago. Nobody would recognise *me* as an author. Bryan Mailer never went public. Hardly anyone knows we're the same person.'

'Then we need to change all that: get these books out there again – get *you* out there. You've clearly not lost the bug, or you wouldn't be writing your memoir. I can't believe I didn't twig what was going on! Did you write all these shorthand?'

'Of course. Computers haven't been around forever, have they?'

Ollie grinned. 'I can't wait to tell Thea!'

'Now hang on, Ollie.'

'What is it?' She knew she was coming across like a giddy schoolgirl, but this was incredible news. It was almost, *almost,* the best thing that had happened since she'd moved to Cornwall.

'They're a few old stories that were popular several decades ago, and I doubt anyone would care a jot that I wrote them.'

'I think you're wrong,' Ollie said. 'I really, really do. Does Melissa know about them?'

'No. I finished writing them in the late Seventies. Briony was a teenager then, and Melissa wasn't born until eighty-eight, so the books were all put to bed long before she was old enough to be aware of them.'

Ollie looked around Liam's study, the window still open, letting in air that made the curtains shift and the decorations dance. It was the study of a writer: of course it was. She couldn't believe she'd been so blind to it. She looked at the book, the title that was so familiar: *The Legend of Kerensa's Handprint.*

'So you based all your stories around well-known Cornish legends?' she asked. 'So many of them correspond with the book you lent me. People love that blend of fact and fiction. When you think about the way true crime and thrillers have merged, or the scripted reality shows like *Made in Chelsea,* it's just—'

'Ollie.' Liam put his hand on her knee, stopping her in mid flow. His apprehensive look morphed into something else: something more apologetic.

'What is it?'

'Your little book of Cornish legends?'

She nodded.

'I wrote it. There's no name on there, because it was a . . .' He huffed out a breath. 'It was a marketing tool conjured up by my publishers: a companion piece. An anonymous book of the supposedly famous legends that accompanied the stories.'

'You wrote that too? Wow!' Her mind began to race. 'How did you unearth all the details? They're so thorough. All the history, that's—'

'Ollie Spencer,' he said firmly. 'I made them *all* up. All those legends. I invented them in the Roskilly and Faith books, and I invented them for the book you've been carrying around with you.'

The whirling thoughts in Ollie's mind came to a sudden halt. It was as if she'd walked into a brick wall. She blinked. 'But . . . but no. But I . . . I saw the handprint. Max and I found one of those incredible shells. This is not . . .'

'I've lived here all my life,' Liam said. 'I know the landscape like the back of my hand. I found shells on that beach, and they were so stunning, so unusual, I invented a story around them. I found that rock with the markings, and thought it looked like a handprint. I imagined how one could have got there. I wanted to map the landscape, to work meaning into what I found on my long, solitary walks. This place is beautiful, and I wanted people to find that out for themselves. What better way than to imbue it with history: tragedy and love; unsolved mysteries; ghosts?'

Ollie pressed a hand to her mouth. Her shoulder twinged, but she ignored it. 'I've been following them,' she said. 'Max and I . . .'

'I thought it might help you get to know the area a bit more: help you find your feet here. And when you started taking Max with you, well . . . I can't say I felt guilty, because it had achieved what I'd been hoping for. It had brought you closer to Port Karadow, and the people in it. My whimsical tales captivated you, and perhaps stopped you worrying so much about the bookshop: about moving here, all on your own, to start your new life.'

Ollie sipped her tea, even though it was lukewarm, and tried to get it to sink in. Liam was a writer: he was Bryan Mailer. He wrote books about myths and mysteries, and he'd created the legends she'd been so caught up in, that she'd asked Max to help her track down.

'I suppose the ruins of a church have to have *some* kind of sinister story attached to them,' she said.

'I'm so sorry, Ollie. I just—'

'What on earth are you sorry for?' She laughed. 'This is amazing news!'

Liam sat back in his chair. 'It is?'

Ollie pressed her lips together to stop her idea bursting out of her before she was ready to explain it. Liam had said it was all behind him, which meant she needed to tread carefully. She would work everything out and come up with a failsafe plan. Her thoughts back to racing, she got up, went to the desk and offered Liam another mince pie.

Max was going to be OK, and, in a move that was highly ironic considering what they'd been searching for on their walks, he'd helped her to discover one of Port Karadow's hidden treasures. She hoped that, soon, they would be able to return it to its former glory together.

Chapter Thirty-Four

'Did you know?' Ollie asked Marion, when she had finished telling her about her discovery. When she'd finally left Liam's study the evening before, taking another two mince pies with her, Marion had already slipped off home, like she so often did.

Now it was Monday morning, still too early for the sun to have fully risen, and Ollie was bleary-eyed after a night full of worrying thoughts about Max that, she knew, would linger until she'd seen him for herself. Hopefully, that would be later on today.

She stood in her dressing gown at the kitchen island, Marion on the opposite side, both of them clutching mugs of coffee. This time, Marion hadn't even pretended to have an ulterior motive for turning up. The first words she'd said when Ollie had opened the front door were, 'How are you doing, Ollie Spencer?'

She had remembered something Melissa had said to her once, the words staying long after she'd forgotten the context: *Hard times bring people together, Ols. Human connection matters more than anything.*

Ollie was grateful to have Marion to talk to on a day when she was going to have to tell Thea that the grand, spangly author launch she'd set up for A New Chapter, that they'd all been working towards as their impressive Christmas event, was about to become a big fat failure. They'd been selling tickets for Sophia's launch – which was supposed to include a reading and a Q&A – and promoting it as if it was a Dolly Parton concert. And now they would have to do the one thing Thea had told Ollie she wanted to avoid: admit defeat and suck it up, not to mention refund all the ticket money. It wouldn't just be disappointing: it would be a disaster.

'Of course I knew,' Marion said, scoffing as if any other scenario was utterly absurd. 'You think Liam could keep a detail like that hidden from me? Don't forget who's been dusting those shelves.'

'He kept it from *me*,' Ollie said, unable to hide her disgruntlement.

'I've known him for decades,' Marion pointed out. 'When he was younger, and prouder of his achievements. He always wanted the pseudonym, though: didn't do any events at the time, and without social media and whatnot, it was easy to keep his true identity hidden.'

'He didn't want to bask in the glory?'

'He's always been a quiet man,' Marion said. 'He loved writing, giving people pleasure with his stories, but he's never been a "look at me" sort of person. He doesn't need me, you know, apart from a few bits here and there. I like being busy, and Adam still works in London four days a week. It's more like a partnership than one old farmer and his faithful housekeeper.'

'I guessed it was mostly about the company.'

'And now he has you, as well. I'm sure he could type that book all on his own, arthritic fingers or no.'

'I'm quicker, and I know my way around a laptop.'

'Still. The man could go out of an evening, to the Sea Shanty or the Happy Shack. He doesn't need to employ people just to have friends. He's incredibly personable, but he's glued himself to his farmhouse these last few years.'

'Well.' Ollie put her cup down. 'I'm hoping to change that, as it happens.'

Marion raised her eyebrows but held her silence, until Ollie started to squirm and was compelled to fill it.

'I want him to do an event at the bookshop,' she said. 'He's such a brilliant storyteller: he'd have everyone transfixed. I've been so intrigued by the Bryan Mailer mysteries since I found them, and a lot of people I've spoken to here love them too. Revealing Liam as this talented, popular author would be such a brilliant thing. His publishers are no longer in business, and the books are out of print, but I don't think that matters. He's local, and he's a legend himself – never mind writing about them!'

Marion's gaze was steady, but Ollie thought she could see a twinkle there.

'You like it,' Ollie went on. 'You've turned into this silent, wise old woman, but—'

'Less of the old, thanks. And yes, I do like it. I think it would be wonderful for A New Chapter, and the residents of Port Karadow, and Liam, too. Good luck getting him to see it that way, though.'

'I know. I need to come up with a plan to convince him.' She drummed her fingers on the countertop. 'Do you want some pancakes? I feel like making pancakes, and it's still early enough.'

'Oh! Are you sure? I'd love some.'

'Settle yourself down, then. I think it's a myth that you need to leave the batter to stand, anyway.'

As Ollie prepared the pancake mix, she and Marion talked about Liam, about the town and the legends he'd invented, and Ollie admitted that she'd been completely fooled by them.

'I assumed they were traditional Cornish stories that everyone knew. I spent a whole lot of time asking people if they'd heard of Bryan Mailer, but I didn't ever think to ask about the legends: didn't even consider that nobody would have heard of Kerensa and her handprint, or the ghostly battle at St Ethel's church, outside of those books. Mind you, Max didn't know about them, and he was keen to visit the locations with me.' She chewed her lip, thinking back to the way he'd reacted. 'Although . . .' She spun round, but Marion held her hands up.

'As far as I'm aware, Max didn't know Liam had anything to do with them.'

Ollie waggled her whisk. 'I bet he sussed it, though. I bet everyone would have, except me.'

'Ollie, you're not from around here. Of course the people who have grown up here, when faced with some supposedly traditional stories they've never heard of, might question where they came from. You were at a disadvantage from the get-go.'

'Maybe I just wanted to believe,' she said, pouring oil into the frying pan and waiting for it to heat up. 'I found it comforting to think of those people, centuries ago, being out of place, struggling, but still leaving a legacy. Isn't that what we all want?'

'To be the subject of some mythical story?'

'To make a mark on the world. Though at the moment, I'd settle for not fucking up completely at the bookshop, and getting to spend all my free time with Max.' She flipped the pancake, irrationally pleased when it landed right in the centre of the pan, not even one edge sticking to the side.

'You really like him, don't you?'

Ollie glanced at Marion, then turned back to the hob. 'It's gone a bit beyond that,' she admitted. 'It's like we're hardwired together in my thoughts. Found something on a walk with Henry – I must tell Max; worried about something at the bookshop – Max will make me feel better. I rolled over in bed this morning, and before I was properly awake I was reaching out for him. The shock when he wasn't there . . .' It hit her, suddenly, that if things had gone differently, he might not be in a hospital bed, recovering: that she might not have been mentally preparing to see him today, after being sick with worry. That it might not have been possible.

She swallowed, and poured too much batter into the pan, so that she knew the next pancake would be burnt on the outside before it was properly cooked.

'I love him,' she said. 'I am in love with Max Holden.' She held her whisk up and spun to face Marion, whose smile was accompanied by distinctly watery eyes.

'I'm so glad he's going to recover,' the older woman said. 'That he's as strong as he appears.'

'Do not start me off, Marion,' Ollie warned, pointing the whisk at her. 'I have just about stopped crying, and if I'm going to achieve all my missions today, I need to push the emotions back as far as they'll go.'

'What are your missions, then?' Marion crossed her arms on the counter and sniffed loudly.

'Make us pancakes for breakfast without burning them. Go to the bookshop and fix the very tiny problem that cropped up over this already traumatic weekend. Convince Liam that he wants to out himself as Bryan Mailer and do a reading from one of his books at the Christmas event on pageant day. Go to the hospital and tell Max that I'm in love with him.'

'Gosh.' Marion exhaled. 'Just a small list, then.'

'Basically, I need to fix Christmas. For me, Max, Liam and Thea. For Port Karadow.'

'Cornwall, England, the UK, the world . . .'

Ollie grinned. 'It feels a bit like that.'

'But why do you need to fix it, when you're not the one who's broken it?'

Ollie put bacon in another pan and turned the heat on under it. 'Because the grand author event that I promised Thea and the town, that we have been promoting to the max, and that everyone, it seems, is excited about, is no longer happening.'

'What?'

'I had a call from Sophia Forsythe-Hartley's editor on Sunday. Can you believe that? Even though she didn't know what had happened, the timing's pretty off, don't you think?

Sophia's had some sort of crisis, and can't make the event. And . . .' She huffed. 'I'm sure it's genuine. I don't think they'd cancel if there wasn't a real issue, but it's a disaster, Marion. I hadn't let myself take it in until now, but I've got a lot of fixing to do.'

'And you think Liam could be part of that?'

'He could be the saviour,' Ollie admitted. 'Like Santa Claus, but with stories as his gifts.'

'So tell him that,' Marion said. 'He's a stubborn old man – he hasn't broken the mould there, let me tell you – but he's a kind soul, and you're the perfect weapon against stubbornness.'

'I am?'

Marion levelled her with a look. 'If you can make me believe I need to order Victoria's Secret underwear, then you can convince Liam he needs to dust off his author persona and treat the town to his storytelling. You're persuasive, Ollie: you know you are. Use all your charm, your quirkiness, your lack of inhibitions to show him that he needs to do this.'

Ollie bit her lip. She nodded absent-mindedly, but already, a plan was forming in her mind.

Once they'd finished their pancakes and Marion had left, Ollie got ready for work. She would allow herself one more day of not telling Thea about Arabella's call: she would much rather go to her with a problem *and* its solution, and she wouldn't know if she had one of those until later that evening.

She spent extra time on her make-up, because she needed the confidence boost – she still looked washed-out after too little sleep and too much stress – and because she hoped, more than anything, she would get to see Max today.

Her phone vibrated from the duvet cover, and she picked it up.

The name at the top of the message made her heart skip, and the words turned her legs to jelly, so that she had to sit down on the bed and reread them over and over again until they sank in.

Please don't be scared. I don't want to live without you either, and I've got the best possible reason to get better this time. I promise you I will. See you later, I hope? Mxx

Chapter Thirty-Five

Ollie got the call from the hospital when she was on her way to the bookshop, and rang Thea straight away. Her boss picked up on the second ring. 'Ollie, how is he?'

'He's awake, and his mum told Liam that the doctors are confident he's going to be OK.'

'Oh thank God! Are you on your way to see him?'

'Would that be all right? The hospital have just called me.'

'Of course! I have Andrea in all day, and look – Becky's just got here. Do you mind if I tell her that Max is allowed visitors? I know Dylan has been really worried about him.'

'I don't mind at all. I expect the more friendly faces he sees, the better, as long as we don't tire him out.' She swallowed. 'Listen, Thea . . .'

'Yes?'

She thought of her plan, thought she could hold onto her secret for one more day. 'I'll be in by lunchtime, OK?'

'Take your time, Ollie,' Thea said gently.

Once they'd said goodbye, Ollie squeezed her eyes closed for a beat, then hurried back to the barn and got into her car.

The sight of the mini Christmas tree standing jauntily on the nurses' desk was so familiar that it confused Ollie for a second, until she remembered that she'd stared at it for hours on Saturday night. It wasn't a surprise that it had imprinted onto her brain.

'I'm here to see Max Holden,' she told the nurse behind the desk, who seemed to have her attention on a computer, ringing phones, bits of paper and several colleagues all at once. 'Someone called me and said I could come in?'

'Right, hang on a second.' She typed on her keyboard. 'He's in Acute Medicine. It's up on the second floor. Come out of the lift or stairwell and take a left, then it's all the way down the corridor. There's another reception there.'

'Thank you,' Ollie said, feeling stupid that she'd come straight to Accident and Emergency. She followed the nurse's instructions, the stairwell cold and windowless, its light a sickly yellow. The corridors were busy, reminding her that all sense of normal time disappeared in hospitals. She remembered the time right after her injury, when she could barely focus on anything but the pain, and had got that impression then, too.

She followed the signs to Acute Medicine, where there was a man with neat grey hair behind the reception desk. Two figures were sitting on chairs in the waiting area, and as Ollie got closer, one of them stood up and walked towards her. She tensed when she realised who it was.

'They won't let Dylan in to see Max,' Becky said. Ollie noticed she had mascara smudges under her eyes. 'Apparently he's not on the list.'

Ollie frowned. 'I'm sorry, I didn't . . . I just thought they were letting close friends see him, now that he's well enough. I didn't realise there was a list.'

'Of course you didn't,' Becky said. She kept her voice low, but Ollie could hear the anger in it. 'Why would you know that when you're always on them? When you never have to face barriers, when it doesn't matter what you get wrong because you always get a free pass? Dylan is *twelve.*'

Breathe, Ollie thought. 'Let me ask the nurse, OK?' She didn't want to get into this, not when she was so close to seeing Max, or with Dylan within earshot.

'Because of course they'll listen to you, and not me.'

'Becky, I'm just trying to help. That's all I've *ever* tried to do. I know you don't like me, but I honestly haven't been trying to make your life – anyone's life – harder. You think I moved to a brand-new place, miles from anyone I knew, with the sole intention of messing up the status quo?' She realised she was hiss-whispering, her hands clenched into fists. She loosened her fingers. 'Please, just let me ask. Maybe Max's parents gave names to the nurses, and they weren't aware how close he is to Dylan?'

Becky glared at her, then flourished an arm in the direction of the nurses' station.

Ollie walked up and put her hands on the desk. 'Hi. I'm Ollie Spencer, here to see Max Holden.'

The grey-haired man looked at her, then glanced down the corridor. 'Let me check he's ready to accept visitors.'

'Actually,' Ollie said, not wanting to point out that he must be ready, otherwise they wouldn't have called her, 'there's a boy here who knows Max, and who'd love to see him. Is there any chance he can go in? Apparently he's not on a . . . his name's not been given to you?'

The man turned to his computer screen. 'We need to monitor the number of visitors he sees. What's this boy's name?'

'Dylan,' Ollie said. 'Dylan Cowling.'

'I can't see him here.'

'No, that's what I'm telling you. But could he go in and see Max for five minutes? I'll give up some of my time, if that's how it works.'

The man looked at her, assessing, and then at Becky and Dylan. The boy had his head bowed.

'Five minutes,' he said. 'Room twelve. He can go in first, then you can see him.'

'Thank you.' Ollie glanced down the corridor. Room twelve was just there, with the door closed and the curtain drawn across the window. Max was inside. It was only five more minutes, she told herself. She walked over to Becky and Dylan.

'Hey Dylan,' she said. 'You can see Max for a few minutes.'

When Dylan looked up, she saw that he had tear-tracks down his cheeks. Her heart squeezed.

'For real?' He looked from her to his mum.

Becky nodded. 'Take it easy on him, OK? He's probably really tired.'

Dylan scrambled to his feet and Ollie walked him to the door, then turned away when he pushed it open. If she saw

Max now, she wouldn't be able to stop herself going in there too. Instead, she sank onto the seat next to Becky.

'I know that Sophia Forsythe-Hartley isn't coming,' Becky said.

Ollie had been half-expecting a thank you, and certainly not this. Her stomach clenched. 'What?'

'Thea told me when I got to the bookshop this morning. Arabella called A New Chapter yesterday, too. Thea said not to mention it to you, because of Max: that we could deal with it later.'

'When Thea called me this morning, I – I wanted to tell her in person. It wasn't a good time.'

'When would it have been a good time? You've put so much effort into this one, huge event, and now your author's backed out. Thea's been working towards it, coordinating with Anisha on the planning team at the council, so it fits in with everything else that's going on for the Christmas pageant, and now we don't have a guest.' Becky's laugh was humourless. 'Of course, Thea will forgive you, but I want you to know how much damage you've done.'

'I've got a plan,' Ollie said.

'Oh of *course* you have! You've always got a bloody plan.'

Ollie glanced at Max's door. 'I'm really sorry, Becky, if I've hurt you in some way. I thought we were getting along, that you liked the Book Wars event. I am *really* trying here, and I just . . .' She gulped down the lump that had solidified in her throat. 'I want us to work well together, and for the bookshop to be a success. Of course this is a blow, and I'd never have approached Arabella if I thought there was a chance she and Sophia would back out. But these things happen, and we can come up with something else.'

'You think it's all so easy, don't you?'

'I think what's easy?'

Becky gestured around her, though surely she couldn't mean this, here, right now: a hospital with one measly glowing snowman on the nurses' desk, and Max unwell in a bed nearby.

'Everything,' Becky said. 'You've got your job, which you're treating like some kind of homework project; your perfect boyfriend; your swanky barn and your cute dog and your friends. You're toying with it all, and if something doesn't work out, so what? You drop it, then move onto the next thing.'

Ollie frowned. She really, *really* didn't want to cry in front of this woman. She honed in on her anger instead.

'I'm not dropping anything.' She turned on the plastic chair so she could look Becky in the eye, trying to keep her voice even so the nurse wouldn't hear. 'I am embracing *everything* about living here. I love working at the bookshop, I feel incredibly lucky to be living in Foxglove Barn, and I am not taking any of it for granted. Maybe I put on this front where I seem happy all the time – blasé, even – but it's only because I try and stay positive. It doesn't mean I don't care: it's the opposite, in fact.

'I was lucky that I was able to move down here, to Cornwall, but it didn't come out of the best circumstances, and I promise you it hasn't all been easy.'

Becky fiddled with a button on her coat, her eyes trained on the floor.

'And as for Max,' Ollie continued, because this was where

322

she felt most betrayed by Becky's words, 'does this look perfect to you? He told me he'd been ill in the past, and then I . . . I watched him collapse, and I've felt guilty ever since, asking myself if us spending time together contributed in some way, if I pushed him too far. But I promise you' – her voice was thick with tears, now – 'I am not toying with Max, and I'm not going to leave just because it's got tough. I care about him, and I'm not walking away from him.' She rubbed her cheeks with the heel of one hand, and searched for a tissue in her handbag with the other. 'Fuck.' She spotted a visitors' toilet further down the corridor, and hurried to it.

She went into a stall and pulled off several sheets of paper, pressing them to her eyes. She felt defeated and blindsided by Becky's accusations, when all she'd been focused on was seeing Max.

Ollie splashed water on her face, dried it and looked at herself in the mirror. Whatever happened with Becky, she needed to be strong for him. No more tears, she told herself, and strode back out into the hospital corridor.

Chapter Thirty-Six

Becky wasn't in the waiting room, and the door to room twelve was open.

'You can go in now,' the nurse said.

Ollie shoved her hands into her coat pockets and walked up to the doorway.

The first thing she saw was Max sitting up in bed, his dark curls a tangle against the white pillow. Early morning sun filtered through the window, hitting the side of his face, emphasising the purple smudges under his eyes. But he was smiling, saying something to Dylan while Becky stood beside her son.

She hesitated, not wanting another confrontation, but as she shifted, her boot scraped the floor and Max looked up. His smile widened, his eyes latching onto hers, and he beckoned her forward.

'Ollie. Come in.' He sounded just like normal, no hint of weakness in his voice.

'I don't want to interrupt.' She hovered at the end of his bed.

'You're not,' Max assured her. 'Please.'

He held his arm out, and Ollie couldn't hold on for another second. She rushed forward and put her hands on either side of his face, lifting it gently so she could kiss him. Seeing him, touching him, pressing her lips to his felt overwhelming after the hours of fear and uncertainty. She wanted to pull him tightly against her, wrap him up forever, so instead she kissed him again, kissed his nose and then his forehead.

'Hey,' he said, laughing softly. 'I'm OK. I'm all right, Ollie. I didn't mean to scare you.'

'Well, you did,' she said. 'But I forgive you, as long as you'll let me look after you.'

'I don't need looking after. The doctors have said I'm going to be fine. I just need to take it easy for a bit.'

Ollie pushed away her guilt. 'You have to let me make you tacos, at the very least.'

'You do make excellent tacos.' Max took her hand as she sat on the side of his bed.

'We should go,' Becky said. 'I have to get back to the bookshop, and Dylan needs to go to school.'

For a moment, Ollie had forgotten they were there.

'Mum.' Dylan drew the word out with a long-suffering sigh.

'Thank you for coming to see me,' Max said. 'It means a lot.'

'I'm glad you're getting better,' Dylan said solemnly.

'I am, too,' Becky added. She glanced at Ollie, then dropped her gaze.

'Wait,' Ollie said. 'What I told you – outside? I meant all of it. I never wanted to offend you. I've just been trying to . . . to fit in.'

Becky pressed her lips together and took her son's hand.

Ollie felt suddenly frantic. It wasn't the right time or place to have this conversation, but Becky didn't seem to want to give her a chance. Perhaps if she said it in front of Max and Dylan, she would listen.

'I suppose for me that means shouting loudly, making my mark,' she went on. 'How will anyone know what I'm capable of, if I don't immediately show them?' She chewed her lip, wondering how to say what she wanted to, and felt Max squeeze her hand. 'I knew when I moved here that some people would always see me as an outsider, but I still wanted to try and prove them wrong. Maybe I came across as cavalier, perhaps I tried *too* hard and it looked like I was throwing things at the wall and seeing what would stick. But it has never been because I didn't care, because already, being here feels like . . .' She looked at Max, took courage from the way his eyes held hers. 'It feels like home, and I don't want to give that up, not so soon after I've found it. But if I haven't listened to you enough, to anyone, then I'll stop shouting and start listening instead.'

'Mum,' Dylan said, in a loud whisper that nobody could miss, 'what is she talking about?'

Ollie laughed, and even Becky cracked a smile.

'I'm trying to apologise to your mum,' Ollie said.

'What for?'

She sighed. 'For not being thoughtful enough. For—'

'She's apologising for things I've accused her of,' Becky cut in, 'but that aren't true.' She rubbed a hand over her

326

eyes. 'I was surprised when Ollie came to work at the bookshop, and I suppose I didn't like the way she did things: how she was so positive, all the time.'

Dylan frowned. 'You didn't like her being happy?'

Becky laughed. 'Not when I was feeling grumpy, no. But it wasn't fair of me. I've not been fair, I've—' She looked at Max. He smiled at her, but stayed quiet. 'I didn't give you a chance, Ollie. And I still think some of your ideas are batshi— ridiculous, but what you said outside . . .' She shook her head. 'I assumed you came here with tons of money and this grand idea about how you could make things better. In the bookshop, I mean.'

'I do want to make things better in the bookshop,' Ollie said, shrugging. 'But not because I think I *know* better. I just want to work with you and Thea, to be a part of it. In my last job, I needed to take some time off and my boss sort of . . . gave up on me. She filled the position with someone younger, and I tried to challenge that by being over the top, I suppose. I've held onto that here, but I promise I'll tone it down.'

Becky shook her head. '*I'll* be more accepting.'

'How about we just both try and understand each other a bit more? And please, tell me if I'm being a dick– pain in the bum,' she amended, glancing at Dylan.

'And you can tell me if I'm not listening,' Becky said. 'I'm sorry, Ollie.'

'I'm sorry, too.'

'My teacher, Mrs Cardigan, says that Christmas is all about forgiving each other,' Dylan piped up. 'Tomorrow, I have to read out an example in front of the class. Can I tell them about you?'

Becky patted his head. 'Are you going to write it all out beforehand?'

Dylan nodded. 'Or I'll forget.'

'Good. Will you let me check it? I don't want you making Ollie out to be in the wrong, OK?'

Dylan frowned. 'Didn't you both do things wrong?'

'Yes,' Becky said. 'But it was me more than Ollie. I can help you later, if you like. But right now, buster, you have to get to school.'

'All right.' He sighed. 'Bye Ollie. Bye Max. I'm glad you're OK now.'

'See you later, Dylan,' Max said. 'Thanks for coming, Becky.'

'See you at the bookshop?' Becky said to Ollie.

'I shouldn't be too late.'

'You can tell me what you're planning to do about Sophia, and we can work on it together.'

'I'd love that,' Ollie said. 'Thanks, Becky.'

They walked out of the room, Becky closing the door quietly behind them.

'I'm sorry about that,' Ollie said to Max. 'I didn't mean to use up our time hashing out my and Becky's issues.'

He shook his head. 'I didn't realise it had got that bad between you.'

She laughed. 'Neither did I: I thought we'd fixed things.'

'You have now, though. What did you say to her outside?'

Ollie scooted closer to him and took his other hand, lacing their fingers together. 'I told her that I wasn't just playing at this new life, that it hadn't been as easy as she assumed, and that I wasn't giving any of it up, least of all you: I told her that I cared about you too much to let you go.'

He swallowed. 'Even when I'm this much trouble? What happened on Saturday, Ollie – I'm so sorry.'

'What could you possibly be sorry for? If anything, I'm responsible.'

Max squeezed her hand. 'What are you talking about?'

'I've blazed my way into your life, upended it. All those long walks in the cold and the rain, everything we did—'

'None of that had *anything* to do with this and, even if it did, I wouldn't give it up. Ollie.' He took a deep breath. 'Ollie, look at me.'

She raised her gaze from the bedcovers.

'This was just bad luck,' he said. 'The doctors told me that, even though recurrence is rare, because I had it before, I was more at risk of getting it again. That's all it was. Not going on walks with you, not eating tacos or tying ribbons round Yule logs. They want to monitor me for a few days, and I'll have to have weekly check-ups for the next couple of months to make sure it hasn't done any permanent damage, but they're hopeful: I've been hooked up to monitors, had every test possible, and as long as I take it easy for a while, don't agree to run a marathon or swim the Atlantic, I should be fine. I am so sorry I scared you.' He pressed his lips against her forehead, and Ollie closed her eyes.

'I went through so many scenarios,' she said. 'So many horror stories.'

'My parents said that you and Liam were here all Saturday night.'

'I didn't want to leave you. I would have come in the ambulance, stayed in the emergency room, even if it meant sleeping on the floor, being kicked by doctors. I was worried that . . . that they would come out and tell me . . .'

Max let go of her hands and wrapped his arms around her, pulling her tightly to him. Ollie resisted for a second, worrying about his heart, then let herself sink against him. Max was here, and he was going to be all right: he was going to come home to her.

'I love you,' she said into his chest, whispering the words against his hospital gown and, beneath, the organ that had put him here. She waited for the pause, for him to tense up, but he just tightened his hold on her, and it made her bold. 'I am in love with you, Max Holden, and I want you in my life.'

'Good to know,' he murmured into her hair, 'because I'm in love with you, too. I was trying to find the right time to tell you, but I should have said it the moment I felt it.' He pushed her back, so they were looking at each other. 'I was going to say that I'm hopelessly in love with you, but hopeless feels like the last thing this is.'

'Hopefully in love?' she suggested.

'Much better. I am hopefully in love with you, and I intend to spend the next sixty years showing you just how much.'

She grinned. 'That doesn't sound *too* terrible.' She pressed a hand to her chest. Could *her* heart cope with all this emotion, this flood of happiness after so much worry?

'And I want you to know,' he went on, 'that I'm committed to looking after myself. The doctor says I couldn't have predicted this, but there are things I can do, things that will make a recurrence less likely.'

Ollie ran her hand down his arm. 'You were already doing those things. Unless you were secretly eating fifteen of

Beryan's sausage rolls a day, and even then, it's mainly about exercise, isn't it?'

'That's a big part of it, but there are other ways I can look after my heart.'

Ollie nodded. 'I can help with that. I think it's my job now, anyway.'

'Why's that?' All the flippancy had gone between them. The air felt charged, and Ollie could see – because she knew him well, now, despite the short time they'd been together – that he was scared. Who wouldn't be, after something like this?

'Because,' she said, 'a piece of your heart belongs to me, so it isn't just your responsibility anymore.'

Max's eyes flooded with emotion. 'Ollie . . .'

'I'm serious, Max. We're in this together. You have my heart to strengthen yours.'

'Ollie Spencer,' he said, his voice catching, and the next moment she was in his arms again, and they were kissing each other as if they'd been given a second chance, and both of them realised just how precious it was.

Chapter Thirty-Seven

'I should get going,' Ollie said. 'I told Thea I'd be at the bookshop by lunchtime.'

Max tightened his arm around her. 'Why did Becky mention Sophia? What do you need to sort out?'

'Ugh. Arabella called me on Sunday, would you believe? She told me that there's been a crisis, and Sophia can't do the event anymore.'

Max's eyebrows rose. 'What? You are kidding.'

'Nope. Anyway, I wasn't as focused as I could have been, so the first thing I need to do is call her back and find out exactly what's going on, and if there's anything we can do to change her mind.'

'And if you can't?' Max tucked a chunk of her red hair behind her ear, then slid his fingers down the strands.

'If I can't, then I have an idea that currently has a *lot* of hurdles in its way, but, if I can pull it off, will be incredible.'

'Tell me your idea,' he said, his eyes alight with amusement.

'Are you laughing at me, Max Holden? On the inside?'

He shook his head. 'I don't understand how anyone could be put off by your enthusiasm. It's infectious.'

'Yes, but sadly, on this occasion, I have proved Becky right.'

'Nope. It's just a blip. Tell me your new plan.'

Ollie looked out of the window. All she could see were rooftops, dusted with a light sprinkling of winter sunshine, and a cold blue sky. If Max had been staying here longer, she would have brought her garlands from home to cheer the place up. One fibre-optic snowman was not enough.

'Why are you stalling?' Max asked. 'What is it?'

She sighed. 'On Saturday night, in Liam's study, you were getting a book down from the shelf.'

'Ah,' he said softly. 'No tiptoeing around this, Ollie. We need to be open with each other. If you're worried, just say, *This relates to when your myocarditis came back and I'm worried you won't like it,* then I'll say, *I'm fine because I've got you, so go ahead and talk to me.* Fair?' He tugged gently on her hair, and something loosened inside her, some more of the tension that she'd told herself had gone, but was still lingering.

'Fair. So, this is about Saturday night.'

'Shitty night: I ruined a great evening. Tell me.'

'Do you remember why you were interested in the book? The one on the top shelf?'

He looked at her, his face blank, and then his eyes widened. 'It was one of Bryan Mailer's mysteries, and you told me that Liam hadn't heard of him.'

'Exactly. And, it turns out, there was quite a significant reason why he had given me the brush-off.'

Max waited, lips parted.

Ollie smiled. 'It's because Liam Byrne *is* Bryan Mailer. He's the author. He wrote all those books.'

Max stared at her. 'What?'

'It was his pseudonym. Apparently he never revealed he was the author, so all these people – all the Port Karadow residents who love his books – have no idea their mystery writer is the slightly reclusive, kind-hearted owner of Foxglove Farm.'

Max rubbed his forehead. 'That is nuts.'

'I know! And those legends, the ones we've been following?' She took a deep breath. 'So—'

'I think I know what you're going to say now,' Max cut in.

'Huh.' She shook her head. 'You're spoiling my second big reveal. And you might not like it, either. It might really piss you off.'

He grinned at her, and despite his obvious tiredness, the fact that he was lying in a hospital bed, his smile lit her up inside.

'What are you looking so smug about?' she asked.

'I'm looking smug because *this* is the secret I thought you were going to tell me. That you'd discovered the book of legends you've been carrying around have no real historical basis: that we've been chasing fictional fairy tales.'

Ollie's mouth fell open. 'You . . . How did you know?'

'I didn't *know*. I suspected.'

'For how long?'

'Ever since I came to meet you at St Ethel's church.'

'What made you suspicious? Come on, Max, this is like getting blood out of a stone.'

He sighed. 'That legend was completely new to me, and I've lived in this area my whole life. And then, when you told me about the others, I hadn't heard of them either – not a whisper. With the mystery series, when you said some of the legends were the same, I just assumed the author, Bryan Mailer, had taken his inspiration from your little grey book. I had *not* considered that Liam was behind all of it, that he's been hiding this huge secret. I'm guessing, now, that he wrote the stories in the grey book too?'

'He did. It was a companion piece to the series. A publicity stunt of sorts.' She shook her head. 'Why didn't you tell me what you suspected?'

He put a finger to her cheek, turning her head so she was looking at him properly. 'Because I didn't want you to stop inviting me on those walks. It was as if I got a charge off your excitement: I felt more alive with you than I did anywhere else. Of course, then I realised it had nothing to do with the walks or the legends, because I felt that way whenever you came into Sea Brew. I realised that charge I was getting, it was me falling in love with you. So . . . anyway. There you go.'

'OK,' Ollie said. 'Wow. I will forgive you for not telling me, considering your explanation is the most romantic thing I've ever heard.'

He gave her a soft smile. 'So, what's your plan? Get Liam – Bryan – to replace Sophia at the pageant event?'

'He's local, he's loved, and it would be a huge coup to reveal him as the author of such a popular series. He's a wonderful verbal storyteller, too. Everything about it is perfect, except that—'

'He doesn't want to do it.'

'Right. He says that part of his life is over – his memoir aside – and he never outed himself as Bryan Mailer. He doesn't want to change that now.'

'You think you can talk him round?'

Ollie fiddled with the sleeve of Max's hospital gown. 'These things are ridiculous. Are you even warm enough? Do you want me to get your dressing gown from home? Or a nice soft blanket?'

He didn't reply, and when she looked up, her stomach flipped at the look he was giving her.

'What?' she laughed.

'You're perfect,' he murmured. 'I don't know how I got so lucky.'

'It's only a dressing gown.'

He shook his head. 'I don't need anything from home. I have my clothes from Saturday night for when they discharge me. Mum and Dad are feeding Oxo.'

'Oh, yes. Of course.' She'd forgotten about his cat. 'I should have thought about Oxo.'

He gave her an exasperated look. 'Ollie! You don't need anything else adding to your to-do list, and what I said, about you being perfect . . . I wasn't trying to put pressure on you. But what's the point of not telling each other how we feel? What good does it do?'

'Leaves us with a little dignity?' She smiled to show him she was joking.

'Dignity can sod off, if it means not telling someone you love the truth. Nobody will get to the end of their life and say, *I wish I'd been more reserved with the people I cared about,* will they?'

'Nope,' Ollie agreed. 'So I suppose I have to tell you that you are the hottest, kindest, most incredible man I've ever met, and I never want to spend a day without seeing you or talking to you. Also, I'd quite like to have sex with you every day, too, because you turn me on in ways I didn't think were possible. I've reached the age of thirty-five, and suddenly that clichéd phrase, *I never knew it could be like that*, makes a whole load of sense.'

Max's eyes darkened, and his gaze dropped to her mouth.

'But maybe we should leave those truths for a different time,' she murmured.

'Yeah,' he said. 'I do want you to elaborate on that at a later date, though. Really.' He cleared his throat, and Ollie grinned, her own pulse thrumming. 'What's your plan for talking Liam round?' Max's head shake told her it was an effort for him to change the subject. 'I'm 100 per cent convinced that you can do it, but I'm obviously going to miss it, so you need to tell me all the details.'

'It's pretty out there.' Ollie settled back onto the bed, so she was sitting next to him.

A nurse appeared in the doorway, wheeling in a complicated-looking machine on a trolley. Ollie was heartened to see that the trolley had tinsel wound around its legs.

'I should go.'

'Five minutes,' Max said to the nurse. 'Ollie was about to tell me something really important.'

'It's not *that* important,' Ollie protested.

'It's incredibly important, to you and A New Chapter. And it'll be entertaining, too.' He smiled at the nurse, and Ollie watched the older woman's face soften. Max

Holden, she thought: bewitching women every single day of his life.

'If it's entertaining,' the nurse said, 'I need to stick around to hear it.'

Ollie exchanged a look with Max, saw the amusement in his eyes, and marvelled at how he could be so positive after everything he'd faced. She kissed him and got off the bed. 'OK,' she said to the nurse, whose name tag read *Gillian*. 'But in order for it to make sense, I need to give you context.'

'Let me check Max's vitals. When I've done that, I'm all ears.'

It was a good idea, running her plan past Max and a total stranger. It was Thea's business and reputation, and she'd only just built a tentative truce with Becky. She didn't want to bring everything crashing down just as they'd begun to understand each other.

She stood against the wall and watched the nurse busy herself around her patient, the machinery beeping occasionally as she marked things down on his chart. When she'd finished, she clipped the chart back on the end of the bed.

'You're remarkably well, Max,' she said, 'considering where you were thirty-six hours ago. Doctor Riordan will come and assess you later this morning, and I'm confident he'll move up your discharge.'

Max nodded, and Ollie wondered if Gillian had noticed the relief flash across his face. She thought that, even though he was recovering well physically, the mental impact of something like this must be huge. But Ollie would look after him, in any way he needed: she would do anything for him.

'Now then,' Gillian said, turning to her. 'What's this entertaining plan all about?'

Ollie pushed herself away from the wall. 'It's about A New Chapter, the independent bookshop in Port Karadow. I'm going to rescue their Christmas event – that I, admittedly, am in charge of – and unearth a local legend that has stayed buried for far, far too long.'

Chapter Thirty-Eight

A New Chapter looked like a magical fairy grotto, a hidden, twinkly den, with only the lights at the back of the bookshop on, the Christmas decorations sparkling, and darkness outside.

'He's definitely coming, isn't he?' Becky spoke in a loud whisper, even though they knew Liam wasn't here yet because the bell hadn't dinged.

'I don't think he'd ignore the message I sent him, and I got the "read" notification almost immediately, so I think he's keeping his antique mobile with him.' Ollie pulled down the skirt of her dress. It was incredibly short, but made out of a thick, velvety fabric, so she felt both too hot and entirely exposed.

'Won't he be mad that you used Max's situation to lure him here?' Thea asked, from her position behind the counter. The till screen's blueish glow lit up her face, and she looked striking, her pretty features enhanced.

'I didn't mention Max,' Ollie said. 'I just asked him to meet me here, and told him it was urgent.'

'But he'll probably think the urgency has something to do with Max.'

Ollie shook her head. 'I called him when I left the hospital, told him Max was doing really well, and passed on his and his parents' thanks for calling the ambulance, and for being at the hospital on Saturday night. There's no way I'd make Liam – or anyone – believe there was a problem. I don't ever want to joke about Max's health.'

There was a moment's quiet, then Thea said, 'I'm sorry. I shouldn't have suggested—'

'Oh no, it's fine,' Ollie cut in, from her place at the top of the stairs. 'I would use almost anything to my advantage, but Max . . . God. It scared me so much.' She shook her head. She didn't want to lower the mood. 'But he's recovering well, and he and Gillian, his nurse, totally approve of this plan – and that was *before* they saw the outfit.' She looked at Becky, who was on the top floor, leaning over the railings and holding a paper bag, inside which was a crucial element of what they were about to do.

Becky grinned. 'It was the only Christmassy thing I could come up with at such short notice, and it's ancient.'

'It's also ridiculous,' Ollie said. 'But hopefully it will work in our favour.'

She pulled at the fabric which was too tight across her shoulders, then dipped down to a stupidly low neckline trimmed with white fur. It was a sexy Mrs Santa Claus dress, and when Becky had brought it to the bookshop that evening – her children were being looked after by Lola,

341

their neighbour – Ollie had laughed for five minutes straight.

'I'll take a photo of you afterwards, and you can send it to Max,' Becky said.

Ollie looked down at herself. 'He might not be ready for this,' she murmured, thinking of the check-ups he would be having over the next few months, to make sure his heart hadn't suffered any long-term damage. She would be with him for every one of those, if she could.

The door pinged, and Ollie watched as a tall, slender shadow stepped through it.

'Hello? Ollie?' Liam's voice was deep and sonorous. It was *perfect* for telling spooky stories.

'Hello, Liam,' Thea said cheerfully. 'So lovely to have you with us.'

'For what?' he asked. 'What is this?'

'And . . . *go!*' Becky whispered, as if she was directing a play, which, Ollie supposed, she was. Sort of.

Ollie opened the book, her finger already on the right page, and, moving down a step, so she was directly under the spotlight in the ceiling, began speaking.

'*Megan Roskilly knew that taking her first posting after graduating from the Police Academy in the sleepy Cornish village would be an experience, but she hadn't expected this.*' She projected her voice, adopted a Cornish accent that she knew, without a doubt, was terrible, and took another step down as she continued to read:

'*As she stared at the unusual formation in the rock, her short, blonde hair dancing in the chill breeze of an early April morning, she had a sudden longing for the grimy streets, the harsh predictability, of London. "What is it again?" she asked, because when Mr Merrick, the old farmer who had called the station – the phone startlingly loud when all she'd had for company the last several hours had been the ticking of the clock – had explained it a moment ago, she hadn't quite understood.*

"'Kerensa's handprint," he said, which told her nothing. And then, "A young girl who died here, centuries ago, left 'er mark behind." Megan nodded, hoping her superiors were on their way, because it wasn't the girl, Kerensa, or her handprint she was concerned about right now: it was the body beside it, the young woman who'd died here mere hours, not centuries, ago.'

Ollie stopped and raised her head. Liam was standing at the bottom of the stairs, his arms folded over his chest, staring up at her. She tugged on the hem of her dress.

'Bloody hell,' Becky said from above her. And then, 'Oh shit!' There was a rustling sound, and then Ollie's hair and skin were peppered with the glittering confetti Becky was supposed to have thrown over her sooner, before she stopped speaking. As performances went, it was pretty haphazard.

'What is this?' Liam said again. 'Why are you reading from that book in that ludicrous outfit, Ollie? It's as if I've stepped into some sort of parallel universe.'

Ollie walked down the rest of the stairs. 'Don't you think it sounded good, though?'

'Not in that accent.' Liam's brows were creased, and while Ollie didn't think he was angry, exactly, she could sense his frustration. Had this been the wrong thing to do?

'Forget the accent,' she said. 'Forget the get-up. That is a killer opening.'

343

'Quite literally,' Thea added. 'I'm desperate to know what happens next.'

'Me too.' Becky hurried down the stairs to join them. 'I'm borrowing it off Ollie after this.'

Liam just shook his head.

'Liam,' Ollie said. 'I really hope you don't mind that I told Thea and Becky you were Bryan Mailer. If you decide you don't want to come clean, then I promise we will all keep your secret. But you're *such* a good writer, and your books are set here. I know the exact spot Megan has been called out to: I know that rock. Of course, I thought Kerensa's handprint was a traditional local legend, but we'll skip over my gullibility right now . . .'

'I wasn't trying to make a fool of you,' Liam said.

'I know!' Ollie beamed at him. 'Max got it, though. He said that if you grew up here, then you'd know the legends hadn't been passed down through generations, because that book – along with your novels – are the only places they appear. The point is, I was completely drawn in. Don't you think, if you came here on pageant day, read the opening of this mystery, that customers would be overjoyed? So many people adore your stories: they would be thrilled if they knew you were the author.'

'You're part of this town,' Thea added. 'Everyone already loves you. If they knew this side of you, knew that you'd written these books, they'd just love you more.'

'They're all out of print,' Liam said.

Ollie felt a skip of hope, because if this was his biggest counter-argument, then maybe he was coming round. 'I found copies on AbeBooks,' she said. 'Ages ago, when I started reading the series. I've ordered a whole load of them, and they'll be arriving here over the next few days. Some won't make it before the event, but people can come and buy them afterwards.'

'Why on earth did you do that?'

'Because I believe in you, because I think you're a local treasure and everyone else will feel the same, once they know. Also, we no longer have a star author for our pageant event, and we want you to fill that space. I'm sure our customers will be as excited to meet Bryan Mailer as they would have been meeting Sophia Forsythe-Hartley.'

'You're trying to flatter me into accepting?'

'Flattery, honesty, straight-out begging,' Ollie said. 'I've already messed this up once. Please say yes, or I'll have messed it up twice and Thea will fire me.'

'Emotional blackmail now, too?' Liam raised an eyebrow.

'I won't fire you,' Thea said, sounding put out.

When Ollie had arrived at the bookshop and told Thea how sorry she was about Sophia and the problem she'd created, her boss had been sympathetic. Ollie thought she'd got away with it because of what had happened with Max, and it made her even more determined to fix it, because she didn't want to accept a free pass or fail to be accountable for her actions.

'You'd be brilliant, Mr Byrne,' Becky said. 'My Dylan's just getting into scary stories – I've got him a copy of *A Christmas Carol* for his stocking – and if he sees you reading from this book, here, on pageant day . . . I reckon it'll make him love books even more. And not just him, either. Those mysteries are really popular, so there'll be fans, people who will be surprised that you're Bryan Mailer, and new readers, too.'

345

Liam cleared his throat. 'I was never the public face of those books – there wasn't one – so I have no performance skills to speak of.'

'That's not true,' Ollie said gently. 'You tell your stories out loud as well as you put them on paper. You have it in you.' She pressed her hands together. 'And I promise we'll look after you. We were thinking of promoting it as the first ever public appearance of Bryan Mailer, keep the fact that it's you a secret until the night. You could come out of the upstairs storeroom, step onto the stage . . .' She could imagine it so vividly. 'We'll put the spotlights on you, and you can start reading. It has the potential to be magical.'

Liam leaned against the bookshop counter. Ollie could tell he was considering it, and she looked at Becky, their eyes widening in unison as they communicated their hope to each other. Thea grinned, as if it was already a done deal. And Ollie, more than any of the ideas she'd had for the bookshop since she'd been here – more than Sophia Forsythe-Hartley, more than Marcus Belrose or Book Wars – wanted this to happen. Not just because it would save her skin, but because it felt so right for everyone involved.

A loved local author, and a well-loved member of the community were one and the same. It was a story that would appeal to children and adults, women and men. She had been fascinated by the legends, even when she hadn't known the area. It would be so much better than a straight-forward author talk: it would be about the community she had become a part of.

She realised, as she saw Liam's frown turn into a smile, saw warmth replace the confusion in his eyes, that she was holding her breath.

'I'll do it,' he said, but before any of them could cheer, he raised a finger. 'On one condition.'

'Anything,' Ollie hurried.

'You do not make me do it dressed as sexy Mrs Santa. That, Ollie, would be a step too far.'

She spluttered out a laugh. 'OK. Done. That wasn't a hill I was going to die on anyway.' She did a little twirl and a curtsy, then rushed forward and pulled Liam into a hug. 'Thank you,' she murmured, while Thea and Becky whooped and clapped. 'Thank you so much.'

Liam pushed back, holding her at arm's length. 'Thank *you*, Ollie. I don't think you realise quite how special you are. I'm glad Max does.'

Ollie felt a prickle in her eyes that she wouldn't give in to. She had no time for tears now, not when there was so much to do to get ready for their magical new headline event. They had to pull out all the stops, and they only had three days to do it.

When she crawled into bed that night, Ollie felt simultaneously wired and exhausted. The last few days had been an emotional rollercoaster, more extreme than anything she'd find at Disneyland. She wished she was climbing into bed alongside Max, even if it was a hospital bed, but he needed rest, and so did she, if everything was going to work out.

She selected the photo Becky had taken of her in the Santa dress, attached it to a message and typed:

Liam's on board! This was the only Christmassy outfit we could come up with. How are you feeling? xx

The dots popped up immediately, and Ollie was delighted that he was still awake. Perhaps he'd been waiting for the verdict. His reply appeared:

> Just calling the doc – think I might be having a heart attack! Bloody hell though, no wonder Liam said yes! Are you keeping the outfit? 😎x

> Don't joke about your ♥ 😔. Dress is Becky's. Don't worry, I'll surprise you with something else. Sleep lots, get better, I love you. xx

> I love you too. Sweet dreams, Ollie. Mxx

Ollie held her phone against her chest, grinning stupidly, and then, instead of getting the beauty sleep she so sorely needed, she clicked on to the Victoria's Secret website and checked whether she was too late to get something delivered in time for Christmas.

Chapter Thirty-Nine

Ollie's walk to work the following morning took her past several of the light displays that had been appearing around the town over the last few weeks. Meredith had told her that on the twenty-third, the day of the pageant, there would be a treasure hunt of sorts. She wished she'd have time to take part in it.

There were the traditional displays: stars in the crooks of lampposts, a giant Christmas pudding twinkling down by the harbour, a group of snowmen at the top of Main Street, near the community hall. Then there were the unusual ones: a pink crab, pincers shimmering, near the Happy Shack; a row of seashells stuck to the wall outside Sea Brew, the flashing, chasing light pattern making it look like they were dancing. Ollie wondered if Max had had a say in what went where, and made a mental note to ask him.

She walked into Sea Brew, and found Stu and Molly, two of Max's colleagues, behind the counter. They had already been given the news that he was recovering well – Max's mum, Cath, had made the phone calls – and that he would soon be back, ruling over his cake-laden empire.

Their relief was obvious in their wide smiles, and in the tight hugs they gave Ollie, slipping out from behind the counter to embrace her. When she ordered a box of cinnamon and brandy butter doughnuts – she couldn't wait to meet Beryan, then perhaps kidnap her for her own culinary ends – they refused to let her pay.

'I hope this isn't going to become a habit,' she said, after she had gratefully accepted the box.

'Oh no,' Molly said, her ponytail swinging as she shook her head. 'As soon as Max is back all this special treatment will stop.' She grinned, and Ollie laughed.

'The problem is,' Stu added, leaning on the counter, 'if he gave freebies to everyone he knows, he'd be bankrupt in weeks.'

'The love of his life might be a tad different though, no?'

Ollie turned, surprised, and found Lizzy smiling at her. She was wearing a knee-length, berry-red cagoule and Hunter wellies, and was carrying a large sprig of mistletoe.

'Love of his life?' Stu frowned. 'I knew they were close, but . . .'

'There was a love declaration at the hospital worthy of a Hallmark romcom,' Lizzy told them.

Ollie's mouth fell open.

'Who are your spies at the hospital?' Molly asked.

Lizzy tapped the side of her nose. 'Never you mind.'

'I need to get to work,' Ollie murmured. She wasn't sure how she felt about Lizzy's gossip. She would happily shout her love for Max from the roof of the Old Post House, but

350

what they'd said at the hospital – how emotional she'd been, how personal some of it was . . . For the first time, she felt uncomfortable that the Port Karadow rumour mill was fully operational, and turning its attention to her.

'Ollie.' Lizzy put a hand on her arm as she passed. 'Don't take offence. I can't think of anyone who isn't wildly happy about you and Max. Jealous too, of course, but not in a serious way. From the moment you got here, nobody else stood a chance.' Her smile was uncharacteristically gentle. 'Bask in the glow. Don't worry about me, or anyone else.'

Ollie muttered a 'Thank you', then took her box of dough-nuts up the hill.

She arrived at the same time as Becky, and could imme-diately feel her and Thea's jittery panic. The entire bookshop was abuzz with nervous anticipation, and the enormity of the situation hit her. They had three days, not including Friday itself, to get word out that Sophia Forsythe-Hartley was off the programme, and that Bryan Mailer was on it.

'Right,' Thea said. 'We have posters, social media, phone calls to the customers who've already bought Sophia tickets. Whoever is doing the social media mans the till, too.'

'Posters.' Becky put her hand up. 'I'll print them and go round town, slapping them on everything. Marcus Belrose will have to have at least three up in the Happy Shack: I won't take no for an answer.'

'I'll do the phone calls,' Thea said. 'Just because some of the people who've bought tickets are customers I know quite well.'

'Or the Port Karadow glitterati,' Ollie added, opening the box of doughnuts.

Thea rolled her eyes. 'Don't you start. You're as bad as Adrian, who thinks this town has its own set of socialites.'

'Oh, Liam's told me all about them,' Ollie said. 'We need them *all* to come to our grand event.'

Thea waggled the bookshop phone. 'That's what I'm planning. Though maybe I should leave it to you, seeing as how you persuaded Li— Bryan to change his mind.'

'I think it was Becky's speech that did that,' Ollie said, taking a doughnut when nobody else did.

'No way,' Becky replied. 'It was your outfit, and that reading.' She guffawed. 'I wished I'd recorded it. If things don't work out here, you can always join the Truro am-dram society, work your way into the Minack theatre group. Hey.' She turned to Thea. 'Isn't Finn's aunt an actor?'

Thea nodded. 'She's in *Estelle*, actually. The new series is starting on the BBC on New Year's Day.'

'Whoa, really?' Ollie said, through a mouthful of doughnut. 'That's proper stardom.'

'And I've met Sam Magee and Lila Forest,' Thea went on, her expression uncharacteristically smug. 'Meredith's quite friendly with Charlie, Lila's cousin, and Charlie owns the Cornish Cream Tea Bus, which is based in Porthgolow—'

'Great cream teas,' Becky cut in. 'I take the kids there sometimes for a treat.'

'And Charlie's husband, Daniel, owns Crystal Waters, the spa hotel on top of the cliff.'

'I did yoga there with Max,' Ollie said, her brain fuzzing at the bombardment of information. 'Wait, hang on – this is too many connections. What do these people, Charlie and Daniel, have to do with what we're talking about?' She rubbed her eyes. 'Sorry, I'm still trying to catch up on sleep.'

Becky squeezed her arm. 'You've had a rough few days. And I know I didn't help, at the hospital. I'm really sorry, Ollie. And I didn't thank you for letting Dylan see Max. It was so kind of you: Dylan commented on it, too.'

Ollie smiled. 'Luckily for us, there's enough Max to go around.'

'And I think the original point was,' Becky went on, 'that your reading was really something. You should extend your role: participate in Book Wars, not just introduce it.' She stretched along the counter, reaching for a doughnut. 'What did Max think of your Santa outfit? I assume you sent him the photo?' She waggled her eyebrows, and Ollie took a moment to marvel at the about-face Becky had done. Perhaps the other woman had simply wanted her to show some vulnerability, prove that there was more beneath the surface.

'He was quite taken with it,' she admitted.

Becky laughed. 'I'll bet.'

'What did he say?' Thea asked. 'Sorry, that's probably really personal, but—'

'He made a terrible, obvious joke about having a heart attack,' Ollie said, 'which I told him off for, then he said it was a shame I wasn't keeping it. Which reminds me, Thea, I've got a personal delivery coming here today. I hope that's OK?' She hadn't wanted to risk her Victoria's Secret purchases being gathered in by Liam or Marion, when she knew the branding would be on the box.

'I bet it's a kinky maid's outfit,' Becky said. 'You'd look great in black and white, with all your red hair piled up. Scarlet bra strap showing. I can see that.' She nodded sagely, and Ollie doubled over.

353

'What the hell, Becky?'

Becky grinned. 'You would, though!'

'This is a lot classier than a maid's outfit. I'll show you when it arrives, if you like?'

'I'd love,' Becky said. 'I've got a third date with a guy, Jerry, who I really like. I need some ideas.'

'Oooh, who's Jerry?' Thea asked.

'I met him at this—' Becky sighed. 'Shit. Should we do this later? We really need to start promoting Secret Bryan, or we're going to have a lot of pissed-off customers.'

Thea grimaced. 'You're right. Let's make a start, then we can reconvene at twelve for a quick strategy update, coffee and doughnuts, and you can tell us about Jerry. OK?'

'Sounds good,' Becky said.

'Perfect,' Ollie agreed.

She opened Instagram and, smiling to herself, switched from her personal account to the bookshop's. The last few minutes had felt close to the early days of her and Melissa's friendship, when they'd been giddy and inseparable, sharing the most personal details of their lives. Was it really possible that, after all these weeks where she'd still felt slightly on the outside – down, in part, to her own attitude – one of her new, genuine friends might actually turn out to be Becky? Wonders, she thought, would never cease. Except that it was nearly Christmas, and so even the most unlikely things were possible: that's what she was counting on, to make project Secret Bryan a success.

Chapter Forty

As Ollie drove through Port Karadow in the darkness, 'It's Beginning to Look a Lot Like Christmas' playing on the radio and the festive lights frosting the town, she realised that, for the first time in a long while, her heart felt full.

She still had no firm plans for Christmas Day – the upheaval of the last few days had left little room for any organising – and she knew she might end up entertaining herself and Henry, but that suddenly seemed unimportant. It was only one day, and she was finally building a real life here, with real relationships that would last into the future.

She had been working furiously with Thea and Becky to get everything ready for the event tomorrow night. Most of the ticket holders had wanted to keep their tickets, thrilled at the thought of meeting Bryan Mailer, and some were coming simply because it was on pageant day and they wanted to be a part of it.

There was a lot to do, and Ollie had left the bookshop later than usual, then gone straight to the hospital. Max had seemed better, more cheerful and less pale, and she had stayed until Gillian told her that, unless she planned on bunking up with him all night, it was time to leave. When Ollie had told her she would love to stay all night, Gillian had laughed and shooed her out, saying they would all get in trouble if that happened. Max's kiss, the strength of his embrace, had sent her on her way with less anxiety than when she'd arrived.

Now, she was taking a meandering route home that no satnav would ever advise, because she had deliveries to make. She had no idea if the occupants would be home, or if they'd welcome the intrusion.

The first house was the one she was most nervous about. It was a neat terrace to the south of town, not too far from the Happy Shack. She parked outside and admired the bushy wreath on the front door, with silver baubles nestled between the pine fronds, and the subtle snowflake lights shimmering above the windows.

Ollie took her first gift out of the boot of her car. She loved the meaning, the sentiment behind it, but it was undoubtedly unusual, and she was prepared to be met with blank faces or bafflement.

Becky answered the door wearing penguin pyjamas, her hair damp from a shower.

'Ollie!' She stared at her, then at the item she was holding.

'Becky.' Ollie smiled. 'Happy Christmas, to you, Dylan, Meg and Billy. This is for all of you. Careful, it's quite heavy.'

'Have you been pilfering from the woods behind Foxglove Farm?' Becky bent her knees and accepted the slender tree trunk.

'Something like that. It's a Yule log.'

'It doesn't *look* like chocolate,' said a voice from behind Becky, and Ollie peered around her to see Dylan standing on the bottom stair. 'If it is, then that is a *lot* of chocolate.'

Becky put Ollie's gift down and turned to him. 'Bedtime, you.'

'I heard the doorbell,' he said. 'Why have we got a *tree*?'

'It's not made of chocolate,' Ollie told him, 'but there are peppermint creams in the bags tied to either end.' Dylan's eyes widened. 'I don't know if you have an open fire, but if not it could go in the garden, as a bug hotel or something.' She rubbed her cheek. 'Or I can take it back, if you don't want it.'

'We've got a fireplace,' Becky said. 'And thanks . . . I think?'

Ollie smiled. 'Max told me about them – about Yule logs. When it's burning, you're supposed to stop doing any sort of work. You're meant to rest, to celebrate the holiday season. And I wanted to say . . . if you ever need a babysitter – or a child-sitter,' she amended, glancing at Dylan, 'then I'd love to help out. But only if you want me to. And also, if you ever fancy coming to mine for a drink, a natter . . . then I would really like that.' She laughed. 'Usually I'm quite articulate. Basically, this is a Yule log and an olive branch rolled into one.'

Becky grinned. 'That sounds great. Especially the drink and the natter. Let's sort something out after Christmas. Are you ready for tomorrow?'

'So ready,' Ollie said. 'The comments on our social media posts have been mainly understanding, only a few disgruntled ones, and there's a lot of excitement about Bryan Mailer.

He's much more popular than he thinks he is, and I'm confident we'll still get a good crowd.'

'Did Liam really write a whole load of mystery books?' Dylan asked.

Ollie nodded. 'It surprised me, too.'

'Don't worry,' Becky said, 'I've only just told him. And he's promised me, on pain of having to do all the washing up over the entire Christmas break, that he won't tell a soul.'

Dylan mimed zipping his lips. 'Did you make these?' He pulled out a Christmas tree-shaped peppermint cream from one of the bags tied to the ends of the Yule log.

'With help from Marion,' Ollie said. 'They're for all of you.'

'Billy and Meg are asleep,' Dylan pointed out.

'So will you be, soon. Now is not the time for a sugar rush.' Becky turned back to Ollie. 'Thank you for this.'

'I hope it's not too weird.'

'Not with the explanation.'

'And the sweets,' Dylan added. 'Is Max going to be OK now?' He asked it casually, his gaze not meeting hers.

'He's doing really well,' she told him. 'The doctors are happy with his test results, so he should be able to come home soon.'

Dylan chewed his bottom lip. 'Are you giving him some peppermint creams, too?'

'If the nurse will let me sneak them in.' She winked at him, and Dylan grinned. 'I'll leave you to it. See you tomorrow, for the big day?'

'Can't wait,' Becky said. 'Take care, Ollie.'

'You too.'

Ollie hurried down the path, trying not to skip with happiness. Olive branch extended; one Yule log delivered; three more to go.

Meredith and Finn were delighted with their Yule log, and Ollie – predictably – spent twenty minutes explaining the tradition and its variations after Finn asked her an endless stream of questions. They were relieved when she updated them on Max's condition – as much the reason for her visits as gifting them the logs and peppermint creams – and she had to turn down a cup of tea because she still had two more houses to visit. She sidestepped their questions about how she had managed to track down Bryan Mailer, and gave their beagle, Crumble, and Smudge the cat, a healthy dose of affection on her way out.

Lizzy's farmhouse was a little way out of town, but Ollie found it easily due to the large tree at the edge of the driveway that had been wrapped in golden lights. When she drove onto the gravel in front of the house, she was met with a laser show of snowflakes, that spun and drifted over the brick building in a way that made her feel slightly dizzy.

'All right, love,' Lizzy said when she answered the door. 'What's all this, then?'

'It's a Yule log,' Ollie told her. 'It's for your fireplace. But don't burn the bags at the end – they're full of peppermint creams.' Two sleek black dogs appeared at Lizzy's side, their noses raised eagerly towards the sweets.

'Did Adrian from Cornish Keepsakes send you? He delivers Christmas hampers about the place.'

'No, this is all me,' Ollie said. 'I wanted to apologise for the way I left Sea Brew the other day. You've been kind to me since I arrived, I was just . . . a bit put out, I guess, that mine and Max's conversation at the hospital was doing the rounds.'

Lizzy's expression softened. 'That's just the way it is here, I'm afraid. Even as far away as Truro, news runs as swiftly as the clouds over the sea. But I didn't want to make you uncomfortable. Come on in.' She took the log, then turned and disappeared, giving Ollie no option but to follow her into the bowels of the farmhouse. 'Do you want a drink?'

'No, thank you.' Ollie watched as Lizzy took the gift bags off the ends of the log and put it in the basket by the fire. It dwarfed the other pieces of wood, and looked ready to upend the entire thing. 'This is just a flying visit.'

'I appreciate the gift.' The fire was already crackling, the smell conjuring up cosy nights in snug rooms with mulled wine, and Ollie could hear voices somewhere else in the house. 'My teenagers,' Lizzy explained, gesturing behind her.

'Ah. Well, I hope you all have a wonderful Christmas.'

'I'll see you tomorrow,' Lizzy said. 'Pageant day in Port Karadow is a special occasion, and this is only the second year they've run it. I have to admit, I was half-surprised, half-not, when I saw that you were bringing in Bryan Mailer to replace Sophia Forsythe-Hartley.'

'Why half-not?' Ollie asked, laughing.

'Because it's you,' Lizzy said. 'It's as if you have a big neon sign with the word *determination* flashing above you. I wouldn't have been *that* surprised if you'd got Richard Osman to come and do a reading tomorrow night.'

'I couldn't hold onto Sophia,' Ollie pointed out.

'And who else in your situation would have pulled off an equally exciting alternative in a matter of days?'

'It has very much fallen into my lap, this new event,' Ollie said. 'You'll see what I mean tomorrow night.'

Lizzy stood up. 'You make all the excuses you want, but you're just what that bookshop needs. And Max, for that matter.'

Ollie's heart shimmied. 'Really?'

'He was a sunbeam before you came along, but now he's positively glowing – last few days aside, of course. You were meant to come here, Ollie. Remember that whenever anybody looks at you askance.'

'I will,' she said, the words lancing straight through her. 'I will remember that. Thank you, Lizzy. I'd better be off.'

The older woman walked her to the front door. 'See you tomorrow, and thank you again for the Yule log.'

'It's my pleasure.' Ollie hurried to her car, sat for a few moments, transfixed by the snowflake laser show, then reversed down the driveway and out onto the road.

Thea lived with Ben in a gorgeous cottage overlooking the sea, and as Ollie pulled up in front of it, she could see their tree glowing in the window, its rainbow lights pulsing blue to red, green to pink. The wreath on the door was a twirl of gold and blue ribbon, interspersed with holly, cinnamon sticks and dried orange slices. When she knocked, she heard voices and barking inside.

Ben answered the door, his smile widening when he saw her and, despite the hefty piece of wood she was holding, he pulled her in for a hug.

'We've just been speaking to Meredith and Finn.' He stepped back and gestured for her to come in. 'They said that Max is firmly on the mend?'

'He is,' Ollie said. 'God, I'm so relieved.' She didn't like the way her voice cracked on the last word, but as she stepped into their beautifully modern front room, Ben took the log from her and Thea embraced her, even though they had been together until a few hours ago.

'You've seen him this evening?' she asked, sitting down and patting the sofa cushion beside her. Ben's dog, a soft-hearted Australian shepherd called Scooter, came and rested his nose on Ollie's knee, letting her stroke him.

'He's looking a lot better,' she told them, as Ben put the log next to their wood burner, and carefully extracted the bags of sweets. 'He's got more colour in his cheeks, and he doesn't seem quite so exhausted. Sometimes you don't realise how worried you are until the worry starts to lift. And I suppose I didn't . . .' she shook her head. 'I wasn't sure if I could really feel the way I did, because we've been together for such a short time.'

'Love can't be measured,' Thea said. 'It doesn't matter if you started loving him after a minute or a decade, and you shouldn't ever worry if what you're feeling is appropriate. I'm so glad you're here! I wanted to find out how he was, how *you* really were, but I didn't want to ask at the shop in case you were only just holding it together.'

Ollie smiled. 'It's not been the easiest few days, but there's so much good stuff to focus on, with the event tomorrow—'

'Stop, Ollie.' Thea held a hand out. 'You don't need to do anything for the next hour except relax.'

'Hot chocolate?' Ben asked. 'And thank you for the Yule log and the peppermint creams. You really didn't need to.'

362

'You've made me feel welcome here – both of you. Max was the one who told me about the Yule logs. You're supposed to stop working for the entire time it's burning.'

Thea grinned. 'I can understand why he brought it up. And, before the madness of tomorrow, I want you to know how happy I am to have you at A New Chapter. It hasn't all been plain sailing, but I never expected it to be, and you've done so much for the shop already.'

Ollie looked down at her knees. 'I'm going to be more collaborative from now on.'

Thea's smile softened. 'You've been great, and I'm looking forward to working on more events, prioritising the Book Wars tournament and the book club in the new year. But after tomorrow . . .'

Ollie looked up. 'After tomorrow?'

'You need to get hold of a Yule log of your own. Focus on Max, on Christmas, on whoever you're spending time with. Read a massive pile of books, but don't think about anything book-related beyond that.'

'Understood,' Ollie said with a laugh. 'What are your reading plans for Christmas? How many books have you set aside?' They were mid-discussion when Ben returned carrying mugs of the most decadent hot chocolate she had ever seen, with whipped cream, marshmallows and a chocolate flake slowly melting on top. 'Oh my God,' she murmured. 'This looks incredible. Thank you.'

As she told Thea and Ben about her visit with Max, how relieved she was that he had someone as funny and as kind as Nurse Gillian looking after him, and what her plans were when he was discharged, she hoped that neither of them would notice that she hadn't mentioned Christmas Day. The truth was, despite her love of festivities, her garlands draped around the barn and the leftover peppermint creams waiting in a tin on her kitchen island, she didn't think her first Christmas in Cornwall was going to be as rich or indulgent as she would like it to be.

Chapter Forty-One

It was the day before Christmas Eve, which Ollie thought was one of the best, most anticipatory days of the entire festive season. You were often busy getting last-minute presents and food, but still looking forward to that slide into Christmas Eve, when everything started to feel magical and otherworldly. This year, however – and her first in Cornwall – it was the day of the town's Christmas pageant, and their hastily re-shuffled, much-promoted author event.

When she'd got back from Thea and Ben's the night before, she'd knocked on the farmhouse door. She'd wanted to check Liam was still happy, and was relieved that he seemed quietly satisfied with their plan. There were no signs of cold feet, and even if there had been, Ollie wouldn't have been worried: if he didn't turn up, she could simply go home and fetch him.

The day was grey and serious – peak December, she thought – but the muted winter colours, the slates, browns and soft greens, and the deep, steely blue of the sea in the distance, were a balm to her senses as she walked. Then, as she left the fields behind, and Port Karadow appeared in front of her, the sombreness was replaced by Christmas. There were windows with boldly decorated trees, wreaths adorning doors, lights dripping from gables, twinkling feverishly to brighten up the day.

The lights the council had installed were glowing, and families were already working their way around the treasure trail, giddy children dragging still-sleepy parents wearing Santa hats. She could hear 'Last Christmas' playing somewhere in the distance, someone else singing Mariah Carey with wild abandon, and she inhaled deeply, as if she could breathe it into her soul, become the epitome of Christmas, her skin turning shimmery for the festive season.

Inside Sea Brew, with its Yule log bunting and the tantalising smells of cinnamon and gingerbread wafting through the air, she felt even more festive.

'How's Max doing?' Stu asked.

'He's better,' Ollie said. 'He might be discharged in the next couple of days.'

'In time for Christmas? Oh, that would be wonderful,' Molly added, as she made Ollie's latte.

'His parents will be overjoyed to have him with them,' Ollie said. She thought she'd kept the sadness out of her voice, but Max's colleagues exchanged a look. 'And it would be a million times better than having Christmas Day in a hospital bed. Are you preparing yourself for a busy day?'

'Yup.' Stu rubbed his hands together. 'And your blast from the past, Bryan Mailer, is arriving at six thirty?'

'That's right. Don't miss it!'

'Like we would.' Molly grinned and held out a box. 'Here.'

Ollie shook her head. 'I've had so many freebies from you recently.'

'Come on.' She waggled the box. 'It's Christmas!'

Ollie accepted it, told them she'd see them later, then strode up the hill – her thighs at least 30 per cent stronger than when she'd first moved to Cornwall – and walked into A New Chapter.

'I Wish It Could Be Christmas Every Day' was blaring almost aggressively out of the speakers, and the first thing Ollie saw was Becky rush past her, her head a mane of different-coloured tinsel.

Ollie laughed, bemused, just as Thea shouted from the top floor, 'Fucking *hell!* What is wrong with this fucking thing?'

Ollie put the box of goodies and her takeaway cup on the counter, and took off her coat. It was clearly time to swing into action.

'The coffee machine's not working,' Thea said, when Ollie reached the first floor.

'We'll sort it.'

'How can we?' Thea's face was pale, her long hair somewhat less than sleek where it looked like she'd been tugging it.

'We'll have a look at it,' Ollie said calmly, 'and if we need to call someone, we will.'

'But Max isn't here!' Thea blurted, and Ollie felt like a stone had been chipped off the road by a car tyre and lodged itself in her heart.

She smiled, pushing the sensation away. 'We can do this, OK?'

'Sorry,' Thea said quietly. 'I'm stressed.'

'There's no need to be. We've got wine and elderflower cordial for tonight, so it's not going to get in the way of the event, and Stu and Molly are working in Sea Brew today. If we need one of them, it's a five-minute walk. But that's a big *if*.' She opened the top of the coffee machine, remembering everything the salesman had shown her in the shop, while Max had stood quietly by, his calm confidence transferring itself to her. It all looked as it should, as far as she could see.

'What is it?' Thea asked.

'Not sure yet. Why is Becky running about downstairs like the tinsel monster?'

'Oh. This morning Meg told her their house wasn't Christmassy enough, had a huge meltdown about it, apparently, so Becky went to the supermarket first thing. She bought up their entire supply of tinsel, and is intent on making her house, and this place, genuine fire hazards. So that's nice.'

Ollie laughed. 'This is Christmas stress, compounded by event stress.'

'And yet you seem perfectly calm,' Thea observed, just as Ollie found the problem. A bit of plastic from one of the bags of beans, which were inserted into the machine upside down and supposed to be emptied automatically by the mechanism, had ripped off and got stuck in the workings. She untangled it, held it up, and Thea clapped. 'Yes! See! How did you do that?'

Ollie put the machine back together, then set it up to make a cup of coffee, to check it was working properly. 'This is the kind of atmosphere I thrive in,' she admitted. And then, thinking of Max, of Sophia Forsythe-Hartley, of

368

Becky's antagonism, added, 'Besides, all the worst stuff has already happened to me. Today, Thea, is going to be nothing short of incredible.'

The day was relentless, the savoury pastries from Sea Brew – sausage rolls and cheese pies, the turkey and stuffing rolls Max had commissioned from Beryan – proving welcome and entirely necessary. The shop was extra busy, the town humming with Christmas cheer and happy customers, people coming in to pick up last-minute presents while carrying burgers and burritos from the food stalls; one small boy with his arm, up to the elbow, in a bag of candyfloss.

The music from the bands playing down by the harbour drifted up the hill, and Becky, Thea and Ollie sang and swayed along in their newly enhanced, book-filled Christmas grotto. Ollie didn't know how Becky had secured all the tinsel to the ceiling, but it hung down in swathes, making her fancy garlands at home seem paltry by comparison.

'I'd like every Lee Child book, if possible,' said one woman, her cheeks red from the cold, a poinsettia sticking out of her tote bag.

Ollie winced internally. 'I'm not sure we have every single one in stock right now. We can order them in, of course, but they won't be here until after Christmas.'

'Oh, fiddlesticks,' the woman said. 'I tried to get them on Amazon, and they tell you that they have them, that it's all fine, and then – bam! You get an email saying your order has been cancelled for no reason.'

'That's the problem when you're dealing with an algorithm rather than a person,' Ollie said, giving her a reassuring smile. She looked up the details on the computer. 'We have seventeen of them here, including the first five. Why don't you get those, give the lucky recipient the first ones under the tree, and then, by the time they've finished the fifth book, you'll have the others waiting. You could even add in some kind of cryptic message, something about there being more to come, then leave the rest wrapped up and hidden about the place, so they keep discovering more.' She shrugged. 'It's a bit silly, maybe, but more fun than getting them in one huge, overwhelming bucketload.'

'What a brilliant idea,' the woman said. 'Everyone loves a bit of mystery, don't they?'

'I think so. As long as you get a good payoff at the end.'

'Like getting hold of Bryan Mailer. My friend, Pam, and I used to read those Roskilly and Faith mysteries together. We'd take it in turns to be the first to read one, then whoever did would annotate the pages for the other. I can't believe you've tracked him down!'

Ollie's heart sped up. 'I'm so glad people are excited.'

'It sounds like the perfect night. Wine and book chat, and his reading, of course. I love a good reading: if they've got a mellow voice and you can lose yourself in the story . . .' she sighed. 'I listen to audio books for that very reason.'

'They're really popular now, which can only be a good thing.'

'You don't mind everyone downloading books to listen to rather than buying them from your shop?'

'People won't ever stop buying physical books, and if audiobooks introduce reluctant readers to the joys of story-telling, then I can't be mad with it.' She grinned. 'Let me get those Jack Reachers off the shelf for you. Will you be OK carrying them? Seventeen books is a lot.'

'My two grandsons are in the YA section picking something out. I've bribed them with another Christmas Eve Eve present, so they'll help me carry the books to my car.'

Ollie laughed. 'You've got it all figured out.'

She tapped her tote bag. 'You have to be prepared, especially in the run-up to Christmas. I was cursing Amazon before, but now, thanks to you, I've got a much better plan.'

'Glad I could help,' Ollie called, as she walked over to the Crime and Thriller section.

As the afternoon slipped into evening, the Christmas lights took over. They were wound around the banisters, all the way to the top floor, draped along the windowsills and curled along the top of the till. With all Becky's added tinsel, it made the bookshop seem like the inside of a glitter ball.

None of them had managed much of a break, but Ollie could tell that Thea and Becky were as excited about the evening as she was, adrenaline powering them through. At six o'clock, after the last customer had left, they shut the doors for half an hour, so they had a chance to get everything ready.

'I told Liam to come in the back door, in case there's anyone outside,' Thea said. The back door, she had told Ollie, was part of the renovation that had turned the Old Post House into A New Chapter. Thea hadn't wanted anyone getting stuck inside if something happened to block the front exit.

Ollie got the wine out of the storeroom and fridge, while Becky arranged the copies of Bryan Mailer's mysteries that had arrived from AbeBooks on a circular table close to the till.

'The chairs are all laid out,' Thea called, hurrying down the stairs. 'I think we're mostly there.'

'Now all we need is Liam,' Ollie said.

'And a quick change of clothes,' Becky added. They had all brought outfits to change into, and now they did, one by one, in the bathroom at the back of the shop. Ollie's dress was midnight blue with tiny gold suns on it, and looked festive even though the design wasn't, the metallic shimmer picking out the blonde streaks in her hair.

'Gorgeous,' Thea said, when they'd all reassembled. Her dress was dark red, flatteringly cut, and Becky was in a simple black dress that she'd paired with silver jewellery and heels.

'Ready to do this?' Ollie asked.

Thea nodded. 'All we need is our special guest, and we'll be good to go.' They exchanged nervous smiles, and Ollie noticed that people had started to gather outside. Now, after everything, the moment there was nothing they could do to change the course of the evening, the nerves started to flutter.

Chapter Forty-Two

'Getting through Port Karadow right now is a nightmare,' Liam said, when he arrived five minutes later to heavy sighs and relieved grins. 'Have you seen how busy it is out there?'

'Uh, Liam, that's sort of the point.' Ollie put herself between him and the front of the shop, glad there were bookshelves blocking the view of the glass-panelled door. 'Pageant time, lots of people.'

His brows lowered. 'I haven't done anything like this.'

'But you've told me legends,' Ollie said. 'You had me hanging on your words, desperate to find out what happened next. You're going to be wonderful. And I'm here – we're all here, supporting you. If you freeze then I'll step in, but I'm sure I won't need to. Now, hood on. We need to get you upstairs, then you can have a glass of wine in the back room while we let the guests in.'

'When Ollie says back room,' Thea added, 'she means storeroom. But there's a box you can sit on.'

'I should have asked for a rider,' Liam muttered, as he pulled his hood over his head and Ollie made him stoop, then the three women stood around him, walking him to the front of the shop and up the stairs, ensuring he was hidden from view of anyone peering in the windows. They were like some kind of weird human insect, Ollie thought, but not the human centipede: that was a whole other ball game.

With Liam safely settled on his box in the storeroom, a glass of wine in his hand, Becky went downstairs and opened the door, letting in a stream of eager people. They were fresh from the delights of the pageant, smelling of sugar and fried onions, cheeks flushed from the cold and the beer served at the mobile bar down by the harbour.

As Ollie took up her place behind the wine table, she heard snippets of conversation: speculation about how they had tracked down Bryan Mailer; people listing all the books they were going to buy to finish their Christmas shopping; comments about Sophia Forsythe-Hartley and her rudeness. Ollie didn't want anyone thinking the worst of Sophia, so she made a mental note to fully exonerate her in her opening salvo.

She greeted people and poured them wine, and it slowly became apparent that most of Port Karadow had come to A New Chapter, to be here for the local mystery writer's grand unveiling. There was Stu and Molly from Sea Brew, Adrian and his wife, Tillie, and Lizzy had turned up with her husband and teenage sons in tow. There were two tall, striking women who both asked for white wine, and who Ollie thought must be Finn's actor aunt and her partner: she had looked up the cast of *Estelle* after Thea had mentioned it, and was sure one of the women was Laurie Becker.

Sylvia turned up with a woman who looked like a younger version of her, and squeezed Ollie's arm before she'd even said anything.

'Looks like it's gone as you'd hoped,' she said.

Ollie couldn't help laughing. 'Glad it seems that way, because I can assure you it very much has not. But I am happy with the outcome.'

'That's all that matters: you got here in the end.'

Ollie puffed out a breath. 'We really did.'

Sylvia raised her glass, then let the woman Ollie presumed was her daughter lead her to a seat near the front.

Maisie, all blonde curls and sunny smile, asked for a generous pouring of red.

'Is there anyone left at the pageant?' Ollie asked.

'Only the food vendors, I think,' Maisie said. 'Anisha's wangled it so there's a break in the entertainment, and then, when this is over, the choir are going to perform.'

'Where? At the town hall?'

'Down by the harbour,' Maisie said. 'It's so pretty down there, with all the boats lit up and the stalls selling snacks.'

Ollie nodded. She'd seen it from the window.

'It looks great in here,' said a voice behind Maisie, and Ollie looked up to see Finn, his arm around Meredith's shoulders, and Ben, who was wearing a beanie hat over his short hair.

'How are you, Ollie?' Meredith asked. 'Everything OK?'

'We've been so busy all day,' Ollie said, pouring them all wine. 'And I can't believe the turnout tonight. It's amazing!'

'Is Port Karadow's most famous resurrected author ready to take to the stage?' Finn raised an eyebrow.

'Of course,' Ollie said.

'And, as your friends,' he continued, 'do we get any sort of a clue?'

'Absolutely not.' Ollie gave him a serene smile, and Meredith laughed.

'He's just annoyed because Ben knows.'

'And I've been sworn to secrecy,' Ben said. 'My life wouldn't be worth living if I told you, not even now, minutes from the big reveal.'

'Fair enough,' Finn grumbled. 'I won't hold it against you. Or you, Ollie.'

'Very generous of you.' She grinned, then handed them glasses of wine and told them to get good seats in front of the stage.

She served Anisha and her family – her husband, her two young children and her parents – elderflower cordial, and there were a couple of fishermen she recognised from the harbour, the petite wine glasses looking dainty in their weather-worn hands.

'Got a good crowd for it,' Marion said, approaching the table. 'You look wonderful, by the way.'

'Thank you,' Ollie replied. 'You look gorgeous yourself.' The older woman was wearing a shimmering silver top and black, wide-legged trousers. She looked classy and beautiful. 'Go and get a seat at the front.'

'I'd rather be near the back, but thank you. Everything set?' She glanced around her furtively, and Ollie stifled a laugh.

'As we'll ever be.'

'You'll be grand. And so will Mr Bryan Mailer.' She waggled her eyebrows, took her glass of wine and went to get a seat at the back of the room.

The next face Ollie saw in the queue made her do a double-take.

'Hello,' Arabella said, her smile reserved.

'Arabella,' Ollie stuttered. 'Are you – is Sophia—?' Her heart was suddenly thudding.

'Sophia's mother is being moved into a care home today,' Arabella explained. 'It all happened so quickly, and she's so terribly sorry she can't be here. But we'd love to do something in the new year.'

'That would be great,' Ollie managed, 'but you—'

'I wanted to show my support. And when I heard Bryan Mailer was appearing, I couldn't not make the journey.'

'You've *heard* of him?'

'I love Roskilly and Faith,' Arabella admitted. 'Such a shame the publisher went out of business. If you could wangle me an introduction to Bryan afterwards, I'd be ever so pleased.'

Ollie nodded, dumbfounded, then handed Arabella her wine and watched her find a seat. It took all her willpower not to rush into the storeroom and squeal at Liam.

When the upstairs of A New Chapter looked fit to bursting, and Ollie had got over Arabella's appearance and finished having a brief panic about fire regulations and all their extra tinsel, Becky came up the stairs and gave her a thumbs up. It seemed that everyone who was planning on coming, was here.

Thea, who was standing close to the storeroom door, nodded and pressed a nervous hand to her lips.

Ollie put down the wine bottle she was holding and strode onto the stage. The remaining chatter died out, and Thea lowered the lights, plunging all but the front of the room into darkness.

'Good evening everyone, and happy Christmas Eve Eve,' Ollie said. 'Welcome to A New Chapter, and our festive pageant event. As most of you will know, our plans for tonight changed recently and suddenly. It *is* disappointing not to have Sophia Forsythe-Hartley here, but a family emergency prevented her from coming tonight, and I'm sure you will all join me in wishing her well. We're hoping to reschedule our event with her next year. In the meantime, however, we have been very lucky to secure someone who, frankly, I could not be more excited about!'

She paused, taking in the eager faces, feeling the hum of anticipation in the air. 'Soon after I moved here I picked up a book called *The Legend of Kerensa's Handprint* by one Bryan Mailer. I devoured that mystery, and then the next, and the next, in huge, hungry chunks, and when I started asking around, I discovered that I wasn't the only one who was hooked by the locally based series. It became obvious that he is well known – and well loved – around here. What I struggled to do, despite hours of searching, was find out more about the man himself. He turned out to be as much of a mystery as his stories – and we all love a mystery at Christmastime, don't we?'

There were several enthusiastic 'Yes's', and some quieter murmurs of assent.

'Luckily,' Ollie went on, 'the man is no longer a mystery, and I hope you will all be as surprised, as delighted, as I was to come face to face with the wonderful writer who sometimes calls himself Bryan Mailer.' She took a deep breath. 'He's one of our very own Port Karadow residents, already a well-loved member of the community, and he's agreed, for us, tonight, to come clean about his previous life as a successful author.'

She clasped her hands together. Becky, at the back of the room, caught her eye, and they exchanged gleeful grins. 'Ladies and gentlemen, boys and girls, please give it up for esteemed mystery author and the darkest horse I know, Mr Bryan Mailer – otherwise known as Liam Byrne!' She turned, and Thea opened the storeroom door.

Liam stepped out, looking handsome in a moss green shirt and charcoal trousers.

There were mutters of *Seriously?* and *Liam?* and *What the hell?* and Ollie heard someone say, *Is this for real?* But all of that mingled with the applause, which got louder and rowdier, a few cheers and whistles thrown in, as Liam took his place on the stage, the slim volume of legends – that Ollie had temporarily returned to him – in his hands.

Once the cheering had died down, he cleared his throat and began to speak. Ollie was relieved at the strength, the steadiness, of his voice.

'I had intended to take this secret with me to the grave,' he said, 'but when you let Ollie Spencer rent the barn on your estate, it turns out nothing is sacred anymore.' He turned to her and smiled, and she grinned back, while several members of the audience laughed. 'Although, in this case, I am perhaps doing her an injustice. It was Max Holden who overturned the first stone, then evaded my ire by landing himself in hospital.' The laughter died, and Ollie felt the weight of several stares on her. Everyone in town knew what had happened to their beloved café proprietor. 'I am only making a joke of this,' Liam went on, 'because

Max is recovering well, and has given me his express permission to blame him for this predicament: me standing up here, in front of all of you. I'll go easy on him, however, and will only demand one sausage roll per day for the next decade, as penance for his nosiness.' He lifted his glass of wine and said, 'Let's raise our glasses to Max, and wish him a full and speedy return to health.'

Everyone in the room raised their glasses and chorused, 'To Max!' Ollie felt, briefly, as if her chest might explode.

'And now,' Liam continued, 'to my tawdry past as a mystery writer. I thought I would explain a little about how I ended up writing the Roskilly and Faith books, why I chose to do it under a pseudonym – simply, because I was more interested in the stories themselves than having any kind of notoriety – then finish by reading one of the legends I wrote to accompany the series. I've picked one that I hope you'll approve of, as it has a distinctly Christmassy feel.'

The last of Ollie's nerves dissolved as Liam addressed his audience like a pro. He was funny and dry, and recounted his journey to publication with as much nuance and interest as there was in his novels. The audience were rapt, Finn leaning forward with his chin resting on a hand, Lizzy's eyes bright, everyone slowly accepting, and enjoying, the fact that the slightly reclusive farmer had moonlighted as a skilled, popular author several decades ago.

When he began reading the legend – one Ollie hadn't got to yet, about a mysterious figure called Misty Nicolas who left Christmas wreaths on doorsteps on foggy, December nights, every household who received one having some good fortune befall them – the bookshop was silent apart from Liam's deep, mesmerising voice.

Ollie loved studying the happy customers, and she loved that they could all feel proud of Liam, as well as enjoying his stories. This event felt exactly right, for A New Chapter, Port Karadow, and, she hoped, for Liam, too – she thought of Arabella's appearance, and suppressed a grin. He certainly seemed to be having a good time, holding his listeners in the palm of his hand. He thrived on it, she could see, even if he'd told himself he had never been interested in the public side of being a writer.

She caught Thea's eye, and her boss gave her a discreet thumbs up.

When Liam finished his reading, the room erupted into wild applause, as if they'd been treated to a night with a famous rock band or world-class opera singer. Liam seemed taken aback, and Ollie walked onto the stage and put her arm around him.

'Wasn't he wonderful?' she shouted, and the applause got louder and faster, showing no signs of dying down.

'Enough!' Liam said, holding up his hands and laughing. 'Good lord, people. Thank you, thank you.'

Ollie waited for the clapping to subside before she spoke. 'We are in the process of ordering copies of Bryan Mailer's – Liam's – series from second-hand sellers, but it could take some time. We have a few sets of his mysteries downstairs, and I've also had some pamphlets printed up. It's a small selection of his legends, and something for you all to get signed by him tonight: it also gives any of you who aren't yet a fan, a taster of his brilliant writing. If you could form an orderly queue . . .' She raised her voice, having to shout all of a sudden, because the crowd had started murmuring, their applause returning, quiet and patchy to begin with, then once again filling the room, thrumming through the building like the tremors of an earthquake.

She frowned, confused, and looked to Liam for clarification. He squeezed her hand and pointed.

Ollie turned towards the stairs, and her breath caught.

Max was standing there, wearing a soft grey jumper and jeans, his curls and his green eyes and his smile like water to her parched body.

'Oh my God!' She rushed over to him, then paused. 'Max?'

'Come here,' he said, and wrapped his arms around her.

'I didn't know you were coming.' She kissed him softly on the lips. 'I didn't realise you'd been discharged.'

'They let me out an hour ago. I wanted to get here earlier.' He rubbed his cheek, embarrassed as people continued to cheer and clap. 'I didn't mean to interrupt.'

'You're here,' she said, squeezing him. 'You're OK?'

'I'm better than OK.'

'Not one surprise,' Liam said to the crowd, 'but two. Max and Ollie are the reason I'm here tonight, so let's give it up for both of them. Come on, everyone!'

It was Liam who led the next round of applause, while Ollie held Max tightly and rested her head against his chest. He brushed his lips against her hair, and laughed softly into her ear, while the whole of Port Karadow welcomed him home.

'It's a Christmas miracle!' shouted a voice, and when Ollie looked up, Lizzy caught her eye and winked.

382

Chapter Forty-Three

Ollie woke on Christmas morning and stretched out, finding a warm body at her side: hot skin and dark hair, and delicious stubble for her to kiss.

'Hey,' she said, turning over.

'Happy Christmas,' Max said, his voice gravelly with sleep.

'Happy Christmas,' Ollie whispered, smiling against his lips.

The kissing lasted a long time, and Ollie was debating whether to ask Max if he wanted coffee, or if they should just stay in their duvet cocoon until Henry demanded his breakfast, when Max said, 'How long do we have to get ready?' and Ollie remembered that she was not going to have the lonely Christmas she had been imagining. Instead, she was hosting Max, Max's parents and Liam, and then later, Meredith and Finn, Thea and Ben, Becky and her kids.

'Shit.' She flopped back onto the pillow.

Max laughed. 'I thought this was what you wanted? I thought you were desperate to show off your sparkly garlands and your culinary skills?'

'Of *course* I am. This is like all my Christmases come at once, and on Christmas Day, too: Christmas stacked upon Christmas. It couldn't get any better.'

'So?' Max asked, drawing the word out.

'I just want a bit longer here, with you.' She slid her leg over his. 'If that's . . .'

He cupped her face in his palms and kissed her softly. 'I'm good. No marathons, triathlons, or Iron Man competitions. Let's take it slow, OK?'

'OK. So just kissing, for now—'

'That's not what I meant.' Max trailed his fingers down her neck, his touch teasing as he reached her back, setting her nerve endings alight. When he squeezed her hip, he said, 'I meant let's take this slowly, right now.' He kissed below her ear, ran his lips down the sensitive skin of her throat, and she hummed into him.

'Slow is better, sometimes,' she murmured.

'Yeah.' He tugged her gently until she was on top of him, the duvet over her shoulders like a cloak. 'Slow can be perfect.'

It was, Ollie thought, as she bent to kiss his stubbled jaw, a great way to start Christmas morning.

Her beautiful barn was full. She'd cooked far too much, had got over-excited about hosting and bought a turkey and a beef joint, a small salmon and a nut loaf. There were enough roast potatoes to feed an army, Brussels sprouts which she'd cooked with butter and bacon, and a vat, rather than a jug, of gravy.

The morning – after Max had finally let her get out of bed – had been a whirlwind of cooking. They'd worked together, though she'd made Max sit at the kitchen island, giving him chopping and sorting tasks to do, so he didn't get too tired, and Henry had constantly got in the way, but had done it so adorably that they couldn't be cross with him.

It felt like domestic bliss, and Ollie hoped she was getting a glimpse of her future. Max might not cook his own pastries and cakes at Sea Brew, but he had a great tip for getting the roast potatoes extra crispy, and he knew how to make the creamiest, most indulgent brandy butter, and when the spread was laid out on her dining table, she felt an overwhelming sense of achievement.

Max poured her a glass of champagne, himself a lime and soda – doctor's orders – and clinked his glass against hers. 'Happy Christmas, Ollie.'

'Happy Christmas, Max,' she said, taking his hand. She wanted to be close to him all the time, even if it was just their thighs touching as they sat beside each other. 'I'm so glad you're here.'

'I'm not going anywhere.'

She grinned. 'Excellent! When shall we move your stuff in? Do you think Oxo will get on with Henry Tilney?' She'd meant it as a joke, had expected him to grin back at her, to laugh, but his eyes went wide with shock. Of course, right at that moment there was a knock on the door, and Ollie had to go and answer it, and then the barn was full of people and laughter and clinking glasses and Christmas music, and she was the host, with Max at her side, and she'd just managed to make things impossibly awkward between them.

'I couldn't eat any more, thank you,' Max's dad, Philip, said, leaning back and patting his flat stomach.

'It was delicious,' Cath, Max's mum, added. 'Ollie, you are a marvel.'

'It was lovely to have people to cook for.' She was surprised at how calm she was in the company of Max's parents – though they were both warm, down-to-earth people, which was unsurprising, considering who their son was. 'Until a few days ago, I thought I'd be having Christmas alone.'

'Tush,' Liam said, topping up wine glasses. 'Even if you hadn't bagged your fella, I would have had you over at mine. It would have been shepherd's pie, but we'd have made a go of it. This, I have to say, is a real treat.'

'I didn't want anyone to go hungry,' she said with a shrug.

'Were you picturing the whole of Port Karadow when you set yourself that goal?' Philip asked, a twinkle in his eye.

'I'm going to leave it all out, and the others can pick at it when they get here,' Ollie said.

'And what about Henry?' Max pointed at her chocolate Labrador, who had his nose on Max's lap and was looking longingly up at the table.

'If I give him some more pigs in blankets, and some sprouts – which he loves – then he shouldn't be too much of a terror.'

'Wishful thinking,' Liam said mildly. 'We'll all keep an eye on him.'

'Until we fall asleep,' Philip added, holding up his wine glass.

'Oh no.' Ollie stood and started to collect their empty plates. 'That's not happening. We're playing charades.'

There were groans around the table, and when Ollie caught Max's eye, he grinned at her.

'What?' she asked.

'Nothing.' He shook his head, his eyes dancing with amusement, and Ollie had to turn away as love swelled inside her and she risked making a fool of herself in front of his parents.

The charades became a hundred times more chaotic when Ollie's other guests arrived. Dylan, Meg, Billy and Finn threw themselves into it with wild abandon, assigning teams and team names, talking in hushed whispers as if it was possible to strategise a game of Christmas charades.

Ollie watched them with growing happiness. Her home was full of talking and laughter, the new arrivals looked like they might actually make a dent in the mountain of food, and everyone was having a good time. She had always prided herself on her event-organising skills, but she'd never put it into practice in her personal life. After today, she was going to make it a more regular thing.

'Hey,' Thea said, coming to stand beside her at the kitchen island. She was watching Finn and Dylan try and communicate their book or film to their team, while the other team – Ben, in particular – tried to sabotage their efforts. 'This is wonderful, thank you.'

'Thank you for coming,' Ollie said. 'It's the best Christmas I've had in a long time.'

'Me too,' Thea admitted. 'It's my first with Ben, and my first in Cornwall – my two favourite things.'

'What about A New Chapter? A close third?'

Thea nodded. 'But Ben and Cornwall are home to me. The bookshop is important – I'm so happy with how it's going, in no small way thanks to you – and I'm proud of it, of course.'

'But?'

'But having the right people, in the right place: that's what really matters.'

'You've got good people in the bookshop, too.' Ollie gestured to Becky, sitting on the arm of the sofa and ruffling Meg's hair, the little girl calling out nonsensical answers to Finn and Dylan, trying to join in.

'I have,' Thea said. 'You, me and Becky, I really think we're making something of our little bookshop. I'm so glad to be working with you both.'

'I can't imagine not being a part of it. And I . . .' Was it too soon to say it out loud? Was it tempting fate?

Thea nudged her gently. 'What?'

Ollie turned to her. 'I've found my home, too. Here. Max. This motley crew.' She nodded towards the living space, the chaotic game of charades. 'And I'm including the bookshop in that.'

Thea grinned. 'OK, you're right. I only left out A New Chapter so you wouldn't spend Christmas Day thinking about work. But I can see you've found something else to keep you busy.' She reached over and stole a pig in a blanket from the pile.

Ollie laughed. 'I had help with the feast: it wasn't just me.'

'Well, it's all delicious.' Thea held up her glass, and they clinked. 'This is the last thing I'm going to say about it today, but I really want to focus on the Book Wars competition in the new year, and maybe organise some writing workshops, too.'

'Writing workshops? That would be amazing!'

'Yeah. I just . . . people were *so* excited about Liam being Bryan Mailer, and the fact that he lives right here, in town.'

She gestured to where he and Philip were talking animatedly on one of the sofas. 'I want us to encourage new writers as well as new readers, be aspirational. Book Wars will help, because it forces people to talk about their favourite stories and why they love them so much.'

'More children's events, too?' Ollie asked.

'Yup. And launches. We're going to do more author talks and signings. Speaking of authors, what happened with Liam and Arabella?'

'They had a long chat after the event, apparently, and he's going up to London to meet with her in her swanky office in the new year. He won't say if it's about his memoir, or re-publishing his mysteries, or both. I'm going to wait until he's had a couple more glasses of wine, then get it out of him.'

'That's amazing!' Thea sighed happily. 'We'll have to get him to come and do more events for us. I want to do everything, basically.'

'Good! Me too.'

'But we don't have to rush into it,' Thea said. 'We've got time, Ollie. If you're planning on staying, now. If this really is home for you, and you want to . . .' she hesitated.

'If I want to what?'

'I know that A New Chapter is small. You might grow out of it, look further afield, in Truro or Padstow or . . . I don't know.'

Ollie shook her head, and took a moment to drink in the scene in front of her. Liam and Max's parents, her new friends playing charades, Becky and her kids right in the thick of it. Max, wearing a Christmas jumper with a reindeer on the front, Santa's legs sticking out of a chimney on the back, and still managing to look utterly gorgeous as he went to pick a slip from the selection of films and books that Ollie had written out the day before and put in a large bowl.

She watched as he took out a piece of paper and unfolded it, his expression one of intense concentration, reminding her of earlier that morning, the way he'd been so focused on giving her pleasure.

'I've asked Max to move in with me,' she admitted to Thea, her insides flipping. 'It was spontaneous, and he might say it's far too soon – he was shocked, which was understandable, seeing as I said it as a joke to begin with – but now I've thought about it, I really want him to. I want us to walk into work together, him to Sea Brew, me to A New Chapter, and I don't care what other people think about it.' She exhaled. 'I'm telling you this because I need you to know that I'm not going anywhere. This place – the town, and your bookshop, Thea. I never expected . . .' She laughed. 'I never expected to love it all so much.'

Thea squeezed her arm, and they watched as Max and Meredith acted out something that Ollie had a suspicion might be *The Lost City*, but in such a chaotic way that she couldn't be entirely sure.

'That's the thing about this place,' Thea said.

'What's that?'

Billy shouted, 'Christmas crackers!' and a cheer went up from the charades participants, followed by laughter. Henry joined in with a generous bark.

Thea turned to Ollie, her smile warm and 100 per cent smug. 'Once you've let it into your heart, even a little bit, you're stuck loving it forever.'

'Oh, well.' Ollie lifted her shoulders in an exaggerated shrug, then held her champagne glass out in front of her. 'No point fighting it then, is there? Better just to accept it and go all in.'

'Hear hear,' Thea said, and clinked her glass against Ollie's.

Chapter Forty-Four

As Christmas Day turned to Christmas night, the skies darkened, cold and clear, with no hint of precipitation in the air: not rain or sleet or snow. But, as Ollie and Max stepped outside, shrugging on their coats and giggling like teenagers absconding from school, she decided she was happy to trade snow for the twinkling blanket of stars that greeted them. It was almost too beautiful, almost too many stars to be believable.

'Wow.' She stopped on the grass close to the yew tree, her head angled back to take it all in.

'It's a good night.' Max slid his arms around her waist, and rested his head on her shoulder.

'Just good?' Ollie asked lightly.

'Great, at the very least. Epic, possibly. If I say perfect now, though, then I'm leaving no room for improvement, and with you in my life – and after what you said earlier – I have a feeling things are about to get even better.'

Ollie stilled, then turned around in his arms. 'What do you mean?'

He gazed down at her. 'I know it was an off-the-cuff remark, and that you might not mean it right now, but I've been giving it a lot of thought, and I really think that Oxo would get on with Henry. He's quite tolerant – which I know is surprising, given that he's a cat – and Henry is a laid-back dog. I'm guessing they'd get along famously.'

His words were mischievous, but his expression couldn't have been more serious.

'Did you . . . have you been sneaking champagne when I wasn't looking?'

He shook his head. 'I'm not going to mess with the doctors' advice, and me being sober means you can't mistake it for drunken enthusiasm when I tell you, Ollie Spencer, that I would love to move in with you – here, at the barn, or at my place, if you'd prefer – if there was any part of you that meant it. You don't need to say anything now, but—'

'Yes,' she said in a rush. 'Yes please. Please move in with me – you and Oxo. Here, in the barn?'

His eyes were smiling before it reached his lips. 'OK. I would have picked the barn too, but I didn't want to assume.'

'Oh my God!' Ollie felt almost dizzy with elation. 'You, me, Henry Tilney and Oxo, all together in the barn. You can come to Liam's while I finish typing up his memoir, you can nose around his books some more, because I'm sure—' She stopped abruptly, her breath hitching.

'Don't do that,' he said gently. 'Don't think that you can't talk about it. It happened, and it wasn't great, but look where we are now. We're here, together.' He turned them in a slow circle, Ollie taking in the party still going inside, her friends silhouetted in the glass doors, talking and laughing and drinking; then the land surrounding the farm, the shadows encroaching where the lights didn't reach, the stars glimmering high above them, the scent of the sea in the air.

'We're here, together,' she repeated, those three words, spoken while she was in Max's arms, grounding her better than any meditation could.

'It was the biggest possible reminder that life is too short to put off what you really want,' he said. 'And I want you, Ollie. I want us to have a life together. If we delayed moving in with each other, what would we be doing it for? You already feel like the person I was always meant to find.'

She leaned into him, her throat thick with emotion. 'And you're my home,' she murmured. 'The barn is just fixtures and fittings.'

'We're agreed then? No time to lose?'

'Life is too short not to,' she said.

Max reached out to push a strand of hair away from where it had fallen in front of her eye. 'I think that—'

His words were swallowed up by loud bangs, and Ollie jumped, startled, until Max turned her gently so she was facing the darkened countryside, lit up by the red and gold spray of a firework charging up into the sky.

'Who's doing this?' she laughed.

'No idea,' Max said. 'They couldn't wait for New Year's, clearly.'

'Someone else seizing the moment.'

'Maybe we're starting a trend.'

His arms tightened around her waist, and they watched the display sending jewels and twirls, sparkles and glitter up into the darkness. The short bursts of explosion lit up the sea in the distance, turning it silvery-grey as if it was made of moonlight, and the trees nearby shivered in the breeze.

It was, Ollie thought, a magical Christmas night. She turned and reached up to cup Max's face, then pulled him down to meet her, so she could kiss all her happiness, her hope for the future, into the man who had given it to her: who had made her see that she could be herself and be loved; who had shown her that she could achieve all she wanted to, and who didn't hold back. So she didn't hold back either, instead kissing him with every ounce of love she felt for him.

Soon, cheers and applause joined the bangs and whistles of the firework display, and they broke apart to find everyone inside standing at the glass, unashamedly cheering them on. Ollie couldn't bring herself to mind, and when Max pulled her against him and continued their kiss with even more passion, she knew he didn't mind either.

Why hold back? she thought again, and couldn't for the life of her come up with an answer.

By the time the sky had quietened, Ollie's ears were numb with cold, and Max's hands were like ice. They walked back to the front door of the barn and, just as Ollie was about to push it open, Max stopped her.

'What is it?' she asked.

He bent down and retrieved something from the shadows of the doorstep, then held it out to her. It was a small, perfectly adorned Christmas wreath. Ivy, holly and mistletoe were wound around a glittering, gold twine frame, and in amongst the foliage were little paper books, the details intricate, each of their covers a different colour.

'Who made this?' Ollie asked, her voice softened by wonder.

Max paused, then said, 'Misty Nicolas?'

'No.' She laughed. 'No way!' She walked along the front of the barn, looked in through the glass and saw that Liam was on the sofa, with a sleepy Meg on his knee. 'That's just one of Liam's made-up legends.'

'I didn't hear anyone come outside,' Max said.

'The fireworks were loud,' Ollie protested. 'It could be *anyone*. They were all there last night: everyone heard that story.' She thought for a moment. 'Except you. You didn't get to A New Chapter until after Liam's reading. How do you know about Misty Nicolas?' She narrowed her eyes at him, and he laughed.

'I might have snuck a peek at the little grey book a few times when you've been otherwise occupied. Liam's stories are pretty good, after all. It doesn't mean I'm behind this.'

'Fair enough,' she murmured, then turned in a slow circle. 'Anyway, the night's clear. It's not even misty.'

But as she spoke, drifts of thick grey fog wafted through the darkness to meet them.

'Smoke from the fireworks,' she said.

'They were too far away for that.' Max's voice was matter-of-fact. 'But you know what the legend said.'

'That everyone who gets a wreath gets some good news straight afterwards?'

He nodded. 'And technically, as of five minutes ago, this is my front doorstep, too.'

'Oh.' Ollie laughed. 'I suppose it is. So you're hoping for a bit of good fortune now, are you?'

He stepped closer, the beautiful wreath between them. 'I've already got it,' he said. 'It's you, Ollie Spencer. I can't think of anything that could top having you in my life; you wanting a future with me. Misty Nic's dropped off his talisman after the good news has already happened.'

'How very sloppy of him,' Ollie whispered, tilting her face up to meet Max's, shivering as his lips brushed hers, as the first chords of 'Have Yourself a Merry Little Christmas' rang out from inside, and she heard Meredith and Thea, Finn and Ben, start to sing along.

Max laughed, ran his thumb along her bottom lip, then pressed his smile against hers. 'Give him a break, Ollie,' he murmured. 'It is Christmas, after all.' Then he took her breath away with a kiss that made her truly believe, for those few minutes at least, that Christmas magic really did exist.

Acknowledgements

How did I get to book number thirteen before I wrote about a bookshop? Come to think of it, how did I get to book number thirteen? Here it is, anyway – I really hope you like it. And here are all the people without whom it wouldn't exist, or look as beautiful as it does, or be in your hands, so you can read it. A huge thank you to all of the following:

Kate Bradley, who is the most brilliant editor, a wonderful friend, and my longest-serving cheerleader in the book-writing world. She always knows what's missing or what I've got too much of, and helps me hone my original story into something brighter, sparklier and more compelling.

Alice Lutyens, the agent of my dreams! I feel so, so lucky to have her in my corner. She makes *me* feel brighter and sparklier, never mind my stories, and brings everything into sharper focus.

The entire HarperFiction team, who do so much – lots of which I don't even know about – to turn my stories into those desirable paperbacks, to get them into shops and reviewed in magazines and on websites, so my characters can find their perfect readers. Chere Tricot, Susanna Peden, Sarah Munro, Namra Amir, Sarah Shea, Lynne Drew, Kim Young. Thank you to Anne O'Brien and Penny Isaacs for going through the pages with your sharp combs and eagle eyes, and for ironing out the wrinkles.

Is it me or do my covers just keep getting better? This slice of twinkling Christmas magic was created by Holly MacDonald, Caroline Young and May Van Millingen, and I love it so much.

Jayne Barratt, who very kindly and generously bid in the Good Books auction run by Young Lives Vs Cancer to have a character in this book named after her mum, Marion Proctor. I hope both Jayne and Marion are happy with the Marion in this book.

The writer friends who keep me going when it gets hard, who make me laugh and fire up my enthusiasm. Especially Kirsty Greenwood, Shelia Crighton, Pernille Hughes, Katie Marsh and the Book Campers.

My mum and dad, who put up with endless chat from me and who always preorder my books, even though I give them copies. It's such a joy for me that, after all the unpublished books that they gave me feedback on over the years, and the emailed Word documents they had to scroll through, my dad can read them on his kindle, and my mum can listen to the audio book.

To friends and family, Lee, Kate G, Kate and Tim.

My husband David, who is also my best friend and number one supporter, who is always there to help me through the tough bits, celebrate the good bits, go with me on random drives to the coast when I need brain space, be a listening ear and a world-class hugger. I couldn't do any of this without him.

Lastly, to all of you, the booksellers, librarians and readers who pick up my books, shout about them to friends and family or online, who love my characters as much as I do. Your enthusiasm and encouragement, the joy you get from reading my stories, makes every difficult moment more than worthwhile. Please keeping reading, loving and talking about books, and never, ever stop going into bookshops.

Cosy up with more delightful stories

from Cressida McLaughlin

All available now.

Don't miss Cressida's latest bestseller!

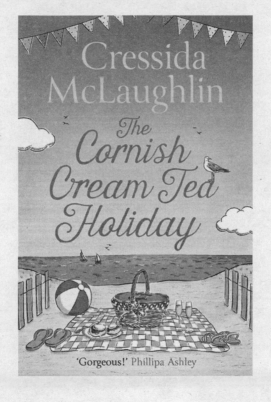

Fern
Britton
Picks
Exclusively for
TESCO

EXCLUSIVE ADDITIONAL CONTENT
Includes an exclusive piece about Cressida's favourite Christmas reading and details of how to get involved
in *Fern's Picks*

Dear lovely readers,

The nights are drawing in, so it's the time for log fires and hot chocolate, and cosying down with a good book or three! A New Chapter, the seaside bookshop in *The Cornish Cream Tea Bookshop* by Cressida Mclaughlin, is just the place to lose yourself for an hour, browsing amongst the bookshelves.

For the heroine, Ollie, who moves to Cornwall and takes a job there, it seems just perfect, and she has a lot to offer. But sometimes fitting in isn't easy and Ollie has a lot to prove, not just to the townspeople of Port Karadow, but to herself too. Luckily, there's always a Cornish cream tea close by at Max's coffee shop next door!

Do you like your cream tea with the jam or the cream on top? I'd love to hear about that and what you think about this month's pick!

with love
Fern x

Fern
Britton
Picks

Exclusively for
TESCO

Look out for more books, coming soon!

For more information on the book club,
exclusive Q&As with the authors and
reading group questions, visit Fern's website
www.fern-britton.com/fernspicks

We'd love you to join in the conversation,
so don't forget to share your thoughts using
#FernsPicks

My Christmas Reading List by
Cressida McLaughlin

Christmas is a time for traditions, and I know for quite a lot of people that extends to reading. I have friends who have one or two particular books they re-read every December, something unashamedly festive or a favourite classic. It's a pause in normal proceedings, so it makes sense to hunker up in your corner of the sofa, where the cushions are moulded just right, while *Mary Poppins* plays for the eighty-billionth time, or when you need a break from peeling five-hundred sprouts, or on Boxing Day, when there is nothing left to do except loaf about and eat leftovers.

I wish I had a reading tradition. I certainly have favourite books that I would read again and again without getting bored, but I am always excited by new books, too. So sitting down with a story I know the ending to, however much I love it, isn't quite as thrilling as the prospect of discovering a new book or author to gush over, especially with the extra, slightly magical time you get at Christmas. Despite all this, there are definitely certain types of books that I gravitate towards at this time of year.

When I was little, Santa Claus put a beautiful copy of *A Christmas Carol* by Charles Dickens in my stocking. I remember the sharp corners warping the shape of the very long, forest-green socks we had as stockings when I was growing up. It's a slim hardback with a maroon cover and an oval illustration of people in Victorian dress dancing at a Christmas party on the front, and all the pages have turned yellow. It's one of my best-loved physical books, it feels really old – though the edition I have was printed in the 1970s – and it's one of the most famous Christmas stories ever written. It's got some genuinely sinister, horrifying parts – Ghost of Christmas Yet To Come, anyone? – and the best, most heartwarming ending. It is a perfect festive story, and I also wonder if, reading it at such a young age, it's part of the reason I'm so fascinated by the supernatural.

I *love* a good ghost story. Anyone who knows me or follows me on social media already knows this. And when is the best time for a ghost story? What about a dark, wintry night when the wind is making tree branches scrape menacingly down the window pane, the glow of moonlight just highlights all those shadowy corners, and the only place you want to be is next to a roaring fire, wearing fluffy socks, clutching a mug of hot chocolate or a glass of whisky?

I love M. R. James's ghost stories, the classics like *Oh, Whistle, and I'll Come to You, My Lad, The Mezzotint* and a particularly creepy one called *The Ash Tree*, with a conclusion that, the first time I read it, gave me a full body shudder, and almost made me drop the book in horror and run screaming from the room. If you love being scared, then I would definitely recommend Michelle Paver. Her ghost stories *Dark Matter* and *Thin Air* are two of the most terrifying, atmospheric books I've ever read. Perfect when there is just enough light to read by and the Christmas tree is sparkling encouragingly from the corner of the room.

At the other end of the spectrum, I love curling up with a Christmas romance. One of my favourite things to do in recent years – a bookish Christmas tradition, in fact! – has been going to a bookshop and, along with getting presents for friends and family, buying the new, festive Karen Swan book. I am a huge fan of my Kindle, but for some reason I need to have physical copies of all of Karen's books. They're always sweeping stories set in exotic locations, with glamour and drama and an epic, all-consuming love story. There is nothing more indulgent than curling up under a blanket and losing myself in the snowy Alps or Canada with Karen's characters, knowing there is heartbreak and redemption in my immediate, fictional future. *The Christmas Secret*, set on the Scottish island of Islay, is my favourite, but you can't go wrong with any of her books.

Another favourite author who writes magical Christmas stories is Sarah Morgan. Her Manhattan with Love series is particularly brilliant, and the two Christmas books – *Miracle on 5th Avenue* and *Moonlight Over Manhattan* are my favourites of the series. They both have heroines you root for, gorgeous, gruff heroes, the New York setting is to die for (I want go to NY so badly!) and the love stories are gripping. Who doesn't want to spend some of their festive break in snowy New York with a sizzling hot hero, trapped inside a penthouse apartment with breathtaking views over Central Park? They are utterly perfect and, now I'm thinking about them, I can see all that stuff about never re-reading books at Christmastime that I wrote in the first paragraph going right out of the window.

Other recent Christmas romances I've loved include *A Winter Kiss* by Annie Darling, who writes pitch-perfect love stories with characters who, at the beginning, you think will NEVER get together; *This Time Next Year* by Sophie Cousens, which is set over the course of a year but has a distinctively festive and celebratory feel, and is life-affirmingly, gorgeously romantic; and *On A Night Like This* by Lindsey Kelk, which has fairytale vibes, a deliciously escapist plot and setting, and Lindsey's trademark humour and swoon.

If you like the darker end of the reading spectrum but aren't a fan of ghosts, then a good locked-room mystery often feels like ideal festive reading material. Obviously, Agatha Christie is the queen of these, but recently there have been some brilliantly sinister chillers that I've loved cosying down with after the roast potatoes are all gone: sometimes Christmas reading just has to be macabre. *The Hunting Party* by Lucy Foley, set in an exclusive but remote Scottish retreat as the weather closes in, is particularly suited to December, but *The Guest List* and *The Paris Apartment*, while not so wintry, are equally gripping, the type of book where you need a few empty hours stretching ahead of you because they're so hard to put down.

Whatever books you decide to read this festive season, whether they're old favourites, a treat you've been saving for the down time, or an unexpected delight you've found under the tree, I hope you have the opportunity to light that Yule log in your fireplace, curl up with a buttery mince pie and a glass of mulled wine, switch off everything except the twinkly lights, and indulge yourself for a few hours. After all, Christmas is the most magical time of the year, and what's more magical than losing yourself in a good book?

Questions for your Book Club

Warning: contains spoilers

- What do think about Ollie's decision to move to Cornwall? Have you ever moved to a new town or made a life-changing decision quickly?

- Do you think Ollie is as confident as she seems about fitting into life at Port Karadow? Or is she hiding some worries underneath?

- Henry Tilney is Ollie's cute dog with an unusual name. Have you ever had a pet, and did you give it a name that meant something to you?

- Ollie starts her new job at A New Chapter. Do you like spending time in bookshops and if so, which one is your favourite?

- Why is Becky so antagonistic towards Ollie, do you think she has good cause to be sceptical about her, or is she being unfair?

- Ollie and Max have an instant attraction, what do you think are the qualities that define a charismatic fictional hero? Do you have a favourite?

- Do you think Ollie is setting her sights too high in her plans for the bookshop? Should she have anticipated some of the problems at the outset?

- Did you pick up on any clues about who Liam was? Did you see it coming? Have you ever found a hidden gem in a charity shop?

- Cornwall is a very popular location in novels and TV series. What makes it so appealing and what is your best-loved book set in Cornwall?

An exclusive extract from Fern's new novel

The Good Servant

March 1932

Marion Crawford was not able to sleep on the train, or to eat the carefully packed sandwiches her mother had insisted on giving her. Anxiety, and a sudden bout of homesickness, prohibited both.

What on earth was she doing? Leaving Scotland, leaving everything she knew? And all on the whim of the Duchess of York, who had decided that her two girls needed a governess exactly like Miss Crawford.

Marion couldn't quite remember how or when she had agreed to the sudden change. Before she knew it, it was all arranged. The Duchess of York was hardly a woman you said no to.

Once her mother came round to the idea, she was in a state of high excitement and condemnation. 'Why would they want *you*?' she had asked, 'A girl from a good, working class family? What do you know about how these people live?' She had stared at Marion, almost in reverence. 'Working for the royal family . . . They must have seen something in you. My daughter.'

On arrival at King's Cross, Marion took the underground to Paddington. She found the right platform for the Windsor train and, as she had a little time to wait, ordered a cup of tea, a scone and a magazine from the station café.

She tried to imagine what her mother and stepfather were doing right now. They'd have eaten their tea and have the wireless on, tuned to news most likely. Her mother would have her mending basket by her side, telling her husband all about Marion's send off. She imagined her mother rambling on as the fire in the grate hissed and burned.

The train was rather full, but Marion found a seat and settled down to flick through her magazine. Her mind couldn't settle. Through the dusk she watched the alien landscape and houses spool out beside her. Dear God, what was she doing here, so far away from family and home? What was she walking into?

When the conductor walked through the carriage announcing that Windsor would be the next stop, she began to breathe deeply and calmly, as she had been taught to do before her exams. She took from her bag, for the umpteenth time, the letter from her new employers. The instructions were clear: she was to leave the station and look for a uniformed driver with a dark car.

She gazed out of the window as the train began to slow. She took a deep breath, stood up and collected her case and coat. *Come on, Marion. It's only for a few months. You can do this.*

Available now!

Our next book club title

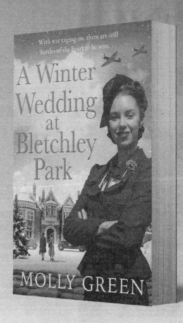

When Rosie Frost was jilted on her wedding day,
she didn't think life could get any worse.
But six years later in the throes of the Second World War,
she is unceremoniously dismissed from her dream job
after they discover her illegitimate child.

Thankfully, top secret war office Bletchley Park recognises
Rosie's talent and recruits her to decipher their Italian naval
signals. Happy to be doing her bit for the war effort,
Rosie settles into her new life.

But when she spots a familiar face at the Park, Rosie's world
threatens to come crashing down once more.
Can she put her heartbreak behind her? And will wedding bells
ring out across Bletchley Park before the year is out?